King Maybe

Also by Timothy Hallinan

The Poke Rafferty Series
A Nail Through the Heart
The Fourth Watcher
Breathing Water
The Queen of Patpong
The Fear Artist
For the Dead
The Hot Countries

The Junior Bender Series
Crashed
Little Elvises
The Fame Thief
Herbie's Game

The Simeon Grist Series
The Four Last Things
Everything but the Squeal
Skin Deep
Incinerator
The Man With No Time
The Bone Polisher

FOR DIANE

King Maybe

A Junior Bender Mystery

TIMOTHY HALLINAN

With all our
very Best

SOHO CRIME

Published by Soho Press, Inc.
853 Broadway
New York, NY 10003

Library of Congress Cataloging-in-Publication Data
is available upon request.

ISBN 978-1-61695-432-1
eISBN 978-1-61695-433-8

Interior design by Janine Agro, Soho Press, Inc.

Printed in the United States of America

10 9 8 7 6 5 4 3 2 1

For Munyin Choy.
Now, as ever,
better than I deserve.

PART ONE

THE STAMP ACT

Next time I send an idiot, I'll go myself.
—Director Michael Curtiz

1
Achy Breaky Heart

Bad luck, as my mentor and surrogate father, Herbie Mott, used to say, arrives on the wind. I'd tried without success to track the saying to its origin, but with or without an attribution, it was hard not to think of it as the wind slammed the sides of the house in which I was risking my life to steal something I wouldn't have bought for a buck-fifty.

But whether I wanted the damn thing or not, there was work to do. I searched for good news and found some. The color looked okay, and that was about half the battle, considering what I'd been sent to swipe.

The little metal penlight gripped between my teeth had a halogen bulb, meaning it put out something very close to natural sunlight, if your idea of "natural" is reading by the illumination of a massively carcinogenic and totally uncontrolled thermonuclear reaction burning seven billion tons of hydrogen every second and perpetually on the verge of exploding, a scant eight light-minutes away.

Out loud to myself, I said, "Oh, cheer up."

I hated this job like I hadn't hated anything since the Great Rope Defeat. When I was eight years old, my father, who hadn't gotten tired of us yet, made me join the Cub

Scouts, either to improve my character or to get me out of the house so he could argue with my mother. This was before it was universally decreed that no child should ever be allowed to fail at anything, so we Cub Scouts of that era grew into our Cubness only through passing certain tests. The very first of these, the test that proved that you were a real human boy rather than a skillfully assembled ventriloquist's dummy, was climbing a rope. A short rope. A short, *fat* rope.

I couldn't climb a rope. I *still* can't climb a rope, even today, as a relatively mature burglar, despite belonging to a profession whose members might reasonably be assumed to have occasion to scale the occasional rope. And since I never did climb that rope, I never progressed up the ranks of Cubness, and Cub Scouts for me was mainly several years of being photographed in the middle of a group of shorter and shorter children as the kids of my age moved on to knot tying and forest survival and pubic hair and . . . I don't know, skydiving. Finally, when the Scout troop leader had taken to having me sit in a chair so I didn't tower over all the kids of my rank, my father gave up on me. A few years later, he left us. I'm not saying the one thing led to the other, but I'm not saying it didn't either.

Anyway, I hated this job as much as I hated the moments before and after I failed to climb that damn rope.

Putting childhood trauma aside, where it belongs, the color *did* look good. It's amazing what you can do these days with the machines that Staples will let you use, right out in the open, in front of God and everyone. I'd gone into the store to copy a tiny, high-definition digital picture—courtesy of Google Images, unwitting accomplice to millions of crooks—of a bald, mild-seeming, bespectacled man, his shoulders wrapped in something that looked like a sheet, gazing benignly down to his right as though he had a kitten in his lap, posed against a background of a slightly brownish rose color. In black type, printed oddly across his chest, was the word SERVICE, all caps, in an institutional, uninteresting sans-serif type. Over the course of an afternoon, I'd made about sixty copies with minor adjustments on both sides of the color scale, messing with hue and saturation and brightness and contrast, feeding the machine with exotic paper prepared by bleaching away the images from entire sheets of old stamps of the correct size, breaking the laws of dozens of countries as the Staples staff members nodded and smiled at me and asked if I needed help. After a couple of hours, I had what I needed.

What I had was a passable replica of a little rectangle of paper, the 1948 ten-rupee Gandhi "Service" stamp, which was issued immediately after the assassination of the founder of modern India and was the least printed of all the world's valuable stamps. Only one set was produced before someone noticed the overprinted mistake, the word SERVICE, and yanked the whole run off the press. In the entire world, only ten copies are known to exist. In 2011 one of them sold for $205,000, making it the most expensive of all modern stamps, which I was certain would have amused the ascetic Gandhi.

The man whose huge, almost threateningly ugly house I was temporarily inside owned one of those ten stamps. And I had a pretty good copy to swap for it. Not that it would fool him for long, but all we thieves need is time for the trail to cool.

Stealing stamps is (1) easy, (2) difficult, and (3) stupid.

On the *easy* side, they're small enough to hide and, in a pinch, can be eaten before one is searched. On the *difficult* side, they're valuable enough to demand extremely frustrating locks, finding a buyer for the rare ones is essentially impossible, and there's always the possibility of accidentally boosting a fake, what with Staples' copy machines, et cetera. On the *stupid* side, valuable stamps are essentially mistakes. Stamp collectors are the only people, except maybe coin collectors, who shell out millions for screwups. Someone who collects paintings or first editions is subscribing to the best of people, people working on tiptoe, and the lucky burglar through whose hands these objects pass is getting a little whiff of genius. A collector who lusts for upside-down airplanes and typographical errors or missing colors is amassing the work of people on their worst days. What a burglar gets from handling *these* things is a whiff of the desperation felt by someone who's just about to lose his job, often in an impoverished country. The average album of truly rare stamps has enough bad karma to sink a cruise ship full of philanthropists.

So the intelligent burglar, a category to which I like to think I belong, steals stamps only on assignment, and even then only when the assignment includes a guaranteed buyer, the location of the stamp, the kinds of locks it's behind, the security status of the house, and a very good idea of where the inhabitants are going to be on the evening of the grab.

And I'd been given all those things, in addition to assurance that this job would end the deep and chilly rift between me and the San Fernando Valley's top premium-swag fence, Stinky Tetweiler. But as important as Stinky was to me, I'd already been inside this house far too long, almost double the twenty, twenty-five minutes I allow myself. The album containing the stamp was where it was supposed to be, but so were a dozen *other* albums, each in several time-consuming layers of swaddling clothes, including a moistureproof and dustproof box, inside which was a rigid slipcover, inside which was the album. The albums had large, stiff pages that needed to be turned slowly and carefully, with twenty to twenty-four stamps per page, laid out in five or six rows of four stamps each. The stamps were in transparent mounts made by a company named Hawid, whose founder, Hans Widmaier, accidentally invented the protective stamp mount back in 1945 when his Berlin neighborhood was getting bombed almost hourly for its *führer*'s sins. Widmaier decided to bury his stamp collection, and as an improvised protective measure he wrapped them in polystyrene before shoveling the dirt over them. When he dug them up several years later in a city that had been reduced to rubble, they were undamaged, and an industry was born.

I knew all about Hawid mounts because I had spent nearly six hours putting stamps into them and taking them out again without leaving a visible trace—no ding on the stamp, no scratch on the mount, no disturbance to the adhesive that held the mount on the page. Then, just to be on the safe side, I'd done it again for two more hours, in the dark.

But owing to a little scuffle, what with the lock on the safe and the twelve albums and the dustproof boxes and the slipcovers and all those awful stamps, I was way beyond my comfort zone for the old in-and-out. I'd been assured that the owner of the stamps was going out to dinner at eight, and it was now almost nine. I was beginning to hope he hadn't decided on fast food when finally I spotted Gandhi and started comparing the color.

It was, as I've said, a pretty good match. But my heart dropped like a stone when I saw that I'd *screwed up the perforations*. There were a lot of them on all four sides of the stamp, and the bleached blank I'd chosen to print on was short by one on each of the two long sides. There should have been twenty-two. My blanks had twenty-one.

Squinting helplessly at the perforations, I could almost literally hear my watch ticking, and it's a digital watch. You can go blind counting stamp perforations, and apparently I had, because I'd skipped one. I popped a modest sweat, just a film of water on my forehead, but for me that's the equivalent of dropping to my knees and chewing my fingers.

For the money the guy who owned this house had spent on his collection of mistakes, he could have bought 5,000 prime acres in Oregon with a river running through them, a 25,000-square-foot house in the best part of Bel Air—which, actually, he already had, and I was inside it—or a third-rate Vuillard, now that prices have dropped for the impressionists. I knew that if I'd bought any of those things, I would have spent a *lot* of time looking, respectively, at my view of the river, at the zip code on my incoming mail, or at my painting. It didn't seem possible that this man would spend an equivalent amount of time looking at these desiccated, fading pieces of paper. Surely he wouldn't notice two missing perforations.

With a nail file, I eased the real Gandhi stamp out of its mount and into a glassine envelope, smooth, waterproof, and acid-free, and then slipped the file beneath the fake stamp so I could drop it into the mount, the missing perforations suddenly seeming bigger than Lake Superior. At that moment the cell phone in my pocket buzzed.

Normally I don't carry a phone when I'm working. In addition to all the obvious reasons, if eventually the situation goes so far south that you're a suspect and the cops can demonstrate probable cause, they can subpoena your cellular records and put you within a few hundred yards of whatever crime they're trying to stick you with. If you were there, I mean, which, naturally, I never was. But in this case I hadn't had time to circle the mark for a week or two to confirm his habits, so I'd set up a lookout. The house was on a cul-de-sac, which is Los Angeles French for dead end, and I'd stationed my girlfriend of the past eight months, Ronnie Bigelow, in a nice Jaguar temporarily stolen to harmonize with the neighborhood, just outside the entrance to the cul-de-sac to tell me if anyone was coming in. Ronnie had said it was her first crime, and I had acted like I believed her.

I carefully put the nail file, with the fake stamp balanced on its tip, on the table, took out my phone, which displayed UNKNOWN, and said, "Yeah?"

Jake Whelan, in his patented seventy-million-cigarette rasp, said, "Please hold for Mr. Whelan."

I said, "I know it's you, Jake." I took a step toward the window, just a nervous fidget, at the same time a gust of wind knocked on the wall, and some of it found its way into the room. The fake stamp took a hopeful-looking little leap and fluttered to the floor.

"This is Bertram, Mr. Whalen's personal assistant. Mr. Whelan will be with you in—"

"Damn it, Jake, I haven't got time for this."

I heard a click on the phone that sounded a lot like a

mouth noise. I didn't want to fumble around one-handed for the stamp, so I studied a hangnail for a moment. This one reinforced my conviction that hangnails don't change very fast.

My watch almost tapped my wrist for attention. *Tempus* was in full *fugit*.

"Junior," Whelan said, voice pumped full of his usual Hollywood brothers-beneath-the-skin enthusiasm. "How's the best burglar in Hollywood?"

"Figure of speech, of course," I said. "Since I've never been charged with a crime, much less convicted. Jake, I'm in a hurry here—"

"Back when I was working with Bob Towne," Whelan said, figuratively putting his feet up and leaning back, "you know, the guy who wrote *Chinatown*? I opened every phone call with, 'How's the best writer in Hollywood?' and Bob would say, 'Who's listening?'"

"Well," I said, "who is?"

"You should be writing, Junior, wit like that. Hey, how you doing for money?"

I knew that Whelan, once the most dynamic producer in Hollywood, hadn't made a movie in about twelve years and that he'd put the British Crown Jewels' worth of imported powder up his nose, but surely he wasn't hard up enough to borrow from me. Even broke, he went through more money in a week, between blow and short-term leases on high-end females, than I spent in a year. I said, "Plowing a modest furrow, Jake. Enough for groceries."

"Haven't got eight, ten million lying around?"

"Jake, I really am tight for time right—"

"Yes or no?"

"Probably got about as much as Bertram. Interesting voice, Bertram."

"That's a no, then." He was heading toward brisk.

"Yes, no is no." In fact, I had quite a bit of money, much of which had once belonged to Whelan. "I got bus fare, Quarter Pounder money."

"Well, that's too fucking bad," Whelan snarled, demonstrating the talent for instant mood swings that had terrified writers and agents for decades. Whelan was like a human pregnancy test; one minute everything's fine, and a second later the stick turns pink and your whole life changes. "Because you're going to need a fucking *houseful* of money, you little prick, if you want to—"

"Jake," I said. "Are you mad at me?"

"*Oh, no,* you insignificant shit, why in the world would I be mad at you?"

"I have no idea," I said—except of, course, I did, and my stomach muscles tightened as though someone were about to punch me in the gut.

"One word, putz," Whelan said. "Clay."

Bad, bad, *bad.* I said, "As in *feet of?*"

"As in Paul, funny man, *Paul* Klee."

"Oh," I said, stalling to give inspiration a little more time to drop by. "It's funny, you know, 'cause when you said *clay*, I wasn't thinking of K-L-E-E, which I used pronounce *klee*, to rhyme with that TV show where everyone's singing all the—"

"You're going to need a *lot* of money," Whelan said, "if you want to buy off the guy I've paid to put a couple through you."

"Put a couple through you" was twenty-four-karat Jake Whelan, the kind of clenched-teeth, popped-sweat excess that had ruined dozens of otherwise perfectly good scripts. No one ever just got shot in a Jake Whelan movie. They got "stitched up" or "nailed to the wall" or they "caught twice their weight in lead" or got "ventilated like a nursery" or something.

But still.

I said, "You've hired someone to do me?"

"Keep your eyes in back of you, Junior."

I started to explain that I'd get a stiff neck, but there was a click on the line, a real one this time, and I looked to see RONNIE on the screen.

"Hang on," I said as Jake's voice scaled up. I hit a button.

"Incoming," Ronnie said. "And fast."

"On the way." I clicked back to Jake, said, "Gotta run," and hung up. The phone vibrated again instantly, but by then I was on my hands and knees on an extremely soft carpet—scented, swear to God, with lavender, so maybe its owner spent more time on the floor than I did—with my little penlight between my teeth again, looking for the stamp. Since it was nowhere in sight, I had time to register that the fragrant carpet was that kind of mealy-mouthed beige favored by people who are afraid of color, so the Vuillard, or even a Paul Klee for that matter, would have been lost on this guy. He deserved his damn stamps.

It had *wafted*, the stamp had, naturally. Had to fall fancy with frills on, had to catch the merest suggestion of a breeze, couldn't just drop like a rock. It had wafted well beneath the circular mahogany table on which I'd put the stamp album and, like a mook, the nail file with the fake on it. I picked up the fake, a bit hurriedly, and made a faint crease across the upper right corner, which, when I got it back onto the table, I immediately began to smooth on the blank side. I heard a metallic squeal that I recognized instantly as a bad hinge on the gates, about thirty yards away, at the other end of a curving driveway. I'd heard it from around the corner when he left.

The Slugger was home. The Slugger ate babies for breakfast.

Smooth the crease in the stamp, put the stamp on the nail file, ease the whole thing into the Hawid mount, *don't hurry*, center it, square it off, work the nail file out without moving the stamp. *Not enough perforations.* Close the album, make it third in the pile, which was where it was before, pick up the pile of albums—

A car door opened and then closed, the resolutely untinny thunk of a good, solid, six-figure vehicle, a Bentley, in fact.

—slide the albums back into the safe, close the safe, and lock it. Figure out which door he was going to head for.

He was *whistling* out there. Not—not . . . no, it couldn't be, not—yes, it was—"Achy Breaky Heart," regularly voted the worst earworm in the history of ears, just completely indelible, so now in addition to going to prison I was going to get beat up regularly for whistling "Achy Breaky Heart."

Well, what did I expect from a guy who collected mistakes?

The Slugger usually traveled armed, according to Stinky, and with good reason, since when he wasn't poring over his collection of misprints, he collected debts for the kind of people from whom one should never, ever borrow money. He'd started small, working for local bookies, and then demonstrated the pep and zip that define the American character by building himself into a kind of nationwide brand, a sort of chain operation contracting beatings (and the occasional pop off when a client ran out of patience), carried out by a handpicked squad of broad-shouldered, short-necked local sadists who could be depended upon to deliver precisely the quantity of pain selected on the sliding scale that Daddy set up for his customers, a one-to-five spectrum in which "one" was a couple of black eyes and a new nose, and "five" was a week in intensive care. Five-point-one was the old "sleeps with the fishes" option, which cost extra.

He'd innovated, too, the Slugger had, offering punishment designed to damage the psyche as well as the bones and muscles: moving beyond crude force to inspired refinements involving spiders, snakes, rats, and in one widely described instance, two buckets full of garden worms, a rectal thermometer, a large funnel, and a recording of tango music. For targets with pathologically inflated concepts of their own masculinity, he'd retained three young women, chosen because they looked like someone with whom you might strike up a conversation in the checkout line at the library, who could begin a session with a blown kiss and end it with full-body trauma, all of it accompanied by a monologue on how a *real* man would defend himself.

He was called "the Slugger" because his persuader of choice was a Louisville Slugger Prime 915, made entirely of "composite," such an informative word, with what the company's advertising copy refers to as "a massive sweet spot" and a relatively light swing that gives the user "the best possible feel" when he brings the bat through the zone. I was pretty sure that "the best possible feel" was a one-sided experience, but the point was that the Prime 915 was the Slugger's preference when he decided to keep his hand in personally, and he ordered them in such quantities that the company engraved his name on the barrel, just like they do for Yasiel Puig.

Too much detail? Okay, in short, the Slugger was packing and willing to use it, and I wasn't. In keeping with sane burglary policy, I never went to work strapped because it automatically ups the charges into a zone where it's very difficult to avoid spending several years in jail, which is essentially a cage full of anger-management case histories who are just waiting to rip the ears off someone suicidal enough to whistle "Achy Breaky Heart."

Which door? Front or back? (*Don't tell my heart*) Either way it made sense for me to get to the big room's single door, if only to be in a position to decide which direction to run.

I was most of the way there (*My achy breaky heart*) when I remembered that the combination of the outermost lock on the safe had been set to 9 when I opened it, and I'd left it on 4, which was the last number, the open-sesame number, in the combination. I was so anxious to fix it that I almost skipped over to the safe, risking my penlight once more to illuminate the dial and twirl it back to 9. (*Don't tell my heart . . .*) The combination lock might seem like a trivial detail, but someone whose idea of a good evening after a day spent crushing kneecaps is poring over tiny, badly printed paper rectangles probably remembers which number he left the combination knob at.

And how many perforations there should be on his Gandhi stamp.

Later for that. For the amount of time it took me to get back from the doorway to the safe and then back to the doorway, he'd stopped whistling. Now, where the hell *was* he?

When I first arrived, I'd walked the place as I always do before going to work, getting a sense of the space and identifying potential escape routes. It was, I'd discovered, a remarkably insensitive re-creation of a Mississippi plantation house, which is to say it was essentially a giant square, two generous stories tall, plus an attic I would have visited on a freelance basis if I'd had the time. Attics make a burglar's palms itch, because people so seldom check on the things they keep there. The grand rooms—living room and dining room downstairs, matching master-bedroom suites upstairs—were in front, and the relatively minor rooms—billiards room, den, book-free library, breakfast nook, lesser bedrooms—were toward the back. What made it unquestionably a plantation house were the gigantic marble stairway that curved up the right side of the grand entrance hall to a second-story landing straight out of *Gone with the Wind* and—behind and between all the fancy rooms—the wooden, unfinished servants' stairs that led up from the back of the house so that the slaves, in the old days, could get from level to level without even momentarily intruding on all that southern serenity.

The aristocracy of the Old South may have loved and nurtured their slaves as much as they claimed they did, but they didn't want to have to say hi on the stairs.

The big differences between the house I was in and the real thing were that the Slugger's monstrosity had cost a hundred times what the finest plantation homes of Georgia and Mississippi had gone for, even allowing for inflation, and the fact that the kitchen was inside, whereas in the antebellum houses it was in a separate room near the slaves' quarters, which both protected the big house from fire and generously gave the slaves a stove to shiver around in the winter. When I'd come in through the back, I'd also seen three tiny bedrooms at the very rear of the house, but Stinky had been right about the house being empty; the people who slept there were all out, possibly attending a neighborhood whipping.

The stamp room I was so anxious to vacate was one of the twin master-bedroom suites, the one on the left if you were inside looking toward the front. If the Slugger was heading for the front door, he'd be coming up the grand stairway. If he came in the back and he felt like slumming, he'd use the servants' stairs.

I stood in the doorway of the stamp room, breathing the way Herbie Mott taught me to breathe, openmouthed with the tip of my tongue touching the roof of my mouth, by far the quietest mode of respiration, and trying not to listen to the chorus of "Achy Breaky Heart" ricocheting brightly around in my forebrain. Seen in a graphic rendering of my body, drawn to a scale that illustrated the extent to which any system was in use, I would have been a vertical line with ears like a fruit bat's and underarm sweat glands big enough to fill an Olympic-size pool. Listening and perspiring, perspiring and listening, I waited to see which door he was going to use so I could pick my stairway.

And heard nothing. I had heard no door open, which was, unfortunately, not the same thing as no door actually having *been* opened.

He could be anywhere, and this (*Don't tell my heart*) was not good. My phone vibrated against my thigh, and I cupped my hand on top of it, frantically going over everything I'd done, now that I'd reset the combination lock, looking for other telltales that might tip him that someone was in the house. Couldn't think of anything: I'd relocked the back door, reset the alarm, not used any lights except the penlight, which I'd pointed away from windows, my back between it and anyone whose eye might be drawn by the gleam. I'd followed all the rules Herbie had laid down for me during my long apprenticeship. Except for overstaying my welcome.

And then I *did* hear something, a tapping sound (*My achy breaky heart*) that brought to mind the hollow, terrifying sound of Blind Pew's cane stubbing along on the pavement outside the Admiral Benbow Inn at the beginning of *Treasure Island*. It took no imagination whatsoever to identify the sound as the tip of a baseball bat being bounced lightly, even playfully, off the marble steps of the grand staircase as someone came, slowly and deliberately, up it.

2

Hypotenuse

Okay, so the bad news was that I'd broken the rule about how long to stay inside, and my carelessness had earned me the potential attention of a man with a gun and a baseball bat and expertise with both.

The good news was that he was coming up the front stairs. Which left the back stairs open.

Sliding my feet over the marble floor—I love marble floors: they never creak, you can't leave patterns in them as you do on carpets, and they're *great* for sliding—I made my way noiselessly and quickly down the hall to the door that led to the servants' stairs. I'd left it ajar, since I usually try to get out of a house the same way I get in. It was a surprise to hear the bat-tapping that was echoing off the marble stairs bounce back from the wooden ones, but then surprise turned to a faceful of black liquid dread as the tapping from the wooden stairs caught up with and then *passed* the tapping that came from behind me.

Echoes don't do that.

Two stairways, *two* guys, two bats. No other way down, at least not in the amount of time I had available to me. I'd identified an emergency exit on my walk-through, but it would take a good minute or even two to open it and close it again, and even then it might just turn out to be the shortest distance to a broken leg.

One coming up the front, one coming up the back. I needed to get to the right-hand bedroom, but not by running down the center hall to the landing, which would put me directly in the sight line, momentarily at least, of someone coming up the marble stairway. I peeked at the rear stairs, saw that he hadn't yet rounded the switchback, and darted straight across the hall to the door into the bathroom that connected to the bedroom I wanted.

Who was the second guy? How did they know I was inside the house? An answer to that question presented itself in my imagination, immediately and with such force that it ended the earworm in between "achy" and "breaky." The answer—betrayal—had to be the right one, but there was nothing I could do about it now.

The bathroom was the architectural equivalent of a hairy calf, so male that it looked contrived. The wallpaper featured a pattern of green pine trees accented cleverly with brown log cabins and a few more-or-less taupe moose and mooselets, a design that might have been drawn personally by L.L. Bean on a bad day and intended for children's pajamas. The seat on the toilet was up, and the water in the bowl was suspect. A broad leather strap hung beside the oak-framed mirror, and it took me only a tenth of a second, which seemed like quite a long time, to identify it as an old-fashioned strop for a straight razor. I pulled open the mirrored door, which yielded with a sound that I would have spelled *bock* had I been in a spelling mood, and there it was, gleaming at me, so I took it out, steel folded into bone of some kind. I'd never used a razor on anyone, and I never wanted to use a razor on anyone, but it seemed like a good thing to keep away from the Slugger.

The tapping stopped, both front and back. The guy in front, whom I automatically assumed to be the Slugger, called out, "We gotcha. Come onto the landing *right now*, because if we have to look for you, you're gonna be horse glue."

I knew with absolute certainty that I was not going onto the landing. Unfortunately, that was the only thing I knew with absolute certainty. The alternatives—and I was sure there were dozens of them—refused to line up and say hi. I stood there in that bathroom wondering why none of the servants had lowered the seat or flushed the toilet, and then three things happened at the same time. "Achy Breaky Heart" started up in my head again, and the guy in front slammed his bat against the floor with a bang like a pistol shot, but that was instantly drowned out by a crashing noise of industrial proportions, a sound that could only have been caused by something the size of a cruise ship taking the gate outside right off its hinges. I actually heard both stages: first the crash with the attendant shriek of hinges being torn away and then the clatter of the gate, probably flung backward, hitting the driveway.

"What the *fuck*?"

That was the guy in front, the Slugger, and the words were still echoing when I heard him sprint down the steps. The one behind me called a question, but I wasn't paying attention to the words: I was already in the right front bedroom, opening the window on the right-hand wall as quietly as I could.

It had an old-fashioned twist-lock at the top, so that slowed me down a second, but then I had it undone and

I'd eased the window up about half an inch and retwisted the lock to the secured position, meaning that the window would look to anyone who didn't take the time to come over for an up-close inspection as though it had been closed from the inside. Then I stood absolutely still, breathing openmouthed, back in fruit-bat mode, listening.

I heard the guy in back call another question but couldn't make out the words, except for "Morrie," which made sense, since the actual name of the Slugger was Morrie, or perhaps Maury, depending on whether it was short for Morris or Maurice, and my guess would be Morris, because—

Stop it. Not germane. *Listen.*

Nothing. Goddamn marble floors, can't hear anyone who's smart enough to slide his feet over them. The whole USC marching band could be sliding down the hall, heavily armed and wearing taps, and I wouldn't hear them. I *hate* marble floors. Then, over the silent marching band, I heard a sound that I attributed to a shoe on wood and then a squeak, which I identified as the fifth stair down—it had creaked beneath my weight when I came up. Then another foot on wood and then another, getting softer, not louder. Going away.

Mr. Back Stairs wasn't so brave without Morrie or Maury to tag team with. Moving as quickly as I could without making noise, I slid the window the rest of the way open. Then I pried up the little V-shaped metal piece at the bottom of the screen, the one that snapped down over the post set into the windowsill to lock the screen in place, and, holding on to the V with my left hand, I used the straight razor in my right to make a cut about two inches inch long in the mesh, exactly where the screen met its wooden frame. It would be invisible unless someone pushed out on the screen.

It was time to listen again, but the Slugger was making it hard for me to hear anything by screaming at the entire neighborhood as a way of expressing wrath over whoever had battered his gates, since that person had seemingly fled the scene. I personally knew and had used every single word in the Slugger's stream of invective but had never heard them grouped in so many short strings of such force and elegance. It had a rare kind of public-restroom eloquence to it.

Then I heard the second man's voice, and it came through the open window, which meant he'd gone outside. This was the best news I'd had in some time. For half a second, I thought about running down those back stairs and out the door, but once I was on ground level, the only way off the lot was through the large space where the gates had been and where the Slugger was now. Instead I stuck with Plan B. I pushed the window all the way up and then angled the screen, which hung from hinges at its upper corners, away from the building. I climbed out onto the windowsill, holding the screen open above me, and found myself looking down at a drop of about eighteen feet to a flagstone path that ran beside the house. Chez Slugger was a relatively recent build, in a style that in the late 1990s was referred to as an "Iranian teardown," meaning that a very nice house of standard size for the neighborhood— say, 12,000 square feet—had been bulldozed and replaced by a self-conscious, oversize architectural boil that could barely be shoehorned onto the lot, stopping only about eighteen inches from the property lines on the left and right. It also lowered the tone of the entire block.

The original house had been surrounded by a serious wall, still standing and fourteen feet high, into which the now apparently destroyed gates had been set. The wall was about a foot wide, and the thickness of its ivy cover—the kind of verdant overachievement that British universities put on postcards—testified to the age of the house that had been knocked down; it had probably been built in the 1940s. As close as the wall was, if I jumped from the window and missed it, I would be falling past the ghost of a stately home that had undoubtedly housed several generations of interesting people, none of whom would be around to sympathize when I hit the flagstone.

I was crouched on the windowsill, putting a little bend in the nail file—which is harder than it sounds—when the Slugger started hollering at Mr. Back Stairs, telling him to get various parts of his anatomy back inside. That supplied a spike of energy that made the bend a bit easier, and, holding the nail file in my left hand, I backed all the way out onto the sill, still in a crouch, until I was clear of the window's path.

Now for the first hard part.

The window casing was a good, thick, dependable two-by-six, and the wall was shingled, giving me little spaces between the casing and the tops of the overlapping shingles into which I could insert my fingertips. With nothing but that and the four inches of windowsill beneath my feet to support me, I leaned in just far enough to reach up and pull the window down. It wouldn't go *all* the way down, because the latch on the inside was in the closed position, but at least it would look locked. I was breathing heavily when the realization hit that I had just eliminated my only quick and easy route back into the house, and the psychological effect was instantaneous: the space beneath me suddenly yawned, darkened, and deepened until those eighteen feet between me and the flagstones felt like eighty.

Now for the second hard part. *And wouldn't it be cool,* I thought, *to be able to climb a rope?*

But I couldn't, and I didn't have one anyway, so it was jump or die, or perhaps jump *and* die. A step four feet down and eighteen inches out separated me from the top of that ivy-clad, one-foot-wide wall. *Piece of cake,* I thought. On level ground it would be a long step. Of course, on level ground it's not such a *deep* step. I thought of Rocky the Flying Squirrel, my father's favorite cartoon character and one of the few things we both enjoyed, Dad and me watching reruns of good old Rocket J. Squirrel together, me laughing whenever he did.

Rocky flew with his arms spread wide, and I thought, *Who am I to argue with Rocky?* I slid the nail file into my pocket, turned around very carefully, opened my arms, and pushed off. In midair I spread my legs, too, guiding myself to the top of the wall along an imaginary path of the sheerest, purest yearning and landing flat on my belly on top of it, gripping it for dear life with my arms and my knees. I knotted my fingers into the ivy in case of . . . I don't know, an earthquake and just lay there, thinking briefly about breaking into tears but remembered that I wasn't finished yet. I still had to lock the window screen.

As I got onto my hands and knees, I reviewed my next steps and found them wanting, an unsettling blend of high risk and low value. I was ninety-nine percent certain that what I was about to do, like having reset the combination dial and making sure that the bedroom window looked locked—all the time-consuming precautions that distinguish the skilled burglar from the chemically addled smash-and-grab, soon-to-be ward-of-the-state thug—was pointless. It had sounded from the beginning as though they'd known I was there. As though I had, in short, been betrayed.

But there was that one-percent chance that I was wrong, that in fact I hadn't wasted my time making the replacement stamp to delay discovery of the theft and doing all that other tradecraft, and then there's also habit. When you can, says Herbie Mott's unwritten masterwork, *The Burglar's Handbook*, you leave the scene exactly as you found it. The longer it takes the mark to discover the theft, the colder the trail.

So what the hell. The Slugger's unwearying stream of invective had ranged off to my right, as though he'd jogged in that direction to try to locate the vehicle that had taken out his gate, and now it was swinging left again, as he came back down the street. The other guy was presumably inside the house by now, although he might be skulking behind a couch or something, waiting to spring into courageous action until the Slugger arrived. Of course, he might also be more frightened of the Slugger than he was of me—I knew *I* would have been—and might be diligently searching the second floor by now. Time to move.

Under normal circumstances, getting from one's knees to one's feet is a skill learned in toddlerhood, requiring little preparation and less courage, but doing it on top of a one-foot-wide wall some twelve feet in the air, above an unforgiving flagstone surface, when you're a guy who couldn't learn to climb a rope and whose phone is once again vibrating insistently in his pocket, turned the whole maneuver into an Olympic-caliber feat: The Rise and Fall or something.

Both my knees and my palms told me that the wall was an uneven, somewhat treacherous surface, a tangle of ivy vines, some of them as thick as my thumb, designed by a malignant God to trip people up and make them turn their ankles just before they fell to their death. I crawled back and forth within an eighteen-inch stretch until my knees found a couple of places where they could actually feel the cinder blocks on top of the wall. One at a time, I slid my feet into those flat spots, and then I rose to a crouch and very, very slowly straightened.

I'm about six feet two, so all I had to do to get to the window was lean forward a foot and a half and break my fall with my hands. It sounds so *easy*, put that way. Once I was standing, I spread my feet on top of the wall, widened the space between my hands to miss the plate glass, filled my lungs just to remind myself what it felt like in case this turned out to be the last time, and leaned toward the house.

No problem, except for a little thump when my left palm hit the side of the house. With my knees locked and the rest of me deeply, deeply aware of the fall waiting patiently beneath me, I pulled my right hand away from the wall and felt in my pocket for the nail file, moving the razor aside to get to it. Beneath my left hand, the wall of the house vibrated very slightly, which my imagination translated into someone walking the second floor. I leaned a little closer to survey the master bedroom, which was still empty.

But probably not for long. So I folded the elbow that was resting against the wall so my weight was being borne by my left forearm, which put me closer to the screen, and went to work. *Slip* the bent nail file through the slit cut into the screen, *position* the downward-bent tip over the little triangle of metal that needed to be popped down over the tiny upright post in the center of the sill. *Press* my fingertip down on the midpoint of the nail file as a fulcrum, meaning that both hands were engaged for a moment, which the space beneath me saw as an opportunity to fill my imagination with a cavernous-sounding *Come on down*, giving me a short but intense bout of head-spinning vertigo. I had to focus very closely on the edge of the windowsill to stop the world's whirl, so I missed the moment at which Mr. Back Stairs came into the room.

But there he was, slope shouldered, thin necked, and round headed, with a prison haircut, an extra-long upper lip that looked red and chafed, as though it got a lot of wiping, and the permanently puzzled expression that distinguished the members of *Spinal Tap*. All those unthreatening characteristics were sharply offset by the baseball bat in his left hand and the small automatic in his right. He was coming into the bedroom very slowly, the gun extended and the bat over his shoulder, and his gaze was directed at the floor beneath the beds.

Anyone who (a) comes into a bedroom searching for someone, (b) thinks first of looking under the beds, and (c) is more than twelve years old is, charitably, someone it should not be difficult to outwit. Nevertheless, considering the gun and the bat, I rolled to my left to get clear of the window. In doing it I caught my right toe beneath a particularly ropy length of ivy, and my left knee bent beneath me as I fought to control the trip. I slammed both hands against the side of the house, got my knees straight and both feet on the wall, and hung there, as rigid as the hypotenuse of the world's sweatiest right triangle, gasping for breath.

I felt him hear me. Steps came closer, then stopped, and then a flashlight snapped on, pointed straight out the window. A bright circle brought the top of the wall out of the darkness, and right there, just below the perimeter of the circle was my left foot, in the black Chinese sneakers I use as work shoes. No choice: I pulled the foot off the wall and let it hang in space, my back and shoulders pressed against the house and all my weight on my right leg.

Which began to tremble.

A tap on the window glass announced that he'd put the end of the flashlight against it. He moved the circle of light up and down and then side to side, briefly illuminating my black-clad foot and the shaky leg above it, also in black, but the dark ivy apparently swallowed them up. It might also have been, I realized, that he was peering through the light reflected on the surface of the window, which had probably been cleaned by the same servant who didn't flush the toilet. Then the light started to move left, toward the front of the house, and as I released a huge sigh, I was dazzled by the gleam of the nail file, sticking straight out of the bottom of the window screen, bright as a politician's promise, winking at me as the light left it behind. When he brought the flashlight back in this direction, there was no way he was going to miss the nail file.

I was reaching slowly for it, keeping my hand below the windowsill and hoping he wouldn't sense the movement, when he turned the flashlight off. Until then the angle of the beam had told me which way he was looking, but now I had no idea, and there was nothing to do but freeze, one foot on the wall, one dangling down, one shoulder against the house and the other contorted forward to let me extend my arm, like someone playing a game of three-dimensional Twister, until I felt him walking again. A moment later a light came on, pale and diluted, that I figured had to come from the hypermasculine bathroom I had briefly explored. I got my left foot back against the wall, wiggled my way back to the window, and managed to snap the little triangle down over the post. There. The screen was officially locked from inside.

That meant one of two things, both good. First, if they hadn't actually been certain I was there, if they'd been reacting to some little trigger, perhaps a glimmer from my penlight against a window, there would be no evidence that anyone had been in the house until some point in the distant, Junior-long-gone future, when the Slugger opened his album and counted the perforations on his damn stamp. Second, if they *still* believed that someone was inside or had been inside, or if they'd been tipped off after all, I had just eliminated the master-bedroom window from the list of possible escape routes. It's always progress to eliminate the place where you are from the list of places people are likely to think you'll be. Then I heard the toilet flush, and the bathroom light went out. No one came back into the bedroom. This was the most secure I'd felt since their car pulled in.

So I screwed up.

I got both feet on the wall, extended my arms, and pushed my center of gravity back toward the wall. After all, it was only eighteen inches, and I damn near made it. In fact, I made it and went *past* it by about three inches and found myself teetering backward on the wall, windmilling

my hands but . . . definitely . . . going . . . over. Instead I
stepped back and let myself fall.

Dropped faster than I'd expected, but about four feet
below the wall's top I managed to grab some ivy with
both hands. There was a tearing sound as quite a lot of
ivy got yanked free of the wall that its tendrils had so
assiduously woven themselves into. Part of the bit I was
holding on to pulled away, dropping me another eighteen
inches or so.

Above me the light came on again in the bedroom.

I panicked. Hand over hand I scrabbled monkey style
along the side of the wall toward the gate, one yank of
ivy after another, not wanting to go down to ground level
and trip the motion sensors I'd seen fill the yard with light
when a car pulled in to the drive about ninety minutes
before I'd entered the Slugger's house. I'd traveled four or
five yards before I realized I should have gone in the other
direction, toward the rear of the property, because they'd
certainly assume I would head for the street.

And they had. Flashlights traveled the top of the wall,
reflecting off the windows of the house behind me, and
I figured it was just moments before the owners of that
house would be out to see who was shining lights into
their windows. Thus far, though, the place was dark, so
maybe I was in luck and everyone who lived there was
in their nineties and they'd all been asleep for hours, and
maybe they were insomniacs who took sleeping pills of
veterinary dosages and sank into a nightly coma or were
under a witch's spell, and maybe they all bunked on the
far side of the house, so even if one of them were pulled
from his stupor by the demands of an aging bladder, he'd
be way over there and wouldn't see or hear any—

Something bumped my leg, hard, from behind.

My feet were about two yards above the ground, and I turned my head, expecting to see a human face staring up at me, perhaps a human face attached to an arm that ended in a hand with a gun in it, but I didn't see anything at all. From the other side of the wall, the Slugger shouted, "HEY!" but I figured it was a lot more tentative than it sounded. I was a good fifteen feet from the window I'd gone out through, and he was still about eight, ten feet behind me, if the light was any indication.

Whatever it was, it hit my leg again, harder this time, and I looked straight down and saw my assailant, front feet spread wide, rump in the air, brown eyes looking up at me hopefully: a chocolate Labrador retriever, tail whisking back and forth like a windshield wiper, hoping desperately that this strange human traveling sideways along the wall would come down and play.

My phone started to vibrate again.

I like dogs that don't want to kill me, and I particularly like Labs, but this was not the time for a romp. I whispered a sharp *No*, and the dog sat down and regarded me critically. My stock with the dog was dropping, my phone had massaged my thigh for so long that it was beginning to hurt, and from the far side of the wall I heard a clank of metal on stone that it took me no time at all to identify as a ladder.

I decided to go hell for leather through the ivy in the direction of the front gate. For a second the dog stayed put, but then it made its will known: it barked. Just once, but quite loudly.

Once was enough. There was an urgent little windstorm of whispers from the other side of the wall, and the ladder clanked again, this time much closer to me. And a light went on in the house the dog lived in.

I let go of the ivy and fell, landing on my feet. The dog promptly jumped high enough to rest its front paws on my shoulders and lick my face, giving me a quality sniff of dog breath, but then it furrowed its brow questioningly and looked back over its shoulder, which meant to me that the front door was about to open.

I dropped to my knees and grabbed two huge handfuls of ivy and tore it upward, away from the wall, but only about eighteen inches of it came free, so I put a foot against the wall and yanked again. The dog barked joyously and took off for the door. I lifted the ivy in as intact a sheet as I could manage and crawled behind on hands and knees. I had my right side pressed against the wall, and I was facing the house the dog had run to.

Up until this point, I'd avoided tripping the lights, but now they came on with the intensity of klieg lights at a Hollywood premiere. Motionless, I peered between a couple of big leaves to see an old dude with fierce eyebrows and a nose like an eagle's beak step onto his front porch. He wore a shapeless white T-shirt and a pair of gray gym shorts and had something black and hard looking in his hand, and my stomach muscles did a little tango step at the sight of it. He glared in my direction and shouted, "You!" Then he pointed the black thing toward me.

I said, "Uhhhh," and a couple of the many-legged things that live in ivy dropped down the back of my shirt and started trying to dig their way into my skin. The sheer shock of it choked off my reply, which was a good thing, because from above me and to my right a familiar voice said, "What, you old fart?"

"What the hell are you doing up there?" Eagle Beak said.

"I'm looking at my wall. Whaddaya think I'm doing?"

"I think you're shining your fucking flashlight through my windows, is what I think you're doing, trying to get a look at Lizzie in her nightie and making my dog bark in the goddamn middle of the night."

"I got a burglar," the Slugger said, "and he's in your yard."

"Yeah?" Eagle Beak called back into the house, "Moron thinks we've got a burglar in our yard." To the Slugger, he said, "You see any burglars down here? Jee-zus peezus, *burglars*. Any burglars in this neighborhood, they'd be waiting in line for your autograph. Now, get offa that wall."

"It's my wall."

"Like fuck it is. Seven inches of it is on my property, and that's the seven inches you're hanging your big fat face over right now. And I'm tired of looking at it." He raised the dark cylinder, and a supernova of hard white light erupted from the end that was pointed at the Slugger.

Above me the ivy shivered and trembled, and the Slugger said, "You blinded me, you old clown!"

"Shine lights in *my* window, will you?" Eagle Beak shouted. He wiggled the black cylinder, which I recognized belatedly as a Streamlight UltraStinger 1100, the agoniz-ingly brilliant flashlight favored by cops in dicey areas all over the country. "Here, take a good look at this." He made tiny circles with the Streamlight, and I heard a scrape of metal followed by a much *longer* scrape of metal, then a despairing scream cut short by a heartfelt yelp and a really rewarding compound sound, half the clatter of aluminum and half the dull thud of human muscle, both striking the unforgiving surface of flagstone.

"And *stay* down there!" Eagle Beak shouted. "Asshole!" He stepped back and slammed his door.

If it hadn't been for the whimpering from the other side of the wall, the night would have been blessedly silent. On the other hand, the whimpering had a kind of plaintive musical quality, a descending arc of tones in a minor key, lovely if heard from the right perspective. If it had had a beat, I might have danced to it.

"I *still* can't see." It was the Slugger's voice, just barely not sobbing, and that was the cue I needed. I clawed back up the ivy until I was about halfway to the top and then headed right. When I got to Eagle Beak's gate, which was about three feet shorter than the wall, I climbed up onto it, stepped over, and then ivy-rappelled down to the sidewalk and took off up the street, away from the Slugger's collapsed gate. Turning the corner, I yanked my shirt away from me and shook off my passengers, one of which bit me by way of goodbye, and pulled out the phone, which was vibrating again, or possibly still. I put it to my ear, and Ronnie said, "Come uphill to Tigertail and turn south. I'm in your car, two driveways down."

3

The God of Spring

I think it was the immortal Chuck Jones, creator of the Road Runner and Wile E. Coyote, who invented the trope in which a character runs off the edge of a cliff and keeps right on running on thin air until it looks down, at which point it falls like a stone.

As busy as I'd been trying to stay alive in the Slugger's house, the moment I heard that car hit the gate, I had the unmistakable sensation that I'd just left the cliff behind and that there was probably a considerable drop beneath me. But I hadn't had time to look down and see just how far the fall might be.

Now I *did* have the time, and as much as I wanted to speed-walk up Tigertail and get into that car with Ronnie so we could motor out of the Slugger's orbit, I stepped back into a hedge instead and thought for a couple of minutes about the person who had just snatched my butt off the barbie.

The question was simple: Who the hell was she?

When I met Ronnie, she was a suspect in a situation I'd been forced into working on. My assignment was to make sure that my client wouldn't be charged with the murder of someone he'd had a lot of reasons to murder.

The victim had been Ronnie's husband, and the first rule of murder when the victim is married is *look at the spouse.* So, during that first week we knew each other, even as we were falling in love, we were both lying for all we were worth, me trying to figure out whether she was guilty and her trying to look as innocent as lamb's fleece. It was, let's say, a layered relationship.

Eventually I figured out who'd killed Ronnie's ex, and that would have straightened it all out between us except that she refused to tell me *anything* about her past, including where she'd come from or what she'd been doing with all the crooks she'd been hanging around with back wherever it was. I knew they were crooks because she'd come to Los Angeles from some dreary East Coast town—Trenton and Albany had been claimed at various times—by being lateraled every thousand miles or so, like a living football, from a car thief to a drug dealer to a blackmailer, the last of whom she'd married.

I know it feels like it must have taken me some time to consider all this, but I was cranked up pretty good and my mind moves fast when it needs to. I knew I'd missed something in the past couple of minutes, and I was trying to dig that out when headlights swept the street, turning down from Tigertail, not up from the Slugger's. I stepped farther back into the hedge as my inoffensive, inconspicuous little white Toyota glided by instead of the Jaguar I'd been expecting, the one we'd stolen so we'd blend into the neighborhood better and which had undoubtedly been the heavy beast that had hit the gates. As it went by, my mind replayed Ronnie saying, *I'm in your car.*

For a moment I thought about zigzagging surface streets, avoiding her completely, until I got someplace where I could call a cab. Just to give me some time to sort out what had just happened and what it might suggest.

Also, I realized I was shivering, a delayed reaction to what had nearly happened at the Slugger's. Ducking Ronnie for a while would also let me get that under control. But then I heard Herbie saying, *The longer you delay facing something important, the longer you give it to kill you*, so when I pushed myself out of the hedge and started uphill, figuring she'd turn around and pass me on the way back up to Tigertail, I still had no idea what I should say once I got into the car.

"So?" she said, pulling away from the curb.

I sat back and worked on not shaking. "Piece of cake."

"I ask because you look like the god of spring, with green stuff all over you, twigs in your hair, and bleeding knuckles."

"Piece of cake," I said again.

"And you're shaking."

"Okay, it was a piece of stale hardtack laced with rat poison."

"That's better," Ronnie said. "I get all warm and fizzy when you confide in me."

"I don't usually talk after a job," I said.

"No shit," Ronnie said, making a right. She headed uphill, toward Mulholland and the San Fernando Valley. We were in a neighborhood where even the weeds were expensive. I don't spend a lot of time in areas like this. Too much temptation and too many security cameras.

I said, "Where are we going?"

She turned and regarded me just a moment too long, given the number of curves in the street, and I hit an imaginary brake pedal with my right foot. "You're asking me?" she said. "We're going to that man with the little tiny nose and the Filipino folk dancers, right? You said he wanted the stamp tonight."

"I'm not sure now. There are a lot of balls up in the air." My phone vibrated. I pulled it out, looked at caller ID, put it to my ear, and said, "Fuck off, Jake." Then I turned it off.

"What a relief," Ronnie said. "It's not just me. One of the balls?"

"How'd you get my car?"

She drove for a moment, and then she said, using the exact same tone she'd used the first time, "One of the balls?"

"Yes," I said.

She said, "How do you *think* I got your car? I drove the Jag back to where we borrowed it, left it there, and hiked up to where we parked this awful little Toyota. I have to say it's a real step down, going from the Jag to this heap. On the other hand, this has brake lights. I left about a third of the Jag's rear end in that gate I knocked down." She drove a few hundred yards and repeated, "That gate I knocked down."

"Yeah, yeah," I said. "And thanks. I might not have made it out if you hadn't done that."

"It was nothing. Really, nothing."

"Just . . . you know, want to be sure you understand I'm grateful."

Ronnie took us around a turn, stopped at an intersection, and then took us further uphill. "It's written all over your face."

"I'm thinking."

"My father always said, 'Never interrupt a man who's

thinking. You might prevent him from having his only idea.'"

"Your father said that, did he? Where did he say that?"

"I *knew* we were getting to this," she said. "And let's not. Let's do what we were going to do, before I saved your ass and you got all crazy. Let's drop the stamp off like you planned and then . . . I don't know, go to the park and search for poisonous mushrooms, something that suits your mood."

"You nailed the gate, swapped cars, and got back to the meeting point."

"It sounds so impressive boiled down like that."

"It *is* impressive. And amazingly fast thinking for someone who's never committed a crime before."

"Are you going to *continue* to be awful?" she said. "Listen, if we're not going to that man's house—"

"Stinky."

"To Stinky's house. I mean, if we're not going there, where *are* we going?"

"I'm working on that. So . . . about your criminal skills, if I were to get someone—say, a cop—to comb through the criminal records in Toronto—"

"I've never been to Toronto."

"Or Ontario."

"Or Ontario. Oh, *look* at my knuckles on the steering wheel. They're all white. Such a stressful line of questioning, when what would be appropriate is appreciation and maybe a kiss."

"I appreciate you. Where was it, then? Montpelier?"

"This is a very peculiar reaction toward someone who just saved your—"

"And demonstrated an unexpected set of skills, at a speed

that suggests well-worn neural pathways. Which, as we both know, are developed through repeated use. Trenton?"

"Fine, sure, Trenton." She swerved the car violently into the oncoming lane and then brought it back. "Cat," she said.

I hadn't seen a cat.

"So we're not going to Stinky's, so you're in this foul mood, because you didn't get it? The big hotshot burglar didn't—"

"I got it. I always get it. I'm a professional. And I flatter myself that I can *recognize* a professional."

The word made her pause just a bit longer than she should have. Perhaps she hadn't expected me to be so blunt. "Whatever that means. Look. You got your stamp, you got out in a single, not badly shaped piece, with your fairly attractive face intact. You've got that stamp in your pocket, and you should be ready to hop on over to your fence's house—" She bit her lower lip. "That's what you'd call someone like Stinky, right? A fence?"

I just looked at her.

"You throw that term around a lot," she said. "Fence this, fence that. 'I'll just run this over to my fence.' Like that. You know?"

"So if I were to send someone to comb through the criminal files of Trenton or Albany under the name Veronica—wait, what's your maiden name?"

"This is territory we haven't covered," she said. "And I *appreciate* that we haven't covered it. I know it's taken willpower on your part."

"It has. What was it?"

She did a little warning drumroll on the steering wheel with her nails. "LeBlanc."

We shared a moment of silence.

"You do realize," I said, "that LeBlanc is not a name that really rings with credibility."

She pulled the car to the curb, hard enough to put the front tire halfway up it. We were most of the way to Mulholland, in an area where the houses were sealed behind gates that made the one she'd driven through look like a saloon door. There were no streetlamps, and we were on a tight curve to the right, practically begging to be hit from behind. The top of the ridge, a few hundred yards ahead, was a curving, pillowy line of solid black against the diffuse glow of the Valley's zillion lights. "I come from a long line of LeBlancs," she said between her teeth. "LeBlancs all the way down."

"Down to where?"

She sighed heavily, a sign that she needed time to work on the answer and its tone. "Down to 1209 A.D.? The Albigensian Crusade? When Pope Innocent III, of all the ironically named people, decided to kill every single Cathar in France because they didn't like the cookies the pope served at the altar. That was when we changed our name, because we'd been Cathars, and burning at the stake didn't seem like an option. Okay?"

"Changed it from what?"

"LeNoir," she said. "Later anglicized to Leonard."

"Anglicized when? That makes no sense at all. I mean, if your name is still LeBlanc—"

"LeNoir was an embellishment," she said with fraudulent candor. She shook her head fondly at her own foolishness. "I can't resist embellishments."

"You're telling me. So your family was Cathar?"

"Still is."

"I thought all the Cathars were dead."

"Yeah, well, don't tell the pope. Can we get going now?"

"And you? You're a Cathar?"

"To the center of my clean little bones."

"So you believe that the world is the result of a war between God and Satan and that everything that's visible was created by Satan and is therefore evil?"

"Explains a lot," she said, "when you think about it."

"And that human beings are the genderless spirits of angels, temporarily trapped inside evil bodies designed in hell, sort of like good champagne in a paper cup?"

She squinted at me. "*What* kind of spirits of angels?"

"Genderless."

"If only."

"So, at the risk of abandoning this endlessly interesting digression, if I were to have someone probe the criminal files of Newark and Poughkeepsie—"

"Trenton and Albany." A pause. "I might have said Newark."

"For arrests and charges involving Veronica LeBlanc, of all the silly names, there'd be no record of—"

"For heaven's sake. If I don't even remember which *town* it was, if I can't say for sure whether I have a record, surely you can understand that it's because I've blotted it all from my memory, that something happened back there—"

"Wherever it was—"

"—so terrible that I've drawn a dark veil over it, even for myself, even blocked it from my dreams. There are areas of experience for a woman that a man can't even begin—Why are you grinning?"

"Because you're so fast, which is what gives you away, and because you know instinctively which buttons to go for. Problem is, I don't have many buttons."

"Yeah, well . . ." She reached over and punched me in the vicinity of my heart. "You've got a big red one in the middle of your chest that says OFF, and I just prevented someone from pushing it. Don't I even get a coupon?"

"I'm just dazzled by your chops. Makes me think about broadening the act. I could use a partner."

"I thought we *were* partners."

"Oh, well," I said. "In the sense you mean, I suppose we are. In the sense *I* mean, we've barely even compared our credentials." A car came around the bend, hugging the right curve, and gave us a couple seconds' worth of irate-sounding horn. "Could we move to someplace where the odds of being killed are a little lower?"

"Sure." She started the car. "I suppose I'm flattered by the partnership offer, but I think it's probably a ploy, a conversational can opener to get at my past."

"Could be." I craned back to check the street. "You can go now."

"I can go," she said, "any damn time I like."

I don't know who else it could have been."

We were maintaining a polite truce as Ronnie took us on a prolonged up-and-down zigzag over the streets south of Ventura, plush by my modest standards but a trailer park compared to Brentwood, just on the other side of the hill. She was keeping an eye on the mirror to humor me while I tried to describe the events of the evening in a way that qualified as a life crisis.

"I hear what you're saying, which is more than you do,"

she said. "So let me say it out loud to you while you listen. You think it's possible that your longtime fence, Stinky Tetweiler—"

"Who did in fact take out a contract on me about seven months ago."

"I'm going to get to that. Stinky, who got grumpy with you six or seven months ago and wanted you dead but accidentally hired someone who's sort of sweet on you—"

"Was. *Was* sweet on me."

"You'd know more about that than I would. So Stinky decides *again* to kill you, and this is the plan he comes up with: he goes to the trouble of finding the person who owns that stamp, he digs up all the information about how you could get into the house, which had to be expensive info, and then he tips off the owner of the stamp so he, the owner, can beat you to death. This means that, first, Stinky doesn't get the stamp and, second, he has to explain to this Slugger person, who doesn't sound like a very forgiving guy, how he knew you were going to be in his house."

I said, "Well, when you put it *that* way—"

"Instead of just . . . you know, hiring another person to shoot you or sending you into a dark, empty house full of ninjas."

"There's no such thing as a ninja."

"Ninjas are everywhere."

"And if ninjas *were* everywhere, a house full of them wouldn't be empty."

"You're dodging the fact that I'm right."

"Two guys," I said. "Baseball bats. I'm ninety-percent sure they knew I was in there. Who else could have tipped them?"

"No one," she said, turning right for the third or fourth time on Hayvenhurst, "which means that you have to go to the other ten percent. The ten-percent chance that you somehow tipped them to your presence, expert though you are, with your little flashlight. *N'est-ce pas?*"

"'*N'est-ce pas*'?"

"That's how we Cathars talk. '*Bonjour, n'est-ce pas?*' We say it on the slightest provocation." She pulled to the curb again, leaned forward, and rested her forehead on the wheel. "I'm hungry. Either I want something to eat and a cup of coffee or I want to go to bed."

I looked at my watch. Ten thirty. "Trade you something to eat for the name of the place you were born."

She said, "Eat where?"

"We're not doing it that way. I'll suggest someplace, you'll say no and suggest something else, and we'll wind up going to the place you suggested."

"Since we're nearly on the other side of the hill, let's go to K-Town. The barbecue places are open late."

"Fine, K-Town." I waited long enough to see a coyote trot past the car, looking professional. Coyotes always look professional. "Well?"

"All right," she said. "Newark."

I braced myself for a surge of elation that didn't arrive. "That's it?"

"Why? Too easy?"

"I don't know. I don't feel like I actually won."

"You didn't," she said. "I lied. Tell you what. Turn on your phone and see whether Stinky's been trying to get you. Or call him, see if he answers."

"I thought you were hungry."

"I am, but this way my going hungry pays me back for

having lied to you, so you can't be mad at me. See? We're even."

I turned on my phone, and it rang with the information that it was Jake, so I turned it off again. "Fine, we'll go to Soot Bull Jeep and get our clothes all smoky and Korean. But change places so I can drive, and give me a little more time first, okay?"

"What for?"

"To take a discreet look at Stinky's house."

4
The Baronial Elite

Stinky Tetweiler had once referred to himself, in my hearing, as "a member of the baronial elite." He's also been known to let his choice of first-person pronoun slip from *I* to the royal *we*. If that gives you the impression that he could be an overprivileged, insufferably smug, self-satisfied twit, you would have an accurate impression.

He came by his smugness in the traditional baronial way, which is to say he inherited it through the dumb-luck accident of birth. He was the scion, albeit in disgrace, of the family that created that most pernicious of innovations, the perfume strip. After earning hundreds of millions with a product that made sensitive people's uvulas feel like a thumb down their throats, the Tetweiler family had diversified by buying one of the seven global companies that create molecules that mimic natural fragrances for commercial use in detergents, artificially flavored food and drinks, room deodorizers, new cars—everything from mosquito repellent to the seductive smell of a fake leather jacket.

He'd grown up in a 20,000-square-foot house with a scratchy little two-horse imitation ranch around it, way out in Chatsworth, in a nouveau riche area now occupied by Justin Bieber and some rising basketball stars. Give him credit: he knew from childhood what he wanted and what he didn't want. What he wanted was the money. What he didn't want was any part of the family business.

He tried, God knows he tried, to remake the fragrance racket in his own image and likeness. He created two spin-off companies. Celebrity Sweat was an attempt to market T-shirts with chemical reproductions of the perspiration of people like Tom Cruise and Arnold Schwarzenegger. The Church of Scientology sued on Cruise's behalf, and that was that. Tokes Without Smoke attempted to appeal to people who had managed to divorce themselves from their addictions but still felt a sort of nostalgia toward them. The advertisements offered the scents of five kinds of marijuana, two varieties of opium, and the pungent reek of cooking meth, all dead-on imitations and all drug-free. Taken together, between the chemistry, the manufacturing, and the marketing, these two ventures cost the company almost a hundred million.

By the time his father started paying attention, Stinky had embarked on his third venture. He'd learned some-where about the condition called synesthesia, in which there's a kind of sensory crossover that results (in some cases) in fragrances being associated with sounds, and he'd decided that synesthetes were guaranteed to be a commercially under-served group. Within a month he'd co-opted the services of a bunch of the company's chemists and a trio of people who either had synesthesia or claimed to, and he'd managed to create scent blends that were roughly equivalent to the first three chords of Mozart's "Dissonance" Quartet. The foundation had been laid for the world's first scratch-and-sniff music book when his father changed the locks at the office and installed Stinky's younger brother in the heir apparent's seat.

So Stinky turned to crime.

He became a high-end fence as a cheap route to nice things, for which he had an inexhaustible appetite and a keen eye for those that would yield a healthy profit. The stamp I'd bagged that evening, for example, would be sold to his client for about a quarter of a million, while Stinky had promised me only $35,000 to lift it. Or he might decide to keep it. There had always been rumors that Stinky held on to about as much loot as he sold.

"He's got room for it," Ronnie said, leaning across me for a better look at the house. She smelled like Ronnie, blessedly free of fragrance molecules. Stinky's house, a fifth-generation Los Angeles mansion, rambled aimlessly around the crown of a big, hilly Encino lot, the back end of which bordered a golf course. The neighborhood, which had aspired to being mildly upper-middle-class when I was a failing Cub Scout, had been plowed under by the relentless bulldozer of big money and replaced by long gleaming strings of mini-mansions, as mismatched as freshwater pearls; gated communities, which I've always thought of as an opportunity to be locked in with people you don't even want to say hello to; and not one but two country clubs, complete with Disney heraldry on their logos: a lion passant and a nine-iron rampant on a field of green.

"From what I hear, he'd need something the size of Versailles to hold it all." I said aloud for the first time a thought I'd had often over the years, "Might be nice to figure out where it is."

"Looks like he's asleep."

"That's the bad news," I said. "Stinky has stayed up all

night since he was ten years old. He never goes to bed until he's read the morning paper."

"He still takes a paper? How quaint."

"The important word in the phrase *morning paper* was *morning*. Stinky regards staying up all night as aristocratic behavior, flaunting the fact that he never, *ever* has to get up until he's good and ready. Baronial elite and all."

"Maybe he's dead," she said.

"It would have to have been awfully fast," I said. "It's only been about an hour and twenty minutes since you pancaked that gate."

She looked over at me as though she were thinking about getting out of the car. "I was kidding. About his being dead? I was kid—"

"I'm not." I pulled away from the curb, leaving the dark house behind, and turned the corner. Halfway down I settled the car against the curb and opened the door. "Sit behind the wheel and leave the engine running. Give me ten minutes, and if I'm not back by then, go home. If you see anyone except me coming down this street, floor it."

"And leave you?"

"Exactly," I said. "No heroics."

She sniffed. "And no Korean food."

My cheap little runner's watch has two features that make it indispensable to someone in my line of work: a diplomatically dim blue light that lets me check the time without drawing an unfriendly eye, and a stopwatch. I put it in stopwatch mode, said, "Starting now," and climbed out.

Walking briskly, but not fast enough to attract attention, I took twenty-nine seconds to get back to the corner I'd just turned and another thirty-four to get to the foot of Stinky's driveway, putting me sixty-three seconds in, with less than nine minutes to go. The driveway was long enough to eat another twenty-five seconds or so, and by the time I hung left to go around the house, which looked completely dark, even on this moonless night, I was almost two minutes in and already wishing I'd asked for twelve minutes rather than the punchy, macho-sounding ten. *Gimme ten minutes,* I heard myself say in my mind's ear. All alone and in the dark, I had the grace to blush.

Stinky had once spent a week in London and had brought home with him a spotty British accent, a weakness for scones, and—as I discovered when I slipped my foot into a wicket and fell flat on my face—an enthusiasm for croquet. Had he known his history, I mused as I tried to catch my breath and listened for any indication that anyone had heard my *whoooof* when I hit the ground, had he indulged his Britophilia beyond the occasional broad *a*, Stinky would have known that croquet actually originated in merry old France. It was first written about in the thirteenth century, being played by small-town French peasants with willow wickets and broomstick mallets. Early in the nineteenth century, the game was transplanted to Ireland, whence it became the plague of Blighty, disfiguring stately lawns all over that blessed isle and eventually tripping burglars in far-off California. A complete Victorian croquet set with decent historical associations can go for five, six thousand bucks, but they're too bulky to swipe and too specialized to fence.

Two minutes and forty-three seconds and I was breathing hard and hadn't looked through a single window.

I hauled myself to my feet and got as close to the house as the bushes would allow. The plan was simple: keep the house on my right and do the complete circle, looking for signs of life.

Chez Stinky was an absolutely style-free one-story burst of misplaced enthusiasm, maybe 6,000 square feet of unadorned stucco and glass—with no obvious architectural ancestors—that had views of the Valley to the north and the big, burglar-friendly windows such views demand. I'd been inside the front part of the house, which is to say the entrance hall, the living room, and the big formal dining room right behind it, often enough to have a sense of where the other rooms were apt to be: contractors like to economize on things such as plumbing and gas lines and often build very different-looking houses on the same plumbing schematic. My guess was that there was a kitchen, a service area, four bedrooms—or three and a den—and at least three bathrooms, each of which would have its own external window.

Los Angeles architecture is like one of those 1950s horror movies in which radioactivity produces terrifying mutations. In this case the radioactivity was the whimsical influence of the movie studios, the employees of whose art departments moonlighted as architects for decades and built whatever the hell they'd liked from the last film they'd worked on. I'd just escaped from an ersatz southern plantation house, and if it had been light enough, I could have seen from Stinky's yard a French Provincial, a Cotswold cottage, several faux-Spanish haciendas, a Moorish mini-palace with scalloped arches, two half-timbered Tudors, a Japanese teahouse that wouldn't have been out of place in Kyoto, a streamlined nouveau-deco hybrid, and a couple of the hard-to-heat glass-and-concrete slabs that became so popular in the nineties.

Stinky had probably looked long and hard to find the resolutely anonymous place he'd bought. He needed it to be that way because he swapped out entire interior decors as often as most people vacuum, and if one morning he decided to trash the Frank Lloyd Wright Craftsman furniture in favor of a Louis XIV motif, he didn't want anything as stubborn as architecture to get in the way of his plans.

The last time I'd been in the living room, I'd been beaten into library paste by his then-resident Filipino houseboy Ting Ting, but before the blood began to flow, I'd seen that Stinky had made one of his infrequent decorative lapses, a leathery assembly of Texas Marlboro Man junk, so six-gun butch that you would have worn chaps to dust it. It *deserved* to have me bleed on it. This two-fisted idyll had replaced a longer-lasting and much preferable Marie Antoinette period, Stinky having an instinctive sympathy for martyred royalty.

Whatever was in there now—and for all I knew, it could have been the Hall of the Mountain King or a twelfth-century peasant's cottage, complete with peasant—it was too dark to tell. About the only things I could make out were a couple of unadorned dark rectangles against the dining-room window that had an angular simplicity, a lack of frill that said they might be Early American.

But no lights and, as far as I could see, no people.

Like most crooks, Stinky was not a trusting soul, and he'd dispatched me, a thief, to score a little piece of paper that would probably earn him a quarter of a mil. *And* he'd told me to bring it straight to him. The Stinky I knew would have been pacing the floor waiting for that stamp, feeling the kind of anxiety I always experienced when my ex-wife told me that our thirteen-year-old daughter, Rina, was at a sleepover. Since the divorce I'm no longer allowed to live with them, but mentally I'm frozen in their living room with my nose pressed to the window, checking my watch every ten minutes and arguing with myself about going to toss the house where she's staying. Stinky should have been anxious about the stamp, eager to brush his broad, spatulate fingers across the surface of the holder. Stinky had fingers like hams but a touch as delicate as a pickpocket's.

He should have *been* there. Cool as the evening was, I was perspiring.

Four minutes, fifty-two seconds.

From what I could see through the living room's side windows, the furniture was still looking Early American, perhaps even Shaker. The Shakers were a group of radical Quakers who included women among their elect and who, because they trembled in worship when the spirit seized them in its teeth, became known as the Shaking Quakers. They believed that owning an ornament led to the sin of pride, and so the furniture they made was as pure and beautiful a statement of function as any I've ever seen. As an influential religious force, the Shakers were a single struck match in the long-burning fire of faith, but if we believe that beauty is God's aesthetic default mode, we have to acknowledge that God employed the Shakers to bring a disproportionate amount of it into the world.

At the big dining-room window at the rear of the house, I was compelled by those classic silhouettes to risk the penlight that had probably gotten me into so much trouble earlier in the evening. The furniture was Shaker for sure, but there was no one sitting or standing in there to appreciate it. Nor could I find anyone either prone or supine on the carpets, no hair-raising pools of dark liquid, no overturned antiques. Stinky's exquisite seventeenth-century

French cylinder desk—like a rolltop but with a curved, solid piece in place of the hinged slats and decorated with floral inlay in wood of six colors—was closed. Stinky closed it whenever he wasn't actually sitting at it, so he almost certainly closed it when he left the house, too.

But why would he leave the house? He should have been shifting from foot to foot, waiting for his Gandhi stamp.

And why was I still here? Six minutes down and all those other rooms to go. I got into a rhythm: shove myself through the brush to the next window, press my nose against the glass, turn on the penlight, swipe it around, move on. I learned that Stinky's enthusiasm for Shaker stuff, or value of any kind, didn't extend to the bedrooms, all but one of which could have been furnished from IKEA; any more generic and the carpet would have had a bar code woven into its center to let people order the whole room with a single misguided click. The exception, and what an exception it was, was the master bedroom. Stinky slept in what seemed to be an authentic, water-warped Venetian gondola, hauled up onto a custom-cut frame to keep it from rocking side to side on the waves of sleep, and the rest of the furniture in the room could have come directly from the Doge's Palace.

Don't dally. The bathrooms were just bathrooms, except for Stinky's, which looked like the pope's pissoir, with what I think was a holy-water font in white alabaster dead center in the room. More mirrors than I would have expected, although I immediately realized I should have known better: Stinky *liked* the way he looked, had in fact paid hundreds of thousands of dollars to have his face sculpted into an aerodynamic cutting edge, streamlined as a Modigliani, with high cheekbones and a tiny nose that plastic surgeons had been sanding down for decades. His hair had been plucked into a widow's peak that was probably inspired by Bela Lugosi. Stinky had apparently fallen in love with an alien who had landed at Roswell and had been remaking himself in its image ever since.

Okay, so the bathroom slowed me down. I was almost nine minutes in when I rounded the final corner of the house and found myself at the front door. I checked my watch, figured what the hell, and pulled on a plastic food-service glove. When I pressed the latch, the door swung open in front of me—always a bad sign—until it bumped against something. As dark as the hallway was, I could still make out the two little pictures I coveted hanging to my immediate right and, on the floor where it had served as a doorstop, a man-shaped consolidation of darkness that the penlight revealed to be Stinky's latest houseboy. He was on his back, but not restfully. His jaw had been shattered so that it yawned open on one side, and his right leg was bent, and not just at the knee. It was bent in three places, and the foot looked like it had been put on backward. It must have taken him many long minutes to die.

A sight like that demands a *lot* of attention, and my sense of time went a little elastic, because when I looked at the watch again, I'd been away from the car for ten minutes and forty-six seconds. I backed out of the hallway to the drumbeat of my heart, closed the door, removed the glove, and pulled the phone out of my pocket. The moment I turned it on, it buzzed. Jake Whelan. I answered and instantly disconnected as I trotted down the driveway, went a few steps farther, and then pushed the speed dial for Ronnie. And listened to it ring. And ring.

And ring.

5

Jejomar

The car was where I'd left it, and Ronnie was craning backward, still in the front seat but looking out the rear window, either for me or just toward me. I gave her a tentative little wave, but she didn't respond. Nor did the car seem to be running. I realized I was distracted by what I'd just seen in Stinky's hallway and slowed to give the night a belated look.

Quiet neighborhood, an architectural patchwork but nothing threatening except perhaps aesthetically. Nicely spaced streetlights, the lawns beneath them shining with dew, a thin, tardy sickle of moon just barely afloat above the trees. No one on the sidewalk but me, no moving cars and not many parked ones. Lights off in almost all the houses.

Ronnie continued to regard me neutrally as I got closer. I might have been a bowl of goldfish for all the interest she showed. I made a little shrug, meaning, *What?* but got nothing in response. My right hand began to itch, which usually means I wish I had a Glock with me. I did have the Slugger's razor, and I took it out and palmed it in my right hand so I could keep the left free to open the door or do whatever else might be called for.

Checking the surroundings again, I went to the passenger side, glanced into the car, and got in beside a wide-eyed Ronnie. The moment my butt hit the seat, I smelled perfume, and the moment I smelled perfume, I heard movement behind me and felt something cold prod the back of my neck, and Stinky Tetweiler said, "Say hello, Junior."

I said, "If that thing touching my neck is your finger, you've got circulatory problems."

"Where's my stamp?"

"Somewhere between here and there. Where's your houseboy?"

A long, long pause. I eased the blade of the razor open one-handed, and Ronnie's eyes went down to it and bounced back up again. When Stinky finally spoke, his voice was shaky. "Back at . . . at the house."

"You get a lot of loyalty from your houseboys," I said.

Stinky sniffled. "I get what? Oh, right, right. I'd forgotten. Ting Ting put you p-pretty well on the c-c-carpet, didn't he?" Stinky didn't usually stutter.

"He did."

"That was the last time I smiled," Stinky announced with another sniffle. He pushed the gun barrel into the back of my neck for emphasis.

I said, "I'm glad to have given you some amusement."

"Yes," he said. "One of the highlights of a b-bumpy relationship."

It seemed like a good idea to keep him talking. "What was this one's name?"

"Jejomar." He had physical difficulty getting the name out, as though it were fighting him.

"Sorry?"

"F-for . . . for Jesus, Joseph, Mary. Filipinos like to combine—" He began to weep.

"They got him pretty bad."

"I heard it." He cried for a moment, sounding like a dog in pain, then swallowed loudly. He pulled the gun away, presumably to wipe his face, then put it back. "I even saw a little of it, although they didn't see me. But what could I do?"

"Yeah, well, you cling to that in the middle of the night. Especially considering that you've got a goddamn gun in your hand."

"Junior!" Ronnie said.

I said, "You should see what they did to him while Stinky was getting his over-upholstered ass down the driveway."

"Onto the golf course," Stinky said. He could never resist an opportunity to correct.

"Not hard to figure out what the weapon was," I said. "And I didn't even see it happen."

He shoved the gun into the base of my skull, hard. "This is what I should have done the *first* time I wanted you dead. Not hire a bunch of palmy hitters who—"

"Don't mess up my car," Ronnie said.

"*Your* car?" I said, and immediately tried to erase it with, "Yeah, don't mess up the lady's car." I turned the razor so the blade was facing away from me.

"Whose car is it, then?" Stinky said.

"Hers," I said as Ronnie said, "Mine."

Stinky said, "Looks a *lot* like the one you drive, Junior."

I said, "I borrowed it from her," as Ronnie said, "I bought it from him."

There was a pause. My fingers were cramping around the razor. Stinky said to Ronnie, "You're fast."

I said, "I was just telling her that a few minutes ago."

"Maybe we shouldn't be sitting here," Ronnie said. "What with Jujube or whatever his—"

"*Jejomar,*" Stinky said, his voice rising.

"Tell me why you want to kill me," I said.

Ronnie said, "You mean *this* time."

"Well, *yeah,*" I said.

"Just looking for clarification," Ronnie said, sounding aggrieved.

"Don't act even dimmer than you are," Stinky said to me. "You told those beasts with bats that I sent you for the stamp, and they came to kill me."

"Really." I let go of the razor and said, "I'm moving slowly here, Stinky," and reached into my pocket. "Explain this." I had the stamp pinched between my fingertips.

"It's the fake?" Stinky said, but the question mark deprived the sentence of most of its authority.

We all sat there for a minute. Then he said, "Gimme."

"In your fucking hat," I said, pulling it away. "You do anything I don't like, and I mean *anything*, and I swear I'll use the last bit of life I have left to chew it into a spitball."

"You guys are both lunkheads," Ronnie said. "*He* thought—Junior here did—that you found the stamp, sent him after it, and tipped off that bat fetishist, all as a fancy way to kill him."

"Preposterous," Stinky said. He settled his weight farther back in the seat, which made the car dip. "As you should know from recent experience, Junior, when I want to kill you, I'll hire someone to shoot you."

"Like that other man just did," Ronnie said.

Stinky said, "What other man?"

I said, "Never mind."

"And *you* thought," Ronnie said serenely to Stinky, "that they caught Junior in the act, as people say, and he told them you sent him, and they said, 'Well, all right, then, thanks, here you go,' and gave him the stamp as a reward and came after you."

"Well," Stinky said, "when you put it *that* way—"

"I said the exact same thing," I told him. "When she reacted to *my* theory, I mean. Word for word."

The pressure on the gun eased off. "You going to give me the stamp?"

"You going to give me the thirty-five K?"

"I haven't got that kind of money in my pocket."

"Well," I said, "this will give you motivation to get it."

"You don't trust me," Stinky said, and Ronnie burst out laughing.

I said, "What's so funny?"

"Both of you," she said. "You're hopeless."

Stinky said, "Who *are* you anyway?" He was looking at her like someone who's just seen something new and is trying to count its legs.

"A mere girl," Ronnie said.

Stinky nodded, stopped nodding, and nodded again. Then he shook his head once as though to clear it and said to me, "So you didn't rat me to them?"

"Would I be alive if I had? Would I have *this*?" I waved it around a little. "So you didn't set *me* up?"

"Of course not." He thought for a moment. "Were you ever a Boy Scout?"

"No."

"Really?" Stinky sounded surprised.

"But you were a Cub—" Ronnie began.

"Skip that," I said.

Stinky leaned forward to look at me over the gun, which was now beneath his chin. "You were a Cub Scout but you never became a Boy Scout?"

"One of my early failures."

"Out of many," he said.

"I'd like *not* to point out that *you're* the one who ran away over the eighteenth hole, leaving his valiant houseboy with his legs on backward."

Ronnie said, "Eeewwww."

"So do you remember the oath?" Stinky said. He seemed to have gotten past Jejomar, with the dependable resilience of the sociopath.

"What oath?"

"The *Boy Scout* oath." Stinky sounded like he'd had a long day of talking to stupid people.

"I told you, I was only a Cub Scout."

"Why?"

"He couldn't climb a rope," Ronnie said.

"What're you, Jiminy Cricket? If I want my conscience singing out all the time, I'll take some sodium pentothal."

Ronnie turned back to Stinky, pushing the gun barrel aside. "Careful with that thing," she said. "He's touchy about the Cub Scout episode. He *still* can't climb a—"

"Fine, fine, fine," Stinky said. He put the gun beside him on the seat. "Is there some oath you *do* believe in?"

"Sure," I said. "The oath of the Tarzana Ham Sandwich and Skateboard Club. I belonged to it when I was a kid."

"Then by the oath of the whatever you just said, do you swear you didn't have anything to do with those sadists showing up?"

"I do."

"Okay." Stinky looked down at the automatic as

though he'd forgotten he put it there. "Perhaps we need to reconsider the situation."

"There's a situation?" I said. "One that we're both in?"

Lights swept the lawn to our left and then flared in the rearview mirror. "Everybody down," I said, and we all dove for the floor. My hand rolled on something, and I picked up one of Ronnie's fugitive lipsticks.

The car came down the block slowly and slowed even more as it passed us. The beam of a flashlight nosed its way through the passenger window and zipped snoopily around over our heads. From the backseat I heard Stinky whisper, *"Ama namin, sumasalangit Ka Sambahin ang ngalan Mo—"*

I said, "Shut *up*."

Stinky left off, but I could still hear his lips moving. He sounded short on spit.

The car accelerated, and the noise of it gradually fell away.

"Okay," I said. "There *is* a situation."

"I *told* you we should move," Ronnie said, her voice pitched a little closer to the soprano range than usual. "Why didn't they get out of the car?"

"There are two possibilities. The good one is that they didn't see anything and decided to keep searching. The bad one is that they *did* see something and decided it would be too noisy to take care of us here." I handed her the lipstick. "Found this."

"I looked *everywhere* for that." She pocketed it. "What a relief."

"What a *relief*?" Stinky said, clawing his way back to eye level. "This team of sadists is after us and getting your *lipstick* back is a relief?"

"It's a hard color to find," she said. To me she said, "How long should we give them?"

"Three minutes."

"Why three minutes?"

"*I* don't know. Same reason I asked for ten minutes before. It sounds kind of cool, suggests that I know what I'm doing."

Stinky said, "You don't know what you're doing?"

"If I knew what I was doing, Stinky, would I be here?"

"I'm not good at this," he said. "I should be home, with my things."

"Wouldn't recommend it, not for quite a while. What were you saying back there?"

"Saying? When?"

"During the flashlight."

"Oh," Stinky said. "Then."

"Should I go out the way we're facing," Ronnie said, "or turn the car around?"

I said, "Why does everyone ask *me* everything?"

"Okay," Ronnie said. "Turn around."

"Why?" I asked.

"Oh, for Christ's sake," she said. "If you want to decide, just decide."

"Just looking for . . . you know, the logic of it. I mean, since our lives might depend on it and all."

"I figured they saw something," Ronnie said, "and decided to wait for us up ahead."

"And why do you figure they saw something?"

"I knew you were going to ask that. When I got down, I hit the brake pedal with my hand."

Stinky said, very fast, "*Ama namin, sumasalangit Ka Sambahin—*"

"*That,*" I said to Stinky. "What the hell is that?"

"The Lord's Prayer. In Tagalog." There was a pause that felt like someone waiting for a slap, and he sniffled again and said, "Ting Ting taught it to me."

I said, "Great guy, Ting Ting."

He said, "Have you seen him?" in the tone of someone who has come to think that "hope" is nothing more than a girl's name.

"We don't move in the same circles," I said. "They're a younger, more energetic couple, go out a lot. And then there's her. She kills people."

"Sorry to interrupt," Ronnie said. "Go straight or turn around?"

"Turn around."

"I feel so vindicated," she said. "The three minutes up?"

"Who's counting? Just get us out of here." To Stinky I said, "Give me the gun."

He said, "It's not loaded."

"It's not—"

"If it was loaded, do you think I would have let them do that to Jejomar?"

"Right, right, right. I'm sorry, I really am. So why'd you bring it?"

"I felt safer. It fooled *you*, didn't it?"

"Here we go," Ronnie said, and there we went, into a very tidy three-point turn. We crept slowly, lights still out, to the corner of Stinky's street, and she started to make a left.

"No, no," Stinky said. "Dead end. That way leads to the country-club gate. It'll be closed by now. Have to go right."

"Got it."

"And turn the lights on," I said. "This is like having the Goodyear blimp over us with a big arrow pointing down and flashing the words 'Here they are.'"

"It's *so* easy to criticize." She flipped the lights on and made the turn.

Instantly, headlights went on behind us.

Stinky said, "There's someone *back* there."

"This is the first night I've ever driven this thing," Ronnie said. "Does it have any punch?"

Normally the car has a big fat Detroit gas gulper, wedged into it by Louie the Lost, but Louie's engine developed a cracked block, so the original Toyota putt-putt was back in place. I said, "Not so's you'd notice."

"Well, let's find out." She jammed her foot down, and the car gave a little gargle and leaped forward, accelerating by a good five miles per hour. She slapped the dashboard. "That's *it*?"

"You have to talk to it." I looked back, past Stinky, at the dazzle of light behind us.

"What do you say?"

"It's too embarrassing." The lights behind us doubled in brightness and grew closer.

"Does it have a name?" Ronnie said. She was bouncing backward and forward to urge the car on, as though she were rowing it.

"That's what's embarrassing," I said. A nice-looking house crept by on the left, at a rate of speed that gave me time to appreciate it. I reached back and snatched the gun from Stinky's hand. "Are you sure this thing isn't loaded?"

"Well, *I* didn't load it."

Ronnie said, "Pookie? FooFoo?"

"Get down," I told Stinky, and the moment he ducked, I pulled the trigger.

Both my ears turned inside out, Ronnie screamed, and the back window exploded into a million diamonds. And then the horn of the car behind us began to blare and the car slowly drifted left, bounced right, swerved left again, and jumped the curb. Then it came to a stop.

"What a shot," I said, although I hadn't actually been aiming.

"Oh, my God," Stinky said. "I could have saved Jejomar."

Ronnie said, "Uh-oh."

I said to her, "It *felt* too easy, didn't it?"

Half a block in front of us, a black Porsche pulled away from the curb and immediately telegraphed its intentions by weaving back and forth at about eight miles an hour.

"Shoot him, Junior," Stinky said, a bit imperiously.

Ronnie didn't have to brake much to stay back. She started weaving in opposition to the car in front of us: it went left, we went right. "Slow is good," she said. "This car is aces with slow."

"How far to a turnoff, Stinky?"

"I don't know," he said.

"You *live* here."

"I don't get out much."

The car in front of us was slowing even more. We were going about five miles an hour, and it kept weaving back and forth.

"I am behind people like this *all the time*," Ronnie said between her teeth. "Why don't you do what the nice man said, Junior? Shoot the fucker."

"Fine," I said. "Weave left. That way I can get a good shot at the driver's side."

"Left, Pookie," she said to the car, and we swerved. It was a slow swerve, but it was a swerve.

The back window of the Porsche was tinted, and I couldn't make out the driver's silhouette, but a driver usually likes to be close to the steering wheel, so I aimed at where I thought it would be, closed one eye, sighted, drew a deep breath, and pulled the trigger.

"You were close," I said to Stinky. "It was *almost* not loaded."

"You mean, that's it? There aren't any extra ones stuck in there anywhere?"

"Not a one. I could throw it at them."

"Uh-oh," Ronnie said again, and then for a third time, "Uh-oh."

I said, "Two?"

"Two," she said. "The one in front of us and two behind us."

Stinky said, "Oh, my God. *Bats.*"

I looked back to see two guys who were as wide as they were tall and had those big, sloping shoulder muscles that seem to begin at the ears and make the head look really, really little trotting toward us, holding the biggest baseball bats I'd ever seen. I said to Ronnie, "What's in front—" and canceled the rest of the question because the Porsche was in a very wide swerve to the right, all the way to the curb, and then it pulled left until it was perpendicular to us and stopped, blocking the road.

The door opened, and a much slighter guy got out, no hurry, all the time in the world. He was slender and kind of classical-musician-looking, dressed all in black and smoking a cigarette. He had an elegant swoop of steel-gray hair that picked up the moonlight nicely, and over his shoulder was yet another bat. He paused, found the bright center of the headlights, stepped into it, and, swear to God, riffed his swoop of gray hair with the fingers of his free hand. He was *posing*.

"That's *him*," Stinky said, his voice breaking on the pronoun. "That's the Slugger."

I said, "I'm surprised he didn't bring his mirror."

Ronnie said. "Where's reverse?"

"Two down."

She slammed it into reverse and floored it. I'd like to say we shot backward, but it was more demure than that. We rolled backward at a dignified, favorite-auntie speed, gradually picking up velocity, and then Ronnie cut the wheel sharply left and we all heard and felt a loud thump followed a hoarse scream, and as the other guy's bat landed on the trunk with malice aforethought, she said, "Engine in back?"

"It's a *Toyota*," I said. "The engine is in the fucking ashtray."

"In the Porsche, you idiot."

The bat shattered the left backseat window, and the car filled with flying glass and Stinky's shriek.

"In the back," I said. "I think."

"Okay. Put on your seat belts."

I said, "Oh, for Christ's—" And Ronnie dumped the car into neutral, raced the engine to the red line, and threw it into gear.

We jumped forward with a squealing-tire abandon that was a new element in my relationship with the car, and Ronnie leaned on the horn, one long, pulsating bleat of desperation to wake up the neighbors. The slight figure of the Slugger jumped elegantly out of the way, and Ronnie twisted the wheel left, hopping the curb on the driver's side and, still gathering momentum, clipped the front end of the Porsche at a sharp angle, knocking it cattywampus, and then we were around it and hurtling downhill.

"*Directions!*" Ronnie shouted.

I said, "Go right, then just head downhill."

She tore her eyes from the rearview mirror. "Watch behind us."

I looked back. We hung a gentle curve and then made the right, and even looking backward as I was, in my peripheral vision I could see the Valley opening itself welcomingly below us, glittering a relieved *Hello there.* Ronnie had brought the car's speed down to something like the limit, and she said, "Anything?"

"Not unless he doesn't have his headlights on."

"Okay," she said. "Then he's probably not coming."

"Why not?"

"Either I knocked the front wheel cockeyed or I pushed the fender into it so tightly it'll cut into the tire and blow it the first couple of yards he drives. That's why I clipped him at that angle. I probably screwed up Pookie's passenger side—"

"She's not named Pookie."

"—but I wanted to make sure I hit his wheel just right." She turned to me. "So where are we going? Or do you want to drive?"

"No, really," I said. "Wouldn't hear of it. You're doing fine."

6

The Great Unspanked Baby of the World

"People *live* like this?" Stinky was squinting against the light. The Du-par's on Ventura, just a block from Laurel Canyon, has been uncomfortably bright inside all night long for about forty years, with the shadowless, concentrated glare of twenty-four-hour coffee shops everywhere. I've always figured the candlepower was meant to discourage dopers and draw cops, who convene from the night like moths. In fact, four uniformed motorcycle cops, their leather creaking as they shifted in their seats, were the only other customers in the place. Stinky glanced at them, dismissed them, and pouted at his plate. "Where in the world are we?"

"Studio City."

"On a *deeper* level," Stinky said, making a point of not rolling his eyes. "What kind of place *is* this?" He prodded the coconut cream pie I'd ordered him. "Is this supposed to be food?"

"People who leave their houses occasionally," I said, "have *places*. They might not be great places, they might not earn three stars from the *Guide Michelin*, but they have several things going for them. We're used to them, they stay in the same location, and we have memories set in them."

Stinky prodded his plate. "Gluten," he said, in the tone I'd been saving to say "knot of writhing centipedes," and then touched the tip of his fat little index finger to his tongue. *"Sugar."*

"It's pie," Ronnie said, poking a hole in the top crust of a piece of apple and then licking the back of the fork. One of the things that recommends Ronnie to me is that she loves to eat. She may have lied to me about literally everything else in her life, but her love of food is genuine. I don't trust people who don't like to eat, which is not exactly the same thing as saying I trusted Ronnie. She said, "What *do* you eat anyway?"

"Lean protein in small quantities," Stinky said. "Cruciferous vegetables. Seeds and nuts."

I said, "You're still going to die."

Stinky said, "Do you know how this stuff *accumulates* in the gut, how it turns to putrefactive acids, how long it takes you to *excrete* it?"

"Not my topic." My pie was peach and had more sugar in it than Hershey, Pennsylvania. "I figure I can either die having eaten pie or die without having eaten pie, and as existential choices go, that one's a snap. It requires even less energy than figuring out who to vote against."

"You have memories about this place?" Ronnie asked with her mouth full.

"This was where I received the Gospel According to Herbie," I said. "He brought me here the night we met, and we came back regularly, whenever he had the urge to pass along a lifetime of learning. Du-par's was the soda fountain of knowledge, so to speak."

"Herbie Mott," Stinky said, having sniffed his water and put it down. "Great burglar."

"There should be a Burglary Hall of Fame," I said. "Posthumous, of course, no need to make it any easier for the cops than it already is." I nodded in the direction of the four uniformed officers in the booth, busily turning my tax dollars into burgers and fries. One of them, who had been staring at Ronnie, held my gaze in the biologically approved male-primate fashion. I smiled to indicate submission. "Herbie would be the first inductee."

"The pathological need of Americans to give each other awards," Stinky said. "It's pathetic. It infantilizes us in the eyes of the world."

"We've been infantilized in the eyes of the world for a long time," I said. "Back in the 1920s, after we came out of World War I in a single piece, the painter John Sloan— Do you know that Herbie left me a Sloan painting?"

Stinky put his elbow on his pie, glanced down at it, and left it there. He rubbed his nose with his free hand, the sure sign that his heartbeat had just increased—I'll kill the person who tells him about it—and said, "You have a Sloan?"

"I do."

He rubbed his nose again. "Have you thought about selling it?"

"Of course not. Anyway, after the war ended, with us largely protected by oceans, Sloan referred to America as 'the great unspanked baby of the world.'"

"Very apt, I'm sure," Stinky said. "You have a Sloan?"

"Who retained you to get the stamp?" I said.

"Surely you jest," Stinky said. Ronnie batted his arm away from his pie, pulled the plate over to her, and began to eat around the elbow dent. "You have the stamp, and you think I'll tell you who the buyer is?"

"Lookie here." I took the stamp out of my pocket and

brought it within half an inch of the coffee in my cup. I wiggled it back and forth, feeling the heat of the coffee on my fingers. "What do you think?"

"You wouldn't," Stinky said, his eyes on the stamp. "You have an aesthetic sense, however rudimentary."

"Yes, I do. But I confine it to things that are valuable on *purpose*. It doesn't extend to accidents."

"I can't tell you who—"

"One," I said, lowering the stamp toward the coffee. "Two."

"I hate to be pushy," Ronnie said, wagging her fork at him, "but just to sidestep the melodrama and move things along—and not attract any more attention from *les gendarmes*—look at it this way. It took less than ninety minutes after the Slugger almost caught Junior here for him to show up at your house. So what that suggests to me—and, I'm assuming, to Junior—is that he didn't have to work his way through a long list of alternatives, a random selection of acquaintances. The people who are normally closest to collectors—and to junkies, too, since it's sort of the same thing—are dealers. Ergo, the person who asked you to steal the stamp might well be the person who sold the stamp to the Slugger in the first place, and the Slugger figured that out, and somewhere in the course of being beaten into pâté de foie gras, the dealer spoke your name. Something along those lines, Junior?" She gave me a bright smile and put her fork in her mouth.

Stinky was giving her that look again, the sort of silent *eeeek* he'd unleashed on her in the car, and I felt something like it on my own face, so I just smiled and said, "That's exactly where I was going."

"You don't even have to tell us his name," Ronnie said

as I sat there wondering which act of the play I'd missed. "Just call him and see if he's there."

"It's late," Stinky said.

She patted his hand comfortingly, and he snatched it away. "If you get him, tell him what happened tonight and suggest he go to Colorado or someplace. He'll be grateful." She felt the cop's gaze, returned it, turned her palms up and indicated Stinky and me, and then shrugged, as though to say, *What can I do?*

Stinky pulled an antique cell phone, complete with a hinge, out of his pocket, angled it away from us so we couldn't see the dial pad, and punched a bunch of buttons. His eyes wandered the room, hopscotched over the cops, and came back to the surface of our table. Probably unaware that he was doing it, he pressed the balls of his thumbs to some piecrust crumbs on the table, then licked them off. He looked up at Ronnie and then at me, and Ronnie said, "No answer?"

"He should be there," Stinky said.

"He probably is," Ronnie said, "but in no shape to take calls."

Stinky said again, "He should be there," and I realized he hadn't heard Ronnie. His forehead was shiny with sweat. He closed his eyes like someone fighting seasickness, and then, without opening them again, he put the phone on the table and snapped it closed. The hand he rested on it was trembling.

"It's probably nothing," I said, and at that moment there was a burst of electrified chatter, several people talking at once, coming from the table with the cops at it. The two on the ends of the banquette, including the one who had been lofting pheromone flares in Ronnie's direction, scrambled to their feet, and the other two slid out. One made writing motions on the air, which I interpreted as *On the tab, we'll be back*, and they all pushed their way through the door.

Ronnie said, "It's probably something," and sirens wailed into life in the street, accompanied by blinking red lights, and then they were gone. "Does your guy live near here?"

"I still don't know where *here* is," Stinky said. "I don't drive, and when you're in the backseat of a limo, knowing where you are is the driver's job."

"Okay," I said. "What street does he live on? Even in a limo, you have to give the driver an address."

He hesitated.

"Stinky," I said, "I doubt he's in any shape to make a deal with me."

Stinky closed his eyes. After a moment, without opening them, he said, "Sunnyslope."

Twelve or fourteen silent minutes later, we turned off of Sunnyslope to head back down to Ventura, each of us carrying the vivid memory of a roomy, sturdy-looking Spanish house, all its doors wide open, afire with the red lights of half a dozen LAPD cherry tops.

7
The Bangle King

We had to offload Stinky—first, because I was tired of him and second, to keep him from knowing where we were going—and the mostly empty parking lot behind Du-par's was as good a place as any to wait.

The three of us sat musing quietly in the dark car, Stinky and I probably processing somewhat similar trains of thought and Ronnie thinking about who the hell knew what. Every now and then, I looked around to see whether the car, which its missing rear window had made quite distinctive, was drawing the wrong kind of attention, although there was no reason for Du-par's to be on the Slugger's map.

When Stinky finally called a limo company to come get him, taking obvious pains not to give the dispatcher a destination, what with Ronnie and me both listening, I memorized his account number. Never know when you'll need a free limo.

From time to time, a cool breeze came through the shattered back window.

Stinky cleared his throat. "Your . . . um, your friend here said somebody else wants you killed, somebody other than me and the Slugger, I mean. Who?"

"It's hard for me to see," I remarked a bit loftily, "how that concerns you."

Stinky said, "I worry."

Ronnie said, "It's—"

I interrupted her. "It's no one you'd know."

Stinky said, "I know a lot of people."

"Well, you don't know this one. Not in your circle. A four-time Oscar winner. As though you know any four-time Oscar winners."

"Jake Whelan," Stinky said promptly. "The fence's dream."

"That's who it is," Ronnie said.

Stinky said to her, "What the hell is your game?"

"My . . . my . . . ?"

"Game," Stinky said.

I said, "Good question."

"Who says I have a game?"

"Where did you meet her?" Stinky asked me.

"Interesting you should ask. Her husband got murdered—"

"Did she do it?"

"That was my question, too," I said.

Ronnie said, "I knew it."

"It's always the wife," I said apologetically.

"Obviously not, since I'm sitting here."

"Well," Stinky said, "you might not have done that, but you've done plenty of other things."

"I am as pure as the driven—"

"Oh, come on," Stinky said. "It's written all over you."

My phone did the polite little burp it uses to tell me I have mail. I said, "I don't want to miss this chat, but hold on."

It was from Jake Whelan, who had somewhere discovered a trove of threatening emojis. The screen was full of grimacing zombies, hatchets dripping blood, sharp-looking vampire teeth, black widow spiders, a spitting cobra, and a skull wearing sunglasses. I figured that last one was a future self-portrait, since at some point, unless Jake had medicated himself to the degree at which he literally could not die, he would eventually become a skull wearing sunglasses, Bentley platinum sunglasses, to be exact, $45,000 worth of tinted glass, big enough to hide the bags beneath his eyes. He'd be sporting those shades in his coffin, because even in death, Jake, who had been a phenomenally handsome young man, would be thinking about the bags beneath his eyes. They'd been the topic of a typically sympathetic Hollywood joke back in the days when people still talked about him. Person A, the joke went, would say, "Why doesn't Jake Whelan get rid of those bags under his eyes?" and Person B would say, "Because they're full of cocaine." Then everyone would laugh, making sure that he or she wasn't laughing harder than anyone else in the room. Ahhh, Hollywood.

I showed them the screen. "From Jake," I said. "Just saying hi."

"I keep watching you, waiting for the penny to drop," Ronnie said with some asperity.

"Which penny is that?"

A limousine too long to turn most corners eased itself into the parking lot, and Stinky said, "He'll wait." To Ronnie he said, "Which penny is that?"

"All this attention for little me?" Ronnie said, her fingers interlaced in the general region of her heart.

"Which penny is that?" I asked.

"Nobody tells someone that he's hired hit men to take that someone out," she said. "Much less makes threatening calls about it all night and then sends a sort of death-animation parade. This is *obviously* not a death threat. It's the beginning of a negotiation."

"This is what I *mean*," Stinky said as I tried to assemble a reply. "What's your game?" The door of the limo opened, and a sleepy-looking guy started to get out, and Stinky shouted through his broken window, "Yeah, yeah, yeah! I see you!" To Ronnie he said, "Well?"

"I have no idea what you're—"

"Where are you from?"

Ronnie said, "Where am I *from*?"

I said, "Great question."

"Let's simplify it," Stinky said. "Where were you born?"

Ronnie looked at me as though I'd planned the entire evening to lead up to this question, drew a long breath, and said, "Bangalore."

"Really. Bangalore." Stinky nodded slowly. "And what were you doing in Bangalore?"

"Well, I was *born* there, so no one consulted with me about the itinerary." She paused, but Stinky just nodded again, his eyes on her face. "My father was a bangle merchant," she said, "and Bangalore at the time was the global center of the bangle trade, as the name suggests. *Bangle*, the word, is of course derived from *Bangalore*."

"*Bangle*," I said, "entered English in the eighteenth century, based on the Hindi word *baṅglī*, meaning a glass bracelet."

"Hindi, Bangalore. *And?*" Ronnie said, without giving me a glance. "Shall I go on?"

Stinky said, "Wouldn't miss it for the world." He'd lowered his head as though he were considering goring her with his horns, looking at her from beneath his carefully shaped eyebrows. And as twee as Stinky seemed at times, I wasn't sure I'd like him to look at me like that.

"Well, my papa," Ronnie said. "That's what we all called him, my five sisters and I, Papa, with the accent on the second syllable like that because our native language was French—"

"She's one of the Languedoc LeBlancs," I said.

"LeBlanc," Stinky murmured. "Of course."

"Well, Papa built an absolutely phenomenal business. He became known as the Bangle King. Our house, a palace, really, in the fairy-tale Bangalore style—"

"Describe one detail of the fairy-tale Bangalore style," I said.

Stinky said, "Don't slow her down. She's just getting going."

"Minarets," she said, even before Stinky had finished. "Minarets everywhere one turned. Minarets that had their own minarets. Anyway, the palace fairly gleamed with bangles—even the *minarets* gleamed with bangles. My earliest memory is of gleam."

I started to say something, but Ronnie held up a hand. "And then it happened. Just as Papa was laying the groundwork for a massive move into baubles—"

"From the French," I said, "originally meaning *child's toy*. No beads?"

The eye she turned upon me could be accurately described as chilly. "Beads are vulgar. Would *you* like to tell the story?"

"Not on my best day."

"So as Pa*pa* was preparing for the bauble expansion, it happened: the Great Bangalore Bangle Theft. We came home all veiled from church one day, because we never missed church, and the palace had been *denuded*. Not a gleam anywhere. '*Sacré bleu!*' cried Pa*pa*, slapping his forehead. 'The vaults!' And we ran across the city, we five girls still in our Communion dresses, veils trailing behind us like abandoned hopes, to find the vaults empty except for one cruel detail: Dead center in each vault, like a taunt, was a single bangle. Deliberately scratched."

I said, "*Sacré bleu.*"

"And well you may say that," Ronnie said. "Right there, in the middle of the fifth and final vault, that vault that had echoed with the cheerful clatter of bangles and our hopeful laughter, I knelt beneath my veil, eleven spotless years old, beside that single scratched bangle—all that remained of my father's empire—and I made a vow. I vowed I would recover every bangle we had lost."

"How could I not have seen that coming?" Stinky opened the door of the car.

"So yes," Ronnie said, "I tell you proudly, *yes*. I've devoted my life to stealing back my father's treasures. If I have skills, which I modestly disclaim, they were earned in the pursuit of my patrimony. Does that answer your question?"

"How many have you gotten back?" I asked.

She said, "Eleven. I was hot on the trail of the twelfth when I met you and abandoned my life's work. For a man who doesn't even trust me."

To me Stinky said, "And good luck." He closed the door and then leaned down and said through the broken back window, "Don't follow me."

Ronnie said, "Of course not," and watched him go. When the driver shut the limo door behind him, she said, "Follow him."

We stayed four and sometimes five cars back whenever possible, catching up a little when we neared a signal and falling back on the long stretches. The driver took Ventura, which made things easier, to the 405, which made things easier still, and then over the hill to Santa Monica Boulevard. Even this late, Santa Monica was jammed. In Beverly Hills they made a right on Doheny, and I said, "I know where he's going. The Four Seasons."

"Must be nice," Ronnie said. She'd been quiet ever since she commanded me to tag along.

"I'd think it would be small potatoes to the daughter of the Bangle King."

She said, "Oh, fuck you." It didn't sound affectionate. "Take me home."

"After I make sure," I said. At that moment the stop light one car ahead went yellow, and we stopped, but we could both see Stinky's long car make a graceful turn into the hotel's entrance, which was wide enough to admit armored personnel carriers, two abreast.

"Nice to know where he is," I said. "I guess." I drove past the hotel and made a left to get us on beam for the trip to West Hollywood and said, "Why did you want to follow him?"

She put down her window and stuck her head out of it like my favorite dog used to do, and she kept it there until we pulled up to her apartment, where I'd been staying for a few months, during a quiet patch when no one seemed to want to kill me and I'd gotten tired of obscure motels.

"Come in and get your stuff," she said.

"All of it?"

"Enough for a few nights at least. I need some time to process the idea that literally saving your life twice in one night is the way to earn a space on your shit list."

"Okay," I said. "And I'll try to adjust to the idea that after almost a year together, I'm still not entitled to know your actual name."

"You do that," she said, closing the door. "It'll build character, although it would build more if you already had a foundation." Through the open window, she said, "Leave your key on the living-room table."

8
Sticking Points

The Dew Drop Inn was a holdover from the time before air quotes, the time before an entire generation managed in unison to misunderstand what the word *irony* means and to confuse it with cheap sarcasm aimed at everything cute, sunny, conventionally pretty, whimsical, good-hearted, and sentimental.

There used to be lots of Dew Drop Inns, just as there were restaurants called Sit & Sip and Chat 'n' Chew. Okay, they were mainly in small towns and disproportionately in the South, but they existed, and every day a few thousand people would see one of those signs and smile and think for a second, *How clever* or *How cute*, and while that may not be a hip or sophisticated reaction, I'll take it over a sneer any day. When the face a culture turns to the world has a sneer on it, it's no wonder it has so few positive ideas.

All that said, the Dew Drop Inn was a dump, worthy of three stars in *The Masochist's Guide to Sleepless Nights*. The carpet, which had apparently been shampooed with petroleum jelly, made an alarming little blown-kiss sound every time I lifted my shoe. The wallpaper was in the midst of a long and acrimonious divorce with the walls; it had developed big, unsettling blisters, as though something gelatinous, something straight out of H. P. Lovecraft, were trying to bloom its way through. The biggest, softest, dampest, seepiest-looking blister was on the wall directly above the head of the bed, and I'm not ashamed to say that I squished my way over, the carpet fighting me for my shoes, and pulled the bed about two feet from the wall. I'm also not ashamed to tell you that I refused to look at the area of carpet I uncovered when I moved the bed. Whatever was down there, I could do without seeing it.

Avoiding the couch, the upholstery of which shone like the knees of a preacher's suit, I parked my small suitcase on the table and went out to the car for the backpack that contained my laptop, the few things I'd taken from Ronnie's place, and several other essentials, including a spare cell phone. I also took a moment to refile, in a small document compartment hidden in one of the backpack's straps, the driver's license and credit card in the name of J. C. Leyendecker I'd used to check in to the motel. The actual J. C. Leyendecker pretty much created an entire worldwide aesthetic of male attractiveness—white male attractiveness anyhow—back in the 1920s with a classic series of ads for Arrow shirts. The Leyendecker man was the person Jay Gatsby wanted to look like, and I had leanings that way myself.

I like my false identities to be someone I'd actually enjoy being. It's a kind of karmic nudge.

I put a bath towel, which smelled almost clean, on top of the bedspread, lay down, and opened my computer. Buried beneath ten or twelve graphic threats from Jake Whelan were three emails sent since seven that evening by my former wife, Kathy. They all had the same heading: *RINA'S BIRTHDAY!!!*

This took me aback. My daughter's birthday wasn't something I was likely to forget. Rina, who was set to turn fourteen (where had the *time* gone?) in twelve days, was (and is) the person I love most deeply in the world.

And yet just as the Dew Drop Inn, despite its sweetly dated name, was a smudge on the face of creation, my love for Rina didn't translate into admirable fathering. I was notable primarily for my absence, at first because Kathy and I went through a period of mutual, if juvenile, antipathy after the divorce and later because Kathy— since I had declined to give up my career, such as it was, and get a straight-world job with her father's insurance company—didn't think I was a positive influence. And things didn't thaw when I told her I morally preferred burglary to her father's industry, which I characterized as a heartless swindle that preyed on our most primal fears— death, bereavement, illness, poverty—and then, when the dreaded day came, devoted most of its energy into finding ways to avoid paying off. It's one, I unwisely said, of the many legal crimes that transfer the world's wealth from shallow pockets to deep ones, twenty-four hours a day.

So Kathy and I had been stalemated, glaring at each other over the gulf between us, until Rina put her foot down and insisted that she *would* see me, with her mother's consent or not. Kathy wisely gave in, making the provision that Rina and I, at first anyway, would see each other only in the house we all used to share, and only when Kathy was present to shed motherly light on the difference between right and wrong. And after a period of adjustment, the two of us growling at each other like pit bulls, we'd relaxed into our new roles. As a result I'd been able to participate, a bit sporadically, in my daughter's life from about the time she was seven. I'd been there for the rocky transition from elementary to middle school. I'd been there when the braces went on. I'd watched her blossom into someone with a keen and inquisitive intelligence, an instinctive disdain for pretense, and a clear, strong heart. I'd been on the sidelines as she fell in love, for the first time, with a beautiful and apparently sweet-hearted kid named Tyrone.

And with all that love and understanding only about fifteen minutes away in Tarzana, here I was, solo and self-pitying in the blistering miasma of the Dew Drop Inn. I was, Kathy's emails implied, invited to the party, but still, I should have been a lot more closely involved. I mean, isn't fourteen supposed to be essentially a 365-day hormonal land mine? Isn't fourteen the year when good goes bad and bad goes irremediable? It sure as hell had been for me. Wasn't I supposed to be in the next room, ready with fatherly wisdom at the first question, fully equipped with comfort and advice at the first betrayed sob?

And what in the world did the topic heading "DN'T MISS RINA'S BTHDY PRTY FRI" mean? Aren't birthday parties usually held on birthdays, or on the nearest weekend day?

Chnge of pln, Kathy had written, apparently confusing email with texting. *Prty now this Fri nite, 7P. Pls rspnd asap.* The other two emails were variations on the theme, some with more vowels and each with a new and puzzling piece of information. *Fri Ptrcia's bday so 2sies,* read the first, and *Dn't tlk abt Tyrone,* said the second. I was aware that Rina had a new best friend, and it appeared her name was *Ptrcia*, and the note seemed to suggest they'd decided to combine parties.

Seemed like a rancid idea to me, but I hadn't been consulted, and anyway it paled in significance beside the possibility of a problem between Rina and Tyrone, because why else was I being warned not to *"tlk abt Tyrone,"* so I just emailed, *Wht's up wth th date & Tyrone?* three times. By the time I pushed SEND it was almost 1:30 A.M. and I was unreasonably angry.

I was angry at my estrangement from Ronnie, which was partly my fault; at my isolation from my daughter and my powerlessness to make things better for her, which was *mostly* my fault; at my being in the Dew Drop Inn at this stage of my life, which was *entirely* my fault; and at the idea that people wanted to kill me. *Again.* At what point in a man's life do people stop wanting to kill him?

Even I, the least introspective of men, recognized the anger as my usual way of hiding from self-pity. That didn't mean, though, that I didn't want to take it out on someone, so I picked up my phone and dialed.

"How do you like the Four Seasons?" I asked when Stinky came on the line.

"I've moved," he said. "I didn't want your friend to have any idea where I was."

"You saw us?"

"I assumed you were back there. I figured the first thing she said when I got in the car was, 'Follow him.'"

"You know her better than I do."

"I know people I've never *met* better than you know her. Can she hear you? Am I on speaker?"

"No and no. We're taking a time-out, she and I."

"What a quaint way to put it. I think *time-out* could be used accurately to describe any period when that woman isn't behind bars."

"You no longer have a buyer for the stamp."

"I can find another."

"Good to hear it. And the Slugger isn't going to stop wanting to kill you."

"It's a big world."

"You'd be willing to leave all your beautiful things behind?"

"I wouldn't describe myself as *willing*. But I'd rather leave them behind than get beaten to death with bats."

"Then why don't you hire me to fix things?" I said.

"Hire you. To *fix things*. You mean so he'd no longer want to kill me?"

"I mean so that you wouldn't have to think about it."

A beat while he analyzed my sentence. "How would you do that, if you please?"

"Ah-ah. That would be telling."

"Here's the flaw in the ointment—"

"Fly."

"Pardon?"

"In the ointment," I said. "It's a *fly* in the ointment. An ointment is a viscous liquid. How can it have a flaw in it? In a sapphire yes or, more frequently, an emerald, but an ointment? Not a—"

"Pah," Stinky said. "The flaw in the ointment is that he wants to kill *you*, too. It seems to me that it's in your own interest to fix things, and it's hard for me to see how you could fix things for yourself without also fixing them for me. And free of cost at that."

"It would be a snap," I said. "I could arrange to meet him,

give him the stamp with a heartfelt apology, and sic him on you."

"And you think you'd survive that?"

"I'll take my odds over yours."

Stinky said, "Mmmm," something he'd picked up in England and clung to as a sort of no-fault way of admitting he was wrong. "Then if I thought you could accomplish that—eliminating the threat, so to speak—and if I decided to ask you to do it, what would it cost me?"

"I have the stamp," I reminded him. "And you say you can find a buyer. I think it would be fair—"

"Eighty-twenty," he said.

"I was a lot closer to fifty-fifty." There was a lump in the bed, right under the towel, so I got up and moved the towel.

"It is to laugh," Stinky said. He made a sound he probably thought was a laugh but that sounded more like a cat announcing a hair ball.

"Finished?" I said. "Wiped your eyes yet?"

"Out of the question," he said. "It's against the moral order of things. Anyway, there's no one but me who can sell it for you, so what else could you do with it?"

"Eat it," I said.

If a silence, which is after all just an absence of sound, can be characterized as *appalled*, what we had was an appalled silence. I yawned into the phone.

"You *would*, too," he said.

"I sure would. Look, think about it this way. For half the price of the stamp, you're getting the whole stamp and I'm throwing in your life as a sort of goodwill offer. A holiday bonus."

"What holiday?" he asked suspiciously.

"My daughter's birthday." There was a lump under the towel's new location, too.

"You have offspring?"

"Don't test me, Stinky. The mood I'm in, I could just hang up, find a bolt-hole, and let you wait for batting practice." I put the towel at the foot of the bed and climbed on.

"A counter-offer," he said. "Forty thousand cash, right now, small bills."

"Your life is worth five thousand dollars? You were already going to pay me thirty-five."

"That was when I had a buyer."

"Seventy-five."

"Fifty."

"Tomorrow," I said. "All of it."

"This is what we call a sticking point," Stinky said. "I'm not going to give you the money until I know you've completed your end of the bargain."

"And I'm not going to give you the stamp *or* complete my side of the bargain until I have the money."

"Hmmm." While Stinky *hmmm*-ed, I looked up Jake Whelan's number on my other phone, since I was using the one he had called me on and I've never known how to look up a number without disconnecting my call. I made a mental note to ask Rina to teach me.

"A deal," Stinky said. "We'll do it in tranches."

"I've never known what *tranche* means."

"It's a financial term. It means payment in increments, each tied to the completion of one stage of development."

"Sort of like lay-away," I said.

"If that's helpful to you. I'll pay you a little more, but in stages. I'll pay you sixty. You were willing to hand the stamp to me tonight for thirty-five. You do that, and when

I'm convinced that the Slugger is no more, or is no longer interested in me, I'll pay you another twenty-five."

"No," I said. "You pay me the forty-five in the hope that I can do the job, and when I've succeeded and I come for the remaining thirty-five, I'll give you—"

"Twenty-five."

I began to whistle. I can't whistle in tune any better than I can climb a rope.

"All right," he said. "*Stop* that. But when you get the forty-five, I get the stamp. And all I'll owe you is fifteen."

"Brilliant," I said. "Exactly what I would have suggested if I were as smart as you are."

Stinky said, "You know what, Junior? You *deserve* your little friend."

Even before I said hello, Jake Whelan said, "Fuck you, Junior."

"Everybody's saying that to me tonight." So far I hadn't found any area of the mattress that was lump-free.

"When you're standing in the middle of a hail of bullets, you cocksucker, when time slows down so far that your heart sounds lower than a bass drum, when you know you're a millisecond away from seeing patches of sunlight appear in the middle of your own shadow—"

"Got it, Jake. Before I do the big blink. Before I'm tucked away for the dirt nap. Before I'm date bait for a taxidermist. Before I'm stitched like a pillowcase—"

"Wait a minute, wait a minute," he said. "I'm writing these down."

"Why? You got a script you want to spoil?"

"You're colorful, Junior, I'll give you that. I'll almost miss you."

"Shame you've decided to kill me, then, isn't it?" I said, and hung up. Almost instantly my other phone began to ring. I ignored it and dialed him on the one I'd just hung up. When he snapped a hello, I said, "Sorry, someone's calling me on the other line," and hung up.

Then I got up and turned down the blanket. Nothing scurried out of sight, although the sheets were the gray of a London fog. I was testing with both hands for more lumps, and finding them, when both phones began to ring.

"Hi, Jake," I said. I dropped the phone on the bed and went into the bathroom, where I washed my hands, undid the zipper on my suitcase, and shook out a T-shirt so I could let it unwrinkle on a hanger overnight. Then I went back to the bed. "You still there?"

"You're not taking this seriously."

"You think?"

"Get over here."

"What, I'm going to make it that easy? Actually *show up* someplace so your shooters can autograph my chest in bullet holes?"

"That one's not so good," he said.

"I know," I said. "If I'd been writing instead of talking, I'd have gone back and replaced that with something better. The tragedy of our life, Jake, is that it's a first draft."

"And in your case, it'll be an unfinished first draft."

"Oh, come on. As someone wiser than I once said, 'This is *obviously* not a death threat. It's the beginning of a negotiation.'"

There was a moment, during which I located several more lumps, and Jake said, "Hey, honey?"

"Too late for that Jake. There was a time perhaps, but—"

"Not you, you asshole. Honey, you wanna trot all that

prettiness in the other room a couple minutes, gimme a chance to talk to my acquaintance here?"

I said, "Acquaintance? That stings."

"I don't know," he said in a voice that was mostly edge, "put a fucking log on the fire, do yoga, work up a cheerleading routine, but do it *out there*, okay?"

"That's the tone they all love," I said.

"You have no idea what I just kicked outta the room," Jake said. "You oughta get over here just to make it up to me."

"I'd love to, but you want to kill me."

"Awww, come *on*," he said. "You know I love you."

"Of course I do. Still, you were pretty persuasive earlier this evening, and those emojis took a year off my life. Where'd you find them?"

"Aren't they great? I'm trying to option them as animated characters. Junior-high-school site called Hatebook. Nobody can hate like kids. That's right, you got a kid, don't you?"

"I do. And I'll agree with you that you have to go to the Middle East to match the level of malice you find in the average junior high."

"She pretty, your daughter?"

"Jake," I said, "don't take this wrong, but I can't think of anyone from whom that question would sound creepier than it does from you."

"I know someone," he said, "making a movie. He can't find the girl he needs, and I mean he's talked to everybody. Whatever else I might think of you—and remember, I love you, I'm your biggest fan—there's no getting around that you're a good-looking guy. I'm thinking maybe the apple doesn't fall far—"

"Please, please, please. Just turn off the goo and tell me what you want before the sun rises."

"You ripped me off pretty good," he said, and then he covered the phone not very effectively and said, "Looks great, looks great. You go practice the high kicks and track that back in here in, say, five minutes." To me he said, "The things I do to live up to my reputation. So okay, so the Klee you sold me wasn't. And I paid pretty good for it."

"It was a steal," I said. "Or it would have been if it had been real."

"And I looked like a *shmendrik* when I showed it to someone."

I said, "I can imagine that was embarrassing, but taking out a contract on me seems like an overreaction."

"Oh, quit kidding around. We're past that. Yeah, I was a little pissed off, but then I got to thinking, what does Junior have that I want?"

"Are you waiting for an answer?"

"Listen, give me half an hour with my little friend and then come over here, we'll talk about it."

"I can't. My car's rear window is broken."

"Yeah? How'd that happen?"

"Bullet."

"No wonder you pushed my nose in it. People must take shots at you all the time. You're *used* to it. Hey, *there's* a movie: A crook, maybe Nic Cage, he gets bored 'cause nobody's tried to kill him in a while, so he pushes it, tries to double the excitement—"

"I need to fix the window before I go anywhere unless I want to get pulled over. But I'm not getting near you until I know what I've got that you want."

"Skills," Jake said.

I tested the folded blankets and got right back up. "No," I said. "I've learned my lesson. No more jobs on commission."

In a voice as hard as slate, Jake said, "I actually *can* have you killed, you little *vantz*. No, wait, wait, wait, that was a tactical misstep. Off target, out of tune, wrong key altogether. Here's the pitch: My life is at stake here, Junior. My legacy, my reputation, everything I've ever done, the work of a lifetime, and it's one simple job. An office, in and out in ten minutes. You don't even take anything. You're my only hope."

"God," I said, moving my pillow and blanket to the shiny couch. The bed was lumpy enough to be stuffed with the skulls of the sleepless. "It must be something to be able to change channels like that. And to have those violins available."

"An *office*, for Chrissakes, probably not even locked. Were you listening? You don't *take* anything."

"I don't? Then what am I doing there?"

"You find a piece of paper, you read it, you're out of there."

"One piece of paper," I said, settling in. "In an office full of paper."

"It'll be filed. The guy, the guy with the office? He's famous for his files."

I was interested in spite of myself. "Who is it?"

Jake said, and I could hear the satisfaction in his voice, "It's King Maybe."

PART TWO

TURNAROUND

Hollywood Boulevard is a clogged artery
with no heart attached to it.
—Columnist Louella Parsons

9
Designer Rot

"I'm flattered," Louie the Lost said as I undid the second lock on one of my three storage units. "This is like . . . I don't know, getting a look at your closet."

"I've always trusted you," I said, fingers crossed. I pulled open the unit's door to reveal a cubist mountain of cardboard boxes, stacked any old way across the room, shoulder-high in places. "And, of course, my car's in the shop you took me to, so I have no other way to get—"

"You know, when you called this morning, I said to Alice—that's my wife, Alice—I said—"

"I know Alice," I said. "I've even *met* Alice."

"So I said to Alice, even before I saw the number, I said, 'You know who that is?'"

With a grunt I took a box off the tallest stack. "This is all about you complaining how long it's been since I—"

"I said, ''Cause it's been *so long since he called*,'" Louie said, "'it *has* to be him,' and Alice, she jumped right in and said, 'You mean that nice boy, that burglar George?'"

"George?" I said, opening the box. Many books, spines up, exhaled a hopeful hello. The box was full of A's, with Kingsley Amis and Jane Austen, an odd couple if ever there was one, nestled side by side as though they'd fought their way through the alphabet to find each other.

"It's been so long since we heard from you and all," Louie said. "You can't blame her." He craned into the box. "You read all those?"

"I have, and others, too. And you can't make me feel guilty about not calling. I lack the gene for guilt."

"You don't have shelves?"

"Motels are short on shelf space." Maybe the only thing Louie didn't know about me was that I had a secret apartment in Koreatown with an actual library in it, by which I mean a room full of books that was originally designed to *hold* books, if you can imagine that. Built in the late 1920s, when people still read. Today it'd be a *media room.* "Have you read any Austen?"

"Yeah, sure," he said. "Colin Firth."

"Stinky is on the fade," I said, hauling down another box and opening it. "Be nice if you could figure out where he is."

"Why would Stinky be on the fade? Why would anybody want to find him?" He nudged me aside for a better look. "Balzac, huh? A whole box of Balzac?"

"Two and a half boxes. He's on the fade because someone tried to kill him. I want you to find him because he might decide to get out of the line of fire by having *me* killed to get a piece of merchandise that I currently possess and then returning that piece of merchandise to the person who used to own it, who is also the person who tried to kill him."

Louie nodded. My possible death was just another piece of pronoun-littered information, and Louie dealt in information. "What's the merchandise?"

"The heiress to the Vaseline fortune."

"Okay, fine, be that way. Usual rates?"

"If that means you pick a number out of the air, sure."

"Only way I know. Wow," he said as I took the lid off a third box, "that's a whopper."

"It is," I said, pulling out a bright orange edition, a good three inches thick, of Balzac's *Droll Stories* with illustrations by Gustave Doré, the first English translation and a real showboat item published in London in 1874. "But don't get your hopes up." I opened the book, which was hollowed out in the center to house something wrapped in oilcloth, and then I removed the oilcloth to reveal a Glock and a couple of magazines.

Looking pained, Louie said, "You cut up a nice book like that just to hide a piece?"

"I did not." I slipped a magazine in and listened to the click. "I bought it this way from Duck Dixon." Duck Dixon was well known, in certain circles, as a dealer not only in guns but also in all things gun-related. He was called "Duck" because, as far as anyone knew, he was the only crook in California who'd ever ducked a bullet and lived. Heard the bang, ducked, got up, and ran like hell. I always figured the shooter had just missed, but Duck was touchy about that. "When you've got a lot of books," I said, "hide stuff in books. If nothing else, it slows the thief down."

"Says the expert. But I mean, Stinky? You so worried about *Stinky* you're gonna be carrying?"

"I'm worried about everybody," I said. "It's that kind of day."

"Outta my league," Louie said. We were in a coffee shop on Ventura that Louie liked because he thought the waitresses were motherly, which said a lot about his childhood. "I mean, sure, he's a crook, but not my kind of crook. So what that means, I got history but nothing current." He was lipping a cigar longingly, and a waitress who was passing patted him on the shoulder.

"Ah-ah-*ah*," she said. "I'm not going to have to pour boiling water in your lap, am I, honey?"

I said, "It was nice of her to warn you."

"She loves me," he said. "They all love me. I been eating here for years."

Louie the Lost looked to me like a free sample of middle-aged male Mediterranean genetics, something you might be given a bit of if you were comparison shopping. He had olive skin, eyebrows so heavy they looked like they were planning to spread, and very lively brown eyes beneath a high forehead in a big round face, in the center of which his features gathered snugly in a way that always reminded me of a roomful of furniture that's been pushed together so the walls can be painted. He wore his hair in a short, graying ponytail that at the moment stuck out of the back of a San Francisco Giants cap like a little pump handle. He'd started life as a getaway driver, but a substandard sense of direction earned him a nickname that did not inspire confidence, and after six months of waiting, like some falling movie star, for the phone to ring, he'd repackaged himself as a telegraph, the person you go to when you want either to get some information or spread some.

I said, "When you say he's out of your league, does that mean you don't know anything about him?" I looked at my watch—12:10 P.M. Jake Whelan would be snorting himself into a waking state any hour now.

"Ain't nobody I don't know anything about," Louie said. "But like I said, history, not current, and mostly when laws got broken. French fry?"

"Thanks anyway." I had a Reuben sandwich cooling in front of me, next to a coffee cup that had been refilled half a dozen times. "So what do you know?"

"Okay, Jeremy Granger, a.k.a. King Maybe, producer and studio exec. Started out as a *patzer*, you know, like a personal assistant to well-known jerks: agents, third-season TV stars, Brian Sampson." Sampson was a producer who was noted for having intentionally backed over a meter maid one day when she was writing him a parking ticket and he was late for his tennis game. "Got a rep as a guy who could really put up with it, just eat it all day long, no matter how much the boss shoveled out, and still give you a big grin without caring what was on his teeth. That's a valuable trait in this town, what with all the reincarnated Roman emperors and popes and whatnot running things. So bigger and bigger assholes stole him from each other, and he ate and grinned his way up."

"Nothing illegal?"

"Depends. I mean, in LA plagiarism is like a character flaw, you know? Like, if it was an addiction, you could get over it with a three-step program." He unscrewed the top of the salt shaker, poured a little dune of salt onto his plate, took the cigar out of his mouth, licked a french fry to make it sticky, and dredged it through the salt. "He was an assistant to some development guys for a while— you know, the ones who scout the ideas, if you wanna call them ideas and if you wanna call stealing scouting. So there were some charges that he bagged other people's stuff, like some poor hack in Van Nuys would submit the one inspiration of his life to one of your guy Jeremy's employers, and Jeremy would read it, and it would get returned stamped UNREAD, and a year later that very same movie would come out, only the central character wasn't a superhero anymore, he was one of the Seven Dwarfs or something. Anyway, he got sued a couple times for stuff like that." He picked up another fry, wiggled it, rejected it, and took another. "About eight, nine years ago, just before his big jump—and this is why I know anything about him—he had this little brush up about trafficking in minors."

I said, "Really."

"Yeah, I guess he'd had enough of people his own size. Well, not minors so much as *minor*. One. Starts taking out this little sparkler, said she was seventeen, just graduated from high school—Catholic school no less—went to auditions in her uniform. So your guy, Jeremy, he was working for Barry Zipken in like 2007, when Barry was the head of Farscope Pictures, and Barry had an eye for uniforms. Anyway, Jeremy sets it up for the sparkler to get the standard audition with Barry, but it has a different ending, which is she punches Barry in the eye and then her and her mom press charges. Barry, he tells the cops he thought she was of age and everything, and he says that Jeremy, your guy, told him she was eighteen but actually knew what the game was and intentionally gave old Barry the wrong impression to set him up, and both of them are looking at a lifetime on the sex offenders' registry, the Gucci ankle bracelet, and the whole thing, but the studio springs into action, and suddenly Jeremy's got ten million dollars' worth of lawyers, and then the sparkler changes her story. Says she told Jeremy she was eighteen, even showed him a driver's license. Which she displays on the witness stand.

Jeremy gets off, Barry gets off but gets fired by the board of directors, and all of a sudden Jeremy doesn't even have an office anywhere—he's working out of delis and coffee shops, but everyone knows he's the Man at the studio. Like a ghost executive, not even getting paid on the books. And that's when he started putting his name on movies."

"So she was eighteen," I said. My Reuben was cold, and nothing, up to and including an oil well, is greasier than a cold Reuben. I looked up, found a waitress staring at me like a pointer that's scented a bird, and nodded toward my coffee cup. She sprang into action. I said, "Kind of a long story if she was eighteen. There wouldn't be any consequences—"

But Louie, with his mouthful of french fry, was waving me off. "License was duff," he said, spraying salt. "She wasn't even *seventeen*, she was *sixteen*."

"Where'd she get the license?"

"Ever hear of Garlin Romaine?"

"The painter? Does passports or something?"

"Not just passports, every kind of document there is, all from countries that don't exist," Louie said. "Complete with royal seals or whatever, and all filled with immigration stamps from *other* countries that don't exist. Whatsittoyastan, places like that. And 'cause they're not real places, it's not forgery, it's art,"

I said, "She sells them in albums, right?"

"The whole thing," Louie said. "In a package, like a briefcase, a—what's the word?—a folio. The passport, some letters home from these fake countries in envelopes with fake stamps on them—"

"Don't talk about stamps."

"Even snapshots, painted by hand. A whole . . . a whole

whatchamacallit, a grand tour, all to places that ain't there. With hints of things that might have happened. Like a mystery, but with pictures."

"I'll stick with Van Eyck."

"Garlin's kind of a big deal now, but before she started getting on the cover of art magazines, she used to do documents for people who *really* needed documents. And she wasn't cheap even then, so my guess is that the studio ponied up for that license."

"And what happened to the sparkler?"

"Your guy Jeremy. He put her in a TV series—"

"Which one?"

"You don't watch TV."

"Humor me."

"Just lasted a couple years. Called *Dead Eye*. She was a zombie private eye in the future when the whole world is zombies, but it's far enough in the future that they've smoothed out some and kind of got the lurch thing under control. They've become like executive zombies. The only humans are the ones they raise on ranches like cattle, and even though she's a zombie, too—the sparkler, I mean— she's in love with this handsome alive guy who doesn't own a shirt, the leader of the big human rebellion who's like riling up his herd on this huge ranch."

I said, "She played a *zombie*?"

"A cute zombie. You know, kind of designer rot, and only in the right places. Her blouse was always torn. Or maybe it was falling apart, but, you know, it was falling apart *right*."

"So it only lasted two years. Then what happened to her?"

"Well, first she was awful, okay? No career ahead of her unless there was a show like *America's Most Embarrassing*

Series Outtakes. Anyway, by then she was eighteen no matter what papers you checked, even though she still barely looked it. Show went off the air, he married her."

I found myself rubbing my eyes. I hadn't slept well, I'd been bitten in numerous places by the other residents of my room at the Dew Drop Inn, I was worried about Rina, my car was a mess, and I didn't want anything to do with someone whose idea of recreation was a sixteen-year-old. "Married her," I said. "What was her name?"

"Tasha something, by then. Something kinda shiny, you know, a stage name. Dawn, Tasha Dawn."

"Yes," I said, "just possibly a stage name."

"She's in her twenties now. Goes to art galleries, raises money for one of the major political parties and who cares which one, gets her picture taken with the Dalai Lama wearing big jewelry. Weighs about eighty pounds and looks like most of it is teeth."

"So maybe he got what he deserved."

"How often does that happen?"

"Right. Do you think my car's ready?"

"They'll call me. So what's the deal with him—with Jeremy?"

"I don't know exactly, but he's somehow got Jake Whelan's balls in a bear trap, and Whelan's talking about his legacy, his life, whatever else he can think of on the spur of the moment to get me to do something about it."

"Why would you say yes to Jake? Why would anybody?"

"Oh, don't ask. He says he'll have me killed if I don't, but I guess the bottom line is that I feel like I owe him. I rooked him pretty bad on that painting."

"Conscience," Louie said. He picked up another french fry. "It's a curse."

10
Paying by the Inch

I had a new rear window, but it was dappled with greasy black fingerprints, the car was still full of sharp little cubes of greenish glass, and the front quarter of the passenger side, where Ronnie had swiped the Porsche, looked like it had lost an argument with a train. When I turned the wheel to the right, there was a little tug a few inches into the turn and the axle groaned, and while I was sure it was nothing, I wasn't sure enough to take the freeway. By the time I got to Beverly Glen, I was groaning along with it.

Lots of opportunity for groaning as we did the increasingly expensive zigzags of Beverly Glen, the houses growing more royalist as we neared the crest of the Santa Monica Mountains and then bursting into full Louis XIV territory as we started down into the Brentwood/Beverly Hills side. This was, in fact, the same street Ronnie and I had been parked on when we began our long wrangle, only—good Lord—the previous night.

That realization caused me a moment of paralytic blankness, because I suddenly couldn't remember where I'd put the Slugger's stamp. And that, in turn, told me that I was even more tired than I'd thought, since it only took me a few seconds before I recalled putting it into the concealed document compartment in my backpack, on top of the fake ID cards, after Louie and I finished with the books in the storage unit. Louie actually *liked* books; he was one of the few crooks I knew who took advantage of his plentiful free time to broaden his horizons. He'd now taken three courses on Shakespeare's king plays in four years. "Kings," he'd once said to me, "are just crooks with better hats."

But as much as I liked Louie, I didn't trust him far enough to tell him about the stamp. At this stage of my life, I trusted very few people: my daughter, Rina, who would tell me only the standard, predictable teenage lies; my former wife, Kathy, who believed in telling the truth not just when the truth hurt but *especially* when it hurt; and—it suddenly occurred to me—someone who had arguably never told me a single true thing about herself, Ronnie.

But I trusted Ronnie *emotionally*.

Three people, out of more than three hundred million in America alone. And one of them lied to me all the time. Pathetic.

I *deserved* this car.

Jake's driveway was always a surprise when I was heading south, because it appeared suddenly on the left just after a long curve in that direction; the moment the road straightened up, there was the driveway. I didn't have time to signal, and the clown behind me was practically grafted to my license plate, meaning I couldn't hit the brakes, so I simply jammed the accelerator and cut diagonally across the street, directly in front of an oncoming Humvee, which sounded its baritone drill-sergeant horn, a feature of the optional Testosterone

Package, and swung to *its* left, into the path of the clown
behind me, who leaned on his own horn and almost
jumped the curb, and we collectively had ourselves a real
LA moment, up among the fabulous stars in Brentwood.
Made me feel good all over.

I pulled up to the wrought-iron gates at the bottom of
Whelan's steep, curving driveway and pushed the buzzer.
Then I counted to thirty and pushed it again.

"Whozis?" a woman said through the speaker. She
had the bleary and attenuated sound of someone who'd
recently had more than her fair share of enjoyment.

"For Jake," I said. "Junior Bender."

"Jus' minit. Howdya make this fucking . . ."

"You're Jake's friend from last night, right?"

"Far as I remember," she said.

"Look, there's a button on the left that says—"

"'*Open,*'" she said triumphantly. "So come in already.
Don't know where Jake is. Kin you make coffee?" Texas
announced itself in the "kin."

I said, "I could make coffee in free fall. See you in a
minute."

The driveway was designed to reveal the house in a
series of dramatic medium shots, one gorgeous detail at a
time, before you topped the hill and saw the whole thing
in wide-screen. Back in Jake's glory days, when he was the
most famous movie producer in the world, he'd been given
a medal of achievement in France, a big heavy Christmas-
tree-ornament thing on a tricolor ribbon.

But the prize that mattered wasn't the one they gave
him. The awards ceremony was held in the wine country, wherever that is, and the organization had put Jake
up for two nights in a small castle that he always said

was thirteenth century but I figured as sixteenth, early seventeenth. The day after the ceremony, Jake bought the castle for cash, and in August, when apparently the entire population of France goes on vacation to make disparaging remarks about other countries, he had it disassembled stone by stone and shipped to Bel Air along with a contingent of French craftsmen who put it back together again and added a few frills and gewgaws of Jake's design before returning to France, where they were immediately drummed out of their various guilds for architectural treason. As Jake said to me when he told me the story, "I feel bad for them, but . . . you know, fuck them." Which was pretty much Jake's attitude about everything.

The last time I'd seen the house, it had been a drizzly November evening, and it had come across like a timeless tone poem of gleaming wet stone and yellow light shining through mullioned windows. At 2 P.M. on a workaday Tuesday, the place looked frayed and bleached, like an attraction in a shuttered amusement park. The driveway had gone unswept for so long you'd need to rake it before you picked up the broom, and the wood around the beautiful old windows was dried out and splintering, its once-satiny finish a casualty of the remorseless onslaught of California sunshine.

And another telltale, if one were needed: on my previous visit, I'd been met by a tight little trio of armed muscle, one of whom had been carrying an umbrella to keep me dry and two of whom were there to shoot me to death if I'd revealed bad intentions. Jake was famous in the criminal community for keeping enormous amounts of cash on hand to fund his nasal aerobics and his highly compensated dates; there was a theory that the insulation between the castle's walls was made of stacks of hundred-dollar bills. That made the muscle a necessity.

But the greeting committee this time was a tousled young woman who had somehow smeared her lipstick about two inches up her right cheek and who wore a pair of sunglasses with no left lens, as though to balance the effect of the lipstick. She also wore a T-shirt with a pair of those unsettling staring Tibetan eyes printed precisely over the area you didn't want to stare back at and a pair of extra-brief lavender briefs. She was about an inch taller than I was, which made her six-three.

"That's you, huh?" she said. She was leaning rather heavily on the door.

"It is. Jake up yet?"

"And hi to you, too. Coffeepot's back here." She turned and went in, at the very last moment doing a sort of backward-karate-kick maneuver with her left leg to swing the door open again. "Come *on*," she said. Then she wavered and tried to get her foot back under her but instead went down full length on Jake's sixteenth- or possibly seventeenth-century wooden floor. It was a pretty noisy fall, involving many knees and elbows.

"Help you up?"

"You're not big enough to help me up," she said. "But thanks for the thought." She rolled over onto her stomach and got up on hands and knees, and I left her to her own devices and went into the kitchen.

Which was a mess. And it wasn't a *fresh* mess either, not your standard aftermath-of-a-debauch mess. From the look of it, it had been messy, and getting messier, for months. All the time I'd known him, Jake had been cared for vigorously by a British housekeeper, short, brisk, stout, and—in her fifties—chronologically safe from Jake's impulses. I'd always thought of her as Mrs. Brisket, although that couldn't possibly have been right, and Mrs. Brisket never would have permitted this kind of . . . well, squalor. As I cleared a space on the counter so I could pull out the coffeemaker's filter basket, I found myself thinking, *Jake is in financial trouble.*

The thought had no sooner formed in my mind than I heard it spoken aloud behind me. "You think he's still got any money?"

"I have no idea," I said. Indoors, she'd pushed the broken sunglasses up into her reddish hair. "You'd know that better than I would."

"This is a first date," she said, pronouncing it "dight." She caught sight of her reflection in the side of a toaster. "Why didn't you *tell* me? I look like John Wayne Gacy." She went to the sink, grabbed an extravagantly foul-looking dish towel, and started to run water on it.

"Toss that," I said. "Paper towels, over there, but I'd peel off the three or four outer ones."

"You're a domestic little thing, aren't you?" she said. "When I was a kid, in Texas? I stepped on a rusty nail in a pile of horse shit. *Barefoot.* Bingo, right there in one deep puncture wound, you had everything that's s'posed to cause tetanus. I never even got a headache. Germs are afraid of me." She went back to the sink and soaked the towel, then began to rub it in circles on her cheek. "I didn't cry neither."

Back at the coffeepot, I said, "Other side."

The towel stopped moving. "You sure?"

"I'm looking right at you."

She switched sides. "Maybe I had too much fun last night. Is it off?"

"No, it's bigger. But it's paler."

"I'm Casey," she said scrubbing some more. She looked at the towel, folded it to get a fresh surface, licked it, and went back to work. "Y'all got a name?"

"Junior," I said, "and yes, that's my real name."

"Lot of Juniors in Texas."

"I'll file that away so I know where to go if I ever get lonely." I popped open a can of coffee beans from the counter: Sumatra from Trader Joe's, not the $60-per-pound Jamaica Blue Mountain that Jake usually drank, although it always seemed to me that he liked to talk about it more than he liked to drink it. I filled up the grinder and pushed the button, and Casey let out a brief, agonized, unspellable sound of protest and jammed her fingers into her ears, the wet paper towel dangling from her right hand.

"Pain before pleasure," I said, dumping the grounds into the filter.

"Sometimes during, too," she said. "As well as after."

"Sorry to hear it."

"Aaaaahhhh," she said, slapping the sympathy aside.

I went to the faucet to fill the carafe. "So how did you meet Jake?"

Casey pulled the sunglasses out of her hair, positioned them low on her nose, and regarded me steadily over them, a very effective pantomime for *duhhhhhh*. "A girl in this day and age has an answering service."

"Got it."

"When they said they thought he'd like me, I watched some of his old movies on Netflix. You know, to make chitchat, since all men want to talk 'bout is theyselves.

Hell, half the time that's why they call us. They were pretty good movies, but he didn't know shit about Texas."

"Which one was about Texas?"

"*Pearl and Steel.*"

"Sounds like a pair of mismatched cops."

"Naw, that was *Riggins and Hitch*. *Pearl and Steel*, that's the handle of a gun. It was s'posed to be a western, but everybody sat around pouting when they needed to be shooting people."

I dredged up a title. "Which one was *A and Zee*?"

"That was the one about subatomic-particle physics? It all happens inside the Hadron Collider." She pronounced it "*Hay*dron," and for all I knew, she was right.

I said, "You made that up." The coffee began to drip, and we both hung suspended in the fragrance for a moment, like coffee addicts everywhere. "The Hadron Collider was built years after Jake made his last movie."

"Okay, you got me. *A and Zee* was another buddy movie. See, there's these two Secret Service agents who realize that the First Lady is being blackmailed by a terrorist ring."

"That sounds more like Jake. You watched all of them?"

"In my business," she said, "or at least the business in which I currently find myself shipwrecked, he's known as a *whale*. S'posed to be, if he serves a girl a salad, it's got shredded-up hunnerds in it." She tilted the sunglasses as though to focus through the missing left lens and gave me a long look. "I've got to say, as a professional observation, you seem sort of immune to my state of undress."

"My mother always said it's not what a lady wears, it's how she wears it. Have you seen any signs of Jake throwing money around?"

"Not so much," she said. "That's why I asked, all those weeks ago."

"Might have wasted that creativity," I said. "The cheerleader routine, I mean."

"Oh, well," she said. "I was amusing myself, too. This job is *not* enough to keep the mind alive." She nodded at the coffeepot. "How 'bout you just sort of shove a cup under that thing?"

"Fine." I opened the cupboard and found exactly two clean china cups, a beautiful luminescent pearl color and thin enough to see the shadow of my finger through. I swapped the pot for one cup and poured its contents into the other. Casey got it away from me before I even knew she'd crossed the room. Up close she smelled like cigarettes. I said, "Jake still smoking?"

"Like a locomotive. Although cigarettes are the least of his problems. Guy's got a nose he could vacuum a cruise ship with." She drank half the cup, held it out to me, and said, "Trade?"

"Sure," I said. "What about you?"

"Me? You crazy? I'm a country girl. If it doesn't come in a bottle, I don't do it."

"I think he's in trouble," I said.

"Honey," Casey said, "way he's going at it, he's gonna kill himself. And as brown and leathery and mummified as he is, there's still a real person in there somewhere. It's a good thing this is a commercial transaction, 'cause I'd hate to get all maternal about him."

"About who?" Jake croaked from the door. To me he said, "Isn't she *big*?"

Casey said, "Good thing you're not paying by the inch."

"Please," Jake said, "let's try to maintain the illusion

you're here because you can see through all that tanned leather."

"Uh-oh," Casey said. She fanned her face as though it were hot. "Well, you know what they say about eavesdroppers."

"Give me that coffee," Jake said to me.

I did, reluctantly, and found a big chipped mug in the adjoining cabinet, which I filled for myself.

To Casey, Jake said, without looking at her, "For Chrissake, go get dressed. You may be a tramp, but that doesn't mean you gotta look like one."

Casey eyed him for about ten seconds, chewing on her lower lip, and then she went to the sink and dropped her full cup into it, with a satisfying mini-explosion of coffee and little bits of china, while I silently admired the gesture. She brushed her palms together. "Should I call a cab, too, you old catcher's mitt?"

"Why not?" Whelan said. "Unless you've got some new tricks, something that wouldn't be a rerun. I wouldn't want to have to sit through it twice."

"Really, Jake?" Casey said, and her voice was calm although her face was flaming. "You expect me to *remember* what we did? I forgot before I fell asleep." She turned and left the room.

"You've lost your touch, Jake," I said. "That's a nice young woman."

"They're all nice young women, and who gives a fuck? And in case you think I was kidding about having you taken out, you better wake up."

I went to the sink and dropped my mug into it, too. Thick as it was, it broke into several nicely shaped pieces, and coffee splashed over the edges of the sink and onto the filthy counter. "Tell you what," I said. "Call me when you want to say you're sorry. And don't worry about getting a cab for Casey. I'll take her home."

Jake growled, "You gonna pay her, too?"

"The way things look here," I said, "I can afford it better than you can."

Jake hauled off and threw the delicate cup at me. It spooled end over end across the big kitchen, trailing a spiral of coffee, hit a wooden cabinet about three feet to my right, bounced off, and dropped to the kitchen floor, miraculously intact. On my way out of the room, I detoured to step on it.

Jake called out, "Wait!"

I said, over my shoulder, "She watched all your mind-shriveling movies so she'd have something to talk to you about. Even that piece-of-shit Secret Service thing. Then she put up with you all night. She should charge you a few thousand over and above whatever you pay her for the cheerleading."

"That was a *great* movie!" Jake yelled. "Get back in here!"

"Casey?" I called from the living room. "I'll take you home."

"Just a sec," she called from upstairs, her voice echoing down the stone stairway. "Looking for my earrings."

"Junior," Jake said.

"Fuck off, Jake."

"*Junior.*" His tone turned me around, and there he was, at the far end of the room. I really took him in for the first time. He'd been a fabulously handsome young man who had aged into an extremely well-kept older man. But all that residual glamour was scrubbed roughly away by the afternoon daylight coming through the windows. He looked like he'd spent ten years in a jar. The famous tan was patchy and had the supernatural saturation of early Technicolor makeup. The black hair showed half an inch of silver at the scalp, and the infamous bags beneath his eyes were packed so full of puffiness they'd tugged his lower lids down to reveal an unhealthy-looking line of moist pink tissue below the whites. He wore a T-shirt and a pair of boxer shorts that exposed knees like walnuts, and he weighed twenty pounds less than when I'd seen him last.

I said, "Jesus, Jake."

"Junior," he said, "I'm in trouble." He took a step toward me, and I actually thought he was about to go down. "I'm in real trouble."

"How do you *think* I found out it was fake?"

Jake, looking fairly relaxed for someone who was as wired as the phone company, was stretched out in his butter-colored leather armchair in front of the giant fireplace, in which Casey had built a very businesslike fire as a hedge against the house's air-conditioning. From time to time, she abandoned *Lawrence of Arabia*, which Jake had cued up for her in his screening room, to bring in more wood. In jeans and a long-sleeved T-shirt with vertical yellow stripes, she looked even taller.

"You had it appraised," I said. "At a guess, you needed the money."

He gave me a look I could only describe as grave. "I had three appraised. I've never had to sell one before."

"And I can see why, considering how you got them."

"Oh, there's a market," he said. He smiled, but it wasn't the kind of smile that improves a face. "If anyone should know that, Junior, it's you."

"Were the others straight?"

"Straight enough to hang in the Louvre."

"So why are you selling them? Where's all your *money*, Jake?"

"You don't wanna know. I'm getting fucked on streaming because who ever heard of it back when my contracts got drawn up? More streaming means less TV syndication, and all that means less residuals. Also, who am I kidding, the movies are getting old. Kids don't want to watch them. These days they want giant robots throwing planets at each other."

"Come on," I said. "If that's what they wanted back then, you'd have made them."

"But with *heart*," he said. "Remember the Tin Woodman in *The Wizard of Oz*? Had a clock instead of a heart? That's these movies, got a clock for a heart, and it's set at the exact time to let theaters squeeze in an extra showing every day. Good? Bad? Who cares anymore? What matters is, *Is it a franchise? A tentpole? Will the Chinese like it?* More than half the box office now, it comes from overseas." He sat back, sniffed to clear his overworked nose, and crossed his bare ankles. He'd changed into a brown cashmere sweater, no shirt, beige linen slacks, and alligator loafers, no socks. It was so nineties it made my teeth itch.

"But still, you're Jake Whelan."

"I was," he said. "Now I'm the guy who *used to be* Jake Whelan. These days—Jake Whelan these days—you know who he is? He's Jeremy Granger, that's who he is."

"What's he got on you?"

"My future," Whelan said, showing lots of yellowy front teeth on the *f* in *future*. "Which is the only thing that matters to me now that Ellie is dead." Ellie Newsome, an actress he'd made into an almost-topliner, had been Jake's third wife. He'd lost her—Hollywood's oldest story—to a movie star on a location shoot. The relationship with the movie star had fallen apart in about ninety minutes, but it took her marriage to Jake with it. Still, some habit of affection survived, because she and Jake remained a sort of ceremonial couple, getting their formal wear back from the dry cleaner's when they were invited to fill out the C-list at some event where they previously would have been the crown jewels, smiling like dethroned royalty while the flashbulbs went off for younger faces, slowing hopefully for red-carpet interviews with people who were already craning past them for someone fresh.

Ellie had died of cancer, very badly, about five months earlier.

"I was sorry to hear about Ellie, Jake. But I don't know how I can—"

He waved me off, a bit of the imperial Jake I'd first known coming to the surface. "That's on account of you keep talking. Here's the first thing: you *took* me, Junior. I trusted you, and you sold me crap."

"Not on purpose," I said. "I stole two of the pictures, and one of them was real. How the hell was I supposed to know the other one wasn't? How can anyone *tell* with Klee? They look like the geometry in a nightmare."

"Junior," Jake said. I was in the slightly less swell armchair to his right, and he leaned over and tapped my knee. He was a hard tapper. "I'm not gonna tell you my aesthetics are all outraged. I don't like the picture any more than you do, didn't like it when I bought it, but it filled a hole in my collection, and you know what? *It was supposed to be real.* You wanna serve me Miracle Whip? Fine, I'll choke it down. But don't you fucking tell me it's mayonnaise. Those pictures in my cellar, they *represent* something to me. They represent someone who's pushed himself or herself to the far edge of their talent, someone who was already burning as hot as he could but threw a little more coal on, maybe even burned part of himself away, but he got what he was reaching for. There weren't supposed to be any *fakes* down there."

"I know," I said. "I know, I know, I *know*. I'm embarrassed as hell. I'm *humiliated*. I can usually tell when something's duff. It was a personal lapse on my part." I was rubbing my face with both hands. "And I know exactly how you feel about that, that burning thing, about people at their best."

"And now," he said, as though into silence, "I'm gonna have to sell one I really love."

"Who's the artist? Not that I actually want to know."

"Mary Cassatt."

I said, "Ouch."

"So you can probably see why I wanted to kill you."

"I'm not exactly neutral on that issue, Jake—"

He said again, *"Mary Cassatt."*

"Okay, I *do* see why you wanted to kill me. But that doesn't mean I'm automatically going to do this job for you. And don't threaten me again. You're not exactly invulnerable yourself anymore."

"So what do you want?" he said. "I mean, what do I have to do?"

I nodded toward the production room. "Have you paid her?"

"Fifteen hundred," he said. "That's seven-fifty over." He did something with the corners of his mouth that might have developed into either a grin or a snarl if he'd let it. "She asked did I want change."

"How bad is your situation? Financially, I mean."

"What's that got to do with you?" He gave me a good look at his eyeteeth.

"It's part of the picture," I said. "I don't want to do what you want me to do, so I need to know why I'm going to do it."

He rubbed his nose, possibly checking to see whether it was still there. "It's shit. I'm poorer than the Little Match Girl. I made less than half a million last year, and my expenses are three, four times that. Bank accounts are down to paper clips. I've borrowed as much as I can on this place. House payment alone is twenty-eight Gs at this point, so that's like a third of a mil every year right there. Lawyers are eating me alive, trying to solve this streaming thing. I'm still paying alimony to the first two Mrs. Whelans. I owe a couple mil to the IRS."

"How much is the collection worth?"

He shook his head, and then he shook it again, more vigorously. "More than I need. But you gotta know, Junior, I *can't*. I can't sell them all. I might as well die. Just the Cassatt, it's like getting a leg cut off. Also, I sell a clump of them like that, I'll get busted sure as hell."

"And what's Jeremy Granger got on you?"

"Okay," he said. He drew a rectangular frame in the air with index fingers and then pointed at areas to identify items inside it as he talked. "The money, the house, the IRS, all that? That's my past and my present. Bad as it is, much as it keeps me awake at night, it's *gornisht*." He erased the frame with an open hand. "What Jeremy's got is my future. My legacy."

"Can you be more specific?"

"A movie. My *legacy*. The thing that will stand for Jake Whelan as long as people watch pictures in the dark.

The thing that could make up for all the junk I put out while I was on top." He paused for a moment, blinking into the fire like someone trying to work through some blank spaces in an idea. Then he said, "Back in a minute," and got up. I watched him climb the stairs, moving more slowly than I remembered, off to fill his nose so he could face the moment. Fill himself up again with the jittery, snow-burn energy that passed for Jake Whelan these days.

I got up myself and wandered the long hallway to the projection room. I pushed the door open and looked in. Peter O'Toole, his eyes as cold and as blue as sapphires, drank in the desert like a man lusting for something he hated, or maybe it was the sight of Jake plodding up those stairs that made me see it that way.

Casey turned back to me. "How do the Brits *do* this?"

"Training?" I said. "An actual education? I don't know."

"Well, it works. Have you seen this one?"

"Over and over. How you feeling?"

"I'm okay. I'm like a diamond, I don't chip or scratch. How's he?"

"Sad, old, and fucked up."

"That's about right. Damn, he was handsome when he was young."

"You supposed to be anywhere?"

She reached into her purse and brought out her phone. "Close to this."

"That's all right, then."

"I s'pose." She turned back to the screen. "How long until the sheikh comes back?"

"Not long. They looked at him in the rushes and beefed

up his part. We should be out of here in . . . I don't know, half an hour."

"I'll be here," she said. "With Lawrence. And the sheikh."

"You know his nickname?" Jake asked. He was a lot more energetic, and there was a little sift of snow on his upper lip. "King Maybe?"

"I've heard it. Don't know what it means."

"It means what it says. He's the man who says maybe. Maybe we'll do this. Maybe I'll make your movie. Maybe I can get the stars you want. Maybe it'll put you back on top of the heap."

"Does he deliver?"

"That's really *two* questions, and when you're a supplicant, which is what I am these days, you only ask one of them, and that's *can* he deliver? And the answer to that is yes. Yes, he can deliver, practically without lifting a finger. The second question is *will* he deliver? And the answer to that is practically never."

"Okay, he can but he doesn't. So why would you do business with him? Why would anybody?"

He held up two fingers. "Two guys, Junior. There are probably only *two guys* on the entire planet who can greenlight a movie that costs a hundred fifty, two hundred mil without going through a committee of people whose only job is to say no, and Jeremy Granger is one of them. The other one is someone, if I was being nailed to a cross, he'd be looking for blunter nails. Used to be we had studio chiefs, moguls, and they were awful, a lot of them, but most of them, if you cut them deep enough, you'd find someone who liked movies. Now the studio chief is a spreadsheet and what says yes or no are P&Ls—sorry, profit-and-loss models. And the models have changed. People used to worry about which section of the market a movie would sell to, like slices out of a pizza: male—that was a big slice; female; teens, which was another big one; couples"—he tilted his hand side to side—"sort of *meh*. Now they move the pizza over to the side of the table and worry whether it'll sell to the Chinese. And you know what sells to the Chinese?"

"No idea."

"Guys in tights with capes. Things going boom. Titles they already know. *Tyrannosaurus Terrificus 12*. *Hyperman 14*. No need to market, just put thirty seconds and the logo in prime time on CCTV—sorry, China Central Television—slap the preview on Weibo, and get out of the way. Not much dialogue, because it requires too much dubbing. Oh, and it's gotta flunk the Bechdel test."

"The—"

"Comes from a comic strip," he said. "Woman named Alison Bechdel made it up. To pass the test, there's gotta be like three points: there has to be at least two female characters in it, and there has to be a scene where they talk to each other, and when they talk, it can't be about the guys in the movie. So the movies that flunk that test, you can imagine how the great actresses fight over the female roles. These girls in these movies, the way they're written, they're all Cracker Jack prizes."

"Talking about me?" Casey said from behind an armload of wood. "Sorry to bust in, but I figured you two would freeze to death if the little woman didn't keep the home fires burning. And the movie is really long,"

"I apologize, Casey," Jake said.

"And I accept, Jake. That doesn't mean I'll be coming back, but thanks for the impulse."

"What's happening in the movie?" I said.

"Ya caught me," she said. "That's really why I left. He's getting his ass whipped by those Turks and sort of enjoying it. That, like, brings up some of my issues." She took an andiron and distributed the wood she'd thrown on the coals. "Okay," she said, "real reason? I got a call. No hurry, but I gotta get home and do stuff to my face in an hour or so."

"No problem."

"Nope," she said, hanging the iron up on its stand. "Well, you boys just jaw a little more, and then we'll hit the road." We both watched her go.

"Thirty years ago," Jake said, shaking his head, "I'd have probably put her in a movie and married her."

"Thirty years ago was probably fifteen years before she was born."

"Jesus," Jake said. He rubbed the side of his face as though he'd been slapped. "Really gets away from you, time does. Aaaahhh, you wouldn't know. What're you, thirty-four, thirty-five?"

"Thirty-eight. Okay, so I assume Granger—King Maybe—has his hands on this movie you want to make."

"Exclusive option. One year for starters. He's had it seven months already. Means I can't show it to anyone else. He paid me twenty K for it, and nobody else can even look at it."

"So that's the maybe. Why can't you take it back?"

"He's got a unilateral—that means I get no say—option to extend it for a second year. And a third, which should show you how desperate I was. Problem is, even if he gives it back to me, there's nowhere else I can shop it. I told you, there's really only two places you can take a big movie without having to go lick the shareholders' shoes, and one of them is Jeremy and the other one is closed to me."

"So in the best-case situation, what happens?"

"He likes the script, check: in fact, he says he *loves* it. He develops what's called *coverage*, which is Hollywood talk for a short overview with a few assessments of its commercial appeal or lack of it, check: he says he's done that and it's *fabulous*—that was his word. He won't let me read the coverage, but it's *fabulous*." He kisses his fingertips and releases the kiss to the air like a waiter selling the special in a bad restaurant. "He takes it to a bankable director and a couple of top-money-club actors, check: he says he's done it and that you'd know the names of everyone who's supposed to be interested. He puts together a package: stars, director, rewrite screenwriter, the whole *mishegoss*, and then he tells the studio they're doing the movie, and hi there, Jake Whelan is back in business."

"Not check?"

"Not. And now he's not taking my calls."

"And the worst he can do?"

"He can put the fucking thing in a drawer without ever showing it to anybody and keep saying *maybe* until I die of old age, which won't be that long, the way I'm going. He can commission really disastrous coverage that says it's a flop, it's *Ishtar*, it's *The Lone Ranger*, it's a black hole, it'll bankrupt any studio that makes it, on and on and on. Then he can circulate that coverage really aggressively to everyone in town who might conceivably want to make the picture in the future. Or—and here's the big one— he can take the central idea, put it through a centrifuge, and hire bigfoot writers to kick it out of shape until it's deniable if I sue for plagiarism, and then he can make the fucking thing himself and either earn another billion on it while I slowly lose everything and end up living in a box somewhere, or he could go the prestige route and use it to win his Best Picture Oscar. And then return the treatment to me, with a valentine saying, 'Sorry. Couldn't move it.' That's called putting the project in *turnaround*. Son of a bitch can put my whole life in turnaround. So all of the above. Oh, and he can *enjoy* it."

"Why would he? Why would anybody?"

"He got where he is by eating shit, is why. He worked for the worst people in this town, and that's saying a lot. This is an industry that enjoys the sight of failure and likes to make it just a *little* worse, so all the people whose shit Granger was eating introduced him to their so-called friends, and they, or I should say we, all fed him some more shit. While *he* grinned and nodded and kept his ears open, read people's email, rifled through file drawers, and made notes. By the time he aced Barry Zipken with that teenage fluff, he had stuff, lethal stuff, on everyone at Farscope. They had a choice: either they defended him in court or they got the rug pulled out from under them. These guys had mortgages the size of Manhattan, and they had big, fat, expensive asses, which they didn't want to land on, so the lawyers appeared in a shower of glitter, Barry got fired, Jeremy skated, and—informally at first—he used all that info to take over. The ghost with all the power. And now he does just two things with his life: he makes movies that earn trainloads of money, and he gets even. With everyone. Guy's probably saying maybe right now to twenty, thirty movies, just tying knots in people's lives. Twenty-four hours a day, he gets even."

"Turnaround."

"Sorta benign sounding, isn't it? Like a dance step. Like if they named leprosy *lacyface*."

"But, Jake. Even if the movie never gets made, in the end you can sell paintings, one at a time, and sooner or later you'll get paid for the streaming rights and you'll wind up okay. I mean, come on, this is just another movie. Out of how many? Fourteen? Fifteen?"

"*Seventeen.* Total grosses more than two billion." he said. "Nearly three billion, and those are the *official* figures, so God knows what the real ones are. But see, King Maybe, he's operating in a new universe, a *global* universe, where the grosses are . . . well, it's like there's no gravity, okay? He's been at it less than a *decade*, and he's already pushing eight billion. There's not as many movies now as there used to be, not so much competition, and there's bigger audiences with Asia standing in line over there waving their yuan around, but that's all just excuses. Makes me look like a *pisher*, is what it does."

"Seventeen movies. What makes this one life-and-death?"

He got to his feet, and for a moment I thought he was heading back upstairs for a little elevation, but instead he went to the fireplace, grabbed a couple of wrist-thick branches, and tossed them in. "It's an *apology*," he said to the fire. "It's my way to make up for all the zap-zap, kiss-kiss, boys-being-boys crapola I passed off as art all those years. It's a movie that's actually *about* something, something more important than The Rock's pectoral muscles or the physics of warp speed when you're wearing a tight sweater in outer space. Those movies were about *movies*, Junior. The world in them was pieces of other movies. This one is about life." He turned to face me, ragged at the edges but still as imperially slim as Richard Cory just before he went home and put the bullet through his head. "It's the last thing I want to do before I die."

Okay, Jake was a huckster with decades of experience. He'd been making exorbitant claims for negligible movies ever since some of his early ones thrilled my little-boy pants off. I'd grown up with him giving ponderous interviews and making mythic claims in publications that should have known better—the *New York Times*, for example—about films that turned out, upon arrival, to be lighter than air and a lot smellier. High-concept, low-IQ. Zap-zap, kiss-kiss, like the man said. This was what he *did*, repackage shit as shea butter. It was part of his job description.

Except that I believed him.

Sort of.

I said, "What's it called?"

He focused on a spot over my head, drew a couple of deep breaths, licked his lips, and said, "*Ambient Violet.*"

"*Ambient*—"

"*Violet.*" It was almost a snap.

"Not *Stone and Steel*, not *Nickel and Dime* not *Scratch and Sniff*?"

"That was a *formula*," he said, as though that had never occurred to anyone. "I'm telling you, this one is different." He raised a hand in a way that suggested I'd been poised to interrupt. "Just give me two minutes, okay? You can time me, I don't give a fuck."

"I'm listening."

"I need a second." He picked up the fire iron and messed around with the logs. It was a little stagey, but then I'm a cynic. "I've done it all," he said. "I've *had* it all. However you measure it, there are wide lives—*big* lives— and there are small lives. And I think maybe I've—maybe we've all—been chasing the wrong one."

He leaned the iron against the fireplace. "So I went for the big life, and I got it, bigger than almost anyone. Probably looked great from outside, and you know, Junior, for a long time I lived my life so it *would* look good from outside. For example, books. I never read shit, and when I did, it was junk, you know, the heartrending romance of the week and real-life crime and even those condensed books like they used to have—you know, 'All the story in half the words'? But my bookshelves, they were all Tolstoy and the Greeks, poetry and Shakespeare, biographies of people I never heard of, but the guy I had buy my books for me, he said they were important. And the other thing he did, he wrote a couple paragraphs about each of them so I could talk about them and not sound like an idiot. 'The theme of redemption in Tolstoy,' you know what I'm saying?"

"I suppose. But I don't have any idea where you're taking it."

"See, that's why the *movie* is so important." He pushed himself away from the fireplace and started to pace. "What I can say right now, just you and me in this room, is that I fell for it myself. The bigness was what I thought I wanted, and so I made it, I claimed all that space and then I filled it up with junk, and I *believed* it. Those books, this house, the Ferraris, my name on those theater marquees, me standing around at parties shooting the shit with Harrison Ford. Saying yes and no to the world. I bought it."

By now he'd gotten far enough to my left that I was going to have to shift to keep him in my field of vision, and he turned, so it was pretty clear he was aware of his audience's sight lines. "See, what happens in life, you try this and that, and if you're lucky, you find something that pleases you, that satisfies you, makes you feel good about yourself. If you're not lucky, you find things that hurt less than the other things do. So either way, what you do, you use that information to build a sort of house out of your life, does that make sense? As long as you stay inside those walls, in that floor plan, chances are you won't get creamed." He stretched out an arm, index finger extended, and indicated the rectangle of the room we were in. "Same rooms over and over again, but they're *safe*. You're trapped, but you're safe. And, of course, the joke is that you have to get as old as I am to understand that I could have walked through those walls anytime. That I *should* have. Into someplace small and quiet. Someplace I could get my arms around."

"The unexamined life," I said.

He snapped his fingers and pointed a finger at me, pistol style. "That's it, that's exactly it. And listen, I know this isn't the first time anybody ever thought about this, but now I look back at all that time I was given, that time I spent returning calls and jumping on planes and crossing oceans and getting hair implants and *shtupping* starlets, and you know what I see? I see that every day of my life I've been getting up in the morning and next to my bed there's this, like, chalice, whatever a chalice is, and it's full of these golden, glowing seeds. And every day I've reached in without a second's thought and grabbed one at random and then never thought about it again, and *that was my day*. And it's not until you get *old*," he said, coming back to his chair and sitting on the arm closer to me, only a few feet away, "that you realize that the level of golden seeds in the chalice drops every time you take one out. Gets lower. And one day you look in and you realize you can almost count them, and what did you do with the ones you pulled out? Did you breathe on them, roll them between your hands, try to feed that teeny golden fire just a little bit? Did you say thank you, did you explore them, or did you just pop the seed like an aspirin and forget about it, go make another million, schmooze some actor, buy another yard of books you won't read?" He leaned back and slid the rest of the way into the chair. "Maybe, in your case, steal something that someone loved?"

"And what would have happened," I said, "if you'd tried to feed the fire?"

"Who the fuck knows?" he said. He slapped his thighs with his open hands, the sound surprisingly loud. "That's why it matters: *you don't know.* Whatever kind of life it was, big and shiny like mine or tiny and awful like some street beggar's in New Delhi, sooner or later it's gone, and you didn't *explore* it, you never went all the way to the borders, much less through them. *I* know, I know this sounds like white people's problems, sounds like every old fart who ever lived, but maybe there's some room in the world for something that *suggests* to people that they owe it to themselves to realize that the walls that they built yesterday, they can go through them today. If you built big, you can go small, if you built small . . . well, you know. You don't have to be the person you started out to be. You can walk away from that person the way you'd blow off the bore at a party. Be something different. You can look at each of those little seeds and make the most of it. In my case, center in and go for something small."

"Why small?"

He leaned back and regarded his lap for a moment. "Well, first, obviously, I've had big. But more than that, beyond that, there's a kind of *density* to some small lives, you know? A kind of concentration. Emily Dickinson left a pretty deep scratch on the world for someone who hardly ever went outdoors, Jane Austen in her . . . what, her drawing room? I don't know. How big was Jesus's world? A couple hundred square miles?" He lifted his feet one at a time and brought them down onto the floor, making footsteps like a sound effect. "Covered mostly on foot? I still have a lot of energy, Junior. It's *wisdom* I don't have. Maybe looking very closely at one thing at a time for a while, learning every square inch of a small room, figuring out how to play the first six notes of 'Clair de Lune' on a violin *perfectly* is how you get to wisdom. Maybe I've got enough time left to make a start on that."

"You're going to work toward a small life by making a hundred-million-dollar movie."

"It's what I know how to do." He peeled himself from the fire and headed toward the stairs, but it was movement for movement's sake, and he turned halfway and came back toward me, stopping eight or ten feet from my chair. Raised both hands, palms outward, telling me to sit there and listen. "At this time in my life, I need to *say* something. I need to try to tell people the things I'm beginning to figure out, in a way they won't forget. A movie, okay? And at the same time, it'll be my *discipline*. No more ten things at once. One movie, word by word, idea by idea, inch by inch. Image by image. Like scrimshaw." He made it to his chair and did something that was midway between sitting down and collapsing. "Like how a face ages, one slow wrinkle at a time. Pulling it out of my soul, if I can find my soul."

"*Ambient Violet*," I said.

He leaned forward in the chair, very quickly. "Laugh at me, I'll kick your face in."

"Then don't amuse me."

"The whole thing, the whole movie, it takes place in the moments between the time someone—an old woman—breathes in for the last time and the time she breathes *out*. The opening shot is a wall, just a rough, blank, white-washed wall, somewhere in the Third World, with a crack running down it. And we get a quick glimpse of her face with her eyes wide open, staring at the wall—maybe fifteen, twenty frames, just enough to register her—and then we're back to the wall, and we hear her inhale deeply, a little raggedly, the sound slowed way down, and the camera moves inch by inch toward the crack, and almost imperceptibly the crack widens and turns blue, and we do a tilt-shift, and it's a river with some trees over it, and it's the thing she knew best in her life. And then she's a young girl at the edge of a river, and we're there with her."

"In her memory."

"In her life. And her life, it's *nothing*. It's nothing any-one would ever write down. She lives, she falls in love, she has a couple of children and one dies, she gets old and sick, she finally breathes out, she passes away, and *nobody remembers her*. And the river is still there, the crack on the wall is still there, and *they* don't remember her either."

I said nothing.

"And that was the whole world," he said. "That was all

of life, all of time, that was everything everyone has ever wanted or needed or been afraid of, and she didn't go anywhere, she didn't do anything. She didn't get painted, she didn't get filmed, she didn't get rich. She lived, she loved her kids, she died. The history of the world, in close-up. What would I mean to her? What would you mean to her? We'd be a streak on the horizon, a blemish on the stars. She wouldn't give us a thought. She had—she had, like that girl in there watching *Lawrence of Arabia*—she had fires to build. People to keep warm. Then she was gone. The end."

"Why violet?"

He looked embarrassed, as though he'd been hoping I wouldn't ask. "Violet is the color of memory. To me, I mean."

"Got it." I sat back in the chair, distancing myself from his intensity as I might pull away from a space heater. "You think you can make that movie?"

"I don't know," he said, tight-lipped. "I'd have to become somebody else to do it, wouldn't I?"

"I asked if you *thought* you could make it."

"I think I have to try."

"Well, shit," I said. It was my turn to get up, even though there was nowhere I wanted to go. "If I say no, you'll kill me, so what do you need me to do?"

Outside, the wind rattled the windows.

12

Tired of Being Dead

"So you want to be an actress," I said. We were crossing Santa Monica, heading north into Hollywood. It was late afternoon, still hot and windy. The trees were waving their arms around, and their shadows stretched themselves all the way across the street. The shadowscape felt premature, with daylight saving time gone for only a week.

"Jake told you, didn't he?" she said accusingly. "Bet I know how he made *that* sound."

"Jake doesn't matter. You want to act, right?"

"Who doesn't?" she said. "Especially when you're out on the Texas panhandle, just you and the wind, and the only color you got is what's on the *teevee*." She was looking down at her lap, and I could see why; the neighborhood through which we were driving was the absolute ass end of Hollywood, street after street of buildings neither old enough to be interesting nor new enough to look clean.

As though reading my mind, she glanced up for a second, just a *Where are we?* check, and said, "When I first got here? I looked at all these crappy soda-cracker buildings and I felt like they was just—sorry, they *were* just—inviting earthquakes, daring them, saying, 'Come on in and shake.' It reminded me of trailer parks in the South, just hollering up to the sky for a big fat tornado: 'Git your ass down here and blow me all to shit.' Yeah, I wanted to be an actress. Me and every other semi-pretty chick in Texas."

"Don't short yourself. So you sat around and watched TV and thought about coming out here?"

"Right at the next turn," she said. "Yeah. It looked easy. Learn the words and let them get you all made up, and there you are, going out with some Jonas brother. It's funny, when you're in that gear, wanting it so much, you don't notice how bad some of them are, the girls on TV. If you did, you'd probably consider, 'Hey, maybe it's harder than I think.'"

"Bad actresses," I said.

I made the turn. She said, "Was that the complete thought?"

"No. Did you watch a show called *Dead Eye?*"

"The zombie thing, few years back? That chick, I mean, she was fine-looking, even if she had kind of early-bloomer fifteen-year-old looks, but she was hopeless. She talked like a machine, like Siri on the iPhone, on a bad day And I mean she actually looked at the *camera* some-times."

"Somebody Dawn?" I said.

"Tasha," she said. "Tasha Dawn. We used to have con-tests, like imitating her, in junior high. She had this little wee helium voice? 'I am so *tired* of bein' dead,' she said once in a while. I guess it was supposed to build her char-acter or something. We used to say it in Mr. Winslow's social-studies class. He'd say something extra dull with like a hundred dates in it, and a dozen girls would say, 'I am so *tired* of bein' dead.' But, you know, out there on the panhandle I looked at her and thought, 'If she can make it, I can.'"

"She married it," I said.

"So I learned. *El queso grande*, the big cheese himself. Some girls have all the luck."

"I'm not sure she's as lucky as all that."

"Well, she's not living *here*," Casey said. "Right here, just pull over. *Mi casa*, on the right."

Casey's building was a nondescript three-story apartment house, one of hundreds stamped out of a mold: just a big concrete lower-Hollywood shoe box with pathetic little balconies, all of eight inches deep, protruding below the windows like a patient unenthusiastically showing the doctor her tongue. Casey waited a moment after I pulled up to the curb, looking at me sort of expectantly with one foot tapping, and then she said, "Buy me a drink sometime? I'll tell you some Texas stories."

"Sure," I said.

She waited an awkward moment for me to ask for her phone number, and then smiled and said, "Looking forward to it. I am so *tired* of bein' dead. Hey, thanks for the rescue." Then she got out and leaned back in, reached into her purse, and took out a card, which she dropped on the passenger seat, only her first name and a number. She said, "Just in case," and backed away and closed the door and hurried up the sidewalk to get ready for her appointment, whoever that might be, a rangy, lonely, small-town Texas girl hopelessly lost without a map, a few short blocks south of the Walk of Fame.

I felt like I had a large stone sitting dead center on my chest, a dense mass made up of many unpleasant things: the separation from Ronnie, the aftermath of my brush with the Slugger, whatever tangles had developed in the relationship between Tyrone and Rina, the state of Casey's life, the commitment I'd made to Jake. Plus, of course, Jake's damn, impossible movie and the fact that I was pledged to commit a burglary to find out whether Jeremy Granger, a.k.a. King Maybe, exploiter of teenage girls, was intentionally shredding Jake's legacy.

And the sheer persistence of the wind had stripped the coating off my nerves. My skin felt like a collection of tiny electrical short circuits.

Was anything all right *anywhere*? I gave it a few minutes' thought, sitting there, and didn't come up with a yes. If—as some ironic people used to say as they flashed air quotes—life was a box of chocolates, someone had sat on the box.

It occurred to me that I was about twenty minutes away from Ronnie's neat, bright, book-filled little apartment in West Hollywood, where most of my clothes were. I was either going to have to make up with her and move back in, if she'd have me, or else go pick up my clothes in some kind of final gesture. Or, I thought, defer the whole thing until she was in a better mood and go buy some new clothes.

I drifted my way around the block a few times, literally unable to choose a direction. I didn't have the slightest idea how to put things right with Ronnie. There was no good reason to go back to the Dew Drop Inn and many reasons not to. It would have taken me ninety minutes in the thickening afternoon-to-evening rush to get to Rina and Kathy's house in Tarzana, where I'd probably be pushed aside in all the preparations for the party.

Yikes, the *party*. Rina's birthday, mysteriously moved

to a different night that was not actually her birthday and apparently off-limits to Tyrone. That settled it: go see Kathy and Rina. But first the coward's solution: don't go see Ronnie, call her.

In all the time I'd known her, Ronnie had never recorded a personalized voice-mail message. Either she was happy with the electrically cheerful female voice the phone company supplied or, more likely, she didn't want her real voice hanging out there where it might be heard by someone from her (apparently) permanently shrouded past.

So it was a surprise, when I was idling at the curb half a dozen addresses east of Casey's shoe box with my phone at my ear, to hear Ronnie's voice say, "Hi, this is Ronnie. If you want to leave a message or recite some poetry, please wait for the beep. On the other hand, if you're Junior Bender, go fuck yourself."

I didn't wait for the beep. With my ears burning and the stone on my chest twice as heavy as before, I turned my badly dented white Toyota toward the Cahuenga Pass and the San Fernando Valley, toward the house I once thought would shelter my family and me forever.

The Cahuenga Pass, which derived its name from a Spanish mispronunciation of *Cabueg-na*, a Native American trading post that once occupied much of the space where Universal Studios stands today, was for centuries a footpath through the chaparral covering the Santa Monica Mountains that lie between the Valley and the Los Angeles Basin. By the first decade of the twentieth century, the original trail had been broadened to create a rough and rocky dirt road that led over the hill from the abandoned ruin of Cabueg-na to the booming little townlet assembled from four adjoining sections of land by a developer named

Harvey Wilcox. His wife, Daeida, named the development Hollywood after an estate (which she'd never seen) owned by a friend of hers, back east in Illinois. Although Daeida chose the name for its upper-class intimations of quality and grace, by the 1930s Hollywood would be so linked in the American public's mind with sex, drugs, and moral corruption that the residents of another Hollywood, in Indiana, would change their town's name in self-defense.

In its infancy, though, Hollywood was a model of civic virtue. Wilcox was vigorously opposed to fun of the louder varieties and prohibited the sale and consumption of alcohol within the limits of his new city. The nearby Pass, as it was called, inevitably became rum-sodden outlaw territory, home to high spirits and loose women. Many of the latter operated out of Eight Mile House, the first hotel in the area, which was noted for the extreme frequency with which its rooms were rented, often six and seven times a day, and the heavily armed desperadoes who congregated there. No less distinguished a personage than Cecil B. DeMille had been shot at on the Pass.

By the mid-1920s, Eight Mile House had been reduced to a pile of old lumber, and Hollywood's most socially prominent women were agitating to plant an enormous and reproving cross high in the Pass, a reminder visible to sinners for miles around that the Lord's righteousness did not expire at the Rockies. They won their battle, but eventually the cross went the way of the whorehouse. In the end they were, after all, both just wood.

I saluted mentally as I crept past the place where Eight Mile House had so briefly filled the Pass with the sounds of gunfire, breaking glass, and groans of simulated pleasure.

The footpath was now an eight-lane freeway, cratered with potholes, stained with oil, and choked with carbon monoxide, just another permanent vehicular ordeal to be endured by commuters twice a day. It was enough to make me yearn for a horse, a dirt track, dappled sunlight, and oak trees full of songbirds. Lord, how we've battered and pasteurized the world.

At Woodman I gave up on the freeway and coasted down to the surface streets. I grew up in the Valley, and Valley residents have always seen traffic jams as a sort of noisier weather: they came and went, like smog and heat waves, and there was nothing to be done about it.

But that didn't mean we didn't try. I zigzagged my way across the grid toward Kathy's house, running residential streets and alleys, selecting obscure detours through the east-west streets that only seasoned Valleyites know. In the end I probably added six or seven miles to the trip and subtracted two or three minutes from the clock, but I was feeling vindicated as I made the right onto Santa Rita. On some tiny, meaningless, totally trivial level, I still had it.

I was pulling to the curb when I saw Tyrone standing at the open door. He had his back to me, and the person blocking his way into the house, silhouetted against the light in the hall, was my ex-wife, Kathy. For a small, usually genial woman, Kathy can project a really impressive force field of rejection. If there were ever a *Star Trek* movie set in Tarzana, Kathy's Rejection Force Field would get a story arc all its own.

Tyrone stepped back, and I took my foot off the brake to kill the red lights and let the car roll forward. I heard Kathy's voice, as edgy as a bouquet of razor blades, and then I was out of sight. I drove past a couple of houses to the little circle off to the left, did a 360, and waited as Tyrone slouched toward me, head down, hands in his rear pockets.

When he was about eight feet away I lowered my window and said, "Hey, kid."

Without looking up, he said, "Yeah, yeah."

"Tyrone," I said.

He stopped and looked up at me. "It's you," he said.

I said, "I hear that all the time."

"I don't mean to be rude," he said, "but I already heard all about what a shit I am. And you know what? If you've got something to add, I'd just as soon you keep it to yourself."

"Tyrone," I said. "Please get in the car."

He looked me in the face for a good five seconds. Then he said, "Why?"

"Short version, I don't know what's going on, and I'd like to hear it from you. Long version, I . . . um, I've come to appreciate who you are and the way you are with Rina, and who knows? Maybe I can help."

Tyrone's eyes were the golden brown of autumn leaves. Against the dark skin of his face, they seemed to leap out at me across the dusk. The only expression I could read in them was doubt. An almost-friend, a hit woman named Debbie Halstead, had once taken a single look at him and predicted that Tyrone would spend his life trying to escape from women, and I'd been watching him ever since, searching for a glimpse of the corruption that extreme good looks can bring. So far I hadn't seen it.

He went around and got in. Then he loosed a sigh that practically blew out the windshield. "They know this car," he said. "You want them to let you in sooner or later, right? So you don't want them to see you sitting out here talking to me."

"The conspiracy of the patriarchy," I said, putting the car in gear.

He said, "Say what?"

"Talking to myself." I made the right onto Vanalden. "That happens when you get divorced."

"So," he said. "What did they tell you?"

"Nothing. Just that I wasn't supposed to mention you in front of Rina."

"Yeah," he said. "Sweep old Tyrone under the rug."

"I think the implication was that Rina is in kind of a fragile state where you're concerned. In other words, if you'll excuse me pointing it out, it was more about her than you."

"Well, sure," he said. "Her family, it's about her. Me, sitting here on my side of the car, if you'll excuse *me* pointing it out, it's about me, too."

I said, "I am so weary of everyone having a perspective and all of them sounding so valid. How the hell am I supposed to get anything clear if everybody's *right*?"

We glided in silence past a couple of houses, all lit up and containing theoretically happy families, and then Tyrone said, "Hard day, huh?"

"Don't ask."

"I don't care. I was just being polite."

I found a nice empty stretch of curb in between streetlights. The sharp, bright tip of the moon peeped over a tree, and wind-borne dust danced in the beams from the headlights. "Tell me what's happening."

"Truth is?" He sighed again. "Okay. Truth is, I kind of screwed up."

"How badly?"

"In spirit," he said. "I screwed up in spirit."

"This is either a fine distinction or not, depending."

"You're her dad."

"And."

He put down his window and looked out of it. "And this isn't easy to talk about."

"If you don't talk about it," I said, "I can't do anything for you. Assuming I'd want to, once I hear what you have to say." This was greeted by silence. "I was a kid once, you know."

"Yeah," he said. "All old guys say that."

I had turned off the lights, and now I turned them back on. "Up to you."

"Okay, okay. Just give me a minute." He put the window up and put it down again halfway. "You don't have to worry about Rina," he said, slowly enough to have picked the words out of a bowl.

"In what regard?"

"Boy, does *that* sound stiff. In what regard? You could add 'my good man,' you know. Sound even stiffer."

"The question stands."

"In regard to what *you* probably mean when you say 'a good girl.' No, Jesus, don't *ask* me, you know what I mean."

I said, "*Boy*, is this awkward."

"So she's nothing to worry about in that department, she's got a strong will and she's smart and she's decided not to do anything that would limit the choices she can make. That's what she said to me, she's not going to *limit the choices she can make.*"

"Good for her."

"Yeah, I mean it's not very personal or very romantic, but it's clear, you know? Girl's real clear."

"So I assume that the context of that conversation . . ." I completely ran out of gas.

"Well, sure. I'm a guy, right?"

"I'd noticed that, and believe me, as her dad I've thought about it many times."

"And since you made the point that you were young once, then you know what I'm talking about."

"A minute ago," I said, "I didn't think this conversation could get any more uncomfortable. I stand corrected."

"But you do know."

"I know, if we're going to focus on my own mythical youth, that I wouldn't want Rina dating anybody like me." A sudden gust of wind hit the car, rocking it slightly, and a ragged bunch of dry leaves skittered across the street. Not only was the heat sticking around, so was the fire season.

"Well, then, you can relax, 'cause I'm not like you. But I am a guy. And . . . um, you also know that just because you can't—you know—get a drink of water someplace, that doesn't mean you're not still thirsty."

"You *didn't*," I said.

"No! No, I didn't."

We sat there as the moon inched its way higher. The wind wasn't bothering the moon any. And then Tyrone said, "But it might have looked like I was going to try."

I said, "Would it be possible for us to dispense with the conditional tense?"

"Is that like *if* and *might have*?"

"It is."

"They don't teach us that."

"They don't teach you shit, if you want my opinion. But that's not the subject."

"Yeah, okay, okay. So there's this girl named Denise, and Denise, who is not, like, totally unattractive, told this friend of hers who told this friend of mine that she wouldn't mind hooking up with me."

"As in—"

"Oh, come *on*."

I said, "*Look* at that moon, would you?"

"Yeah," Tyrone said. "There it is."

"You know why you sometimes see it as a crescent?"

"Yes," Tyrone said. "That's one of the things they do teach us."

I drew a breath that seemed to include most of the air in the neighborhood. "So, to summarize, there's a sort of *barrier* to the further exploration of one possible aspect of your relationship with Rina, and you're down with that but not fully satisfied on a sort of hormonal level, and this girl named . . . named . . ."

"Denise. Fine looking—"

"I don't care if she's got six legs. This . . . this Denise, who could probably use a little aggressive parenting, sends you a verbal chain letter to inform you that she has an interest in making the beast with two backs—"

"That's *Othello*," Tyrone observed. "Interesting you should choose *Othello*, with me being—"

"—and you say, what? 'Good to go'? 'Ready when you are'?"

"I don't say shit," Tyrone said. "But I hung around with her a little."

"Hung around."

"Like at school. In broad daylight. In public, with about a million people looking."

"'In public' where?"

"Outdoors," he said. "A park once and the mall once. We were always vertical." He cleared his throat. "But I held her hand."

"Oh, boy," I said.

"So naturally, that was when Rina's friend, this little scab on the world's nose—her name's Patty—"

"*Patricia,*" I said. "They're going twosies, as my wife said, for a dual birthday party."

"And that's like a first-class ticket for Patty, who's been trying forever to get close to Rina."

"Why?"

"Because Rina's tope. Everybody thinks—"

"Wait. Taupe? You mean, like, beige?"

"No, *tope.* T-O-P-E. Like tight and dope, put together. Okay, okay, for you, *cool,* remember cool?"

"We're talking about *Rina?*"

"Top of the ticket. Dudes want to hang with her, sisters want to be her bra."

"Tyrone."

He gave me the first grin of the evening. "Like *bro,*" he said, "but for the other half. You know, like tight with her."

"She never talks about this."

"If she did, she wouldn't be tope."

"So Patty, or Patricia, saw you and . . . uh, Denise, holding hands, and she used that as a way to make friends with Rina."

"To get tighter," Tyrone said. "They were already

on hey-there, nod-in-the-hall terms. But then Patty goes and gets all weepy and says, 'Oh, I hate to tell you this, but— No, never mind, I can't,' and Rina's like 'What what *whaat*?' And finally Patty breaks down and gives her the news. Kleenex everywhere."

"How do you know it went like that?"

"Because Rina told me. 'God bless Patty,' she says, or something like that, 'I practically had to torture her to get her to tell me,' and I'm seeing old Patty just beauty-queening it up in a corner, probably rubbing her legs together like a cricket."

"You saw her?"

"No, that's a figure of speech. Rina told me over the phone, but Patty was in the room. Rina said so."

"What did you say."

"What *could* I say?" Tyrone asked. "I denied it."

"You lied?"

He looked at me as though I'd begun speaking in tongues. "*Course* I lied. What would *you* have done?"

"Yeah," I said. "Right."

"So I denied it, but, see, Patty had *brought someone with her*, another marginal girl, who had seen it or said she did, and she told Rina, Patty did, to break it to me, like, one witness at a time, so she could see whether I'd lie." He looked up at the moon for a moment. "And I did. I said I hadn't done it, and this other girl pipes up and says *she* saw me, too." He lifted his right foot and kicked himself in the left shin with his heel. A tree branch, leaves intact, tumbleweeded across the street.

"But you're telling *me* the truth."

Rubbing his shin, he said, "I am."

"How do I know?"

"You know," he said, "one reason you're double-checking me on that . . . well, it's the same reason Rina believed it so fast, the same reason you picked *Othello*. Black guys are supposed to be dogs, right?"

"I don't think so," I said. "I think it's about insecurity. Rina thinks you're the best thing in her life, and she might be right. And she sees how other girls look at you, and she . . . she doesn't believe she's interesting enough to hang on to you. Pretty enough, I don't know. And another teenage girl, who understands all of that, is playing her like a violin."

He shrugged, "I guess."

"So I'm sorry for doubting you. I believe you, Tyrone."

He sat silent for a moment, and then he said, "I know old people—sorry, adults—don't take this seriously, but I do really love your daughter. Never loved anyone like I love Rina."

"Well then," I said. "We've got to fix this."

"How?"

"Honestly, Tyrone?" I said. "I have no idea."

13
Something Weaselly

I dropped him off at the corner so Kathy wouldn't just happen to look out the window and see my car, as she does with probability-defying regularity, and then I took off down Vanalden. There wasn't much point in trying to talk to her or Rina until I had some sort of agenda.

But just to demonstrate that I had my hand in, I pulled over and used my phone to email Kathy, using her preferred vowel-challenged mode: *Wnt 2 tlk w/u abt Tyrone.* Pleased with having set *something* into motion, I got halfway to Ventura Boulevard before I mentally slapped my forehead, remembering that I was supposed to have been paid $35,000 for the stamp that day.

Stinky didn't answer the phone. I left a message with the phone company's fembot: "Have stamp, clock ticking," and mused for a second about the fact that no one I knew—well, *almost* no one I knew, now that Ronnie had gone over to the dark side—recorded personalized voicemail messages. Maybe it was a crook thing.

I'd no more than pulled back into traffic when the phone rang. I answered it without looking, which is always a mistake. "I saw you," Kathy said. "Skulking around out there and picking up Tyrone."

"How did you see me?"

"I just happened to look out the window."

"You were spying on Tyrone," I said. "You wanted to see whether he was actually leaving. Talk about *skulking.*"

"I knew you'd take his side."

"I haven't said anything about whose side—"

"Well, you should. Poor kid."

I said, "Uhhh."

"You know," Kathy said, and I could practically hear her knuckles going white as she gripped the phone, "when we were married, it really pissed me off when you assumed you knew in advance how I was going to react to everything. And it still does."

"The way you said 'his side' made it sound like he'd been caught raising money for the American Nazi Party."

"You heard it like that because it's what you expected me to think."

I paused, sorting it out. I said, "Only you and I could disagree about agreeing with each other."

"It's a habit we got into. A way to keep talking. There's something I don't like about that Patricia. Something weaselly. When Patricia was here a couple of days ago to break the bad news to Rina, I saw a mean little glint of triumph in her eye after Rina hung up on Tyrone."

"That's what Tyrone says. He says Rina is really popular and Patricia isn't, and this is Patricia's way of worming her way into the circle."

"Even if I do dislike Patricia and like Tyrone," Kathy said, "Tyrone has a good reason for trying to make Patricia look bad. Patricia nailed him."

"Maybe. When he and I were talking, *Othello* came up, which is kind of interesting, because *Othello* is all about bringing someone down by making him jealous, when there's really no cause."

"I hate when you do that," she said. "I like to feel like my life—and Rina's, too—isn't plagiarized. You know, our lives are new to *us* when they happen, even if you've read them in better versions."

"Just thought it was interesting."

"Okay, I'm not being fair. You're not like most people who go all literary every ten minutes. You actually *do* things once in a while."

"I don't suppose Rina can hear you."

"I'm out by the pool. She's in her room with the door closed, wearing her Dr. Dre Beats and looking at hip-hop videos. Probably hoping her father will call."

"She wouldn't talk to me about it anyway."

"No. It's a girl thing."

"If you don't like Patricia," I said, "why are you up for the twosies party?"

"I had to give Rina *something*. She's been crying for days."

We both stopped talking for a minute or so at the sound of that. It brought us back to what mattered. After I finished sighing, I said, "You've done an amazing job with her."

"She was good material to work with."

"You've never been able to accept a compliment."

"I haven't had much practice," she said. "Listen, are you coming to the party?"

"Sure. But let me think about Patricia a little bit between now and then. What's her last name?"

"Are you going to do something illegal?"

"Me?" I said.

"Silly question. It's Gribbin."

"Spelled like—"

"Like *Gribbin*. Whoops, I see Rina looking at me through the kitchen window."

"Tell her that she—" I said, but Kathy was gone, which was just as well, since I had no idea how I would have finished the sentence.

Innocent people can sit in front of a house at night for hours without getting prickles on the back of their neck, but I'm not an innocent person, and I'd been there long enough. In the almost twenty years I've been breaking the law for a living, I've never been arrested. It would be really stupid to have a run-in with a cop because some citizen saw me through his window too many times and called the law. People are so distrustful these days.

So I rolled down to Ventura, made a right, toward Hollywood, and turned over in my mind the question of whether I was really ready to set in motion the only plan I had, which was to persuade a young girl to commit a criminal act. It seemed to be something a decent person would hesitate about, and I was proud of myself for hesitating. When I felt I'd hesitated enough, I turned right onto one of the north-south streets, pulled over to yet another curb, and dialed.

"I thought you'd lost my number," Anime Wong said.

"Actually," I said, "I'm having a kind of moral crisis, and I was hoping you could help me with it."

"This is the Moral Crisis Hotline," Anime said. "Lilli says hey."

"Hey, Lilli." I heard a young girl's voice, prematurely dry, in the background. While Anime greeted whatever the world threw at her as though it were the first sunrise ever, Lilli had dry, as well as world-weary, down cold.

"You guys still working?" I said.

"Of *course* not," Anime said. "You told us to stop."

Anime and Lilli, both fourteen, worked for, or perhaps *with*, an elaborately tattooed cyber crook named Monty Carlo, breaking through the computer shields that surround the substantial funds that states create when they assume ownership of the contents of abandoned safe-deposit boxes. Once through the firewalls, the three of them helped themselves to an amount of money that they determined, through an algorithm Monty worked out, could be plausibly attributed to a rounding error or a normal short-term fluctuation. Of course, a sum that represents a rounding error to a state is a fortune to a teenager, and Lilli and Anime intended to go to a top-line East Coast college together, probably holding hands, and emerge with advanced degrees and zero student debt, having paid their way in stolen cash.

"Fine," I said. "Glad to hear it. I'll call someone else."

"I was just bagging on you," Anime said. "We're still crooks. Whaddaya got?"

"I need to know about a kid," I said. "Patricia Gribbin. Lives in Tarzana or Reseda, around there."

With the almost infinite weariness of the computer geek adrift in a world of idiots, Anime said, "Have you looked at Facebook?"

"No. I'd need to friend her to read her stuff, right? Did I say that right? *Friend*, like a verb?"

"Yes, and we were impressed. Depends on her privacy settings."

"In any case, I think it would be a bad idea to friend her."

"You could snoop her through a ghost account."

"Anime," I said, "I still don't know how to play an MP3 file."

Lilli muttered something in the background, and Anime said, "Lilli wants to know, do you mean her any harm?"

Well, *did* I? "No. I just need to get the basics. Where she lives, how old she is, what she's interested in—you know, the kind of stuff that would tell me who the hell she is. Whatever you can get. And tell Lilli that Patricia Gribbin may be messing around with my daughter, and I need to know whether she can be trusted."

Anime said, carefully, "When you say 'messing around' . . ."

"I mean maliciously."

"So not like a girlfriend. Not a girlfriend the way Lilli and I are. You know, romantically."

"No. She seems to be trying to make my daughter unhappy. She's messing with Rina's private life."

"Private life," Anime said. "What a droll concept. Isn't that droll, Lilli?" Lilli seemed to be agreeing that it was droll.

"So will you?"

"Sure. I'll get back to you in a little bit. How are you?"

"Same as always."

"You were kind of *off*, last couple of times we talked."

"Thanks for noticing."

"Well," she said. "We were worried about you." Lilli said something, and Anime said reprovingly to her, "You were *too*." To me she said, "Lilli always has to seem tough."

There were lights on in Ronnie's apartment, although the blinds were down. The pale blue ghost-glow of my watch told me it was about ten to nine.

The apartment house where she—and, until recently, I—lived was constructed in the 1940s and consequently was both attractive and well built, although it featured that odd bricklaying technique that forces out little pillows of excess cement between the bricks, thoughtfully making a wall easier to climb. The building, only two stories tall, was shaped like a squared-off U on three sides of a nicely tended garden, which had been planted long enough ago that ivy had used the protruding cement as handholds to scale the wall. Looking up at the ivy, I thought again of Ronnie bravely driving the stolen Jag through the Slugger's gate, and my conscience, which doesn't get out as often as it should, gave me a belated little squeeze.

I knocked on the door and stepped back so I wouldn't seem to be crowding her when she opened it. It was a nice touch, I thought, sensitive yet still manly, but it was wasted, because the door remained closed.

I knocked again, a bit more briskly this time, and stepped back yet again. Prepared my most spontaneous smile.

Nothing. Well, her lights were on a timer, so they'd still be on if she were in Timbuktu. So leave a note. No point in driving all the way over here and not even leaving a note. Although part of me was relieved not to have to go through the conversation, I still wanted credit for making the effort. I was most of the way to the car to get a Post-it from the dash compartment when my phone rang.

"I'm not here," Ronnie said.

"You do know that's an impossibility. Wherever you are, you're there, so you can't possibly say, 'I'm not here.'"

"Fine. Then I'm not there."

"Where?"

"Wherever you are. And it'll probably be quite a while before I *am* wherever you are."

"Can't we talk about this?"

"We just did." But she didn't hang up.

"I finally realized something, an hour or two ago," I said. "You're the only person I know whom I trust emotionally."

"Do I win a candy bar?"

I rested my hand on the hood of the dented Toyota. Warm as the night was, it was still warmer. "I thought it might matter."

"I'm sure it does, to you," she said. "And it probably will to me, when I've given it some time. And I'm not trying to go all *Fatal Attraction* on you here, but you're making it totally about you, which is a very masculine approach to life."

"What does that mean? I'm saying I *trust* you. Emotionally, I mean."

"Well, even setting aside the partial disclaimer at the end, it's still all about how *you* feel, isn't it? If you give this more than a moment's thought, Junior, smart as you are, you'll come up with another explanation of this situation."

One occurred to me, and I said, "Oh."

"There we are," Ronnie said. "One possible reason for the fact that you don't know very much about me on a factual level."

"*You* don't trust *me*," I said.

"See?" she said. "Other people are as real as you are. Surprised?"

I had nowhere else to go, so I went to my secret home, Apartment 302 at the Wedgwood, in Koreatown. The

Wedgwood is one of the "China" apartment buildings, so called not because they were an LA rip on Chinese architecture but because they'd been named, back in the late twenties, in honor of three makers of fine china: Wedgwood, Royal Doulton, and Lenox. Today, random neon-sign failures had turned them into the WED WOOD, the ROYAL DOULT, and the NOX.

The China apartments were among the most deceptive addresses in a highly deceptive town. They'd been left behind like a trio of abandoned outposts as the town's money moved west toward the sea in the 1930s and had gone precipitously downhill. About fifteen years ago, an anonymous Korean syndicate had bought the buildings for cash under the table and furtively fine-tuned them for the kind of people whose lifestyle dictated secret luxury, people who would benefit from living in a palace with a dump wrapped around it. Now, despite exteriors so distressed they looked like the Bates Motel in drag, the interiors had been meticulously restored to their original burnished Art Deco glory: high ceilings, polished hardwood floors, double-wide doors everywhere. As an added attraction, the three huge underground garages had been knocked into one, so that someone could dip down the driveway of the Wedgwood and conveniently emerge, a moment later, from beneath the Royal Doulton, around the corner and out of sight.

Someone, in short, like me.

I was sitting in the library in my apartment, surrounded by twenty years' worth of books. I was waiting for the calming effect that's usually exerted by rows of books seen spines-out, especially when they've been alphabetized by author and arranged by topic: fiction here, biography there, science (mostly cosmology) over there, art—heavy on Flemish and Renaissance painting—running along the top, close to heaven, where the visual arts belong—and, in an especially solid-looking block on the right, three high-density shelves of nonfiction.

Books, despite the fact that they can be so messy and even incendiary between the covers, are reassuring in bulk, especially when they've been massaged into the kinds of categories that are so conspicuous by their absence in life. Properly presented, everything they contain—the spilled blood, the envy, the plagiarism, the striving and failure and betrayal and disappointment and bad ideas and heartbreak—are combed out, like burrs from a horse's mane. The very sight of the regimented, unrebellious rows somehow puts the world into past tense. The *safe* tense. The best piece of advice I ever heard about how to get through things was Alfred Hitchcock's. When someone asked him how he kept his calm when he was confronted with production crises, difficult actors, uncooperative weather, rising costs, and the light-blocking, soul-sucking bulk of producers, he said, "I try to live my life as though it happened three years ago."

I *knew* all that. I knew about Hitchcock and the books and the calming influence, the broadening of one's worldview, that those things were supposed to provide.

But.

Ice tinkles differently when there's alcohol in the glass, and I had a little marimba in my hand, a couple of inches of good scotch and three nice clear cubes in heavy crystal. The books and the scotch had so far failed to muffle the world and dull its edges, to cushion me in bubble wrap and get me to the point where everything that hurt right now, everything that had begun to go wrong when the wind started to blow, would seem like a memory. I'd screwed it up with Ronnie. I was allowing Jake Whelan to shuck me. I was an absentee father and an unsatisfactory ex-husband. My daughter was crying. Everybody I knew wanted to kill me.

But I couldn't see why. It seemed so evident, so *obvious* to me that I was the hero of my story that I had trouble understanding why other people didn't see it that way.

Oh, yeah. It's their story, too. *Other people are as real as you are*, Ronnie had said. It's one of God's best jokes: to give you a perspective, even visually, that suggests you're the center of the universe and then to rub your nose in the fact that you're clinging for dear life to the far edge.

I drained the scotch, rattled the cubes, and poured more. Getting drunk was no solution, but it had its own misleadingly hearty appeal. A sort of burrowing sensation in my stomach reminded me that I hadn't put anything into it since those two or three sips of coffee at Jake's. I thought about getting a steak out of the freezer. I thought about not getting a steak out of the freezer. I thought about getting up and going into the living room to look at the nighttime skyline of downtown Los Angeles. I thought about calling a taxidermist and having myself stuffed, right there in my reading chair. The management's Korean maids could dust me when they came in to dust the books.

In the end I just sat there, dead center in a small but sharply fought war of conflicting emotions and mutually exclusive impulses until the combatants limped off the field with their issues unresolved, and then I got a pen and a piece of paper and began to make a list of things to do the next day.

14

The Tinkle of Doom

After the Toyota, which I'd driven for years, the big black Town Car that Louie had supplied felt wider than the *Queen Mary*. I kept shying away from the cars to the left and right of me, earning glares from those who passed, as though they suspected I'd had a few.

"You're making me seasick," Jake Whelan said from the backseat.

"Would you prefer to get out and run alongside?"

"The car is narrower than you think it is."

"Well, if I'd had an hour in it before the rush started, I'd probably know that by now."

In fact, Louie had shown up an hour late, at almost a quarter after four, at Musso & Frank's, where I'd enjoyed a late lunch. He deflected my complaints by taking me on a hike to the back of the car to show me the license plate, which read CHAUF 90. "Took an extra hour," he said proudly. "The real thing, I had someone bag it off a limo at LAX. The studio guys, they know these cars. You don't got a chauffeur's license, they're gonna phone you in."

"It doesn't *matter* if they phone me in. The person I'm driving has an appointment. What happens if the chauffeur at LAX notices his plate is missing?"

"He won't," Louie said. "My guy put a fake CHAUF plate on, just painted but looks kosher. No one will notice it until they wash the car."

"And then?"

"It'll run like Alice's mascara when she laughs too hard. But by then *these* plates will be in the city dump, so no connection."

By the time I got to Jake's, waited for him to finish smoothing out his tan, and then plowed into the traffic, it was after five.

From behind me he said, "So how's that girl?"

"That girl? As crappy as you treated her, you could at least do her the honor of remembering her name. It's Casey."

"You don't have get all morally correct about it," Jake said. "That's not even her real name."

"How do you know?"

"When she was in the can, I went through her wallet."

"You did not."

"Hey, she's in my house, I get to know what her name is. Suppose she walked out with something and I'm telling the cops to look for a hooker named Casey and that's not even—"

"The way you say 'hooker,' you make it sound like a life," I said. "She wasn't born a hooker, she won't die a hooker. It's a job, kind of a rotten job, but she's too smart to do it for long." I veered away from a silver Rolls that was almost wide enough to serve as a garage for the Town Car.

"Wants to be an actress, like all the rest of them," Jake said. "They come into town by the trainload, all high hopes and low IQ. Actual name is Cindi Jo, if you can imagine that. Real big-hair name. Cindi Jo Gilman, not even really from Texas. A baton twirler from Baton Rouge."

"Right on the Mississippi," I said, feeling like turning around and taking a bite out of him. "I'd think you'd be a little nicer about that, given your current inspiration. Girl grows up on the bank of a river, you said, '*and that was the whole world.*' Everything that matters, remember?"

"Habits are hard to break," Jake said. "This is really smart, this whole limo thing. The only guy in a studio no one pays attention to is the limo driver. Nice suit, by the way."

"Three hundred forty at the Hollywood Suit Outlet this morning. You owe me."

"For the limo, too," he said.

"Forget it," I said. "It's stolen."

"I admire flair. The gate is the next right."

"I know where it is. It's been there, under one name or another, since 1937."

"They've got a night shoot and a couple of live-audience sitcoms on the lot tonight, so the commissary will be open. You tell the waitress to verify that you're Arthur Rundle's guest so they'll let you stay there and put you on his tab. You'll be all comfy-cozy until it's time."

"And *time* is—"

"Granger's proud of the fact that he's out of the studio by seven every night. He thinks people who work late, who burn the midnight oil like Selznick did, are either showboats or badly organized. Or both. You're not gonna have any problem getting into the office. The hard part of breaking into a studio is the gate, and you've come up with a brilliant solution for—"

"That's enough butter. To recap, I'm going in, finding the file on *Ambient Violet*—"

"Files are in his office. The active stuff is in an old wooden filing setup against the left wall as you come in, *old* like an antique."

"Got it." We were coming up on the gate, a nice piece of Streamline Moderne from the thirties, all high vertical curves and layers.

"It'll be under A for *Ambient* or W—"

"For Whelan. I actually can think these things through for myself." I pulled up behind the Rolls, which had gotten ahead of me again as Jake and I talked. "And then all I do is flip through the file, see whether there's correspondence that suggests he's trying to do something with it, make mental notes of whoever he's pitched it to—"

"Coverage," Whelan said. "Look for coverage. I need to know what it says."

"Got it. So . . . in, out, maybe ten minutes tops."

"Tops," Jake said with all the confidence of someone who wasn't going to be in the room. Then he tapped me on the shoulder and said, "That guard, I know the guy, he's named Tino, lemme handle it." I heard his window go down as I pulled up to the gate, and the guard looked back without even a glance at me and his face lit up like high noon as Whelan said, "Tino! Must be a hundred years. That daughter of yours married yet?"

The institution of the studio commissary, essentially an on-the-lot restaurant, was developed to allow people who were costumed and made up for, say, a production of *Madame Bovary* to sip some soup or eat a burger without being stared at and where stars who were known for knocking back a few during the workday could safely be fed and watered under the eagle eye of their director and producer. Back in the unenlightened old days, it also functioned as a kind of living chessboard where the kings, queens, and pawns of the studio system could make their moves and exercise their prerogatives over breakfast and lunch. Some commissaries served as an adjunct to the casting couch: MGM, for example, was known for its "Golden Circle," a reserved table where heavyweight directors and producers, and even the occasional writer, could be introduced to an unending parade of hopeful and often willing talent. Many a meal was cut short for a personal interview.

The commissary at Farscope, like most of them these days, was your basic proletarian cafeteria, except that the walls were thickly hung with stills from classic films. The moguls and tycoons have given way to shareholders and accountants and taken with them the onyx tables at $300 a square foot and the mahogany chairs. Three pine tables on a raised platform along the back wall, obviously for such heavyweights as still exist, were empty when I went in; it was a quarter after six, and executives all over the lot were presumably dawdling over the last of the day's chores in order to be ready for the call telling them that Granger's car had glided out through the gates and they were free to run for the hills.

The commissary's only customers when I went in were twelve or fourteen actors wearing makeup and the kind of modern-day clothes seen only on television, either too cool for the street or a kind of character license plate that spelled out *dweeb* or *hottie* or some other type for those trying to follow along at home. One corner hosted a little knot of men wearing the sleek suits and narrow ties of the

1960s, actors from a show that Ronnie liked, and I felt a little pang that I wouldn't be able to call her up and tell her I'd just seen the only guy on TV who always made her sit forward when he appeared on the screen. He was shorter in person, but who isn't?

Mentioning Rundle's name got me a smile, a big cup of coffee, and a piece of coconut cake, which seemed like a good idea since I'd had a little too much of that whiskey the previous night. I had that underslept, exposed-nerves feeling that a hangover always produces in me. Coffee and sugar and carbohydrates, I thought, would get me into the performance zone. Breaking into places both requires and produces a lot of adrenaline, even when it's a routine operation. Without that heightened alertness, it's easy to forget to watch the details, which, as has often been remarked, is where the devil lurks, just rubbing his hands together and waiting for a lapse. Granger's office might be easy to get into, but my primary concern is always getting *out* again, and that might demand internal resources that I felt I lacked.

So I had a second piece of coconut cake and refilled the coffee from the pump thermoses and listened to the actors laugh too hard at well-used jokes and watched the minutes shave themselves away in slices so thin they were transparent. All I wanted to do was move, and all I *could* do was wait. I'd spent hours in the morning going over the Google aerial shots of the lot that Anime had found, and I was certain, even without Jake's directions, that I could walk unerringly to Building G—"for God," Jake had said. Building G would have been conspicuous anywhere, a streamlined white structure in a precise half circle that resembled a giant vanilla confection, the second story set back from the first like a tier on a wedding cake. From his big office up there, Granger could look down at the entire lot.

I let the time dribble by until 7:40, and then I got up and took my little bag into the men's room, locked the door, and changed into a pair of black jeans, a black T-shirt, and the cheap black Chinese sneakers I use for jobs because they're as quiet as going barefoot and grip the ground when and if I have to run. The thin plastic food-service gloves were already in my pocket. Then I unlocked the door and went out through the bright commissary to the Town Car. By 7:50 the bag was in the trunk and I was hoofing it down a long alley between sound stages.

It was fully dark but still hot, and the canyon between the stages grabbed at the wind and concentrated it and sent it rocketing into my face, forcing me to squint against the dust and grit. Halfway down the alley, a startlingly attractive young woman in a 1960s cocktail dress passed me in the opposite direction, both hands shielding a Jackie Kennedy bob. When she caught my eye, she said, "Not good for the hair at *all*." and gave me a grin that, pre-Ronnie, might have slowed me down and maybe even turned me around, but I returned her the kind of full, frank smile that can come only from a guy whose conscience is intact and kept on going.

And there was Building G, dazzling white and lit from all sides as befitted the wedding cake of the gods. There were only four parking spaces in front, each designated by a sign in a modified Futura typeface that harmonized with the design of the building and the studio gate: reading from closest to the door to farthest away, Mr. Granger, Mr. Kinsey, Ms. Stradlin, and Ms. Percival. Kinsey and Stradlin were executive producers, meaning they ran errands for Granger and lorded it over everybody else, and Ms. Percival was Granger's administrative assistant. A couple of secretaries, a receptionist, and a projectionist also worked in the building, but they parked in the back of the lot with the peons. All four of the spaces in front were empty.

Three broad steps led up to a pair of frosted-glass doors with handles shaped like giant sea horses. I pushed START on my miracle watch to begin the twenty-minute countdown, took hold of a sea horse, and pulled. It yielded easily, but then the wind yanked it away from me and I had to snag it again before it could slam back against the wall. I stepped inside and closed it behind me and then leaned against the wall beside the door, hyperventilating in a cool, silent corridor. *Wind.*

It took me about a minute to bring myself securely back into the reality in which I'd gotten to the door before it shattered itself deafeningly into bright, gleaming smithereens all over the front steps, ending the job before I even got in. When my pulse was back under control, I looked up and down the corridor and did what I should have done the moment I came in: I listened. Breathing openmouthed, Herbie style, I gave myself a full minute to let my ears wander the building. The light was tinted a cool, slightly green color, as though it were coming through a few feet of water but which was actually a product of overhead light fixtures that had been made with thick glass that might have come from old Coca-Cola bottles. The carpet was white, the walls pearl gray, the light that chilly-water green. Except for an occasional squeak of protest from the glass doors when the wind hit them from outside, I didn't hear anything at all.

I waited one more minute anyway, using the time to

review the building's likely floor plan. The entrance was dead center in the curved wall, and the corridor followed that curve away from me in both directions, meaning that I could see only about fifteen, twenty feet in either one of them. The way Jake had described it, the lesser deities—Kinsey and Stradlin and their secretaries and staff—occupied the lower floor to the right as you came in the door, and about two-thirds of the distance to the left was the receptionist for Granger himself, the widely disliked Ms. Miyagawa, who sorted the wheat from the chaff. On the other side of the door that she guarded were the elevator, which operated with a key that only Granger used, and a flight of stairs for the mere mortals. At the top of the stairs were Granger's office, Ms. Percival's office, a tiny room for a couple of typists or word processors or keyboardists or whatever the hell we call them these days, a conference room, and, at the far end, a small screening room that could hold about a dozen people.

A pretty nice step up in the world, I thought, from negotiating out of delicatessens.

Just to be completely sure I was alone, I worked my way down the corridor to the right. Doors open, offices mostly dark, all empty. Granger's legions obviously weren't bound by fierce loyalty to remain at their desks after hours. The bathrooms were also empty, so I turned and retraced my steps, pausing at the glass door until I was certain that no one was about to come in through it, and then I strolled across the visible area like someone with the whole night on his hands and a godlike right to be there. I followed the corridor to the barrier that was Ms. Miyagawa's desk, which blocked all but about three feet of the width of the hall. Behind it, in the center of the wall, was a mahogany door that undoubtedly opened onto the stairway to heaven.

The door, despite my being armed with all that info from Jake Whelan, surprised me by being locked.

I stood there, not even thinking about going any farther. What was on my mind was, first, that Jake had been wrong about something, and who was to say he wouldn't be wrong again? And second, once I got the door open—if I decided to open it—I'd be doing something I usually avoided. I'd be going into a dead end.

And third, the wind was still blowing.

One of the Unbreakable Rules taught to me by Herbie Mott, in my mind a burglar so great his face should be on Mount Rushmore, was *Always know how you're going to get out before you go in.* When I went into the Slugger's house, I had two sets of stairs and, it later turned out, a window. What I had here, if Jake was right, was a single stairway going up and an elevator that needed a key I didn't have. If I wasn't going break one of the rules that have kept me from getting arrested over the years, the thing to do was to turn around and get the hell out of there.

On the other hand.

I'd stiffed Jake with the picture, so I owed him for that. And while I couldn't make a persuasive case to myself that I actually *liked* Jake, he'd helped me out once in a big way. I owed him for *that.* And despite his tough talk, he might really want to make this movie, which I supposed was a sort of act of contrition.

Not to forget that he *had* promised to put a hit person on me, and it didn't seem like something to be dismissed with a shrug. In this economic climate, hits are cheap.

And the thing about the wind . . . well, that was

superstition, plain and simple. I knew a burglar once who would only hit houses where the address was an even number. He passed up treasure chest after treasure chest to keep himself safe and then got busted in the house at 2222 North Doubletree Drive.

So I added all that up and made a deal with myself. I promised myself that if beneath Ms. Miyagawa's spacious desk there was no buzzer to pop that locked door, I'd be out of the building and into the heat and wind within about fifteen seconds. So I looked, and it was right there. But it *was* still windy, so I gave myself one final out: if the buzzer was loud enough to alert anyone who might be upstairs, then ta-ta, Farscope.

When I pushed the button, the noise sounded like someone snapping his fingers with his hand inside a pillow. I had to do it twice to make certain I'd heard it. The door opened at a touch, inviting me in, and in a second I was through it and into new territory.

The staircase was thickly carpeted and wide enough for three people abreast, and, in keeping with the overall design of the building, it curved. I stayed against the right wall as I went up, ears working overtime and hearing nothing but the almost inaudible whoosh of the air-conditioning. At the top of the stairs, I paused and waited another minute, just a last auditory survey before I committed myself all the way.

I heard no reason to turn around, so I stepped into the corridor. The second story, as I've said, was also a semicircle, so the corridor curved away from me in both directions, with a single door visible a little more than halfway down on the left. If Jake was right, it led to a rather miserly space in which the executive assistant, Ms.

Percival, spent most of her waking hours and, beyond that, to Granger's lair, which took up about half the floor.

Ms. Percival's room was as described, with one exception. The surprise was a square of gray concrete neatly set into the thick carpet in front of her desk; impressed into it were a pair of petite shoeprints and the dimples of hands not much bigger than a twelve-year-old's. Written beneath them, with a flourish that betrayed lots of anxious practice, was the name *Anna Percival*. A custom-made bit of Grauman's Chinese Theatre, a bit of old-time glamour created as a treat for his assistant. His *weensy* assistant. I thought again about the teenage girl, sixteen or however old she was, whom he'd used to clear his predecessor out of this office and then married, remembering suddenly that a wife couldn't be compelled to testify against her husband, a quirk in the law that many dreadful people have found useful. I couldn't actually say I was liking Granger very much.

Okay, back out into the hallway and then a quick pass through the rest of the floor, as empty as the first, the big difference being that up here the walls weren't painted, they were covered in cream-colored suede. It was almost enough to tempt me to take off the food-service gloves just to feel it. The suede, plus the carpet, deadened sound very effectively, and I realized I was going to have to keep my ears wide open while I was working.

It occurred to me that I hadn't seen the elevator up here, and that mystery was solved the moment I sidestepped Ms. Percival's cluttered little desk and pushed open the door to Granger's office: the elevator was set into the left-hand wall, at its corner with the wall I'd just come through. I put a hand behind me to make sure the door closed silently, but it was already slowing, finding its way home with a discreet sigh.

The office was about twice the size of my living room at the Wedgwood, which made it pretty damn big—an oversize architectural piece of pie with three walls, one of them curved. It was lit from overhead by dozens of tiny halogen pin spots about an inch across. The carpet was the color of Jake's old tan, at least two inches thick, and it stretched uninterrupted from the door to a riser eighteen inches high, made of stone that was green enough to be malachite. It stretched about ten feet long and six deep, in front of the window on the rear wall. On top of the riser perched a gleaming satin-finished Regency desk from the early nineteenth century that would have had Stinky slapping at his nose with both hands.

The desk was all status and no storage, nothing as plebeian as drawers, about four feet wide with drop leaves on either end that, when raised, would have doubled its width. The sole object on the desk was a big chrome- or silver-plated antique telephone with an ornate, heavy-looking handset napping horizontally on an elevated cradle. The dial had been replaced with a touch screen.

The chair was an object of beauty, a circle of deep-grained wood with a carved back and delicately shaped arms encircling a cream-colored leather seat cushion. I put it at about 1850, French, and roughly $6,500 retail. The desk cost a *lot* more.

Off to the right, the furniture of a small sitting area had been shoved into the smallest possible space: a red leather couch and chairs in English gentlemen's-club style, the couch pushed against the wall with the chairs flanking it, and in front of it a low marble-topped table, also

English. Facing the couch, at the center of the table, was a twin to the Regency chair behind the desk, making it clear where Granger sat when he chose to descend from his platform.

Two other things were evident from the arrangement of the furniture: first, no one sat down unless asked to do so by Granger, since that would have meant crossing the entire office to get to the couch and chairs; and second, he didn't ask very often. The riser beneath his desk was a time-honored movie-mogul trick that he'd probably borrowed from Louis B. Mayer and Harry Cohn, both of whom were sensitive about their height and both of whom enjoyed the experience of having people look up at them. It would take a good reason for Jeremy Granger to come down to floor level.

In order to take all this in, I'd spent only fifty or sixty of the small number of seconds available to me; that's what the adrenaline is for. To my left stood the open, dark elevator, also nineteenth-century, featuring stained walnut paneling and a shining brass accordion grid that would be pulled closed before the car could start down. I would've liked to have taken a better look, but the clock in my head was running: I was going to spend a total of twenty minutes inside, tops, and I was already about six minutes in. Look what had happened two nights earlier, when I got sloppy about that.

Which reminded me that I was going to have to do something about the Slugger.

Against the wall beside the elevator, beneath a painting of an English racehorse that probably wasn't by George Stubbs although it sure looked like it was, was the old wooden filing cabinet Jake had mentioned, but I'd taken only a couple of steps toward it when I realized that not only was the cabinet a fake, it wasn't even a good fake. In fact, it was prop furniture, probably from some movie that was set in nineteenth-century England. It had been clumsily distressed; a tiny drill had been used to create the wormholes, and the grain had quite plainly been put on with a paintbrush over what was probably plywood. An eyesore at this distance, although I supposed it would have looked convincing enough in the background if the lighting were dim. A nighttime scene, perhaps. In black and white.

What was it doing in here?

I gave it a closer look. Cheap and clumsy. A little alarm went off in my head. This was junk. There were ten of these in every studio prop house in town, and nine of the ten would have been better. Why was it in this man's office?

The watch said I had twelve minutes and a little change remaining. I'd lost some time, distracted by the fake. So speed things up.

"Ambient Violet," obviously, begins with an *A*, and they'd expect me to begin with the top left hand drawer. The fastest plausibility check I could think of was to see whether all the drawers were full, and if they were, whether the documents inside them obeyed the hard-and-fast rules of alphabetical order. If not, I was gone.

I opened the bottom-right drawer. The first thing I saw was a synopsis of *Zoo Station*, a splendid World War II novel by David Downing that I'd thought would make a great movie when I read it. Behind that was a folder titled ZZZZIP, all caps, which, when I opened it, proved to be a continuation of the Sandra Bullock vehicle *Miss Congeniality* in which her character went into burlesque with, it promised, "riotous results." The folder had a large red NO stamped across it in about sixty-point type, which was the only sane judgment.

Nothing else in the drawer, but there aren't that many titles that begin with Z. I opened one approximately in the middle and found myself looking at a folder for something called *Nirvana Candy*, which was subtitled *A Heavenly Comedy*.

I felt a furtive twinge of compassion for Jeremy Granger. Swill in both directions, up the alphabet and down again. On the other hand: (a) this was a guy whose three biggest hits, all with the word *Eight* in the title, starred a four-story tarantula who was actually a handsome ancient Egyptian prince enslaved by a perpetual curse; (b) these ideas, however grim most of them might seem to me, represented (according to Jake) the hopes and dreams of writers, directors, and producers who were targets of Granger's wrath and were being consigned to permanent turnaround; and (c) I hate most movies and am no one to pass judgment.

So, slightly reassured, I opened the first drawer. There it was, five or six folders back, just behind something called *The Always Machine*. Jake's would-be masterpiece was housed in a relatively thick file, more substantial anyway than ZZZZIP. The first thing in the folder was a three-page, double-spaced document on Jake's letterhead that described the film as "a paradigm-shifting filmic exploration of the eternal aspects of everyday life." If that description had popped up on network television, I thought, there would have been broken remotes all over America.

That was followed by three or four letters from Granger to a director and some actors whose names I knew, offering them "something courageously offbeat" that represented

"a uniquely different approach by a legendary producer."
No replies had been filed, which I suppose meant either
that the letters from Granger were fakes that had never
been sent, dummies to deceive Jake, or that the people
who received the pitch decided it would be more discreet
not to reply in writing,

At the end of the file—with seven and a half minutes
left—I found the coverage. Or, more accurately, the *cover-
ages*, because there were two of them. At first glance they
looked identical: title of project; a "log line" ("Cosmic
exploration of the meaning of life through the life and
death of one obscure woman, in the tradition of foreign
[Japanese, Indian] films"); name of producer, synopsis,
and, comments.

The "comments" section of the first document began,
"From one of the great producers in the history of film, a
concept that's almost biblical in its sweep and complexity, and almost a haiku in its simplicity—as much a poem
as a film—using one short life, spent beside and shaped
by a fast-flowing river, as a paradigm for life itself, in all
its . . ." You get the drift.

The second one began, "Unfilmable and probably
unwatchable, this is a sad attempt at atonement by a
once-successful film producer in his dotage. It opens with
a death and goes downhill from there."

I checked again. Yup, two of them, identical in format,
but one was a rave and the other was the kind of pan that
drives writers to alcohol and shotguns. Forgetting about
the time for a moment, I read both sets of comments in
their entirety. Both seemed completely sincere.

What in the world was I going to tell Jake? I checked
behind the second piece of coverage, the pan, but there

was nothing else in the folder. I was putting the whole thing back into the drawer when I thought I heard something.

It wasn't so much an identifiable sound as it was a bump in the silence. It was enough, though, to freeze me where I stood. I couldn't even let go of the edge of the file, off balance but unwilling to adjust, holding my breath.

I gave it a count of five. On *five* I blew the breath out and slipped the file the rest of the way into the drawer, and the instant I pulled my hand back, the phone on Granger's desk began to ring.

It was a muted ring, a soft, melodic ring, the kind of lullaby ring that might be custom-composed and recorded for a highly irritable individual. It was a calming sound, a sound designed to lighten the heart and brighten one's personal outlook. It terrified me.

I stood there, trying not to hear it and knowing that this was a life changer. I was thirty-eight years old. I'd been earning my way through the world by breaking into places and assuming ownership of carefully selected items since I was seventeen, without even a formal brush with the cops, although I knew that one conviction would make me their first stop in any burglary investigation for the rest of my life. And if things went way south between Kathy and me, a record could possibly prevent me from seeing my daughter until she was of age.

All that and I wasn't even *taking* anything. Still, I was frozen in place, unable even to think, listening to the tinkle of doom.

After the fourth ring, an amplified voice said from a speaker overhead. "Get that, would you? It's for you."

PART THREE

KING MAYBE

Don't say yes until I'm finished talking.
—Producer Darryl F. Zanuck

15

One Thousand, Eight Hundred, and Seventy-Four Twenties and Two Tens

Because I had followed orders and gone over to the phone, when the office door was pushed open, the cop's gun was pointed directly at my heart.

"Stay right there," the cop said. "Both hands in plain sight."

Seemed like excellent advice. "You got it."

The cop took a step in and stopped as though he'd walked into a force field, his eyes going to the open door on his left. He was in his mid-forties, plump and round-faced, with a short pug nose, a long upper lip, and a shaggy fringe of hair protruding beneath his cap, and there was something *familiar* about him, which unnerved me even further than I was already unnerved. I've done my best for years not to get to a point where I recognize more than a very few cops on sight. If you know them, they know you. And yet I seemed to know him.

He wiggled the gun back and forth about a quarter of an inch, just a way to put his next sentence in bold type, and said, "Anyone behind the door?"

"No. No one in the elevator either."

"Don't move." He stepped toward me, fast, and used his left hand to shove the door, hard enough for it to bang on the wall. From behind him someone who wasn't visible through the door said in a smoky, emotionless voice, "Don't bruise the leather."

The cop said, "The . . . the leather?"

"On the *walls.*"

The cop said, "Leather walls?"

The other man said, "Discuss it with your decorator. Now, trot on in there so I can get through the door."

The cop gave me a fast, mean look that suggested he hoped I hadn't heard that, so I said, "Just a few steps forward will do it. He's not very big."

The cop tightened his mouth, put both hands on the gun in the approved movie fashion, and sidestepped to clear the door.

Jeremy Granger couldn't have weighed more than a hundred forty pounds, and even with the three-inch heels on his cowboy boots, which I put at about $60,000, he stood no more than five-five. He wore an off-white silk shirt, a black leather vest, and black jeans that looked like they'd been sewn directly on him, except that they were cut too short, undoubtedly to give everyone a chance to appreciate the boots. Young as he was—mid-forties, from what I knew—he'd had work done to redefine his cheekbones, fill the lines around his eyes and the corners of his mouth, and build up his chin. His light brown hair was cut all different lengths, slicked straight back, and gelled into bristling points that suggested a porcupine's quills at rest. He put his hands in the pockets of his jeans and rocked back and forth a little, eyeing me as though I were a car he'd just purchased and he was having second thoughts.

"Nice boots," I said. "Howard Knight?"

He nodded just enough for me to see it, his eyes on mine.

"You don't mind that he makes Dubya's boots? I'm not sure I'd want to wear the same—"

"The second I saw you," he said, and I had to listen because he spoke very softly, "I made you as one of the people who tries to disguise fear with a kind of cheap jocular aggression, like bad private-eye dialogue. When you've sat in the chair behind you as long as I have, you get familiar with fear and all the protective mechanisms people use to mask it. So you can keep it up if you want to, but it doesn't fool me, which should rob you of some of the pleasure, and you should also know that I have a very short attention span and you do *not* want to exceed it."

"Not when you're talking," I said.

He let a second go by, as though giving all of us a little time to absorb the fact that I'd almost interrupted him. "Sorry?"

"Your attention span. When you're the one who's talking, it seems to be infinite."

He nodded, as though mentally checking off another expected response. "Have you ever—this is a silly question, but humor me—have you ever had power?" He raised a hand to shut me up. "Don't bother. That was purely rhetorical. I mean, look at you, standing here, helpless as an invertebrate. Well, having power is a learning experience. A lot of it is abstract; you don't know at first how much you've got and how far it goes. But one thing is immediately evident," he said, craning his neck a couple of aggressive inches in my direction, "and that's that *you can talk forever.* From the moment other people understand the lay of the land, no one ever, *ever* interrupts. They compete to listen more assiduously than anyone else in the room." He almost smiled, the corners of his mouth just edging up. "Isn't that craven? Absolutely *breeds* scorn. And now, just in case you doubt the extent of my power in this specific situation, go over to the window behind the desk and look down."

"Thanks anyway."

"The man told you," the cop said, "to get your ass over to the window and look down, and I don't see you moving."

"*That* window," I said. "I'll just stroll over to the window and look down. Wow, look at that. Two squad cars."

"Got another one at the front door," the cop said.

"Must be nice to have all this clout."

"Culverton is an incorporated city with its own law enforcement," the cop said. He sounded like he'd memorized it so he could recite it on public occasions. "Mr. Granger is the city's primary employer, largest taxpayer, and biggest landowner, and he donates generously to the police and fire departments. Before he arrived, the city leased law-enforcement services from the sheriffs. Mr. Granger provided the start-up funds to remedy that."

"And still do," Granger said, almost smiling again.

An immature little seizure of spite grabbed hold of me and made me say, "Ate a lot of shit to get here, though, didn't you?"

The cop's eyes widened, but in Granger's something *flared*, so concentrated and so malign that I instinctively stepped aside to let it whistle past. He got it under control and stowed it away, leaning one shoulder on his leather wall. If I hadn't seen that flicker in his eyes, he would have looked almost too relaxed to remain standing.

"For years and years," he said. "But I can tell you, it was a microspatter, a teeny bird dropping on a continent-size windshield, compared to the bottomless fecal seas the people who fed it to me are trying to swim through now. Or, for that matter, the tsunami of it you might be facing." He turned his head half an inch to get the cop's attention. "So, Officer—" He squinted at the cop's name plate.

"Biehl," I said. "B-I-E-H—"

"Officer Biehl, I think you can go now. For the moment anyway."

The cop's eyebrows came together over the bridge of his nose, an expression that subtracted many points from his apparent IQ. "Go? Where?"

"*I* don't care. To your car, I suppose. Or the commissary. Go someplace comfortable. Get a doughnut."

"But this guy . . . I mean, you gotta—"

"Mr. Bender is a professional with a rich trove of experience," Granger said, "and he knows when he's fucked."

I said, "Yes, actually, I do."

"So, good, good. You can run along, Officer, Officer . . ."

"Biehl," I said. "You want me to spell it again?"

"Not necessary. Interesting spelling, though, isn't it?"

Biehl said, "Is it?"

Granger raised one hand and wiggled the tips of his fingers at the cop. "Bye-bye."

"Those must be some donations," I said. I was sitting on the couch, and Granger was in the Regency chair across the table from me.

"It takes so little to make them happy," he said. "Now that everyone hates them for shooting unarmed people on what seems to be a racially selective basis, and now that they've been outfitted by the Department of Defense until the friendly old cop on the beat poking, along in his shirtsleeves, looks like one of the emperor's troops in *Star Wars*. And then there's the mind-set that goes with all that firepower."

"You're going to say that thing about the nail, aren't you?"

"As the ancient Japanese saying goes," Granger continued as though I hadn't spoken, "if all you have is a hammer, everything looks like a nail."

"Actually, that ancient saying was popularized in 1966," I said, "by a psychologist named Abraham Maslow. The Japanese saying is 'The nail that sticks up will be hammered down.'"

Granger looked at me, waiting for me to shift in my seat. When I did, mostly to move things along, he said, "I can get that cop back up here anytime you cease to interest me."

"But you won't," I said.

He sucked in the corners of his mouth.

"You've gone through a lot to set this up," I said. "Stringing Jake along about his movie—"

"Not entirely," he said, and then he waved his words away. "I mean, yes, I used *Ultra Violet* or whatever it's called to persuade Jake to get you in here—"

"To set me up," I said. "Good old Jake."

"But you shouldn't blame him. He wants it so badly. And actually, I'm not entirely opposed to the idea of the film."

"Really. Who wrote the coverage about it being . . . I don't know, some old hack's swipe at redemption?"

"I did."

"And who wrote the version you probably showed Jake, about how it could do everything except prevent global warming?"

"I did."

I let my spine touch the back of the couch for the first time. "I had the same reaction, sort of."

"Which one?"

"Both of them."

He treated me to the first real smile I'd seen, giving me a glimpse of either a quarter of a million dollars' worth of cosmetic dentistry or the set of teeth evolution has been working its way up to for millions of years. "Yes," he said, "Jake is a terrible old ball of rags, but the *idea* has something behind it, even if it's only a test of hubris. At first I thought that was why he might have given it to me, thinking that my ego was so big I'd take the dare, but the two times we talked about it, his sincerity was heartbreaking. You know what I mean? He's not *used* to being sincere. He's awful at it. And then, you know, you can't *completely* dismiss his sense of what makes a movie. You've undoubtedly seen the ones that made him famous."

"Not since I was six or seven."

He gave me a gaze that in a more demonstrative face might have been described as *interested*. "Why not?"

"Well, don't take this personally, but I think of Hollywood as the beached whale of popular culture."

"I'm sure you can sustain the metaphor, but—"

"Slowly caving in, crushing itself under the weight of its budgets and its compromises."

Granger nodded, but he was clearly just waiting to get his revenge for my having interrupted him. "Probably more effective left unsaid. And the *other* reason you shouldn't completely blame Jake for roping you in here is because I told him about the upside, for you, of my proposal, and he probably thinks he's doing you a—"

"You went through all this to make a *proposal*?"

"If there were no upside, it would be a threat, I'll admit it. But there *is* an upside, and it's considerable. That makes it a proposal. You're here to discuss how you avoid the threat and profit from the upside."

I leaned back and closed my eyes.

"Here it is, the elevator pitch. You listening?"

"Sorry, I always fade out when people begin to talk about the upside. It's usually so embarrassing."

"You can sit up and listen or you can go take a ride with Officer . . . Officer . . ."

"Biehl." I opened my eyes. "You have trouble with names, don't you?"

He shrugged.

"Why do you suppose that is?"

"Contempt," he said. "Now, listen to me, it's not complicated. I'm going to divorce my wife. She doesn't know that yet. Before I let her in on my plans, I want to remove some things from the list of community-property items. You're going to steal them."

"From where?"

"My house, of course."

"What are they?"

"Odds and ends. Some very good jewelry I gave her in various guilty moments. Most importantly, a painting. By Turner."

I said, "You're shitting me."

"A good one," he said, "even relative to other Turners. Probably the best in private hands. It's a sunrise at sea."

"So you set it up for me to rob the house, and I go in with a shopping list of the stuff you want. And you trust me not to take other things?"

"Of course not," he said. "You can take anything that appeals to you. I'll have pulled out the little pieces I actually care about the day before, but there will be plenty left. Treat the place like a supermarket on one of those shows where people race up and down the aisles with a shopping cart."

"Taking your stuff."

"Of *course*." His tone suggested that we were approaching the edge of his attention span. "If you take only *her* things, it would be a trifle obvious, wouldn't it? You can take all you can carry. That's part of the upside."

"What's the other part?"

"Fifty thousand dollars."

I said, reflexively, "Seventy-five."

"Fine," he said.

I said, "Wait."

"This is the mark of the small-time mind," he said. "Underpricing yourself to begin with and then thinking you can negotiate when the door's been closed."

I can absorb a lot for $75K. "Paid how?"

"In small bills, used and not sequenced, half up front and half when you give me the things I want you to take. You can sell everything else you grab. Do you have a good fence?"

"Do I ever." If I could get hold of him. If, by now, the Slugger hadn't beaten him into a quart of guava jelly.

"Good, because some of the things you choose, if your eye is as sharp for other items as it is for cowboy boots, will need to be handled sensitively. I wouldn't want them being traced back to me."

"Me neither, especially since it would have to be through me."

"So." He tapped his nails, which were covered in clear polish, against the marble of the table. He crossed his legs and looked at his boot. "Does Dubya *really*—"

"He does."

"That stings. Oh, well, it makes sense that he'd know all about cowboy boots. Probably a dab hand with a rope and a heifer, too."

"I doubt it," I said. "He's afraid of horses."

He shrugged. The image of Dubya quailing before a horse didn't engage him. "Aren't you interested in the details?"

"Sorry. I get sidetracked. What about the details?"

"The money," he said. "Half up front, as I said, which means now." He reached inside the leather vest and came up with a thick envelope, which he dropped on the table. Then he pulled out another, from the left side of the vest, and leaned forward to get at his hip pocket for a third. He pushed them across the table at me. "One thousand, eight hundred, and seventy-four twenties and two tens. They ran out of twenties. Too thick for one or even two envelopes. From dozens of sources, none of them directly linked to me."

"What if I'd started at a hundred thousand?"

"I would have been wrong," he said. "But you have no idea how rarely I'm wrong. Anyway, you'll get another fifty from the stuff you take, if you're creative about it. Maybe more. And afterward, of course, the other half."

"When do I go?" I said.

"Thursday night."

"Tomorrow night? Not enough time. I haven't even seen the house."

He shrugged. "That's when it is." He leaned forward

and shoved the envelopes a little closer to me. "Thursday I'm taking the little woman up to San Francisco for the opening night of some opera or other. It's the only night for months that the house will be empty, just you and thirty-four thousand square feet of expensive things. You can go in any time after seven and steal to your heart's content until midnight. Our plane back will land at LAX a little after midnight, unless it takes off late or early."

I said, "Early?"

"Private plane. I'll call if we're going to be early. I'm making it easy for you. You'll have a floor plan with all the interesting places marked. I'm going to give you the code to the gate so you can drive right in. And you'll have the number to punch up to turn off the alarm when you go in and then out again. And all the other alarm info."

"What kind of an alarm?"

"An absolute mother," he said. "I'm going to tell you all about it. The one thing you're going to need to think about is the alarm."

16

Zillow

"I *know* what I told you before," I said to Anime. "And it's still important, but this is urgent."

"More urgent than your daughter?" She was speaking more loudly than I would have liked, but the restaurant was jammed with people in the grip of a late-night jones for Mexican food. This was the second time in a few months we'd eaten in the very same booth.

"They're both urgent," I said. I looked around, but no one seemed to be eavesdropping. "That's why I want to hire both of you. So you can double up." I picked up my beer. "And how can you guys be out at this hour? It's a school night." It was almost eleven.

"Oh, *please*," Lilli said, with a level of exaggerated patience I would have thought it would take decades to acquire. She grabbed another handful of tortilla chips.

"I'm sleeping at *Lilli's*," Anime said, indicating Lilli with both hands to help me follow along. She brought the hands back to herself. "Lilli's sleeping at *my* house."

"We're both staying in the storage unit," Lilli said with her mouth full. "Monty is off somewhere, so we have the vending machines all to ourselves."

Their nominal commander, who called himself Monty

Carlo, had bought an entire storage facility and combined two of the garage-size units into a surprisingly plush headquarters from which to mount computer raids. The kitchen, in addition to a small stove and sink, had a great many vending machines.

"Paradise," I said. "How long will that work?"

"Well, my parents are in Hong Kong," Anime said, "and my brother, who's supposed to be taking care of me, doesn't." She reached for the chips, and Lilli slapped her hand.

"And my mom would miss her vodka before she'd miss me," Lilli said.

"I'm sure that's not true," I said.

Lilli gave me a level gaze. The silence stretched out until I filled it.

"If you're staying at the storage facility, how'd you get here?"

"I drove Monty's car," Lilli said. She was wearing jeans and a T-shirt that said IF YOU HAVE TO ASK, DON'T BOTHER. Anime's shirt didn't say anything; it depicted the black silhouette, on red, of a girl reading a book. A thick arrow rose up out of the book and into the air, then down through the silhouette's head and straight into her heart.

"You're not old enough to drive—" I said, but then someone bumped my elbow, hard enough to make me slop beer onto the front of my pants.

"Food in a minute," said the waitress, without slowing as she passed.

"She's mad at you," Lilli said approvingly.

Anime was messing with her phone. "Here," she said. "Before we get to the new project, whatever it is." She

slid the phone across the table to me. On it was a picture
of the Spirit of Discontent, age fifteen or so: small, suspicious eyes, face turned just slightly away from the camera
as though preparing to dodge, mouth pursed as if about
to spit.

Lilli said, "Isn't she wretched?"

"Patricia Anne Gribbin, a.k.a. Patty," Anime said.

"And also Leatherface," Lilli said.

I said, "That's unkind."

"Don't look at me," Lilli said, giving me arched Lucille
Ball eyebrows. "That's what someone called her on Facebook. Her skin is pretty rough."

"Where'd you get this?" I said as the waitress, who had
flirted with me the first time I ate here with Anime and Lilli,
began to put plates in front of the girls. Anime had a burrito big enough to get its own driver's license, soaked in red
chili sauce. Lilli, who'd said she needed to lose six pounds
and who'd monopolized the basket of tortilla chips since
we sat down, had a large green salad. I had nothing so far.
Without a glance at me, the waitress wheeled and headed
back to the kitchen.

"You blew it," Anime said. "Before, I mean. She's hot,
Maria is."

"I've got a girlfriend," I said. "I think."

"Oho," Lilli said.

I asked, "Where'd you get the picture?"

"High-school yearbook," Anime said. "It was online.
What's with this girlfriend?"

"Don't ask me," I said. "You know men can't talk
about feelings."

"Actually," Anime said, "Lilli and I don't know all that
much about men."

"By *choice*," Lilli said immediately. "It's like trichinosis. I know it's out there, and I'm glad someone understands it, but it doesn't have to be me."

"We're not *that* bad. Not all of us, I mean."

"No," Lilli said. "In the spirit of fairness, some girls are pretty beastly, too."

I said, "You've both, um, done something with your hair."

And they had. They'd cut it off on one side only, blunt and straight as a shingle, exactly at the center of the ear. Left ear for Lilli, right for Anime. "Kind of halfway to Kim Jong Un," I said.

"Eeeeww," Anime said. "He's got *sidewalls*. We've got bobs, like in the twenties. Well, half bobs."

"So, I mean, it's what? It's supposed to make you a pair?"

"We *are* a pair," Lilli said.

"Then why cut it on different sides?"

Anime said, with something like pity, "You tell us."

I looked at them for a moment or two, working on it. Anime crossed her eyes. I said, "Mirror image."

Lilli reached across the table to high-five me, and Anime took advantage of it to grab the basket of chips. "Look," Anime said, tilting the empty basket toward me. "I'm in love with a glutton."

"So get more," Lilli said. She started turning over her lettuce with her fork as though she hoped a croissant were hidden under it.

"The game that this Patricia seems to be pulling on Rina," I said. "It's about . . . you know, social circles— which circles you're in, which circles you're not in. As I remember, it was pretty cruel."

"It's a bastard," Lilli said, digging deeper.

"You girls do something like this with your hair, isn't that sort of asking for it?"

"We don't care," Anime said. "And we're pretty femme, both of us. There's some, like, plaid-shirt girls who are the lightning rods. They get all the attention."

Maria put down a plateful of carne asada, an inch out of reach. I leaned toward it, and just as I closed my fingers on it, she said, "Hot plate." Then she took the empty chips basket and left.

"Patricia," Anime said as I blew on my fingers. "You know if she uses Line? Is she on Tumblr? Ello? Instagram? YouTube? Vine? Yik Yak?"

"Surely you jest," I said. "I just found out about Facebook."

"We'll figure it out." Anime was carefully unwrapping and examining her burrito, like someone looking for a missing diamond. "The personal stuff on her Facebook page is for friends only, but that's easy to get around."

"Whatever you can find," I said.

Maria materialized and dropped a new basket of chips directly in front of Lilli, who pushed her salad aside.

Anime raised a hand, fingers spread wide, and began to tick them off, an item at a time. "So far we've got her full name, her address, her birth parents' names, her stepfather's name—Mom and Dad seem to have split, and Mom remarried—that picture we showed you, her grade-point average in elementary, the fact that she's allergic to peanuts, her birthday, her top-ten movies of last year—"

"Yeah?" I said. "What was her number-one movie?"

"That weepie about teenage cancer patients."

Lilli said, "They're all weepies. Girl likes to cry."

"You tough guy," I said, and Lilli gave me a broad smile.

"Pisces," Anime said scornfully. "They're always reaching for the hankie."

"Wait, wait, wait," I said.

"Which part did you miss?"

"Rina is . . . uhhh, a Scorpio."

"Well," Anime said, a bit stiffly, "if you'd told me Rina's astrological sign was pertinent, I'd have factored it into the equation."

"This girl, Patricia, she's claiming that her birthday is this week."

Lilli said, "We forgot. We should have spotted that."

"Patricia is March twelfth," Anime said, looking at her notes. "We got it from the birth certificate, since we haven't hacked the privacy walls on her Facebook page yet."

"See," I said, "I think she's a liar on every level. She's faking this birthday so she can share the party and get closer to Rina. I think she talked some friend of hers into saying she'd seen Rina's boyfriend holding hands with another girl."

"Men," Lilli said.

"Oh, yeah?" Anime had returned to dissecting her burrito. "What about Katie Mendoza?"

"She had *soap* in her eyes," Lilli said, as though for the ten-thousandth time. "I was walking her to the nurse's office. Uh, guiding her."

"*Was* Rina's BF holding hands with that girl?" Anime said.

"According to the boyfriend, yes. What I doubt is the second girl's testimony. Whether she was even there. Seems orchestrated somehow."

"*Listen* to us," Lilli said. "You'd think there were no real problems in the world."

"Feels real to Rina," I said. "Same way I'll bet Anime felt about Katie Mendo—"

"'Kay, 'kay 'kay." Lilli said. "So what's the new job?"

Three minutes later I was studying the living room of Jeremy Granger's house, in full color. Unfurnished and vast, it looked like the space where the first Boeing 787 was assembled, even on the cramped screen of Anime's phone.

"Zillow," Anime said, as if it were a word.

Looking at her own phone, Lilli said, "Thirty-four thousand square feet. Built in 1982 by a guy who produced game shows. Sold in 1996 to somebody from Qatar who never lived in it. Sold again in 2000 to a woman who's described here as an heiress, pretty much the same thing as saying 'pitiful nonachiever.' Sold to a rock-and-roller in 2004 and then to your guy in 2008."

"These pictures are from when it was on the market the time he bought it," Anime said. She reached over and swiped the screen, making way for a new picture, a formal dining room half a block long. "There's even a movie, a tour of the house. The agents put them online for rich people who are on, like, different continents."

"Or alternate universes," Lilli said. "The rock star the Qatar guy sold it to was Mr. Overdose, you know, Ray what's-his-name, the lead singer of the Thuds. He died there. Probably died three or four times before he made it all the way."

"Explains the lower price," Anime said. "Death'll do that." She was calculating in her head, lips moving silently. "Down twenty-nine, almost thirty percent from the first time it sold. I could bring up a Beverly Hills real-estate median-price graph, but that's probably not what you're looking for."

"This is perfect," I said. "Send me the links so I can go over them. I've got a floor plan he drew for me, but I need to know if it's accurate."

"You want the builder's plans?" Anime said.

I said, "Excuse me?"

"*You* know, the ones the City of Beverly Hills had to approve."

"I know what they are. I just didn't believe my ears." I grabbed a chip out of the basket, evading the slap Lilli aimed at my hand. "If someone makes big changes—you know, structural changes—to a house, would that have to be given to the city, too?"

Lilli said, "You mean, if your guy or the Thud decided to add, like, an indoor pool—"

"Exactly. Or any other change that might come as an unwelcome surprise."

"We can get it," Lilli said, "as long as they filed with the city. Sometimes people don't."

"And you can get me a copy of those?"

"Sure," Anime said. "We know a specialist." She pushed the eviscerated burrito away, rearranged but largely uneaten, and Lilli immediately buried her fork in it. "I'm kind of surprised *you* don't know one," Anime said. "Considering."

"I need you guys to go to work on this, fast. I want aerial pictures if you can find them so I can see what's around the house, I need all those plans, I want information on the alarm system, which he told me the name of and I'll remember it in a minute, I want everything you can get. The names of the neighbors, if you can find them. And for the thing with Rina, everything you can find on Patricia Anne Gribbin. *Everything.*"

"When?" Anime said.

"By two tomorrow, for the house. Rina, you can have until Friday at noon." I reached into my pants pocket and pulled out two fat, crinkled envelopes. "There should be a little more than twelve thousand in each of these. Okay?"

Lilli was eating, but Anime had her hands free, and she made the envelopes disappear so fast it was as though they'd never been there. She gave me a bright smile. "College fund," she said.

17
Shortcuts

As I trailed Anime and Lilli back to the storage facility, just being Papa Bear, I called Stinky again and left a message to the effect that the stamp would be glued to an envelope and mailed to Transylvania at ten the next morning if I hadn't heard from him. In fact, I was beginning to see a better use for it, but I couldn't think of any reason Stinky should be resting comfortably while I was tethered to an anthill.

The electric gate slid open for the girls' car, and I followed them in, scanning the weedy field on the other side of the chain-link fence, the field from which—on another windy night a few months earlier—a skeletal hit man had arisen to kill us, actually wounding Lilli. I got out of my car before they did and waited beside the big garage door. When Lilli unlocked it, I went in ahead of them and looked around as they snapped the lights on.

"Okay," I said.

"Whew," Lilli said. "When I think of all the times we've come in here without you, it just makes my palms sweat."

"Her palms always sweat," Anime said, earning a vicious glance from her girlfriend. "Do you know that doctors made up a fancy name for that? Palmar hyperhidrosis. I mean, seriously, is that stupid or not?"

"Puts the doctor in charge," I said. "You go in and say, 'My hands sweat,' and he says, 'You have palmar hyperhidrosis. That'll be two hundred and thirty bucks.'"

"Well, we're inside now," Lilli pointed out. "Look, we're alive and everything."

"I worry about you."

"Worry about yourself," Anime said. "You're in worse trouble than we are."

Louie said, "Do you know what time it is?"

"Why? Don't you have a watch?" I'd been poking my way east, not paying attention to where I was until I registered the soul-puckering ugliness of the failing mini-malls, chain restaurants, and car washes that characterize the area where Saticoy Street and Van Nuys Boulevard intersect, and I realized I wasn't far from Louie's. So I'd called him.

"That's like a reproach," he said. "You call me too late, and I say that, about what time is it, and you feel guilty."

"I'm bearing up under it somehow," I said. "Have you found out anything about Stinky?"

"Nope. I put lines out, but nobody's called in. Went past his house, but everything was dark."

"Not surprised. Did you try the door?"

"What are you, crazy? I don't do that. I have *people* who do things like that."

"Name one," I said.

"Why? You wouldn't know them anyway."

"I just want to hear what you come up with."

"Edward J. Fensterfoot," he said.

"Little guy," I said. "Yellow ears. You want a cup of coffee?"

"It's midnight. You woke me up. I should be asleep. Why would I want a cup of coffee?"

"You know, male bonding? Mind melding. Hoisting the hearty mug of friendship in the teeth of a cold universe. Sharing a laugh at the pointlessness of it all." I turned south onto what I hoped would be a shortcut to the freeway, some nameless, characterless, beauty-free street, just 1950s apartment houses, broken streetlights, scraggly trees, and bad-luck wind. "So whaddya think?"

"I think I'm going back to sleep."

"Before you hang up, can you think of anyone I could talk to about what's-her-name, Tasha Dawn?"

Louie yawned. "Only person I knew who met her was Garlin Romaine, and that was when Garlin was doing fake paper. Now that she's a big art hotshot, she probably won't be happy to hear from me."

"Well, get me an address if you can. By tomorrow."

"I just know," Louie said, "that it's only your good breeding that's kept you from mentioning money."

"A thousand for the artist. Find Stinky, two thousand."

"I'll try. I mean, Garlin, no problem, I could do that free, although I know you'll forget I ever said so. But Stinky, who does he even *know*? I don't think he's left the house in ten, fifteen years. It ain't like he's got groups he moves in. The way he lives, he might as well be in a display case."

"Thanks," I said. "You've given me an idea."

But before trying out my idea, I slipped beneath the freeway and across Ventura, heading south into the hills so I could drive past Stinky's place, which was as dark as it had been last time I saw it. I went all the way around to the golf course, hung a U-turn, and went past again. Then, throwing caution to the prevailing winds, I drove the big Caddy up the driveway, turned off the lights but left the motor running, took the Glock out of the dash compartment, and waited.

For nothing, as it turned out. I gathered my courage, dismissed my fears, and opened the car door. And then, the precise moment I got out of the car, something *did* happen. A gust of wind slammed me on the back and blew Stinky's front door open, hard enough to make it bang against the wall.

I screamed.

And stood there, gasping for breath. Apparently I hadn't dismissed my fears sharply enough. At least, I comforted myself, I hadn't fired the gun, but that was only because that particular Glock had a stiff pull, which Duck Dixon had described to me when I bought it as "the suicide's parachute." Duck's theory was that suicides are shaky and usually deeply ambivalent on some level or other, and a gun that's just plain hard to fire might be all the persuasion they need to put the weapon down, paste on a smile, and go forth to seize the day, get the girl, win the Nobel Prize. Or he could have made it all up on the spot when I complained about the pull.

It took me five pulse-pounding seconds to realize the significance of that earsplitting bang when the door slammed into the wall. When I was here last and had pushed it open, it had bumped into someone, Stinky's houseboy Jejo-something, who was in no condition to get up and move. *Jejomar*, short for Jesus, Joseph, Mary. I apologized to his

spirit for momentarily forgetting his name as I stepped into
the hall, which was empty. The moon was up, and its light,
which was coming over my shoulder, was enough to let
me see that the floor was free of bodily fluids or any of the
other unattractive residues murder so often leaves behind.
I backed out, into the warm, windy night. I knew I would
have registered crime tape if there had been any, even if
I'd passed it in the dark, but I looked again to make sure.
Nope.

Whoever had moved the body hadn't done it officially.

That left me with three possibilities: (1) Jejomar hadn't
been dead in the first place, (2) the Slugger and his guys
had come back to clean up, or (3) Stinky had arranged for
Jejomar to be picked up and transported someplace more
fitting.

I'm better than I'd like to be at recognizing when someone is dead, so that smoked Number One. The Slugger was
a possibility—in fact, that might have been why he was still
in the neighborhood when we arrived—so Number Two
survived the first sharp pass of Occam's razor.

But the one I liked best was Number Three.

I was actually enjoying the big car, the deference its sheer
mass earned from the other cars on the road, as I headed
for the Wedgwood, one eye on the rearview mirror. At
a point a little less than halfway up the Cahuenga Pass,
roughly at the spot where a decisive battle had taken
place in 1831, an uprising against an unpopular Spanish governor who was probably the inspiration for the
one that Zorro was always fighting, my primary phone
rang. It read BLOCKED, so I let the call bounce over to
voice mail. A minute later the phone did the neurotic little

end-of-its-rope shiver it always puts out when it gets voice mail, and I angled over to the right-hand lane with the phone on my lap—a bright screen at night will earn you a big ticket in LA—and turned on the speaker.

"Have we got stuff for you," Anime said, and, behind her, Lilli shrilled, "Jeez, look at *this*!" and Anime hung up.

Stuff about what? About Patricia and what I was beginning to think of as her campaign against Rina, or about Jeremy Granger's 34,000-square-foot bungalow in Brentwood?

And was I really going to break into that house in about nineteen hours?

The burst of wind that hit the side of the car was enough to make me correct my steering. Even in a car *that* heavy. I got off at the Hollywood Bowl to take a final shortcut, watching the mirror all the way.

18
Liminal

By 1:30 A.M., I could have walked through Jeremy Granger's house backward with my eyes closed, thanks to the links that Anime and Lilli had sent me: high-definition photos on Zillow and Curbed LA, and virtual walk-throughs on VisualTour, all sites that the intelligent twenty-first-century burglar should bookmark. The place was as big as God's house must have felt after the Kid moved out, and there wasn't a square inch of it that wasn't either ostentatiously overornamented or unconvincingly austere. The ceilings on the first floor averaged fourteen feet and sixteen on the second and third, not inappropriate for a medieval chapel but still an odd choice for a guy who was sensitive about being short. Just out of curiosity, I checked the original blueprints and found the first-floor ceilings indicated at sixteen feet, too, so I supposed he'd raised the floor on the ground story, where he'd do most of his entertaining. Spare no expense; add in his $60,000 cowboy boots and he'd effectively lowered the ceilings by two feet, four inches.

Most of the slightly lower first-floor ceilings were painted with vaguely Italianate clouds and rays of sunlight, so banal they could have been copied from budget greeting cards or toilet-paper wrappers. In the dining room, the skyscape had been augmented with baby angels sweet enough to eat on sticks. The master bedroom's ceilings, on the second floor, were innocent of paint, but one wall supported a flaking fresco created in some obscure Italian church in the fifteenth century by someone who definitely wasn't Giotto. It had been sawed out by architectural vandals centuries later for sale to the highest bidder.

Who, according to the records, had been Jeremy Granger, the year after he bought the place. You couldn't blame him for the basic layout of the house, although his buying it was an editorial comment in itself. The floor plan hadn't changed much since the first owner laid it out. The guy from Qatar apparently never set eyes on it; for him it was just an investment on a spreadsheet. The heiress lived mainly on the ground floor, since there was no elevator then and stairs were beneath her. The Thud put in an elevator and constructed a recording studio on the third floor, and when his career went upsy-daisy, he pulled the studio and replaced it with a boxing ring, complete with a microphone that could be lowered into the center of the ring, 1950s style. He'd killed himself quite messily in the ring with an absolutely end-of-the-line mix of pharmaceuticals and an electric carving knife that he'd plugged into the microphone outlet, so it might not have been for purely aesthetic or spiritual reasons that Granger yanked the ring, scattered sand over the floor, brought in a few big gray rocks and some ferns, and claimed that it was a meditation space.

The "meditation space" made Granger, in my book, a Grueddhist, another of the gruesome LA poseurs who claim to follow the Buddha's Way to enlightenment in between bouts of ripping people off. In my forays through Beverly Hills, I'd seen the Buddha meditating on license-plate frames that belonged to cars so big they probably emitted carbon monoxide when the engine was off. I'd seen his likeness offered as a $1,500 "table accent." I'd seen it in the display windows of upscale lingerie shops, flanked by bustiers and garter belts. I'd wondered occasionally what the Christian reaction would have been to a full-scale crucifixion employed as a decorative element in, say, the window of a marital-aids shop in Abu Dhabi, in the unlikely event that there were any marital-aids shops in Abu Dhabi. But while the crucifixion was taken seriously in much of the world as a kind of hair-raising shorthand for "I am the way and the life," to Grueddhists like Granger, the Buddha, wrapped in his eternal calm, was essentially a spiritual clothing label that said, *I'm cooler than you, and I'll be cooler than you when I'm dead, too.*

I was in my dim, silent living room at the Wedgwood, sitting on the couch drinking ice water, with my laptop open on the oak coffee table. Beside it a tiny portable inkjet printer ground out the building plans that Anime and/or Lilli had dug up. The plans were solid gold, because they told me not only where the walls were but also what was *behind* them. I yawned, not because I was bored but because I was tired.

I was also feeling sour.

I had no one to cuddle with, which was a problem, because I'm not an indiscriminate cuddler. In my entire adult life—actually, ever since the thorny thicket of desire that was tenth grade—I've only seriously wanted to cuddle with two people, and I'd screwed it up with both of them.

What was so important about knowing the details of

Ronnie's story when I instinctively felt there was no way in the world she'd intentionally do me harm? When I knew, although she'd never actually told me so, that she loved me, in whatever way she was capable of loving? Is love such a common thing, is it such low-hanging fruit that I should be studying it through a jeweler's loupe, looking for flaws and inclusions? Shouldn't I just grab it and run, hoping I wouldn't screw it up yet again? As, apparently, I had.

Herbie once told me not to be so hard on myself. "That's what other people are for," he'd said. One night during my most difficult period with Kathy, he'd told me, "You can't think about you and the job at the same time. You can't think about *anything* and the job at the same time."

The job.

In a normal month, I might work twice, and if I scored big in one or both of those operations, it could be three or four months before I again found myself easing my way into some locked and shrouded space where I didn't belong. The days were long past when I'd done it just for fun, just to look at the diorama of people's lives, their individuality and their peculiarities as evident in the way they placed the furniture, the things they kept on their shelves and tables, as it was in the houses they built or chose for themselves. At this stage in my life, it was strictly business, and my skill at separating the stuff from the duff allowed me to risk it infrequently.

But now I was contemplating three burglaries in four nights and not liking it at all. The first two had ended badly, and I had no faith whatsoever that the one scheduled for the following evening wasn't going to prove to be the worst mistake of my professional life.

It felt all wrong, completely, totally, one hundred percent wrong. The sensation a steer probably gets as he's being goaded toward the slaughterhouse, not being allowed a moment to pause and get a whiff of what's happening in there. I was being pushed from behind, hurried along before the reek hit my nostrils, by Officer Biehl, by the cops waiting down below with their cherry lights blinking, by the man who'd made the police force possible, King Maybe. According to Jake Whelan, the most powerful person in Hollywood.

Something was bothering me about the cop, Biehl. It wasn't just that I had a feeling I'd seen him before. It was something else.

I found myself at the window, looking downtown at LA's liminal skyline. *Liminal* is the kind of word that makes me want to know who was smart enough to make it up, since what it describes is a complete abstraction, a state of incomplete transformation, something that's caught in the process of becoming something else, like someone partway through the initiation ceremony of a secret society: he's not a member yet, but he's no longer *not* a member either. In spite of my habit of viewing life as a sort of snapshot album, complex moments reduced to bright, hard-edged squares of immobile memory, in fact I know perfectly well that virtually everything is actually in transition. The skyline of Los Angeles, a city that had grown outward for more than a century because earthquakes regularly shuddered the taller buildings into clouds of dust and mounds of rubble, has only lately begun to grow upward, and in spite of its shiny new impressiveness, our downtown is still in the early stages of sprouting skyline that might someday be awe inspiring.

I was also liminal. I was caught in the teeth of something that was forcing me to commit an act that, I felt instinctively, might destroy the precarious life I'd created for myself and turn it into something I didn't want to look at. Even putting the run of bad luck to one side, tomorrow night's break-in reeked of the slaughterhouse.

That brought me back to the topic of Jeremy Granger's power. As powerful as he seemed to be, as real as his power felt to me at this moment, it, too, was liminal. He'd eaten shit for decades on his way to that Regency desk, and no one stays in power forever in Hollywood.

And suddenly I found myself asking why so much of his story, so much of his rise and his public life—even the reason he was forcing me into his house tomorrow night—had its roots in someone with no power at all.

19

Dead Eye

It was a quarter to three in the morning before I used the jerry-rigged password and phony email address Lilli and Anime had created to help me navigate my way into Hulu. And there it was, as promised: the first season of *Dead Eye*.

It raised many more questions than it answered.

The first one was how it had stayed on the air.

It's not all that unusual, in today's media climate, for a television series to be yanked even before it premieres if the network decides during production that the concept has gone irretrievably south. Some shows that made it onto the air have actually been canceled before the first segment was over, based on a combination of low audiences and sheer awfulness: a show called *Quarterlife* that made the leap from YouTube to boob tube and lasted thirty minutes, for example, or the title-tells-all *Secret Talents of the Stars* (George Takei likes to sing country songs! Imagine that!). These quick yanks were possible because there was lots of data available to the networks in real time, and even in these days of declining network viewership those weekly slots represented (and represent) far too much potential money to waste them on series that don't draw viewers or that achieve only derisory levels of quality.

So why had *Dead Eye* lasted two years? It didn't qualify on either account. As far as ratings went, Ping-Pong matches played in the dark would have gotten higher numbers than the first half of *Dead Eye's* first season earned, and in terms of quality the show was the kind of abandon-all-hope bad that makes you curse yourself for every precious moment of your life you crumpled up and tossed by watching it. Not only was the writing unintentionally hilarious and the acting—especially Tasha Dawn's—barely endurable, but even *technically* it was something that American television almost never is: amateurish. Hollywood has developed a supernatural ability to make silver, if not gold, out of used floor wax, but *Dead Eye* was so flat and grainy it looked like it was shot on an old eight-millimeter camera by someone who had run out of film and was using gift-wrap ribbon. Theoretically set in a largely empty America, stripped of people by the zombies' ravenous appetites for human rib roast, the first segment featured location scenes shot in front of roads that frequently buzzed with traffic and over which airplanes gaily sailed, leaving ruler-straight vapor trails across the sky. When they filmed indoors, it was even worse. The ranch set that contained the human herd—of which the heroine's beloved, the big handsome alive guy, was a member—was obviously shot on a sound stage, where the lighting gave everyone three or four shadows, suggesting that the earth had picked up a clutch of extra suns.

And perched in the center of it all, as eye-bruising as a walnut in an engagement ring, was Tasha Dawn's performance.

The camera, as they say, likes some actors and hates others. Tasha Dawn was the rarest kind of actor, one the camera ignores. In scene after scene, she barely registered.

She often seemed out of focus even when she wasn't, and although she was pretty enough from some angles, she *needed* those angles, and in spite of the most basic rules of Hollywood camera geometry she didn't get them. Nor did she get the lighting she needed. As a result, most of the time she looked like a reasonably attractive but resolutely, almost statistically ordinary teenager who'd accidentally stepped into the light while taking a studio tour. And Casey had been right. Occasionally her eyes would dart to the camera and then zoom away, which violates the single most basic rule of film acting: that the characters don't know the camera is there.

Why weren't those moments cut? Or redone? The camera operator must have seen them. Directors watch videotape rushes now after practically every camera setup; why hadn't those terrified glances—because that's what they suggested to me, terror—been spotted and reshot right then?

Her voice was shrill, the unvarying, uninflected high G of an adolescent girl who had discovered that complaint would usually get her what she wanted and hadn't created a backup mode. In her most dramatic scenes, she sounded like someone who couldn't get the ice-cream flavor she wanted and thought it would materialize in the freezer if she was just sufficiently irritating.

Why hadn't she been given vocal coaching? It's simple enough to learn to bring the voice from the chest rather than the nose. Almost anyone can master it in a day or two.

I endured the premiere episode, watched the first three minutes of the second show, and skipped to the fifth, thinking that she *had* to get better, if only through practice. Anyone at the network, seeing that first show, would have ordered a full team onto the set: voice people, acting coach, a new cameraman, a human wrangler who did nothing but watch her and catch the worst moments so they could do a retake while everyone was still in place.

Why hadn't the *director* done that? One of a director's primary responsibilities is protecting the principal actors from their shortcomings. Who'd been watching out for Tasha Dawn? For that matter, where was the most powerful person on the set? Her *husband*?

And so back to the biggest mystery of all: How on earth had this soul-sapping piece of cheese lasted *two years*?

Anime, in what I was beginning to see as her permanent overaccomplishment mode, had also rounded up a clutch of stories about the show from both trade publications and consumer outlets. The reviews were scathing, most brutal when they were hilarious, and the main target was always Tasha Dawn. At the end of the first year, the wiseasses who handed out both the Razzies and the Golden Turkeys, which up until then had honored only the year's worst motion-picture actors, made an exception, creating a television category just for Tasha Dawn.

And then the ratings tide began to change a little, but in a somewhat unpleasant way. Teenage girls were tuning in. They started holding viewing parties, ten or twelve girls gathered around a screen, all over the country, watching the show. T-shirts bearing the words TIRED OF BEING DEAD appeared all over the place and were worn by kids who wanted to demonstrate that their affection for the show was properly ironic.

Someone transcribed the pilot script and put it online, and it began to show up on high-school and junior-high-school stages. So many kids—both boys and girls—wanted to play Tasha's character that multiple students took the role in most productions, dividing up her lines among them. Interschool "Tasha teams" held unofficial "act-offs." *Dead Eye* became a limited phenomenon, a little like *The Rocky Horror Picture Show*, but not as profitable. When the network startled the entire industry by renewing the series, the press release noted that the program's audience contained the highest percentage of teen viewers in the entire schedule. It was still coming in fourth or fifth in its time slot, but the microscopic audience was overwhelmingly under twenty, according to the renewal release, which must have been written by someone who had apparently never met a teenager. "The 'teens' of today are the consumers of tomorrow," the flack wrote, "and NBS is proud that this 'cool' audience wants to 'hang out' with us every week. We see it as the beginning of a happy and 'hip' relationship."

And in case anyone wondered how the star was taking all this, there were a few trade stories about meltdowns on the set and a little fever of speculation when she didn't show up for an event at the television critics' annual conference in Century City, a decision that I thought said quite a lot about her judgment, since she would have been barbecued alive during the Q&A session. The event went ahead as scheduled, but without her, and she was indeed hung out over the rotisserie in absentia.

The most vivid glimpse of what her life must have been like was provided in the hundreds of stories about the 2009 Comic-Con convention, the annual geek Bethlehem, at which Tasha Dawn's live appearance was promoted as one of the top attractions. I couldn't imagine what they'd told her she'd be doing there, but it couldn't have been the truth—that she'd be judging a contest in which thirty teens, girls and boys alike, many wearing designer zombie-chic clothes, did their imitation of what the stories described as her catchphrase: "I am so *tired* of being dead."

She had sat there—all by herself—on the stage, with what must have felt like the whole world looking at her, as she listened to her own nasal voice and wooden line reading being mimicked, exaggerated, sent up, *mocked*, while a couple thousand kids in the audience rolled in the aisles. And then came the moment that got all the coverage; as Contestant 26 finished, Tasha Dawn's will broke, and she stood up so suddenly she knocked her chair over and ran from the stage in tears. After an awkward pause and a lot of murmuring in the audience, punctuated by a few unpleasant laughs, the hunk of Hollywood prime sirloin who played the handsome alive guy came out to say that Tasha had been overcome by the affection of her fans and couldn't come back out, and by the way, Contestant 22 had won the prize, which was a walk-on in the show. Later in the day, when she didn't show up for the autograph sessions, there was a mini-riot, if a bunch of middle-class white and Asian kids dressed in expensive costumes designed and sold by billion-dollar media corporations can be said to riot.

The following week she was a no-show on the set. By then, pictures of her fleeing the stage had gotten prime placement in *People* and *Entertainment Weekly*, and the *National Scoop* plastered supermarket magazine racks all over the country with the headline TASHA: THE TRAGEDY BEHIND THE HEARTBREAK.

Mercifully, I hadn't been sent a link to the article, but I was pretty sure I knew what the tragedy was, and I doubted it was the one postulated in the tabloid.

It was fairly clear what, or rather who, was behind the

show's renewal in spite of the ratings. However high the percentage of teenage viewers, the Nielsen comps had *Dead Eye* in the bottom five except for those rare evenings in which the competition was preempted by presidential speeches and the like. As usual, it was entertainment journalism's reddest-toothed carnivore, Nikki Brink, who was then running the widely feared website Deadline in Hollywood, who broke the scoop. While the other trades were parroting the press release, Brink wrote:

> *Toldja: The real explanation behind the jaw-dropping news that NBS has picked up a new season of TV's most turgid show,* Dead Eye, *is simple: Farscope head man Jeremy Granger said, "Make it so." As the chairman of one of this town's busiest production hubs, he made it clear to NBS execs that they would not be given a shot at any of the five highly anticipated new series Farscope is developing for the Fall if* Dead Eye *gets yanked. With most of NBS's series ratings hovering just above freezing, the net needs Granger's shows, and the price includes keeping* Dead Eye *alive, or as alive as it ever gets. Just a reminder for those who haven't been paying attention: Top-billed Tasha Dawn, who humiliates herself weekly on the show, is Mrs. Jeremy Granger. I gotta tell you, if my husband gave me a present like that, I'd back over him with the Rolls.*

Indeed.

I found myself at the window again, but this time I was looking at my own reflection. I've known a lot of angry people, beginning with my own father and continuing through my career in the modern-day concrete-and-asphalt Sherwood Forest, with all the other outlaws. There are a great many angry crooks. Some of them—and I was willing to bet good money that the Slugger was one—gravitated to crime in the first place because it provides such a rich and varied number of ways to make a living by taking it out on the rest of the world. Why risk ulcers by stifling your anger when you can get paid for beating people to death?

Anger didn't always show. Some of the angriest crooks I'd met were those who on the surface were the most serene. The plausibles, who cozy up to people, befriend them, radiate love and caring at them, cultivate their trust, marry them, make love to them, pretend to be long-lost cousins, while methodically bleeding the marks' bank accounts dry and selling their real estate out from under them, are, beneath their charm, almost uniformly furious. I'd known a dozen of them on reasonably friendly terms, and there wasn't one I would have turned my back on.

The *Übermenschen* of anger, the truly globally angry, were of course politicians and, to a lesser extent, high-ranking military officers. Not all of them, of course; some of them (to give them the benefit of the doubt) actually wanted to serve their country, but others (many of them marked, like Cain, with the inverted facial U that Herbie used to call "Donald Trump Mouth") wanted power, pure and simple. I believed that few of them sought it in order to feed the hungry and clothe the shivering. It wasn't that *complicated*; they were furious at the world, and they simply wanted to impose their wills on it, on the rest of us. Make us dance their way, spend their way, maybe kill a few of *those people over there* to protect the national

interest or the interests of major stockholders or the owners of patents on essential medications or our reputation
as carriers of the Big Stick or our copyright on being the
one and only Land of the Free, should some other country
begin to get uppity and forget to tip its hat to us.

As embarrassed as I am to admit it, I sort of understood how people lived with this kind of anger. I could
see how it would be obliterated in the blizzard of justifi-
cation—*somebody's* got to make the hard decisions—and
the symphony of sanctimony that always accompanies the
application of all-out force.

What had driven me to the window was anger on the
purely personal, black-widow-spider scale. When I'd gotten onto my feet, I'd been looking at a series of photos
of Tasha Dawn taken over the course of the past year or
two. In her present-day incarnation, the pretty, ordinary
teenager had been burned away completely to be replaced
by an anxiety-ridden, emaciated, Giacometti sculpture of
tendons, tension, and teeth. Her collarbone was a bas-
relief of anxiety above the ten-thousand-dollar gowns that
hung like regrets from her sharp shoulders. People stood a
safe distance from her, as though what she had was conta-
gious, when it was so obvious that what she needed most
in the world was a hug. In picture after picture, she winced
at the camera, the fast shutter and the flashbulb probably
freezing her in mid-tremble.

I was certain she shook much of the time.

If what I was seeing was caused by what I *thought* had
caused it, the same cause that had kept that girl in that
terrible show, uncoached and unprotected, that had put
her alone on that stage at Comic-Con in front of an audience of merciless kids only a couple of years younger than

she was . . . well, if that was the driving force behind the way Tasha Dawn looked in those pictures—at the ripe old age of twenty-one or twenty-two—then Jeremy Granger, despite his cool, emotionless exterior, was the angriest, most merciless son of a bitch I'd ever met in my life.

PART FOUR
IMAGINARY COUNTRIES

Much more frequent in Hollywood than the emergence of Cinderella is her sudden vanishing. At our party, even in those glowing days, the clock was always striking twelve for someone at the height of greatness; and there was never a prince to fetch her back to the happy scene.
—Screenwriter Ben Hecht

20

Soju

Ten A.M. came and went with no call from Stinky.

I'd phoned him twice and gotten the same energized female phone-mail voice that answered my phone and had until recently answered Ronnie's.

Louie called a little after nine and said, "Your car's ready. Got you a new right front panel, got it washed, got the glass all vacuumed out. Looks good as new, which isn't saying much."

"Great," I said, rubbing at my eyes, which burned from lack of sleep. "I'll take it."

"You don't like the Town Car?"

"I'll borrow it for funerals."

"Nothing new on Stinky," he said.

"And Garlin Romaine?"

"Her I got. Where are you?"

"Down near K-Town." I was sitting in the living room of Apartment 302, nursing a cold cup of coffee.

"Whereabouts?" Louie said. "I could meet you in the Toyota, pick up the limo."

"Good idea. I'll pay you, too. You know Tom N Toms, the good one, in the 3900 block of Wilshire?"

"I'll find it. We'll swap cars, I'll give you Garlin's info."

"Did you talk to her?"

"Yeah. She said she'd been waiting for someone to ask her about Suley."

"Suley?"

"Tasha. Suley's her real name, I think. Nobody's really named Tasha."

"Glad to hear it," I said. "It's a tragic fucking name."

Tom N Toms is a Korean coffeehouse that's open twenty-four hours, and I could sympathize with the five bedraggled, crumple-suited Korean businessmen hunched together in a vortex of fumes in the far corner, obviously trying to caffeinate their way out of an all-night drunk. I'd started coming down here to sober up at all hours a few years earlier when I was having a little tango with alcohol myself. It's a genetic predisposition from my father's side of the tree, and every now and then it takes a bite out of me. I liked Tom N Toms because it was always open, because the coffee was strong, and because—this being Koreatown—there was usually someone here who was in worse shape than I was, having lost a fight with soju, Korea's deceptively mild-tasting, ethanol-rich rice liquor, the alcohol content of which can reach a semipoisonous forty-two percent. I'd drunk it myself a few times and spent the next day or two searching for my car.

I'd had a scratchy night, not going to bed until almost four and even then just stewing on the pillow until well after the morning began to pale on the other side of the window. When I finally managed to drop off, I had dreams that were all frustration: running through endless airports for planes that had left days earlier, trying to follow maps that faded and reshaped themselves on the page, looking

for someone or something in a dark house and being certain that whatever it was, it wasn't in front of me at all—it
was following me.

That last one brought me awake and all the way up to
a sit.

Dreams may not tell the future, but they sure as hell
animate our fears, cut and paste them into a dramatic
structure, and present them to us in color, and it took no
great rational leap for me to know that particular dream
meant I was scared senseless about going into Jeremy
Granger's overdecorated square mile of house tonight.
And I had no way to get out of it without going to jail.

I popped a sweat just thinking about the dream, and
when I wiped my forehead, one of the guys sitting at the
soju-recovery table shook his head in sympathy and gave
me a pained grin.

"Nice place," Louie said from halfway across the
room, much more loudly than was necessary. A couple of
the Korean guys covered their ears. "Whaddaya recommend?"

"Peach tea, if you don't want coffee. The cakes are
good."

"Anything for you?"

"Yeah," I said, holding up my cup. "Ask the waitress
for a refill."

"Ask the waitress for a refill, *please*," Louie said.

I said, "Oh, skip it," and got up as Louie sat down. He
said, "Peach tea for me."

I said, "You're welcome," and my phone rang. I put my
half-full cup on the counter, mimed a refill, said "Peach
tea," and answered the phone.

"So what about old Tyrone, then?" Tyrone said.

"I'm working on it," I said as the counter attendant topped off my coffee with peach tea and pushed it back to me with a big smile.

"Party's tomorrow," Tyrone said. "Not to try to light a fire under you or anything."

"Believe me, I know when the party is. It's blinking in front of me like an End Freeway sign. Aren't you in school?"

"'Course I'm in school. Between classes. Reason I called you, in fact. Rina just walked past me, going the other way."

"Didn't say anything?"

"Didn't look at me. Didn't even *not* look at me—you know how you can tell when someone's not looking at you?"

"I do." I leaned across the counter. "One more coffee, please."

"Must be nice to be someplace having coffee, 'stead of standing around in a school hallway being not-looked at. I'm kind of feeling the pressure here."

"I've already got something, but I don't know what it means."

"What? What have you got?"

"You'll keep it to yourself, right?"

"Sure."

"Because I'm still working on this, and I don't want it dribbling out, I don't want to use it until it's complete."

"I don't dribble," Tyrone said. "And if you want to keep secrets—"

"Sorry. She's lying about her birthday. Patricia is. It's really in March."

Tyrone said, "Whoa."

"So the question is why? And I actually have people picking away at that right now."

"The question is why?" Tyrone said.

"I just *said* that." I put too much money on the counter, picked up the cup that was half coffee, half peach tea, and took it over to the table, where I set it in front of Louie.

"I knew I'd heard it somewhere," Tyrone said.

I turned back to the counter to get my coffee, but I still heard Louie's gasp at the taste. When I got back to the table, his expression suggested that he'd found a way, without opening his tightly compressed lips, to tie his tongue in a knot. I said, "You didn't say please."

"Off my patch," Louie said. I'd bought him a strawberry shortcake, a piece of cheesecake, and a bottle of Perrier to cleanse his palate, and I'd slipped him the thousand for setting things up with Garlin Romaine, but he was still sulking. "Whadda I know about Philippine dance troupes?"

"You gave me the idea, in a way," I said. "Yesterday or last night or some damn time, you said to me something like 'It ain't like he's got groups he moves in,' and—"

"Doesn't sound like me," he said. Behind him, two of the Korean businessmen had given up and gone to sleep, their heads on the table, and one of them was snoring. "Grammar like that, doesn't sound like me."

"Well, you said it. Probably better, of course."

"I mighta said it better. It's *true*, anyways."

"And the answer is, the group he moves in is made up entirely of his Filipino houseboys."

Louie nodded. "Guy must really like adobo."

"Somewhere in Los Angeles, there's someone who arranges tours for Filipino dance troupes."

"Like I said, way off my patch. But I mean, what's Stinky gonna do? Call up and ask for company? You think the guy delivers?"

"No, I think he'll call to try to locate the one who left him a few months back, a guy named Ting Ting."

"Ting Ting?"

"Ting Ting."

"And why did . . . uhhh, Ting Ting leave him? I mean, aside from the fact that he could?"

"He fell in love. With a hit person, named Eaglet. They're living together—"

Louie's head came up. "Eaglet? She's that kind of delayed flower child? Feathers in her hair? Friend of Debbie Halstead? Like a protégée or something?"

"That's the one. You met her?"

"Back when Stinky contracted me to hire a hit on you and I gave it to Debbie because I knew she'd miss, sweet as she was on you."

"She *wasn't* sweet on—"

"Tell it to your confessor. Anyway, after she missed you the second time, your friend Eaglet called me up, asked did I want *her* to take a crack at you."

"She did?"

"Said Debbie couldn't hit you if you had the end of her gun in your mouth. Offered like a sale price, too. You know, clearance."

"Really." I was feeling betrayed. "Jesus, I took her to Kathy's and introduced her to Rina."

Louie gave me a full-press Italian shrug. "It wasn't personal."

"Not to you, maybe. So anyway, I figured maybe

whoever set up these dance-troupe tours could tell me whether Stinky had tried to find Ting Ting."

Louie looked at me, looked at his empty Perrier bottle, looked at the window letting in the milky November light, at the bushes jitterbugging in the wind. Then he said, gently, "Whyn'cha just ask Ting Ting?"

The Korean girl behind the counter was leaning forward, her chin on her hand and her eyes on me, and although it was obvious she was just daydreaming, it felt as though she, like Stinky, had been waiting for me to ask myself that question.

"Because the only way Stinky could find out where Ting Ting was . . ." I trailed off, distracted by Louie's encouraging nods. "You're right," I said. "The only thing I actually need to know is . . . I'm not sleeping well."

"Guess not," Louie said, with a little too much sympathy.

"Well then," I said, all business. "Let's get to it." I pulled out my phone and brought up Eaglet's number. Ting Ting answered, and I said, "Hey, Ting Ting, it's Junior."

"Mr. Junior," Ting Ting said happily. "You are doing good?"

"Doing great. Hey, have you heard anything from Stinky?"

"Oh," Ting Ting said. Then he hung up.

Garlin Romaine lived and worked in a onetime auto-repair shop south of Santa Monica Boulevard in West Hollywood, less than a mile from Ronnie's place. It took up a double lot, just oily-looking asphalt and a low-slung, architecture-disdaining building to which someone had added, obviously as an afterthought, a slender Art Deco tower probably scalped from a teardown somewhere else in the city. The words HANSEN'S AUTOMOTIVE, painted decades ago in a dark pigment, had ghosted their way through a couple of coats of cheap whitewash, and a battered metal sign out front still said MECHANICS ILLUSTRATED RECOMMENDED! The sign had a couple of bullet holes in it.

When I pulled the Toyota across the asphalt in front, the wheels bumped over a fat rubber tube and a bell chimed inside, an antediluvian way of announcing a customer on the lot. So Garlin Romaine knew that I, or at least someone, was out here. Which put me under a little pressure, because suddenly I wasn't sure I wanted to go in.

All the way over from K-Town, I'd been asking myself why Tasha—née Suley, which probably wasn't her real name either—had become so important to me. I'd been trying to rationalize it by convincing myself that she might direct me to Granger's Achilles' heel, assuming he had one, but on sober reflection it seemed as though my initial assessment of her as *powerless* had been an understatement. When she was a child, he'd used her like a hand puppet to bring down Barry Zipken, his old boss at Farscope, and then, possibly because she could hold that over him, he'd married her and made her rich, put her into a TV show and made her famous, and used all of it to make her miserable. And now he was forcing me to go into his house and remove the most valuable painting he owned so he could divorce her without its being factored into the community-property settlement.

So he could, in short, screw her over one final time.

It was inescapable that I was on the wrong side. I hate,

hate, *hate* being on the wrong side. And if that sounds odd or unconvincing coming from a burglar . . . well, broaden your horizons.

So just sorting it out, looking for some sort of rational explanation for my actions: What the hell was I doing here? Why did I want to see Garlin Romaine? Was I trying to find a way to bring Jeremy Granger down or looking for a reason to refuse to go into that house tonight? An excuse, that is to say, to do something that would get me charged with, and convicted of, burglary in the company-owned town of Culverton.

Putting an end to my life as I knew it.

Without knowing I was going to do it, I looked down at my watch—4:40.

A little less than three hours until I was going to have to go into that house.

Part of me just wanted to flatten the accelerator and leave Garlin Romaine waiting for the knock at her door. Forget learning any more about any of it. I didn't have to be Junior Bender my whole life long. I had money stashed in storage units all over town and in a box secured inside the chimney at the Wedgwood. I had valid identification in many names. I had saving accounts and credit cards with multiple banks under each of those many names. I had escape routes I'd laid out years ago. I had lots of people I could be. I had a well-paved road to freedom.

I had a daughter.

Facing the biggest threat to my way of life in years, I found that I actually cared more about whatever the hell Patricia Gribbin was trying to do to Rina than I did about anything else. I had to remain an active presence in Rina's life.

So no alternative identities. No running away. Stay Junior Bender and work through this.

An amplified voice, a female voice, said, "Hey. White Toyota."

I looked out the window to see that a light had come on over a windowless steel door between the two drive-in repair bays. "If you're the person Louie told me about, come in. If you're not, this is private property."

I put my forehead against the rim of the steering wheel and closed my eyes.

The amplified voice said, "Five. Four. I pay my patrol service very well, and they've got large shoulders and thick necks. Three."

I turned off the ignition and got out of the car. It was actually a relief, having someone tell me what to do.

21

Some of Them Never Forgive Her for It

The metal door buzzed as I approached it. I hauled it open—it was heavy—and trekked down a short, dark hallway with a scuffed chocolate-linoleum floor and dirty walls painted that awful hospital green. At the end was a closed door on the left, a partly open door on the right, and, straight ahead, your basic service-station bathroom, door wide open to show the world a wall-mounted porcelain sink, yellowish beneath the faucet with minerals from LA water, and an old porcelain john, both from the forties. Straddling the opening of the toilet was one of those aluminum-legged hospital toilet seats with the rubber-cupped feet that are used by people who can't handle getting down to, or up from, a lower perch.

Through the door ajar to my right fell a narrow slice of light, almost thick with the nose-stopping stink of tobacco.

"Come in," a woman called. She had a breathy voice, not in any intentional way, not for effect, but just from a lack of air to support it. I pushed the door open.

The room I entered, which seemed to be unoccupied, had once been a repair bay, its ancestry obvious from the hydraulic lift in the center of the floor. The area along the wall to my left, the back of the building, however, was domestic. It contained a hospital bed with side rails, the head raised to about a thirty-degree angle, that was rumpled and looked lived in, with books and magazines scattered across it. The bed stood on a very fine New England hooked rug with a stylized floral pattern, probably from the middle of the 1800s. Beside the bed stood a wheeled table littered with trays and dirty dishes, a couple of big glasses of water, and a little forest of pill bottles. Gleaming at the foot of the bed was a vessel of brass or copper that brought to my mind the imaginary chalice into which Jake dipped each morning to pull out the glowing seed of his day.

I went to the chalice and looked inside. It was full of bright-colored, slick little squares of paper, cut neatly but irregularly, mostly a couple of inches square. They seemed to be bits snipped from glossy magazines.

Where the rug ended, the original concrete floor of the repair bay began, chipped here and there where tools had been dropped, and uneven: a little damp in places and stained with ancient oil, the odor of which threaded its way though the malignant fog of the cigarettes. The long wall in front of me was covered from end to end and floor to ceiling by an enormous painting on what looked like a sheet of heavy plastic—perhaps thirty feet long and ten high—of a snow-covered desert that sloped down to the edge of a pale, ice-green sea. The sea stretched away to the east, behind the painter, so to speak, and the tall cacti threw long sunrise shadows across the bone-white snow, all the way to a jagged horizon that held back a blue-black sky with stars popping out of it. Probably because the plastic was so smooth, the painting had the hard, uniform sheen of enamel.

The painting aside, the most unusual thing in the room was the big, rough, wooden platform, covered with another very nice hooked rug, that had been built on top of the hydraulic lift dead center in the floor. The platform extended about ten feet in either direction down the long part of the room, but in width it was markedly lopsided: on one side it extended eight or nine feet, within a few inches of the wall where the painting hung, while on the other it was built out only a couple of feet. The short side had been counterweighted with a couple of big oil barrels full of hard cement so the platform wouldn't tip toward the painting. That freed up the space on the other half of the room, which was a mass of shelving jammed with cans of paint and solvents, brushes, mirrors, lenses—all sorts of paraphernalia for painting, projecting, and photographing images. A door stood open between the sets of shelves.

I stepped forward and took a good look at the painting: early morning in a frozen, empty desert. At the bottom of the picture—below the white snow, the dark shadows, and the black sky—the green of the sea almost made my eyes ring. Coming toward the water, increasing in size as they neared it, were footprints stamped into the snow, and lying at the water's edge was a small blue rectangle. I tried to make it out, but it was only roughed in, just a slap of blue, in sharp contrast to the almost photographic detail of everything else.

I said, "This is beautiful."

"You think?" a woman said behind me. "I've looked at it so long I can barely see it anymore."

"Why? You get stuck on it?" I turned to see a heavyset, oddly crumpled woman glide through the open door in a motorized wheelchair. Probably in her mid-sixties, but she could have been younger or older; her skin was smooth, but the muscles and tendons of her throat had loosened, and her jawline was a suggestion. She wore a singular full-length garment that owed a design debt to a nightgown, layers and layers of white tulle or whatever that gauzy stuff is that they use on ballerina's skirts. It buttoned at her plump throat, billowed out to fill the chair, and ended demurely at her sock-clad ankles, which were crossed. The gown had seen whiter days; it was dirty to the point of graying and smeared haphazardly with paint.

Bolted to the left arm of the wheelchair, in a rig designed specifically to hold it, was a battered forty-eight-ounce can produced decades ago to hold three pounds of Hills Bros. coffee. It had about five inches of brown water in the bottom, and a little flotilla of cigarettes sloshed back and forth as she powered up the wheelchair and headed past me toward the picture.

She studied the small blue rectangle for a few seconds as I looked down at the chop of salt-and-pepper hair, and then she said, "I never get stuck. I've been *interrupted*, that's all."

"By me?"

She didn't look away from the painting. "Don't be silly."

"What's that? The blue thing?"

"When I can get back to work," she said, wheeling part of the way toward me and fishing a pack of Merits out of one of the layers of her garment, "It'll be Will's passport."

"Footprints to the water and a passport right there?" I said. "Looks like a setup."

She shook out a cigarette and lit it. Then she nodded acknowledgment. "It is. Will is a very undependable boy.

It's a setup from the word go. Will is as alive as you are. In Verdinha, that is, so I suppose he is, as far as you're concerned, fictional." She pointed the smoking tip of the cigarette at the picture. "The east coast of Verdinha. Temperate but with occasional cold winters. Language is derived from a sort of bastard Portuguese, religion has borrowed a lot of lace and brimstone from Catholicism, lot of guilt for leverage. Place has a kind of South American zeitgeist."

"But you made it up," I said.

She looked at me for a few seconds, and said, "I *painted* it. If that means to you that I 'made it up,' have it your way."

"Just out of curiosity, why is the picture so big?"

"Got your phone?" she said, blowing smoke away to her right. I've never understood why people who smoke blow the stuff away from them instead of just sitting happily in a cloud of it.

I tapped my shirt pocket. "Sure."

"Get up on the platform. Center yourself and take a picture of it. A horizontal, obviously."

I edged between the painting and the platform, stepped up, and fiddled with the phone. When I had all of it in the screen, I shot it.

"Well done," she said. It wasn't exactly praise. "Now look at your phone. Does it look like a painting?"

"No. Looks like a photograph of a real place."

"I'm good with perspective," she said, "but the secret is that the painting is so big. By the time it gets shrunk down to photograph size, every detail has those hard edges you only see in photographic images. Whether it's a real place or not . . . well, that's a different question."

"Amazing." I looked at the painting from several angles. "So what's Will up to?"

"He's leaving Janet, I think. It's the first step in his new life. They're newlyweds, on their honeymoon, and he's planned this for months. There's a reason he's doing it in Verdinha. But this isn't why you're here. I don't suppose you smoke."

"No."

"Ahh, to have someone to puff with. Well, you'll have to put up with it."

"Are you going to finish the details on the passport, or is it so small it doesn't matter?"

Her nostrils flared, a mannerism I'd read about but never actually seen before. "*Nothing* is so small it doesn't matter. My assistant quit, and the passport is too low for me to get to. Stuck in this chair, I can't bend down that far."

"So what would your assistant do to help?"

"If I couldn't get to it by raising or lowering the hydraulic lift," she said, "She'd raise or lower the *painting*. The whole thing is on rollers, like window shades, side to side as well as up and down. When I have an assistant, I can pretty much stay on the platform and let the painting come to me."

"So," I said, "this picture, as I understand it, becomes part of a portfolio, a trip to a nonexistent country—"

"No" she said, with some heat, "not a *nonexistent* country. A country I know about but you don't."

"Fine. And there are other items in the folio—"

"Letters, tickets, snapshots, diaries, documents," she said. "It's different from folio to folio, but there are always documents. No civilization can exist without documents.

They're valuable because they tell you what people think is important."

"And the items in your folio tell a story?"

She put the cigarette in her mouth and pursed her lips around it, then blew smoke out her nose. "They tell many possible stories," she said, without removing the cigarette. "The people who look at one, or own it, manufacture their own stories, based on the documents and pictures and other things in the folio, letters or souvenirs or whatever tells them about what may have happened on the journey." She shrugged. "Or may not have happened. Why Will dumps his bride, for example."

"They buy the right to establish the truth," I said.

She tilted her chin up. "Why not? It's up for sale everywhere else."

"Can I see some of the documents for, uhhh . . ."

"Verdinha," she said around the cigarette. "In the wooden box, up on the platform."

The box, which was about nine inches by twelve and maybe three inches thick, was solid on all sides except the top, which had holes bored in it at regular intervals. "So something can breathe?" I said.

She shrugged again. "In your version of the story, maybe."

I opened the box. There were some airline tickets, already torn for boarding, baggage tags, a handwritten letter, a couple of snapshots, a marriage certificate, and a US passport, its distinctive blue cover barely creased. I opened it and found myself regarding a picture—I would have said it was a photo, but now I wasn't so sure—of a bland-looking twenty-something male with a big jaw and small eyes, the kind of guy who gets hired part-time at Abercrombie & Fitch. His grin seemed half formed, as though he'd been snapped before he'd finished putting it on. "'William Leinster,'" I read aloud. "Real name?"

She shrugged, but only one shoulder this time. "If you mean is there really someone named William Leinster, I'd say the odds are strongly in favor. If you mean is William Leinster really *that* person's name, or is it an alias . . . well, that's up to whoever owns, and thinks about, the folio."

I flipped through the passport. It was stamped here and there in various faded shades of blue, black, and magenta, each dated and initialed. The countries were Loringia, Paronal, the Caliphate of Forania, Porraigne, and Outer Hester. "No stamp for Verdinha," I said.

"Very observant. Part of the story, no doubt, another puzzle. Looks real, doesn't it?"

"Absolutely."

"I'm going to roll myself over to the bed, and you're going to help me get up into it. I've been sleeping in this chair for days."

"Because you haven't got your assistant?"

"Of course. I can get in and out of the chair on my own when nature raises its insistent head, but I can't lift myself high enough to get into bed. Once I'm up, we'll talk about the reason you're here."

Following her directions, I got Garlin Romaine out of the chair and up into her messy bed, where she lay, breathing heavily and looking like a Victorian grandmother doll, if there was such a thing. She wrapped both hands around her left leg and towed it to the left, sweeping the magazines aside, then sighed. "What a relief. How bad do I smell?"

"Honestly? Through all the cigarettes, it's hard to tell."

She gave a sharp little bark that sounded like practice

for a laugh. "Showers. Something else my assistant used to help with."

"If you don't mind my asking—"

"She couldn't take my smoking."

"I didn't mean that. I—"

"Of course, you didn't," she said. "Steeplechase accident. I was twenty-four. I went one way and the horse went the other, but somehow we ended in the same place, with Rocketeer—that was the horse—on top of me. Permanently disconnected all those tiny low-voltage lines that tell the bottom half of the body what to do."

"Must have been awful."

"I made it worse. I lay there for months and months, obsessing over all the places I'd never go, and I gradually realized that many of the ones I most wanted to see were places I'd never heard of. That was when I began seeing my countries."

"How does it work?"

She scrunched her back against the pillows, and I got up, and she leaned forward as I put one behind her head. "At first I just saw them. They were *whole*, by which I mean they had their names, their climates, their topographies, cities, towns, languages, histories, religions, all that stuff. I started to draw them, and I kept that up until I taught myself to paint. And then it came to me that every country has documents. So I began to make documents, like Will's passport over there."

"Or Suley's driver's license."

"Suley." She closed her eyes. "The topic at last. She called herself Suley, but her shrew of a mother called her Susan Lynn. Susan Lynn Platz, who thought of herself as Suley, and Jeremy Granger made Suley her legal name, at least on the driver's license and birth certificate I created, and then he named her again, as Tasha Dawn, of all the stupid, stagey things, and then he made her Tasha Granger, and with every new name things got worse."

"Suley's the main reason I'm here," I said. I looked at Garlin Romaine, crippled at twenty-four, and made a bet that she'd be on the side of a girl whose childhood had been stolen from her. "Granger's sort of forcing me to . . . well, cheat her, and I don't want to do it."

"Honey," Garlin Romaine said, "there's nothing left to take. It got worse and worse. The past year or so, what I saw was an animal that had been caged and beaten until it had lost the belief it could escape. Just waited for whatever was going to come next."

"Why would he do that to her?"

"It's his nature. She told me once a couple of years ago that the only thing that really interested him was seeing how far he could push his power. Taking people's lives and tying them in knots, getting people with talent to whore themselves out doing things that were beneath them, just rubbing their noses in it. She said to me she didn't think he'd be happy until somebody killed him."

"Eventually," I said, "I'm sure somebody will." I went over to the platform, where I'd seen a canvas-backed director's chair, toted it over, and sat. "So she kept seeing you."

"I think I was the last person she liked in her whole life. After me it was all Jeremy and the wolves he threw her to."

"How did you get involved in the first place?"

At first I didn't think she'd answer. Instead she took a deep drag off the butt, hit the acrid stench of the filter, and glared at it as though it had betrayed her. "You're a burglar, right?"

It sounded so bald, put that way. "Right."

"Well, you're going to have to pardon a bit of skepticism. You *swear* to me you're on Suley's side?"

"I do. And I will. On whatever you choose."

She dropped the butt, which was almost all filter, into one of the glasses of water on the table. It emitted a short, affronted hiss, and she looked down at it severely, then waved her hand in the direction of the painting on the wall. "When I'd been doing this—this art, this work, whatever you want to call it—for a few years, a friend arranged a show for me in a little gallery in Venice. It was a surprise that I sold three of them, because we'd had a terrible time trying to figure out how to display the stuff, which is supposed to be experienced by going through the folder it comes in. Anyway, it turned out that one woman had bought all three, and that she produced a series about lawyers. *Caseload*, it was called. Or maybe *Hard Case*—they all sound alike to me. Overworked public defenders with good hearts and great hair, and the men wear more makeup than the women. She called me up and came to meet me where I was living then, which was a convalescent hospital in Santa Monica, and made me an offer. She'd seen the documents, the passports and customs forms and so forth, in the folios she bought, and she needed some for her show. Subpoenas, arrest warrants, lawsuit filings, ID cards, on and on. Her actors were a little sticky. If the arrest warrant was for Josephine Blow, they wanted it to read Josephine Blow even if it would never be seen in close-up."

"Actors," I said.

"Might have been silly, but it was good for me. I did four or five pieces a week, all sorts of stuff, everything from crime-scene reports and arraignment forms to laminated name tags, and then word got out. Within a few months, I had more clients than I could handle, and I had to start saying no so I'd have time to work on my countries. Eventually I met the assistant to a real dickhead of a producer named Frankie Greff."

"The assistant was Jeremy Granger," I said.

"I'd said I wouldn't work with Frankie anymore, because he was a screamer." She patted the many layers of her gown and came up with the pack of Merits. "So he sent Jeremy, who was, if nothing else, soft-spoken. We got along okay, compared to Frankie anyway. He even bought a folio from me."

"And then."

"And then a few years passed, and gradually I began to sell my *real* work often enough that I could monkey with the prices, make enough to live on." She put the cigarette between her lips, slapped around the gown for a moment and came out with a lighter. "So I quit the documents. And then, a year later, Jeremy showed up with Suley and Suley's mother."

My phone buzzed, meaning someone had texted me. No one texts me except Rina, so I said, "Hang on, it's my daughter," and looked at the screen.

It wasn't Rina, It was Anime, and it said, MACH ONE? MACH TWO?

"Sorry," I said, putting the phone back. Mach One and Two, whatever that meant, would have to wait.

Garlin Romaine lit her cigarette, and through a cumulus cloud of smoke she said, "How old is your daughter?"

"Going to be fourteen at the end of the week."

"Same age as Suley when I met her, then."

"Sorry? I thought—I mean, Louie said Suley was six-teen when all this happened."

"Nope. Fourteen." She pointed at one of the sets of metal shelves along the wall of the big room. "Shelf on the right," she said. "Second from the top, on the bottom of a stack of four boxes. Says 'Suley' on it. Bring it over."

I eased the box out and took it back to the director's chair. Handed it to her. She parked the cig in the corner of her mouth so she could look down without getting smoke in her eyes and popped the lid from the box. Then she rifled through a few odd-size pieces of paper and brought one out, which she looked at for a moment, her face empty, and handed to me.

The girl in the photo, which had been taken in front of a splotchy, neutral seamless-paper background that said "Yearbook," still had baby fat, the vestigial chubbiness in the face that has little to do with weight and that disappears as the body reshapes itself. She smiled at the camera as though she was afraid it didn't like her, a pretty but not beautiful girl who badly needed to please. The anxious eyes peered out of an aura formed by a dry frizz of white-blond hair that didn't go with her skin and eyes.

"Mama bleached her," Garlin Romaine said, shaking her head. "And bleached her and bleached her."

"She's a kid," I said. "How the hell did she wind up—"

"She *was* a kid, even though she'd been working, so to speak, since she was twelve, thanks to Mom and Dad." Garlin Romaine tapped the cigarette against the glass's rim, dislodging a plug of ash a fingernail long. "She was still in junior high. They'd tried to get her into movies, and you know the rest of it. She got a little part in exchange for an advanced cuddle, and her name got passed around, and a year later Mom and Dad had a new car." She waved her own smoke away as though it bothered her. "We didn't have this kind of thing in Maryland, where I grew up."

I said, "Sure you did. May not have been out in the open."

The line of her mouth made it clear that I wasn't worth arguing with. "So what Jeremy told me was that Suley had been caught in a setup and that her mother and father were headed for jail and she'd end up in a foster home if they couldn't show she was eighteen. I made them darken her hair so she wouldn't look so trampy, and I worked up a driver's license and a birth certificate, both for Idaho. I told them they wouldn't hold up in court, but they did, because it turned out to be a civil case, not a criminal case, and the issue wasn't whether she was really of age but whether Jeremy's boss could show he had good reason to *believe* she was of age. Poor baby was in a panic about being separated from her parents. God only knows why, but I suppose they were the parents she knew, weren't they?"

"I suppose," I said, in lieu of sighing, which was what I wanted to do.

"So," she said, breathing smoke, "I busted my butt over the papers, and it all went as planned, except that she kept coming back here after it was over, with Mom driving at first and then, when she got her permit, without Mom. She liked to watch me paint. She liked to be listened to. Nobody ever listened to her. She'd sit at the rear of the platform and talk and make suggestions. She always wanted animals in the pictures, and I'm not much on animals, but I put a few in to keep her happy, because she was . . . she was one of those girls who drew . . . who drew *horses*, and I'd been one, too. She wasn't, as they say, 'dating' anyone then, because Jeremy was paying her— well, paying her *parents*—to keep her out of circulation. He was getting her parts—you know, 'short teenager,' 'girl with puppy,' that kind of thing. Her mom was telling her that she had Jeremy by the balls and she should push for more, but Suley—she . . . she just didn't have any mean- ness in her. She thought Jeremy was *nice*."

I said, "The very word."

"And then she stopped coming by for a while, but she called to say she was in a TV show. She sounded so *excited*, like it was the best thing that ever happened to her."

"Right."

"Until it turned out to be the worst," Garlin Romaine said. "And even then there was worse to come."

"Why didn't she leave him?"

The cigarette was almost down to the filter, but she hit it anyway. "She was terrified of him. And you know how it is: Every now and then, when he began to sense she was about to break the line and swim away, he'd reel her back in, make nice to her, take her somewhere. Buy her stuff. Tell her he loved her. I don't think anybody ever really loved her." She shook her head sharply, probably at the unfairness of it all. "But then, when I talked to her a month ago—on the phone, she'd stopped coming by, because he didn't approve—she said she'd learned that his first wife had divorced him on charges of mental cruelty, even though he offered her extra money to call it irrecon- cilable differences. And Suley said she was going to do the same, and he wouldn't dare to oppose her because of all he'd put her through. She said no one would ever speak to him again."

"Well, I guess they worked it out somehow, because *he's* planning to divorce *her*."

"A happy ending. The last thing I ever expected. All men come into this world through a woman," she said, "and some of them never forgive her for it."

"So now he's trying to cheat her again, steal a museum-quality painting so it doesn't get into the community-property settlement."

"She should take it," she said. "Take anything he offers. Even if she winds up with a few thousand a week and a used car, she'll have her life back." She was looking at the picture, but not focused on it. "Except that it sounds too easy."

"I know what you mean."

"Things don't work out for her that way," she said. Her eyes wandered the room. The cigarette was dead between her fingers. She looked over at me and then down at the cigarette butt, and she drew a breath, deep enough to make her wheeze. "Every place I paint has a religion. It's one of the first things that comes to me. Generally, the more temperate, the more hospitable a place is, the more benign God is. Or the gods are. A lot of places, most places, have multiple gods. Some have *hierarchies* of them." She pointed toward the foot of the bed. "See that thing down there?"

"The chalice?"

"If that's what it is. Go get four snips of paper from the vase. Don't look, just pick them out."

I did: a pale blue sea with palms, a Greek ruin, a bustling harbor, and a jagged, snow-clad mountain. I gave them to her.

"This is Thontein," she said instantly. "Thontein is a backbone of peaks, the top of a long, narrow mountain range that runs through the Pacific from the approximate latitude of San Diego, down where the palms in this picture are, to the southern reaches of the Arctic Circle and"—she flicked the snippet of mountain with her index finger—"Mount Ice. Ten thousand years ago, Thontein was one landmass, and people traveled freely between the cold and the warm regions. But then a volcano blew its top, about two-thirds of the way up, and the ocean flowed in and cut the country in two, putting ten miles of cold sea between north and south. Over time the language changed into two languages, lots of vowels in the south and bristly consonants in the north, and the god turned into two gods. The southern god is a spirit of affable plenty, worshipped in white stone temples dedicated to the rainbow, and his people grow rich as tourists pack their harbors. The northern god is a trickster who delights in showing his people paradise, dangling it in front of their noses and then snatching it away, leaving them to shiver and die in the snow. The people of North Thontein, asking themselves why their god mistreats them, have happened upon what they call the Rule of Seven. One in every seven people, they believe, is a horrible botch, a mistake, someone God would delete in a moment if he could, but heaven's rules restrict him to mass exterminations, like the legendary volcano or the huge tidal waves that wipe out their coastal villages every generation or so. So they regard it as a religious duty, their way of cozying up to God, to find and kill that one in seven. And then the next one and the next one."

"But they keep being born," I said.

"Of course. So in North Thontein, murder is an unending form of worship."

I said, "And you just came up with that?"

"I don't come up with anything," she said. She dropped the dead butt into the water glass. "It's already there. Hell, it's *here*. That's the kind of god that's in charge of what's been done to Susan Lee Platz."

22
Lots Going on in Mach One

I was feeling a tiny bit better as I cranked the Toyota into compliance. I'd been unwilling to go into the day carrying the image of the gods of North Thontein with me, so I'd gotten Garlin Romaine to say she'd talk to Casey about working as her assistant.

"What's she doing now?" she'd asked me.

"Cheerleading. But she's sick of it."

"Then she's got energy."

"I don't think energy will be a problem. And she's big. I mean, she can . . . you know, pick you up and get you into the shower and stuff."

"Will I like her?"

I shrugged. "I did."

"Good enough. I'll call her today."

"Great." I turned to go, but she reached over and put a hand on my arm.

"And try to think of some way to help Suley," she said.

The day was waning, the sun hanging low in the west, kind of a cheap-floor-polish yellow from all the dust that the wind had stirred up. Looked like a costume-jewelry sun from a discount chain store. Less than three hours before I was supposed to punch in the entry code at Granger's gate and go in to do the dirty.

On the phone Anime said, "It's from some messages we managed to harvest from Patty's Facebook page. 'Lots going on on Mach One,' someone wrote her, and she wrote back, 'Check out Two,' the number written out like that, so we figure it's Mach Two, and then she said, 'And don't talk about those here.'"

"The speed of sound," I said. "Mach Two is twice the speed of sound."

Anime said, "I looked it up. Mach is 'a dimensionless quantity representing the ratio of flow velocity past a boundary to the local speed of sound.' That's the kind of thing that gets Lilli worked up. So we figured maybe it's machone.com. We searched it as one word, machone.com and it's available—I mean, for sale—and machtwo.com comes up as a blank page, which usually means that someone has bought the domain name and parked it."

"Parked it." I was pulled over on a side street about halfway between Garlin Romaine's place and my West Hollywood storage unit.

"They're not ready to use it yet, so they leave it blank. If you put an underline in between *mach* and either *one* or *two*, you get a 'Page not available notice,' which can mean the same thing. Or a bunch of other things that have to do with your browser, except we checked the other things, and it doesn't mean them."

"Do you think it's important?"

"It's the only thing we don't understand," she said, "and Patricia didn't want it discussed on Facebook, so yeah, we think it's important."

"Maybe *Mach* is an abbreviation, or a code word."

"We're thinking abbreviation. If it's code, why tell someone not to use it? We've tried *machine* and *macho* and *Machu* and *machaca* and *mach schnell*—which is, like, German for 'hurry up'—*machicolation* and some other stuff."

"'*Machicolation*'?"

"Oh, good, I really hoped you'd ask. 'An opening high in a castle through which one drops things or pours molten lead on the enemy.'"

I said, "Tyrone is going nuts."

"Tell him to come over and go nuts with us. It won't help, but at least he'll have company."

"Anything else interesting?"

"Well, yeah, if you're easily entertained. She's changed schools twice in four years. She got most of the way through sixth grade in her first middle school, then moved to one farther away, and then in eighth she moved to Rina's school."

"And she hasn't changed her home address?"

"No. Each school is a little farther from her house than the one before. She's definitely not in the default area of the school she goes to now."

"What about quality?"

"You mean, like, did she move because the other school was better or because she couldn't keep up in the first one?"

"Something like that." I looked at my watch. I was now fifteen minutes closer to my scheduled arrival at Jeremy Granger's house.

"None of them is a magnet school or a charter or anything," Anime said. "Not remedial either, just your basic crappy California middle schools, full of kids trying to qualify as average and teachers getting older with one eye on the clock."

"Rina likes her school," I said, and immediately asked myself, *Does she? She was okay with it last year, but*—

"Well, lucky her," Anime said, with a certain touch of frost in her voice.

"Why would Patty change schools like that?" It seemed a safer topic. My phone buzzed, and I looked down to see a number I didn't know. "Hang on," I said, and put her on hold.

"Junior?" Garlin Romaine said. "Tell me, is your father still alive?"

I said, "Afraid so."

"Well, dear, when he dies, you know, you're perfectly free to use your real name. No adult should have to call himself Junior."

"Junior *is* my real name," I said. "My father wanted to name me after himself, but his name was Merle, so—"

"How appalling. When there are so many good names. Rex, for example."

"I don't see myself as a Rex. Listen, I'm on another—"

"I'm sorry, I won't keep you. Just wanted to tell you I called your young woman, and she sounds perfect, if a bit Mason-Dixon. She's coming over in half an hour."

"Good to hear."

"She sounds . . . sunny," Garlin said. "We could use a little sunshine around here."

"Hope you get some. Gotta go."

I switched back to Anime. "So," I said.

"Obviously, disciplinary problems," she said, as though speaking to someone fresh off the boat from Thontein.

"But forget learning any more about it. Not even Lilli and me can—"

"And I," I said automatically. "Lilli and—"

"Oh, my God," she said. "I could have endured a *lifetime* of embarrassment. Wait while I write that down . . . And . . ." she said, slowly, ". . . I. *There*. Now, to return to the topic, the school system buries that kind of information, about disciplinary issues, at the bottom of a hundred-foot-deep pool of radioactive water, full of glowing sharks. You know, even if a kid gets transferred for bringing a weapon to school, the school they stick him in doesn't get told about the weapon?"

I looked at my watch again. "Hard to believe," I said, mainly to say something.

"You think? Well, we'll keep trying to figure out *mach*, okay?"

"Fine," I said, but she'd hung up.

As much as the deadline for tonight was pushing at me, I was worried about Stinky. He hadn't phoned me, he hadn't given me the money he'd promised for the stamp or even tried to talk me down. That was a problem, because when Stinky wants something, he wants it *now*. He hadn't answered my calls, of which there had at last count been five.

It was enough to make me wonder whether the Slugger had found him.

That was worrisome, not solely because I liked Stinky— I didn't, really, or not very much—but also because Stinky was the only way the Slugger would be able to find *me*. And even though I wasn't staying anyplace anyone would associate with me, a name is a *great* start when you want to find someone. Crooks being the way they are, the Slugger could probably locate lots of folks who would agree to set me up for an amount of money that wouldn't strain his budget. Once, years ago, during our usual fight, Kathy had asked me, "Don't you ever want to associate with a better class of *people*?" and I'd made the unforgivable mistake of laughing. At this juncture that question had the aura of fate, ignored while rapping on the window.

So it was important for me to know whether Stinky was alive and just being Stinky or not. If he *was* alive, I was pretty certain I knew where he was. But it was way the hell out in Santa Monica, more than two hours there and back, maybe three at this time of day, and time was getting tight.

I also wanted to stop by my storage unit and get my tools, although I could do without them in a pinch, since I had the codes. The storage unit at least had the virtue of being nearby.

So, with the clock ticking, I wanted to go to Santa Monica and I wanted to pop into the storage unit. But I *needed* to make a call.

Need won. I put the car in gear and headed north, crossing Santa Monica Boulevard until I was only a block or two from Ronnie's place. Then I pulled to the curb and dialed.

"What?" she said.

I said, "Thanks for picking up."

"I decided I can't change you if I don't talk to you. You need changing so badly."

"Change me tonight," I said.

"It'll take longer than that."

"Well, you can *start* tonight. I . . . uh, I need a ride."

A moment passed as I replayed the words in my mind, remembered how Tyrone had kicked himself, and followed suit. It hurt. I said, "Ow," but she'd hung up.

I counted to ten and pushed the button again. Her phone rang.

She said, "What time?"

"Around eight."

"Are you about to tempt fate again?"

"I am."

"I'd have thought you'd have learned by now."

"You're *speaking* to me," I said.

"Yeah, but I'm not through being mad."

"I haven't got much choice. I have to go tonight."

"Or what?"

I told her.

"Well, as much as I don't want to help you put your head into the lion's mouth, I will. But not at eight."

"Why not?"

"I'm not home, and I won't be home until about eight fifteen."

I chewed on my lower lip for a moment. "Are you someplace we can meet up?"

"Not unless the lion lives in the general direction of Disneyland."

I said, "No one lives in the general direction of Disneyland." Granger had said I could go in as early as seven thirty and that he wouldn't be back until midnight. I looked at my watch again, without having consciously decided to do it, and when I stopped looking at it, I realized I hadn't read the time. "Around eight thirty?" I said.

"I guess. My GPS says I'll get there about eight twenty,

but it's always optimistic. Eight thirty is probably safe. What's the plan?"

"I pick you up and we go get another car. Then you go have a coffee or a foie gras or something not too far away until I call you. It should be less than an hour."

"This thing about needing a ride is kind of high school, don't you think? What did you do before you met me?"

"I didn't hit houses in Brentwood," I said. "In most neighborhoods it's possible to park for an hour without your license-plate number being written down by the gendarmes."

"*Gendarmes,*" she said. "*Foie gras.* Aren't we *je ne sais quoi?*"

"*Je t'aime,*" I said. "I think."

I heard her swallow. "*Mon Dieu.* We'll talk about that later. But just to allow myself to thaw a bit, you should know that I'm not entirely without regard for you either."

"Me, too," I said.

"There," she said. "That's the Junior I know and . . . well, have regard for."

"See you then," I said, suddenly feeling ridiculously happy. I waited for her to hang up in my ear, but she didn't. She said, "Goodbye."

Buoyed by this proof of her regard for me, and with all that unexpected time on my hands, I pointed the Toyota west, toward Santa Monica.

23

Open Me First

I'd been to Eaglet's condominium once before, right after she met Ting Ting, which happened when he brought me some apologetic flowers from Stinky. Stinky needs to apologize frequently. At the time Ting Ting held pride of place as the Filipino houseboy who'd put up with Stinky longest. Eaglet was in Ronnie's and my motel room when Ting Ting showed up with the flowers, and the attraction between the two was mutual, instant, and Shakespearean in scale. Ting Ting moved into Eaglet's condo that very night, breaking what passed for Stinky's heart forever, or at least until Jejomar crossed the blue Pacific and his sails hove into view.

Eaglet's condo was confirmation, if any was needed, that murder pays better than burglary. She was still a relative neophyte among LA hitters, and she already had a condo I put at a million-nine and rising, only about fourteen blocks from the Pacific, close enough to smell it and wipe salt off the furniture all the time. It was newer than tomorrow, with pale wooden floors and edgy, angular Danish Modern furniture that had all the heart of a Danish cookie. At the time I visited them, there had been a moment, after Ting Ting left the room to make us some tea, that Eaglet let the harmless hippie-dippie, retro-flower-child thing slip a little, on purpose, to give me a glimpse into the eyes of someone I shouldn't even think about fucking with. I'd given my version of it back to her, and in the course of a speechless half second we met each other all over again.

And now I'd learned that she'd volunteered to take me out. Oh, well, as Louie said, nothing personal.

If Stinky was in Eaglet's condo—and the fact that the ever-truthful Ting Ting had hung up on me made the odds pretty good that he was—then the only way to talk to him would be face-to-face, since phoning again wasn't going to get me any further than I'd gotten last time. And anyway, at this point I was thinking far enough ahead to have a plan of sorts, assuming I was still alive after the break-in at Granger's to put it into motion. I needed Stinky for that plan. In person.

One of the things I liked about Eaglet's building was that it didn't have one of those electronic buzzer gates. Standing out there with your back to the curb and the sun going down and a premature streetlight blossoming on your shoulders and the wind whipping the trees around, those things can cut an evening of crime very short indeed. But here, at 3240 Sycamore in Santa Monica, the builder had his priorities straight; he'd skipped the gate and pocketed the expense, and I could walk right in, virtuous as the dawn.

It never ceases to amaze me that people who pay for an eyehole in their door will open up when there's a thumb covering it. It was Ting Ting, of course; Eaglet would probably have fired directly through the door, and Stinky didn't get up for doorbells.

"Ting Ting," I said heartily, pushing past him. "*Damn*, it's good to see—"

The rest of the sentence evaporated in a slow exhalation of surprise. The long hallway, which, on my prior visit, had been decorator-illuminated to put maximum shine on the furniture, was in semidarkness, except for several chest-high lights a few paces apart, which turned out to be thick white candles flickering in glass chimneys and mounted on brass stands. More candles gleamed in the part of the living room I could see, where curtains were drawn against the sunset, and the air was positively sticky with the scent of tuberose, gardenias, and ginger flowers. Ting Ting put a hand on my arm, but it was a soft hand, not the hand of death he'd used on me that one night.

His eyes were red and puffy. He sniffled. He was wearing dark slacks and a white barong tagalog, the traditional Filipino shirt, but with a mandarin collar and, pinned over his heart, a curled loop of black ribbon.

"Oh," I said, pulling up short with an almost audible screech of brakes as the situation presented itself to me, "yes, I . . . um, I figured it—he—would be here. I wanted to . . . to pay my respects."

"You nice man," Ting Ting said, causing me a pang of guilt, "but I think Mr. Stinky—"

"You know what?" I said. "You don't work for him anymore, and you don't have to call him *Mr.* Stinky. Just plain Stinky would do fine. Anyway, Stinky and I, we're old friends."

Ting Ting looked at me, lips pursed, and then shook his head at whatever he'd been thinking. "Is no time for argue," he said. "Please come in."

He led me down the hall and into the living room. All

the furniture had been pushed to the walls, and the room was ringed with weighty, Mafia-style floral arrangements and more of those big candles. Dead center, so to speak, and up on trestles, was an elaborate casket, the top of which had a decent approximation of Leonardo da Vinci's *Last Supper* painted on it, Jesus and his friends frozen mid-bite by the big announcement. The casket's upper half, where the occupant's torso and head would be, was open, but only by about eight inches. Ting Ting stopped beside it for a moment as he went in, and I waited behind him, looking down at the opening. "In Pilippines we like it open," he said, sniffling again, "for say goodbye. But Jejomar, he not looking so good."

"I imagine not," I said. "Was he a friend of yours?"

"Why?" Ting Ting asked, wiping his cheeks. "You mean, because I crying? Jejomar, he was Pinoy, a Pilipino boy, poor boy, same as me. Dancer, same as me. Come far away from home, same as me. I don't meet him, but, you know, he same as my brother." He swabbed his nose. "So me, I cry for him a little. I think he cry for me, too."

"I'm sure he would," I said.

Eaglet came through the door from the kitchen. Her parents may have been the last Asian hippies in California, but she could shed the stony slacker style just as easily as she could shed Peace, Love, and Understanding when the time came to pull the trigger. Tonight she was sporting a very twenty-first-century look in black, and the glance she gave me wasn't affectionate, but she wasn't going to push it under these circumstances. "Junior," she said, with teeth. "What a *nice* surprise. Are you hungry?"

"No thanks," I said, too unprepared for the question to actually consider it.

"Me neither," she said, "but all day long Stinky's former . . . um, houseboys have been coming by, and they all brought these *flowers*"—she indicated the big, beribboned floral arrangements—"and they all wanted to eat."

"In Pilippines," Ting Ting said, with a tiny edge, "everybody eat at . . . at *paglalamay,* at . . . at—"

"The vigil," Eaglet said, surprising me. "I've been reading up," she said. "*Boy*, do they eat."

"Eat because we alive," he said with a bit of bite in it, and Eaglet, who had a spine of solid brass, took the first step back I'd ever seen her take. I reevaluated the pecking order in the relationship.

"Actually," I said, "I could eat a little something." I hadn't had anything since I swiped part of Louie's pastry at Tom N Toms.

"Right back," she said, but I followed her into the kitchen.

"How's Stinky taking it?" I asked.

"Milking it for all it's worth." She lifted the lid from a big, steaming pot on the back of the stove. "Rice and chicken okay?"

"Absolutely. You mean he's not really all broken up?"

"He feels *guilty*," Eaglet said, wielding a serving spoon with admirable precision, "which isn't quite the same thing, is it? But if you ask me, it's . . . you know, a chance for a soliloquy. His big scene. Ting Ting was the only one he really loved. And himself, of course. Gravy?"

"Sure. Where'd the casket come from?"

"He got it off Amazon," she said. "Stinky has a Prime membership, naturally, so the shipping was free, if you can imagine that. Almost thirteen hundred bucks even *without* the shipping. He wanted to save a thousand, get one that was all wood, but Ting Ting said no, the one in there, with the cafeteria or whatever it is on it, that was the *Catholic* one, and I guess that carried the day."

"You guess?"

"I tuned out." She put the dish on a tray and laid down a white napkin, a fork, and a big spoon plumb-straight beside the dish.

"Why'd you tune out?"

"Honestly? I didn't know the guy, he was nothing to me when he was alive, and now that he's dead, he's a pain in the ass. I mean, I gotta have the houseboy, whatever his name was, here in the condo in that big overdecorated egg carton, all my furniture is useless, these guys and their florists are streaming through all day, the place smells like Hawaii, and then there's Stinky, and you know what? An hour of Stinky is like a week of regular people." She put the tray on a little square table, some kind of blond wood, and pulled out a matching chair. "Eat up, it's pretty good."

"He's here, right? Stinky, I mean. Staying here." I spooned some chicken and the vinegary gravy over the rice. Smelled great.

"Is he ever. He's all over the place. He can be too close to you when he's in the other room."

"This is really good," I said. I skipped the chair and ate standing at the table.

"I've been learning. That's Ting Ting's mother's recipe, although the chicken here, he says, isn't as good as in the Philippines, because there you, like, say hi to it and they kill it in front of you or something. You know, you can't be in my line of work if somebody wringing a chicken's neck gives you the wussies, but I'll still take a nice neat package wrapped in plastic."

"So where is he? Stinky?"

"Oh, who knows. Shaving his legs, maybe."

"I do *not* shave my legs," Stinky said, billowing into the room. Stinky's waist was in the high fifties, and in the loose black barong tagalog he was wearing, he looked like the mourning blimp you'd hire for a celebrity funeral. "More in *your* line," he said, with a precisely calibrated tincture of distaste, "than mine, I should think."

"I'm Chinese and Vietnamese," Eaglet said, "and probably the least hairy person you've ever known. Compared to me, you're one of those primate species we watch through the bars as they groom each other. You know, eating nits."

"Through the bars indeed," Stinky said. "Do you mind if this gentleman and I beg a moment free of your company?"

I said, "Now, now, children."

"He's yours," Eaglet said to me. "Try not to return him in one piece."

She pushed past Stinky, into the living room.

"I'm sure she's a competent little death mechanic," he said, turning to make sure she kept going. "She's certainly soulless enough. And she shows a certain organizational flair. The plan for the burial is entirely hers. The elevator here goes right down to the garage, and she's rented a van so about nine thirty this evening we'll be able to take . . . ahhh, Jejomar—" He stopped for a moment, blinking rapidly, and I fought the impulse to pat his arm. He probably would have slapped my hand away. "Take him up to a place she knows in the Angeles Forest, wherever that is, which is apparently an absolute garden of murder victims. The casket—" He peered at me, still blinking, but more slowly. "Do you like the casket?"

"Aces," I said. "For a casket, I mean."

"Wop overkill," he said, "but it soothed Ting Ting's soul. He apparently feels that the design of the box is a kind of tip to the angels: *Open me first*." He heaved an immense sigh. "So by about midnight, Jejomar should be six feet down, under *The Last Supper*, waiting for the trumpet, or the harp, or the barbershop quartet, or whatever the fuck it'll turn out to be." He looked at the floor with what seemed to be total concentration. "How's Miss Most Wanted, the Bauble Queen?"

"We've taken a little time-out," I said, "but we're seeing each other tonight."

"Well, check your pockets when it's over. Although I don't even know why I say that. She's got just what you need."

I finished the chicken and went to the pot for more. "Really. And what's that?"

"You have modest but solid instincts, a good eye, and a certain skill level. She has imagination."

"I don't have imagination?"

"No more than a lead pencil."

"That's harsh."

"Well, look at you. You're a pretty good burglar, *and* you've got a corner on the market of crooks who are also private eyes. If you had any vision, you could be making a fortune."

I said, "You sound like Irwin Dressler."

Stinky doesn't surprise easily, but both eyebrows went up. "I sound like *Dressler*?"

Irwin Dressler, the world's oldest living still-dangerous gangster, had pretty well headed the mob in Southern California for more than five decades, making things work when the elected government couldn't and scraping off the cream here and there for his efforts, and the mention of his name even now inspired a lot of respect—usually accompanied by a surge of dread—among informed crooks. I'd had dealings with him twice and, to my surprise, survived. He'd even smiled at me a couple of times, and I had moments in which I could actually believe he'd experience a twinge of regret before ordering my death. "That's what *he* says," I said. "He thinks I should franchise."

"That's not what he said," Stinky countered severely. "Surely he said you *had* a franchise."

"Right, sorry, that's what he said."

"And your little mystery playmate has the brains to help you work up a business plan. Look how fast she came up with that blather about the bangles. Look at the way she got us out of the clutches of the Slugger and his orangutans. On the fly, with no time to think at all, she out-strategized both of us. And *I'm* smart."

"I'm not exactly used furniture myself."

"Let's not go over things we've already covered. Actually, you should be pleased, shouldn't you? Here I am, *extending* myself, going out of my way to offer you advice, when you know perfectly well that I don't care what you do."

Sometimes the word *insufferable* just falls short. "Thanks."

"That's settled, then. Why are you here?"

"You were going to give me a bunch of money yesterday."

He said, "Mmmmm."

"Mmmmm?"

"Mmm-hmm."

"Give me a vowel. Yes or no?"

He said, "Do you have the stamp?"

"I do."

"May I see it?"

"Sure." I backed away from him—Stinky's got fast hands—and fished it out of my pocket, sealed in a little baggie.

"Give it to me."

"Money."

"A closer look, then."

I clutched both sides of the baggie tightly enough to turn my knuckles white and said, "Grab it, and it'll tear. I'll make sure of it."

"Barbarian," Stinky said mildly. He brought his eyes within a few inches of the stamp and then nodded. "How much did we say?"

"*We* didn't say anything. I said fifty, you said forty-five, and I reluctantly agreed. With fifteen more due when the threat from the Slugger has been eliminated."

"Forty," he said.

"Stinky," I said, "you cease to interest me." I replaced the stamp in my pocket and turned to leave.

"Do you have another buyer?" he said, inadvertently presenting me with a bargaining chip.

I turned back to him. "I do."

He widened his eyes as much as the Botox would allow. "All the business we've done together. All the good times we've had, the laughs we've shared. Don't they *mean* anything to you?"

I said, "Not a whit."

"Who's the buyer?"

"Turnaround Dave."

He looked like he'd smelled something that didn't belong in a kitchen. "You're slumming."

"I don't know about you," I said, "but lately I've noticed that when I spend money, I rarely think about where I got it."

"Dave wouldn't know what to do with that stamp."

"Not really my problem, is it? I mean, once he pays me, it's not like I'll actually give a shit."

"Philistine," he said. "Football fan."

I said, "Forty-five. Now."

"Can't," he said. "I can do the forty. Madame Butterfly out there is charging me five to bury Jejomar."

I looked at him long enough that anyone *else* with a guilty conscience would have looked away, and then I nodded and let him think I'd fallen for it. "Fine," I said. "I believe you. Get the money." It's important to allow people small victories, especially when they know a lot of shooters.

"Right back," he said, and I used the time alone to call Louie.

"Still got the limo?" I asked.

"I only got it back around noon." Louie sounded aggrieved.

"Sorry. Feels longer. I'm going to need it tonight. Does it still have those hand-painted plates on it?"

"Like I said, I only got it back—"

"Good. Where can I pick it up?"

"The garage on Woodman."

"Okay. Be about an hour and a half."

"Take your time," he said. "It's been demographically established that around this time many of us eat dinner." He hung up just as Stinky came back in, a thick wad of money in his hand. I said, "Is that all of it, or do I need to count it?"

"You wound me," he said.

"Not yet I haven't." I reached out and took the bills. "*Now* I have."

"The stamp," he said.

"Later. And I know this is an outrage and I've betrayed you and all that, but this will get the Slugger off your back forever, and it will avenge Jejomar, and you're still going to get your damn stamp, but not until I'm through with it. Or, if you want, I could give you the stamp right now and forget all about the Slugger, forget all about Jejomar. He wasn't my houseboy, and I'm not the one whose name the Slugger knows. And as a last argument, have I ever promised you anything you didn't eventually get?"

He actually thought about it, the creep. "No."

"So. Want the stamp now, with the Slugger still out there and your conscience a single festering sore over Jejomar's death, or you want it later, with the Slugger gone and Jejomar able to rest in peace, knowing that his killer is in the big ditch?"

"Later," he said, but it cost him a lot. He put out a steadying hand and grasped the edge of the counter.

"Couple of days," I said, shoving the money into my pocket, "and all this will be over."

When I went out through the condo's front door, the wind almost blew me down.

PART FIVE

A HARDER DARKNESS

*And here come hired youths and maids
that feign to love or sin
In tones like rusty razor-blades to tunes like smitten tin.*
—Rudyard Kipling

(Not actually about Hollywood, but it might as well be.)

24

Reconciliation Cruise

Sitting behind the wheel, Ronnie said, "It's kind of a boat."

"Lookit all the mass you got," Louie said, as though he were trying to sell her on it, which in a sense he was. "You get into a one-on-one in this thing, you're the party's gonna walk away."

"She's not going to get into a one-on-one," I said, standing beside the open passenger door. "This is going to be a nice, uneventful evening." The wind slammed the car door closed, and I had to yank my hand back to keep all my fingers.

Ronnie said, "I didn't know you had hurricanes in California."

"Santa Ana," Louie said. "Blows down from the desert. The hills above Newhall have caught fire." He sniffed the air. "I could smell it a while ago. Anyway, a little wind shouldn't bother you. This baby, you couldn't blow it over with a water cannon."

"But it's so *wide*," she said, all eyes. "What happens if I scratch it?"

"Junior pays me." The wind stood his ponytail on end, making him look like a candle. "You don't worry about a thing—"

". . . little lady," Ronnie said, finishing the thought for him. "This is the kind of car, in Jersey they'd use it for a guy with his feet in a tub of cement."

I said, "Jersey?"

"Trenton, remember?" she said, with a smile that meant, *Gotcha.*

Louie said, "Cement?"

"It's a *joke*, guys."

"You say so." Louie shrugged, holding his ponytail down with both hands. "So. Gonna be okay?"

"Easy peasy," she said. "I was just catering to the male ego a little. Let's go, Junior."

I opened the door, and the wind snatched at it again, but I kept hold. "When the hell is this supposed to let up?" I asked.

Louie said, "Tomorrow."

"You can't go in there all superstitious," she said, heading south on Woodman toward Ventura. "It's just going to distract you."

"You sound like Herbie."

She took her eyes off the road and kept them on me long enough to make me fidget. "Really? Like *Herbie*? That may be the nicest thing you ever said to me."

I said, "Oh, don't be silly."

"Well, it might be. He's sort of your gold standard, isn't he?"

"I guess."

"You're pouting."

"I don't pout."

"Of course not. You know, I thought this was going to be sort of an . . . I don't know, a reconciliation cruise." She hung a right. "With music on the sound track and every-thing. 'My Heart Will Go On,' that kind of stuff."

Ventura was unnaturally empty, and at this rate we were going to get there in no time. I said, "How are you planning to go?"

"Would you ask a man that question?"

"Yes," I said. Then I said, "I don't know." Then I said, "Probably not."

"Well, I thought I'd take Beverly Glen up the hill and then Mulholland to—"

"Never mind," I said. "Fine."

"You are really, really jumpy."

"Yes," I said. "I am." We drove in silence for several blocks.

"You've done this before *how* many times?" She made a left, heading uphill.

"Who can count?"

"Oh, well," she said. "Are we going to have a talk?"

"This isn't a talk?"

"No, this isn't a talk. This is a dialogue between a responsible adult and a stunted child."

"I've already told you not to wait for me while I'm in there, haven't I?"

"You have."

The street steepened and began to curve, and I could feel my heart strumming away in both wrists and at the side of my neck. That *never* happened. I said, "Okay. I'm seriously spooked."

She took one hand off the wheel and put it on mine. "I'll wait for you." A car rocketed around the curve toward us with its brights on, and she put both hands on the wheel again.

"Absolutely not," I said. "Not even in the general neighborhood. Go down to San Vicente or someplace where there are a lot of restaurants and eat something. If this is what I think it is, which is a setup of some kind, I don't want you getting snagged in it, too. It's bad enough that I had you drive me."

"I helped last time."

I said, "There's a turn coming up on the right. Would you make it, please, and then pull over?"

She did, and when the car had been put in park, on an appealingly dark stretch of curb, I slid over and wrapped my arms around her. "You saved my ass," I said, my mouth moving against the tickle of her fine golden hair. "*That's* what I should have been talking about that night. No one, not even Herbie, ever pulled me out of the fire like that. In fact, you were brilliant all night long." I kissed her, and she gave a lot of it back. "Stinky says I should go into business with you."

"You were doing great there for a minute or two," she said, sitting back. "Leave Stinky out of it and leave the future to the future. Are you seriously telling me that you're scared to do this job but that you have no alternative?"

"Yes."

"Okay, then let's do this. I'll drive back and forth, east and west on Mulholland, just four or five minutes away. You leave your phone on, and I'll leave mine on. Anything at all that goes wrong, you say 'Mayday' and I come on the hop. If you're not out front, I pancake another gate. If I have to drive this tank, might as well get some use out of it."

I said, "Okay. On one condition. If I tell you to get the

hell out of there, you do it. No hesitation, no heroics. You just peel off and take the car back to Louie. Deal?"

She pulled her purse out from between us. "Here," she said, extricating a length of rubbery wire. "It's a single earbud. Plug it into the phone. That way you'll be able to hear me talking to you but no one else will, and you'll have an ear free for the house. I'm going to be listening until we're together again. If you need to talk about anything, ask advice, call for help, I'll be on the line."

"And if I'm in serious trouble and I don't think it's a good time even to whisper, I'll push a key and hold it down. When you hear that, disconnect and go away. Go away fast."

She looked at me, but I knew she wasn't actually seeing me. She was running scenarios in her head. Then she shrugged. "Will do," she said. "Am I allowed to wish you good luck?"

I put my arms around her again and marveled at the way we fit together. I kissed her hair, then her forehead, then the tip of her nose, and then her lips. "Hell yes," I said.

25

Piece of Cake

I could smell the distant fire, feel it in the back of my throat.

The street on which Granger lived was rich in eucalyptus trees, their topmost branches clawing at the sky as the wind whipped them around, making a sound like a waterfall. The smoke was a sharp edge in the air, just another little something to bring the hairs on the back of my neck to attention. The animal reaction to fire may be harder to awaken in people than it was, say, a thousand years ago, but it still had all its potency, and it was just the spark needed to bring the black stew of my anxiety to a boil. It seethed and bubbled in the center of my chest.

From where I stood at the curb, looking back at the long curve of the street, only one house was visible; up here in the hills of gold, the homes were squared away on huge lots, hidden behind daunting fences aimed partly at people like me and partly at tourists and other lookie-loos. This was a street of gates.

Before punching up the code to Granger's gate, before doing *anything* that would commit me, even emotionally, to the break-in, I waited at the curb until Ronnie's taillights disappeared around the corner that would take her up to Mulholland, where she'd be just one more black Town Car in a neighborhood of black Town Cars. The car had already served its primary purpose in delivering me to the gate. If anyone could get out of a car on this street without drawing a curious stare from a neighbor, it would be because he arrived in a limo.

The way Granger had explained the alarm system to me, it was rococo in its complexity, and I was about to breach the weakest and easiest of its perimeters. Five digits punched into the keypad mounted on a shiny brass pole at the level of a driver's window would slide the gate aside. It was heavy steel, on deep runners, and it snicked into a reinforced vertical slot when closed. I thought it was unlikely that Ronnie could flatten it even with the Town Car. I took a deep breath and then another, looked up and down the block, and keyed the numbers into the pad. The gate slid noiselessly to the left, and I said into the phone, "I'm going in."

"I'm with you," Ronnie said. "And listen, while you've got nothing to do, I don't just have . . . um, regard for you. I love you like crazy."

I stepped over the gate's track and stopped, looking up at the house, which was even bigger than I'd expected.

She said, "Are you there?"

"I'm here. Listen, if there was a Guinness World Cup˙ for Reciprocity, I'd win it."

"The Guinness World Cup for Reciprocity," she said. "If it's engraved, it'd have to be a pretty big cup."

"I reciprocate like mad," I said. "It's kicking things off that gives me the willies."

"I'll bask in the warm glow of your reciprocity and let you get to work. Can you smell the fire, too?"

"Sharp as a razor, red as a pomegranate."

"I'll be listening for you," she said.

I tapped the earplug as a kind of farewell and heard the gate slide home behind me. It took a different combination, keyed into a pad just inside the house's front door, to open it again, and the front door itself had a ten-digit key, seven of which were punched in outside and the remaining three inside, within ten seconds of closing the door. None of the windows could be opened without keying in yet another code—a different one for each of the three floors—from the inside. In other words, as far as getting in was concerned, the windows were an invitation to go directly to the police station, because that's where all the alarms actually sounded, and Granger had told me that response was generally within a span of about eight minutes.

And that was the *easy* part. When you finally got inside, it got complicated.

The house rose up in front of me like Xanadu in *Citizen Kane*, but less welcoming and minus the single lit window. A central tower, with a spiral of small windows climbing it, stretched upward the full three stories, and the two wings sloped back symmetrically with an unintentionally aeronautical effect. It would have been almost comically imposing if I weren't scared senseless. There was nothing funny in its sheer blunt mass, its hulking outline a harder darkness imposed upon a dark sky. Bits of it seemed to shimmer and shift as moonlight flickered its way through the dancing eucalyptus limbs, throwing moving shadows on the walls. Nice, malevolent little special effect. Taken as a whole, it looked like the kind of place where there'd be drains in the cellar to make it easier to clean up after the servants were bled out.

The front door stood twenty or thirty yards from the gate. Granger had told me to stick to the driveway, which was covered in gravel that crunched loudly underfoot. The lawn, he'd said, had sensors that when tripped lit up the place like a football stadium. The hiss and whoosh of the wind pretty much drowned out the sound of my footsteps, but even so I had to fight the impulse to move to the grass, where I could walk silently.

When Ronnie had asked me how many times I've done this before, I'd hurried over the answer, as though it were beyond computation, but it wasn't. More than twenty years in the trade, so to speak, and let's say twenty jobs a year, averaging in the higher numbers during the first four or five years, when I didn't know what to steal and how to sell it. Later, as my eye improved, the need was less frequent. Then add in the so-called practice runs I'd done in my teens, when I didn't take anything, when the victory was in getting in and getting out again. There were probably fifty of those, and after a while I'd started a spreadsheet to keep track of what I cunningly called my B-points, *B* being a sixteen-year-old's code for *burglary*. I gave myself points for elegance, for quickness, for invisibility—the traces, or lack thereof, of my having been in a place—and later, as I got better, for difficulty and the estimated value of the swag I left behind. When, with some embarrassment, I'd told Herbie about my point system, he'd nodded approval. "Pretty much the things you oughta be thinking about," he'd said. "Now, burn all that shit before anyone else sees it."

So let's say four hundred fifty in-and-outs, without ever getting nabbed. Why the hell was this one making my knees so shaky? My knees were *never* shaky.

Kid, Herbie said, *don't go in.*

It stopped me. Not the fact that Herbie was talking to me, even though he was dead, because he did that all the time. It was the fact that he'd said, *Don't go in.* He'd never said that before.

"I've got to," I said. I said it silently, so you couldn't have heard it if you'd been there, but then you wouldn't have heard Herbie either. "If I don't, I'm screwed."

Figure that out later, Herbie said. *Like I told you a hunnert times. One thing at a time. Figuring out not to go into this house, you can do that right now. Figuring out what happens later—you can do that later.*

This was the second time in a few minutes I'd been advised to focus on the present. So I did for a moment or two. I considered *not* going in, and every time I did, I saw the not-very-appealing face of Officer Biehl and thought about going to jail. That was enough to force me to start walking again. I'd gotten halfway to the house, and it looked even taller and grimmer. And then, just as I was about to dismiss Herbie's arguments for good—he was, after all, dead and probably a wishful figment of my paranoia—a light snapped on behind a big picture window on the left, which my memory of the floor plans told me was the living room.

"Right," I said out loud to Herbie. "I'll figure it out later."

As I turned to go, lights came on in two other windows: one to the right of the front door—part of Granger's office suite—and one in what was probably the second-floor drawing room, in the left wing. They snapped on simultaneously, so if it was a single person, he or she had *very* long arms. I pressed the little button on my watch and got a pale blue 9 P.M.

Nine. It wasn't even a full week since daylight saving time had made its final curtsy and tiptoed over the horizon. Back then it had been getting dark at this time. People with timers on their lights tend to set them bang on the hour or the half hour. (Note to homeowners: Set yours at very odd times and in clusters, so that groups of two or more come on about a minute apart. We'll be miles away before the next one clicks on.)

So it was just timers that hadn't been changed.

Timers I could deal with.

The house loomed above me as though it were leaning forward a little to see me better, as I ignored Herbie's urgent *tsk-tsk-tsk* in my mind's ear and made for the front door. I knew the interior layout as well as anyone can possibly know a house he hasn't actually been in, I knew what I was after, I knew where to pick up some bonus goods that could be fenced safely and anonymously, even without involving Stinky, and I knew that the guy who owned the place wouldn't even land until midnight or so.

Optimism on demand: this was going to be a piece of cake. A quick look around to make sure it was empty, grab some of Granger's jewelry, all the while doing light-hearted, witty *Thin Man* banter on the phone with Ronnie, get the Turner last because it'll be heavy, take a final bow, and exit.

There, *that* was the frame of mind I needed. I mean, come on, four hundred fifty times? I punched in the seven-digit code, listened for the click, and opened the door, and as I did so, a gust of wind practically blew me across the threshold. But it didn't, and I preserved my sangfroid, which, I suddenly remembered, is defined as "composure or coolness, sometimes excessive, as shown in danger or under trying circumstances."

I closed the door behind me and punched in the three-digit confirmation code. The door clicked again, and something that sounded heavier than a guillotine blade fell into place inside the door. Note to self: Do not attempt to shoulder the door open. No matter what's behind you or how fast it is, punch in the code carefully and precisely, and when you're on the outside, whatever the hell made that noise will be between you and your pursuer. I turned and took my first look around.

The hallway had vaulted ceilings and had been painted a dark terra-cotta. Since the only available light was coming from the lamp on the other side of the garage-width archway into the living room, it was pretty dim. To my right, a hall stretched off toward that wing of the house, which, I knew from the floor plan Granger had given me and the builder's plans Anime and Lilli had found, housed an enormous home-office suite—an actual office, a secretarial space, and a casual den—plus a "fun room" with a soda fountain and one whole wall of transparent drawers filled with different kinds of candy, a china room, which I was assuming held dinnerware rather than an actual piece of the Middle Kingdom, a gift room, whatever that was, and three guest suites, each with bedroom, sitting room, and full bath. All of that, plus kitchen, dining room, breakfast room, and a few more guest suites in the other wing, was on the first floor. The Turner was in the den of Granger's home office.

There were no lights on in the long hallway into the wing on the right, and the door was closed to the room in Granger's office suite where the light in the window had

come on, the room that housed the Turner. I knew from
the plans that the hall elbowed back at about a thirty-
degree angle just past the gift room, but it was too dark
down there to see the turning. The house was the biggest
I'd ever been in, big enough to have its own suburbs, and I
knew I wouldn't be able to hear someone moving around
in its Pacoima or Palmdale, but I was in its Beverly Hills,
which was to say the entrance hall and the living room,
plus the portion of the hall to my right before it angled
away, and that area was either empty or inhabited by very,
very quiet people. I extended my antennae, their acuity
developed over all these years of being in places where I
wasn't supposed to be, and sensed no one.

Still, I waited, mouth-breathing, until my heartbeat
had returned to normal. A couple of creaks, the kind of
incidental noises you'd expect in a cooling structure on a
windy evening, but nothing that made me want to reopen
the front door and run screaming into the night.

And then there *was* a noise, the sharp bang of something hard hitting something hard, a bit muffled but not
very far off, and since the entry hall was essentially an
echo chamber, I had no way of knowing what direction
it had come from. I invested two full minutes of complete
motionlessness, ears exploring all the directions I thought
were likely, and heard nothing more. Obviously, I couldn't
see any of the other rooms from where I was standing,
but thanks to a pair of floor-to-ceiling windows flanking
the door, I *could* see a slice of outside. I slid my feet over
to the right-hand window, put an eye against it, and saw
the culprit. Perhaps. A eucalyptus branch had come down,
taking with it a good-size birdhouse on a pole, which had
slammed into the brick edge of a reflecting pool. *Hence,*

I thought, *bang*. I tried to remember whether I'd seen it when I was coming in, but I'd been watching the lighted windows and probably wouldn't have registered it. I took a deep, deep breath, flexed my shoulders and shook my head to loosen my neck muscles, and turned my attention back to the job at hand.

Judging from my view of the outside and from what I could see in here, especially the clash between the medieval vaulted ceiling in the entry hall, the Spanish-style arch that opened into the living room, and the 1970s hallway running off to the left, this was what I think of as a Stage Five Los Angeles house, which is to say built in the 1990s or later by people with more money than judgment, a grandiose self-image, and a limited frame of reference. The general principles seemed to be (1) make it better by making it bigger, (2) select the most garish aspects of three or four mismatched styles, (3) throw them together in the dark and take them however they land, and (4) spend money on visible surfaces and economize on dreary details like structural support and materials that can't be seen. *Bingo*, a monument to hubris for twenty or thirty years and a maintenance nightmare after that.

I gave it one last listen, turning slowly in a complete circle. Behind me, to the left, a curving stairway spiraled up to the second floor and possibly the third as well, hugging the wall of the tower. I went to its base and tilted my head upward, listening so hard I could hear the mosquito whine of my blood in my ears. Nothing.

I whispered into the phone, "I'm inside."

"How much time?"

"It's too big for twenty minutes. Half an hour at least."

"I'll start down toward you in about twenty-five

minutes if I haven't heard from you. Koreatown, here we come."

"Can't wait," I said. "Now, shhhhh."

"Shhhh yourself," she said, but then she was quiet.

"Here goes," I said, pretty much all breath. I slipped the phone back into my shirt pocket, suppressed an urge to cross myself, and moved through the entry hall toward the big arched entrance to the living room. My eyes had grown sufficiently accustomed to the darkness to let me see a framed drawing on the wall just to the left of the archway: two nineteenth-century British toffs in dark cloaks and top hats leaning forward on a dock to talk down to a boatman in a skiff, afloat on what was probably the Thames, most likely near Chelsea. James McNeill Whistler had made several quick sketches of a scene very much like this one, and I was looking at either a very good forgery or a part of the series. It was beautiful enough to make me pop a sweat but impossible to fence for anything like what it was worth, if it was genuine.

With my food-service gloves on, I felt secure in passing my fingertips lightly over it, looking, I suppose, for some faint residual warmth from Whistler's genius. It put off a nice buzz, the kind you might feel from the door of a humming refrigerator, that made me think it might be authentic. But it hadn't been among the pieces I'd been invited to take, and the last thing in the world I wanted to do was to discharge this wretched errand and *still* have something unresolved between Granger and me.

I had to take two steps down from the entry hall to go into the living room, and the shift in levels made me think again how much Granger had gone through to raise the floors two feet. He'd had to move the doors, the windows, the electrical, the heating and cooling ducts, and God only knew what else, all to make himself look a little bit taller. It spoke to his vanity, certainly, but more than that it represented a personality that essentially had been folded around, had been draped over, a core of obsession, a perspective that saw nothing untoward about spending hundreds of thousands of dollars and months of messy inconvenience to bring his head two inches closer to the ceiling when no one was likely ever to notice.

And if he could do that to his *floors*, just to satisfy his desire to control by an inch or two the way people saw him, what alterations would he impose upon his wife? She had to reflect him as he wanted to be reflected, had to look at him as he wanted to be looked at; she had to seem to be the kind of woman he wanted people to think he would marry. A huge leap, probably an impossible one, for a little girl who'd been turned out by her own parents, who'd never graduated from high school, who'd daydreamed and drawn horses when left to herself, who'd been humiliated week after week on national television. When he was through humiliating her, he'd needed her to redeem herself in the eyes of Hollywood; whatever her shortcomings as an actress, she couldn't be seen to have any as a wife, because she was Jeremy *Granger's* wife. She had to go with the house and the Whistler and the fucking Turner and all the other glittering trappings he'd spread about his throne to reflect his glory. And he'd bent her to the task mercilessly, using the full weight of that obsession and, certainly, the heat of the fury that I'd seen briefly in his eyes.

I asked myself how she'd stood it. On television she'd seemed frail enough to see a bright light through. Insubstantial, nowhere near enough mass, not enough steel to resist being shaped later into the terrified anorexic, shivering inside those designer gowns in the pictures Anime had rounded up for me.

Not for the first time, I thought how rewarding it would be to find a way to fuck up Jeremy Granger once and for all.

And here I was, in the very place that might give me an opportunity to do it.

The living room, with its single glowing lamp, was bright by comparison with the entry hall. Big enough for two high-school football teams to scrimmage in, it was a symphony in beige. Too much stuff: furniture, objects, bric-a-brac, framed pictures, that awful painted ceiling—it overwhelmed the eye, kept the gaze moving, almost in self-defense, until it struck a ravishing polychrome wood sculpture of the Madonna, probably Spanish from the seventeenth century, her robe the perfect blue we always hope the sky will be and never is, her eyes raised in sorrow to the sight, which the viewer supplied in his own mind's eye, of her son on the cross. Far, far too beautiful to belong to Granger, but not stealable because of its bulk, and even harder to fence than the Whistler drawing.

I was on my way through the room when *my* eye was snagged by a painting over the smaller of the room's two fireplaces. It actually made me break my stride. It depicted an elegantly coiffed woman in a pearl-covered stole whose body and tapering, prayerful hands might have been copied by a good modern craftsman from an old Flemish portrait. The face belonged to Suley Platz at her most beautiful, at the age of sixteen or so, before he'd turned her into a spectral mass of jitters. On an impulse I checked the painting above the other fireplace and found a similar treatment of Jeremy Granger, dressed in the lavish robes of a rich Flemish merchant. Putting the two of them together, they reminded me of nothing so much as the portraits of the rich donors who paid for the great altarpieces and who usually appeared in their own little panels, either gazing inward from the edges or looking up piously from the bottom at the work of genius their guilders had paid for. I've always thought of these as the world's earliest PBS underwriting credits and wondered whether Granger, who was not even a little bit stupid, had been making a private joke.

Jesus. Six minutes gone already, and a huge house in front of me.

The dining room boasted, according to Granger, four important, or at least expensive, paintings, and for that reason it was one of two rooms in the house protected by the most serious of the place's alarm systems, the other being the den, where the Turner resided. The company that had alarmed the house specialized in art museums, and to protect the works in these two rooms—which were apparently more valuable than the Whistler drawing—the company had installed full lockdown triggers and all the hardware that went with them.

The moment museum-security hardware senses that something is on the brink of being stolen, the problem ceases to be keeping someone out. It immediately becomes keeping the artwork *in*. Until recently, lockdown alarms had been triggered by mechanisms in the hanging apparatus, if the piece was a picture, or the pedestal on which a sculpture was mounted. If the piece was lifted when the alarm was engaged, the change in weight signaled a theft, and every door and window in the place slammed into lock mode. The insides of the doors leading out of the house sprouted new bolts. Bars shot across windows. There was no way out for either the artwork or the thief.

So thieves had taken the initiative, razoring canvases from their frames while using a support beneath the frame to prevent variations in the piece's weight. In response, the alarm companies and the museums together had decided that the simple *presence* of someone in a room full of irreplaceable art—when the room should have been unoccupied—was sufficient reason to lock things down and bring in the cops. That was the system Granger had mandated in those two rooms of his house.

When I'd asked him why he couldn't simply turn off the alarm while I was inside, he'd said the company's computers made a note whenever the alarms were shut down completely, as protection against a lawsuit: someone is burgled and sues the alarm company, and the first thing the alarm company does is check to see whether the system was turned off at the time of the theft. Granger's worry, and in his position it was one I would have had, too, was that Suley's lawyers would certainly suspect that he'd stolen the Turner himself. Any indication that the alarm had been out of commission would be a big deal in court.

In order to allow the owners of the house to move around without ringing all the bells and whistles, summoning the cops, and causing a lot of embarrassment, there was a two-step override procedure for those two rooms, and it went as follows: Before entering a lockdown-armed room, I was to step on the square of flooring to the immediate left of the door, which had a pressure plate beneath it, listen for a faint click, and then go into the room. Next to the door would be an electrical switch plate with five normal-looking light switches on it. The fifth from the door would be in the down position, and I was to flip it up. That completed the override operation for the room I would be in, allowing me to walk into that room without setting off alarms triggered by other pressure plates beneath its floor and steal everything in sight for a space of twenty minutes. At the end of that time or when I left, I had to remember to flip the switch back down or the system would remind me with a series of buzzes, like a fancy refrigerator that's been left open. If I did remember to hit the switch when I was finished, the room would silently rearm two minutes later.

I'd have to go through all this foolery to get the picture with no record of a system shutdown.

There was nothing I actually wanted in the dining room, but it presented me with the only chance I could think of to make sure the override worked, simply because it was the alarmed room closest to a mode of escape, which was to say the front door. If there was a problem with the override mechanism—if the house would go into lockdown anyway, regardless of whether the steps were followed or not—I desired fervently not to be the person who discovered it without a prearranged exit.

After another glance at my watch, I moved quickly to the front door, keyed in the "open" code, and pulled it ajar. For insurance I dragged a beautiful old English rosewood coat rack, its wood stolen from the now almost barren hardwood forests of Southeast Asia, in between the door and the frame as a doorstop, and then hotfooted it back through the living room to the entry to the dining room, where I stepped on the plate, listened for the click, went through the arch, flipped up the appropriate switch, and trotted through the entire room, pausing in front of a very nice impressionist pastel and even jumping up and down a little, to see whether all hell would break loose. When it didn't, I returned the switch to its original position, counted to fifty to be on the safe side, and went back to the entry hall to replace the coat rack and close the door.

Okay. I knew how everything worked, and it had taken me eight minutes. Twenty-two minutes to go and all the *real* work still in front of me.

Moving as quickly as I could without making noise, with my penlight providing nice, focused, directional illumination, I bypassed the dining room via a center hallway and went into the kitchen, which had more counter space than my apartment at the Wedgwood had square feet. It was empty, as was the breakfast room between it and the dining room I'd already checked out. Nothing worth bagging in either room. I knew there was a big pantry off the kitchen and that the door at the far end of the pantry led to a stairway down into the basement, unusual in a Los Angeles house.

I don't like basements in general, and when I got down into Granger's, I didn't like his either. Just an enormous space, maybe 6,000 square feet, with a cement floor, a huge gravity furnace, piles of retired furniture, and dozens of yards of plumb-straight shelves full of lightbulbs, cleaning junk, electrical components, tools, hoses, some painting supplies with their own ladder. Four six-shelf IKEA units were jammed sloppily with scripts, more dreams that wouldn't come true. No area had stains that looked as if servants had been bled out there.

Of course, not all violence is physical. I had only twenty minutes left when I checked my watch on the stairs back up to the kitchen, so I decided to skip searching the guest suites. I'd pass by them in the hallway and hit the rooms that made up Granger's office, including the den with the purported Turner in it.

Out of the pantry quickly, ease through a pair of doors with only about a foot between them, the dead space meant to shield the ears of the exalted slumberers in the suites from the proletarian sounds and smells of food being cooked, dishes being washed by people speaking Spanish or Cambodian or whatever Granger's part-time help spoke. No point in reminding the guests that there were people in the world who didn't sleep in beds on which the sheets were changed every day by workers the guests never saw, whose voices the house was designed to silence.

Down through the hallway of those anointed ones I passed, moving on the balls of my feet, listening for all I was worth. With the penlight off, the only light was the faintest of moon shimmers through the open doors to the suites, already filtered through screens and smoked glass and semi-sheer curtains that seemed to be organdy. The entire wing felt empty, and it certainly *sounded* empty, except for a recurrent dry scratching—long fingernails on the inside of a crypt? teeth on bone?—that I quickly recognized as bushes scraping back and forth against the window screens at the command of the wind. Ahead of me I could see a pale oblong of light where the hall angled to the right, back toward the entryway and the living room with its solitary lamp.

Just for the hell of it, I looked into the candy room long enough to grab a couple of chocolate truffles by Knipschildt, $2.50 each for about an ounce and a half of candy and usually pretty far beyond my reach. Not bad, I thought, with my mouth full, for $20-a-pound chocolate, but of course, that was the *point*, to waste more money than most people would ever see, to eat cake, as poor, dim Marie Antoinette had when the people had no bread, and to revel in it. Marie Antoinette at least had the virtue of having been clueless. I ran through a quick mental survey of the very rich through history as the chocolate found its way into my system, and except for supporting artists and painters and starting the occasional public-library system, it seemed to me they didn't amount to much more than a modest hill of toxic mold. Generation after generation of voracious swine, generally more belly than brain, whose idea of trickle-down was urinating on the faces of the poor.

The china room was, unsurprisingly, a hymn to china, much of it hand painted and heavily trimmed in gold. I spotted nine full services for eight, six of them Limoges, complete with tureens, heavy salad bowls, and serving platters, plus shelves upon shelves of Baccarat, Lalique, and Waterford crystal. It was kept out here, the door to the corridor open, to be seen, and even someone at my raggedy end of the economic spectrum knew that setting it out for show was a *lot* less classy than putting it behind cabinet doors, where it belonged.

I whispered into the phone, "This is not a healthy environment."

"You want out?"

"You're still there," I said, smiling in the dark.

"Knucklehead," she said. "Yes or no?"

"Yes, but not yet. Stay within a mile or two, though, so I can scream when I can't take any more."

"Will do."

"Duty calls."

The gift room couldn't have been called anything else. The far end was a tidy pile of wrapped packages, perhaps a hundred of them, with personal little color-coded Post-its on them reading MALE, FEMALE, SPORTS FAN, D-LIST, ASSISTANT, ASSHOLE, TALENT, BLOW-OFF, and a few less generic reminders: WATCH (HIM), WATCH (HER), SUNGLASSES, and so forth. One long wall was taken up by a wrapping table with huge spools of ribbon hanging at one end and rolls and rolls of tape at the juncture of the table and the wall. Seasonal and generic paper hung from thick rolls down all four walls, and the floor opposite the wrapping table was literally knee-deep in flat, precreased boxes that could be snapped into three dimensions in a moment or two. They ranged from little tidy ones—for jewelry, I supposed—to some that were four and five feet long.

It is not more blessed to give than to receive, if this is the way you give.

Of the three rooms in the office suite, the den with the painting in it was the farthest from the entry hall and the only one with a shutdown alarm. So I skipped it, figuring to get the Turner on the way out, and went into the main office, just to take a look. Big and buttery, full of very nice nineteenth-century furniture, none of which looked like it had been dragged out of some prop room. The moment this thought crossed my mind, I realized that my first impulse had been correct: that clumsy piece of Victorian duff in the studio office had been put there solely for my benefit. It was a set piece in the little scene Granger had cast me in. He'd allowed me an easy swipe through a bunch of potential film treatments to convince me that he was indeed considering Jake's magnum opus. It was a way of soothing my feelings so I wouldn't be pissed off enough at being made a fool of that I'd turn down his offer. For all he knew, I was sufficiently hotheaded to tell him to go fuck himself. He would have gained nothing by putting me in jail, and he wanted to make sure I wouldn't be intransigent, so he'd gamed me. Successfully.

I said, out loud, "Son of a bitch."

"Someone there?" Ronnie said in my ear.

"No, no. Just undergoing an ego adjustment."

"Come on," she said. "I can see the flames across the Valley from here, and I don't like it."

"Ten minutes," I said. "And then I'm finished with King Maybe."

Famous last words.

26
Made of Sand

I'd seen the elevator indicated on the floor plan, but it had slipped my mind. There it was, though, in the far right corner of the office, bigger and more modern than the one at Farscope. In a laborsaving frame of mind, I pushed the button, and the door slid silently and obediently open.

Sure enough, the buttons said it went up to the third floor. From my recollection of the layout, that meant it would open directly into the third-floor room where Granger had put his serenity boulders and rock garden. I thought for half a second about going up there just long enough to pee on one of his boulders, but it seemed a little too big-dog to give me any real satisfaction. Also, a new method of developing DNA info from urine is high on the law-enforcement hit parade, so I just pushed 2.

The true sound of money is silence. The elevator was so quiet and gentle that I was almost unprepared, when the doors opened, to find myself on a different floor. But the real surprise was the room the doors opened into. It was from another world, the first truly nondescript room I'd seen in the house, a sort of third-string everything room with two economy couches, a couple of cheap tables, and some mismatched chairs. Unread copies of crap books leaned any old way on the shelves. The walls were hung with the kind of badly framed kitsch people buy on outings to Marin County and Cape Cod. It took me a blank, openmouthed moment to realize it was a museum of the past he had decided never to return to, a kind of memento mori to remind him that things that float can also sink. He rode that elevator every day from his all-butter office to the rancid margarine of his past.

The room's sad, musty gravitation slowed me down for a moment. This was the past that kept the shark swimming forward.

Since I have a fundamentally devious mind, it also occurred to me that this cut-rate clipping from his earlier life would be a great place to hide something deeply, unusually valuable, and I made a note to give it full attention for a couple of minutes on my way out.

Stepping into the corridor outside, I turned left and found myself on the landing for the circular stairway, ascending from the first floor and twisting on up to the third. To the right, the landing opened into an enormous double-door room that had a highly polished wooden floor and furniture almost pasted to the walls in that way that says "dancing," and on the far side of the landing was the hall that led to the second story of the left wing, the ground floor of which I hadn't had the time to explore. A splash of parchment-yellow light fell through an open door thirty or forty feet down the hall, the second-floor drawing room where the other lamp had come on when the timers ticked into place.

Beyond that I knew I'd find the two bedroom suites, three rooms each, claimed by the master and mistress of the domain, his (of course) bigger than hers. His was the one closer to the stairs, and in the anteroom directly off the hallway, he'd said, he had a small, relatively cheap jewelry safe, probably as hard to open as a drugstore diary, containing around $60,000 in second-tier jewelry that I had been invited to pocket. I approached it, pausing long enough for a really comprehensive listen before I reached the lit open door of the drawing room. I heard nothing at all until a giant *whuff* of wind gave the front of the house a huge slap before it divided and whistled around the sides, and I cloaked myself in the noise and hurried past, to the door leading to Granger's suite.

When I opened it, I was surprised to find not the cramped little foot-wiping demi-closet I usually equate with anterooms but a big, open, L-shaped space that was lined with literally dozens of framed color photographs, mostly eleven by fourteen inches, immediately recognizable as studio shots: Granger on the sets of his various series and movies, usually modestly seated in the middle of a bunch of standing actors and production principals, or else standing with most of *them* sitting.

Just out of curiosity, I skimmed them until I came face-to-face with Suley in her Tasha Dawn incarnation, in a row of pictures positioned obscurely below eye level in a not very well illuminated corner. Not exactly pride of place for the mistress of the house. In one shot, obviously taken early in the series, she stood beaming, thrilled, heart-breakingly young, beside a seated Granger, surrounded by crew members, actors playing executive zombies in full makeup, and the handsome alive guy, who was—as he almost always seemed to be—shirtless. In another shot, clearly staged, she was going over script pages, looking older and less sure of herself, while cast members and crew gathered around trying to seem interested. Granger was sitting across a small table from her, and looking over his shoulder at her was—

Why was I wasting time on this?

The little safe was just behind the door, where it wouldn't be visible to someone who'd pushed the door open to peek in. It took me about thirty seconds to pop the lock, and I was shoveling glitter into my pocket when time stopped.

I was looking at my plastic-gloved left hand on the safe, at the open door of the safe, at the useless, ugly, expensive bangles, perhaps stolen from Ronnie's mythical father, that were still inside the safe, but what I was *seeing* was a short upper lip beneath a pug nose, eyes too close together, and the concentrated expression of someone who's long grown used to the fact that most conversations go too fast for him.

At the guy who'd been looking at Tasha over Granger's shoulder in the photograph.

I knew who it was, I was *certain* I knew who it was, but I went back and looked anyway. He was still there, wearing the fade-into-the-background costume of a two- or three-line cast member.

Officer Biehl.

An *actor*. The brass legend on the picture frame said DEAD EYE, SEASON TWO. I'd only watched shows from the first year, but I'd undoubtedly seen him in other stuff.

I'd *known* in Granger's office that I'd seen him before. An actor, in a studio full of actors, in a studio that produced several cop series, that probably owned a whole fucking fleet of police cars, complete with functional cherry lights.

I realized what had been out of focus when Biehl, or whatever his name was, had been in the office: Granger had kept calling him "Officer" and he hadn't been corrected, even though Biehl was wearing a sergeant's badge.

Cops don't take rank lightly, given the crap they have to shovel to earn it.

I had the weightless, unanchored feeling I associate with nitrous oxide. Granger had nothing on me. I was free to stuff my pockets, spray-paint his goddamn Turner, and walk out of there, free as a bird. The only person who'd seen me there was "Officer Biehl," and what was he going to do? Confess to impersonating a cop? For that matter, how much of Granger's monologue about owning the Culverton Police Department was true? It had been persuasive because "Officer Biehl" had backed it up, even volunteered some of it.

I thought, *It can't be this easy.* Distrusted it all the way to the soles of my shoes.

I was experiencing the unsettling sense I sometimes have in dreams, that everything around me is made of sand and that all it would take is one sharp push to reduce the solid world to a collapsing beach castle, leaving me in a flat, dark space without a landmark in any direction.

"I'm coming out," I said into the phone. I could hear my heart beating against the earbud. I'd gone back to the safe and was grabbing another handful of jewelry.

"On my way," Ronnie said.

"It's a fix," I said to her as I went out into the corridor. I wasn't even lowering my voice. "The whole thing is a setup." I came up to the open door into the upstairs drawing room, stopped talking out of habit, slowed, then started past it.

But this time I looked in.

This time I saw her.

There was a click on the phone, and standing there numbly, swaying as though I were hanging from a hook, I said automatically, "Hold on," and pushed the button to take the call. I was trying to turn what I was seeing into something else, *anything* else, when Anime shrilled, "*Machiavelli!*"

Around the stone in my throat, I said, squinting at the drawing-room floor, "What . . . what about Machiavelli?"

"Mach One and Mach Two," she said as I moved unwillingly but irresistibly through the door. "Mach One is the Prince, Mach Two is the Princess."

I said, "I can't talk now," and hung up.

She'd been beaten to death.

From the waist down, Suley was on a thick pastel carpet, and from the waist up she was on a dark hardwood floor. One hand was extended to within a few inches of an overturned table—the sound I'd heard and written off to the wind. With a surge of heart-shriveling self-loathing, I realized that she'd been alive when I came in. She'd tried to call me to her.

She was curled onto one side, her knees drawn up, like a child with a stomach ache trying to find a position that doesn't hurt. Except for a cut on her left cheekbone, her face was unmarked, but the blood on her neck and shoulders said she'd been hit repeatedly with the heavy silver candlestick that lay beside her on the floor.

I was bending over her, hoping to detect a breath, when I suddenly registered the soft click I'd heard as I rushed into the room. I straightened galvanically, leaping toward the light switches. *Three* lockdown rooms, that son of a bitch, not two. *Three.*

I'd gotten less than halfway to the electrical plate when the whole house seemed to shudder, and then from every direction came a heavy clank that sounded like the thing that had clamped down inside the front door, multiplied by a hundred. I ran to the window to the left of the fireplace just in time to see four thick iron bars thrust their way from top to bottom.

Lockdown.

27

Not One Damsel in Distress

Eight minutes.

He'd said the cops could get there in eight minutes.

Of course, literally everything he'd told me had been a lie. Might be eight minutes, might be four, might be twenty. But I had to work with something, so I chose eight.

I was bending over her, holding a finger just beneath her nostrils—I realized belatedly that I'd said "Excuse me" when I extended the finger—trying to feel the warmth of a breath. With my other hand, I set the timer on my watch for eight minutes.

No breath.

No pulse.

Damn, damn, damn, damn.

Okay, I thought, backing off mentally in the interest of not going to pieces and looking at the setup with a professional eye, *good job*. I'd walked into the ideal setup, the only thing he'd been after from the start: burglar, dead woman, weapon of opportunity, otherwise empty house, locked down, cops coming fast. Seeing it that way, it was pretty close to perfect. He'd gotten rid of his wife, she'd never spill anything to anyone about their lives, he was free as a bird, and the burglar was looking at life for murder during the commission of a felony.

All wrapped up for the jury.

And, I thought, the hell with me. What about *Suley*?

I said, out loud, "This can't be permitted."

Seven minutes, forty seconds.

When I was eighteen years old, my father announced that he was coming back to us and we were going to be a family again. The prospect of the reunion drove me to rent a little shack in Topanga Canyon, smuggle my stuff out of my mother's house, and move in, all alone on my mountain. It immediately became apparent that I was *not* alone there, that in fact I shared it with a global convention of rats.

My second day there, I bought two big rat traps, baited them with peanut butter, and went to bed. I dropped off and slept for what felt like thirty minutes, and then heard a WHACK like a pistol shot. It wouldn't have been any louder if it had been caused by someone slapping my face.

I lay there, bouncing to the tom-tom in my chest until it was drowned out by the wood of the trap banging against the living-room floor. Then it scraped. Then it banged again. It seemed obvious to me that the rat was out there, in my new living room, dying in agony.

The only manly, self-respecting thing to do was to get up, go out there, and bring the situation to a merciful end. I summoned my courage and learned a valuable lesson: *it doesn't always come when you call it*. As a lower-impact alternative, I piled the pillows and blankets over my head and stayed that way until it got light. And when I finally ventured into the living room, I found the trap empty except for about two inches of tail trapped beneath the hammer, chewed through by a rat who had no intention of dying.

Sitting there beside Suley, I said, "Me neither."

Seven minutes and twenty seconds.

So. The cops were on their way, and Granger's script called for them to find the body and her murderer, standing around shifting pointlessly from foot to foot. The only thing to do was make us *both* disappear. What could possibly thwart Granger more completely than to send the cops into a nice, neat, empty house: nothing missing, no burglar, no murder victim, no trace of violence? He'd have a houseful of cops and no idea in the world what was happening.

No trace of violence. I could take care of that—well enough at least to stand up to visual scrutiny—while I thought about hiding places. I got up fast.

The door that I'd assumed would lead to a bathroom opened instead onto something even better, a linen closet. That was such an odd enough place for one that I decided it had been *intended* as a bathroom until, late in the building process, someone realized there were no linen closets. Linen closets weren't a priority for a guy who used a whole room to display his china. Can't kindle a lot of envy with a linen closet.

I grabbed a blanket and four hand towels, closed the door, and went back to her.

"Please forgive me," I said. I straightened her legs and her trunk—she was still pliable, she was still warm, she'd only recently gone into the other room, forever. When I had her straightened out, I opened the blanket on the floor beside her and rolled her onto it. There was a lot of blood in her hair.

Beneath her, open and facedown, was a book. It was a children's book, big and brightly colored with a picture on the cover of a young woman in nineteenth-century costume aboard what looked like a pirate ship. The title was *Not One Damsel in Distress: World Folktales for Strong Girls.* My inward breath caught and felt for a moment like a sob, and I swallowed it, sniffed hard, and thought, *Later. First let's find a way to fuck this guy up.*

I picked up the book and placed it on her chest, straight as I could, then folded the blanket neatly over her. I said, "This won't be for long, honest," and then I got to my feet so I could look at the bloodstains. While I was up there, I righted the table and picked up the candlestick.

There was blood and hair on the base. It was Georgian, massive, sterling, sharp-cornered. Judging from the weight, the base had probably been filled solidly with bronze, which is heavier than iron. He'd grabbed it by the slender upright and used the sharp-cornered base as a club. The top half was clean and bright.

I took the candlestick and two of the hand towels and ran across the hallway and into a bathroom, where I scrubbed the silver clean and rubbed it dry. Then I soaked the hand towels and wrung them out so they wouldn't leave a drip pattern and ran back into the drawing room.

She'd bled only on the dark wood; the carpet was clean. I dropped the wet, folded towels onto the blood pattern and used my feet and my weight to scrub the floor clean, turning and refolding the towels twice. Then I put down a dry towel and rubbed it briskly over the damp part of the floor. When I turned it over, there was only a shade of pink on the white cloth, a blush. I backed up to get a broader view of the floor. I rolled the damp towels in the dry ones, studying the scene.

Good enough. Obviously, the blood would show up when and if the cops used luminol, but equally obviously, there was no visible reason to use luminol in this room, at least not tonight. By the time they finished with the first floor and got up here, the cops would believe that the whole thing was an alarm malfunction. The room looked as peaceful as Easter except for Suley, folded in her blanket, and a flipped-back corner of the carpet where he'd probably caught a toe on it, coming in . . .

And there it was in front of me, all of it at the same time, as it had probably happened: her, sitting in that armchair, reading some story about a strong young woman, the chair turned toward the dark fireplace, him coming through the door in stockinged feet and with gloves on, reaching for the candlestick, snagging his toe under the carpet and making a noise, her jumping to her feet, seeing him, knowing beyond any doubt what it meant. Trying to get around him—that was why she was mostly off the carpet—him sidestepping to cut her off, bringing the candlestick down and then down again and, probably, again.

And then his nerve had failed him slightly, so perhaps he was partly human after all. He'd decided, wishfully, that she was dead and then bolted before making sure.

I had five minutes and forty-three seconds.

Where? Three stories, 34,000 square feet, where could I put her? Where could I put myself?

Big house. Big air-circulating systems. Big intake vents.

I pulled a couch from the wall and looked behind it, and there it was, just above the baseboard, maybe fourteen inches square, with an old-fashioned metal grate over it. There would be a filter pad about a foot up. I could push the pad up, ease Suley into the vent, then go in myself at the diagonal, feetfirst, shoving myself back until we were out of sight, pray that the duct held, pull the grate into place again, and then flip the filter down, making us invisible. Except—

Except that the grate didn't pop out or in. It was secured with a screw at each corner. No way to close it from inside.

I heard distant sirens. Maybe half a mile, three-quarters of a mile off.

Jesus, *Ronnie*. I'd never talked to her again after Anime called.

I shoved the couch into place and pulled out the phone. Pushed the button to reconnect, and there she was.

"Something's gone wrong, hasn't it?" she said. "I'm a few minutes from you—"

"*No*. Go away, don't come. I can't talk. Just go somewhere and wait for my call."

"But I—"

"I know. But goodbye, and don't get *near* this place."

"I'll be waiting." She hung up.

"Thank you," I said reflexively, although I knew she was gone. I reached over and centered the candlestick on the table, just to be doing something, and listened to the sirens getting louder.

Five minutes and seven seconds. Hopeless, except. *Except*. I pushed speed dial for Anime.

"It's really *sick*," she said. "What that girl is doing—"

"*Don't talk*. Listen. Granger's alarm company, Armstrong something—"

"Hepworth," she said.

"Armstrong Hepworth. I need to know what happens

when a house goes into lockdown. It must be something they promote on their site, how hard it is to get through it in either direction—"

"Lilli!" she shouted. "Armstrong Hepworth, lockdown mode, *now*!"

"The specific question is, who can get in? How hard is it to get in? Call me when you know."

I hung up, ransacking the house in my mind's eye, both the parts I'd been in and the areas I'd seen only in the builder's drawings and then the drawings for modifications, beginning with the basement, thinking about going down there to see, maybe there was room in the gravity heater, *although if I were a cop I'd check in the gravity heater*, but there might be something else down there, and did the elevator go all the way down to the . . .

The elevator.

The elevator.

Sirens louder now. A couple of minutes away.

The *elevator*.

And I was running, leaving Suley behind for the moment, running on nothing but hope because I didn't have anything else, out of the room and into the hall, barreling down the circular staircase, taking the steps three at a time and keeping away from the spiral of windows, and then I was sprinting down the central hall on the ground floor and through the kitchen into the pantry and down the stairs, losing it a quarter of the way down and landing with all my weight on my right knee on the edge of a stair, feeling an explosion of pain, as if every nerve in my body had gathered there to say hi to the stair, and I knew it was going to be trouble, knew it was going to stiffen up, but that was later, and there wasn't any time at *all* for later. There was only right now, about four and a quarter minutes of right now.

It was where I remembered it, by the painting supplies: the ladder. Narrow, aluminum, lightweight, perfect. I limped to it as fast as I could, realized I'd need to bring the ladder back down here (*no time, no time*) to avoid giving them a clue, and with a sinking heart grabbed a big coil of clothesline that was hanging from a nail in the wall, hung it around my neck, hoisted the ladder, and went.

The leg was *absolutely* going to be a problem. I practically had to drag it up the stairs behind me, feeling like the mad doctor's troll assistant in some old horror movie, keeping the ladder angled up so it wouldn't catch on one of the stairs above me and send me racketing all the way back down again, maybe unable to get up this time, and when I reached the top of the stairs, I had two and a half minutes left.

And the sirens were whoop-whooping away, their tones sliding up the scale in obedience to the Doppler effect, announcing that they were coming toward me, if any further evidence were required.

I'd left the elevator upstairs, in Granger's Room of the Rancid Past, so I hauled the ladder and my stiffening leg up the curving staircase and into the stuffy room. I leaned the ladder against the wall and pushed the button and stood there, swearing under my breath, as its doors opened grudgingly, at a rich man's pace, no problem, the world will wait.

Two minutes, twelve—

The sirens peaked in volume and then shut off. They were *here*. So he'd lied about the eight minutes, too.

The question was, could they get in?

"Or the princess," Anime said. "Remember, two channels: the Prince and the Princess."

"So these kids are all over the country?" Ronnie said.

"It's not like there's a million of them," Anime said. "The channel—"

"You keep calling it a channel," Ronnie said.

"It is. It's an *unpublished channel* on YouTube. Two of them, actually. You can't find it through YouTube the way you'd find . . . I don't know, your favorite Michael Bublé song—"

"Oh, please," Ronnie said.

Lilli said, "You have to know the actual URL—you know, the http et cetera you type into the browser window. We didn't have much time to look at it, but it seems like there's nine boys in the channel on Mach One, the Prince, and about twelve girls on Mach Two, the Princess. They've got some skills, too, these kids. Sometimes they've got two or even three cell phones secretly recording video at the same time so they can cut things together on Pro Tools. I've seen worse-quality stuff on TV."

Ronnie said, "And what they're recording is . . . ?"

"Unpopular kids turning things upside down. Getting in with popular kids. Fucking with them. It's like serials. There's a few new minutes on every story every week, all these stories going on at the same time. The thing where Patty and her drizzly little friend saw Rina's BF holding hands with that hashtag hottie, what's her name?"

"Denise," Anime said. "What a numbskull."

"Yeah, but hot. So that took like three chapters to set up, one where Patty explains what she's going to do, right to the camera like some plotter on *Big Brother*, and then two, she talks Denise into it, not that it would be hard to talk Denise into anything, and then three, when she and her tagalong see them together."

"Did they actually film Rina?" Ronnie said.

I said, "They did. I saw it when Anime was setting up the iPad."

"And then four, the big payoff," Lilli said. "The money shot. Her and the lapdog are in Rina's room, and Patty tells Rina about how the BF is messing with this other girl, and then the lapdog backs her up and Rina calls the BF—"

"His name is Tyrone."

"—and breaks up with him, and then Rina gets weepy, and Patty and the tagalong are, like, comforting her."

Ronnie said, "How did they *film* all that?"

"They had their phones on video, and Patty's lens was sticking out of her pocket and the sidekick's was on a table in Rina's room, propped up on something. They'll be filming this party today like it's *Survivor*. This is triumph time."

"And you guys think this is okay," I said.

"We know you, and we think your daughter is probably nice," Lilli said. "But if everybody was strangers? Yeah, we'd be down with it. You bet."

Ronnie said, "They're selling subscriptions?"

"Looks like," Lilli said. "The audience builds by word of mouth. But it's more than a show, you know? They think of themselves as, like, an underground, like revolutionaries. They think they're going to show a million loser kids how to infiltrate the ranks of the local cools. Like it even matters."

I said, "It matters to Rina."

o o o

"We're about five minutes away," I said into the phone. "Are you sure you want me to do this in front of everyone?"

"I want Rina to see what this little monster did to her," Kathy said, "and I want the other kids to see it, too. They need to know who she is, this Patty, or she'll just start over again with one of them."

"No she won't," Anime said from the backseat. I had the phone on speaker so I could use it hands-free.

"Who's that?" Kathy said.

"Anime Wong."

"Is that a joke? Anna May Wong was an oldtime movie—"

"No, it's her name. Spelled differently."

"Patty's gotten kicked out of two schools for this already," Anime said. "If you catch her, I'll bet she quits, because she'll probably get expelled if she doesn't."

"Anime and her friend Lilli are the people who figured this out," I said, "and if there are questions, they're the ones who can answer them."

"How old are they?"

"About Rina's age."

"Do you have any friends your own size?"

"I've got Ronnie," I said. "I think she's friends with me right now."

"Hi, Kathy," Ronnie said.

Kathy said, "Oh, good. Someone for *me* to talk to."

"Wow," Rina said at the front door, checking their hair. "You guys are a *couple*?"

Anime said, "You *got* it. Your father didn't."

"We try not to let him know how dense— Oh, *hi*, Dad."

"Hey, Rina. How is it?"

She tried on a smile that didn't fit. "It's, like, meh. Kind of like life."

"You're not old enough to think life is meh."

Kathy appeared in the hall behind Rina, looking frazzled, but managed a smile at Ronnie, who returned it.

"I'm a lot older than I was a week ago," Rina said.

"Well," I said, "we're going to see what we can do about that."

Anime said, "We brought a time machine, sort of."

"I really like the hair thing," Rina said.

"Come on, come on in," Kathy said. Now that we were down to it, she was nervous. She can't handle conflict, unless it's with me.

We went into the living room. There were only seven or eight kids there, because Tyrone's friends were missing. It was pretty glum, for a party. A lopsided cake with some unlit candles was being ignored on the dining-room table, a few presents were scattered here and there, and some crap music—to my ears anyway—was playing, just loud enough to be irritating. The party seemed to have fallen into one of those uncomfortable group silences that always threaten to go on forever, or at least until all the adults leave.

Rina introduced Anime and Lilli to the room while I looked at Patty, sitting in the chair I'd usually occupied when I lived there. She had her cell phone hanging around her neck in a little leather holster suspended on a lanyard, and the camera lens peeked just over the top of the holster. She was shorter and more ordinary-looking than I'd thought she'd be, in spite of a skin condition bad enough to earn her the awful nickname, Leatherface, that Lilli had used. She looked sour, as though she smiled only when something dicey happened to someone else. I could see an unpleasant-looking adult trying to push her way through the still-soft adolescent face, and her eyes, as they bounced from Anime and Lilli back to Rina and the others in the room, gave away what it was that would eventually make that adult so unpleasant: want. Absolutely everyone in the room had something Patty Gribbin wanted: friends, self-assurance, grace, wit, clear skin. Lilli's word *thirsty* came to me, and once again I had a pang over what I was about to do.

Then she looked at me and held my gaze in a way that felt oddly like a challenge, as though she knew why I was there. I went over to her.

"You're Patty, right? I'm Rina's dad."

"I figured," she said. "You look like her."

"Really? I've always thought she looked more like her mother."

"Right in the middle," Patty said. "She's got both of you all over her face."

I said, "Happy birthday." And I reached down and put my finger over the lens on her phone.

Her eyes widened for a split second before she got them under control. I had a sudden conviction that she *lived* like this, suspecting every new actor on the stage of possessing the information that would reveal her for what she was, and all I could think of was the despair that had shaped her. She shifted, moving her phone away, and said, "Thanks. It . . . uh, it means a lot to me to have my party with Rina like this."

I said, "I'll bet it does."

She started to chew on the inside of the left corner of her mouth.

I leaned down toward her and lowered my voice. "I'm not going to cover your phone again, so the rest of this is on camera. You can leave now if you want. Tell them you don't feel good."

She said, with some steel in her voice, "What good would that do me?"

"Up to you." I felt Anime's eyes on me, and when I looked in her direction, she had her eyebrows arched in inquiry.

I turned back to Patty and figured, let the kid have a last chance to escape the unveiling. I said, "I've got something for you."

"A present?" Patty said, giving the word a nasty twist.

"I guess." I reached into my pocket and pulled out a little box. She hesitated but then took it. Elsewhere in the room, conversation had finally broken out, and it made the moment more endurable.

She opened the box and saw the key chain bearing the capital *H* with its two vertical strokes curving inward toward the center—the abstraction of two fish bellies that signifies Pisces. When she looked up at me, she'd forced her mouth into a smile. "Well done," she said.

I said, "You understand that I have to tell Rina about Machiavelli. You broke her heart."

Patty said, "It'll heal. She'll break it a dozen times before it breaks for good. But of course, her being *her*, it'll never break for good." She got up and brushed past me, heading for the door.

Rina said, "Patty?"

"Gotta go," Patty said. "I hear my mother calling me." The door closed behind her, and as Rina started after her, Lilli put a hand on her arm and handed her the iPad.

"Unwrap this," she said. "The thing you need to look at is all cued up. Just turn it on and push PLAY." Then she followed Patty through the door.

The clip they'd lined up was the four-minute one where Patty persuaded the dim, beautiful Denise to keep grabbing Tyrone's hand. The lines that echoed in the room were Patty's, after Denise said, "I barely know him."

"Come on," Patty had said, "what's he gonna do, call the cops? He's a nice guy—he'll just let you hang on to his hand." When it was over and all the kids had been drawn to the screen and were looking at each other, Anime said into the silence, "It's sort of an Internet TV show. The whole thing was a setup."

With her fingers raised to her lips, Rina said, "But I . . . I called . . . I mean, I broke up with—"

"It's okay, honey," Kathy said from the kitchen door. "Here's your other present," and she stepped aside and Tyrone came in, looking like someone who didn't know whether his face was about to be kissed or slapped, and Rina choked a couple of times and burst into tears. Kathy said to the kids, "Why don't we all take the cake outside and leave them alone for a minute?"

Fifteen minutes later, as Ronnie and Anime and I were leaving, Rina and Tyrone were still face-to-face, only inches apart, in a corner, and he had her hand between his. As the door closed behind us, we saw Lilli coming toward us from her talk with Patty. I said, "What did you say to her?"

Lilli looked at me, lifted her chin high, and said, "I offered her a job."

31
Dead Will Be Fine

It was almost eight as we rounded the corner that took us back to the storage unit. When the gate opened for us, Ronnie said, "Where in the world are we?" and Anime said, "You've never been here? Come on in."

Ronnie said, "Into a *storage* unit?"

"You'll love it," Lilli said. "Free vending machines."

"Gummy bears?" Ronnie said.

"And some. We've even got Japanese Kit Kats, weirdest candy on earth. Matcha Green Tea, Wasabi, Baked Potato, Shinshu Apple, tastes *exactly* like hairspray—"

"I am so in there," Ronnie said, opening the door. "You coming?"

"In a minute. I've got to make a call, and I'm hoping to get one."

"Your loss."

I watched the three of them go as I tried to organize my mind. Louie was around the corner from the Slugger's, waiting to see if he'd go out to dinner again, as he apparently did virtually every night, and if he did, I needed to be ready. And the man I was calling, the man I had to talk to before I moved to the next stage of the evening, did not cheerfully accept waffling; I needed an agenda. I thought for a moment, eyes closed, took a few seconds to appreciate the apparent end of the windy season, and dialed.

"Yeah?" It was Babe, one of the Man's hired muscle flexers.

"It's me," I said. "Junior. Is he there?"

"He's busy."

"What," I said, "is he watching reruns of *Taxi*?"

"That's funny," Babe said. "Okay, I'll tell him you're calling, see if he laughs."

There was a pause, a snatch of loud music, and then Irwin Dressler said, "So? Make it quick, I'm busy."

I said, "I need a favor."

"And I should do one for you why?"

"Oh, I don't know. The memory of good times past?"

"Ten, nine, eight."

"Because then I'll owe you one."

"This is a joke, right?" he said. "A favor from me is worth twenty from you." Pulling away from the phone, he said, "Just a minute, sweetie."

"Sweetie?" I said. "And what's that music?"

"You don't want to know."

"Of course I do. Everything about you fascinates me."

"You know what it is, you schlub."

"I do," I said. "It's that song from *Frozen*, but that would imply that you have very small female children in your living room."

"Me?" he said.

I said, "Sweetie?"

"I've heard this song three thousand times today alone," Dressler said, "beginning about nine in the morning. About the two-thousandth time, it gets kind of catchy.

Then, around twenty-five hundred, it becomes everything you hope the rest of your life won't be."

"What's that?"

"Repetitive, perky, optimistic, perky."

"You already said perky."

"Three thousand times I've heard it," he said. "And even if it was only two thousand, perky pisses me off. I see someone who's perky, I see someone whose hat I want to shoot off."

"You should look out the window once in a while. Nobody wears hats anymore."

"And I'm why. So what's the favor?"

I crossed my fingers. "I need to tell someone I know you."

"That runs high. You'll owe me big. Who?"

"A hitter."

"Junior," he said, "hitters are out of your league. Petty larceny, okay. Jaywalking, okay. Wait, hang on." He partially covered the mouthpiece with his hand and sang, "'Let it *go*.'" Then he said, "Small-time con games, okay. But for you—"

"You *do*," I said. You've got a kid there. You, Irwin Dressler, the Dark Lord of Los Angeles, are singing along with—"

"I've been running a big part of this town since your whole life. I've been in the business, here and elsewhere, more than *twice* your life. I seen a lot of bright boys come and go—"

"Thank you."

"—and you're not one of them. I mean, you're smart, but it's the kind of smart you can buy a lot of, and you don't got to go to Beverly Hills to get it."

"Ah," I said.

"So hitters, no, out of your depth, take my advice. It may not seem like it—'Let it *go*'—but I have a modest affection for you, Junior. Nothing you could mortgage a house on, just the kind of affection says I wouldn't prefer you dead."

"Here comes the chorus again," I said.

"'Let it *go*,'" he sang, although most of the notes he hit were the ones they store in the spaces between the piano keys. Then he said, "It's Babe's daughter, she's four, and this is what she needs to be happy now, okay? Believe me, *she's* not happy, you don't want to be around."

"It's the Slugger," I said. "And I have to talk to him. If you wouldn't prefer me to emerge from the conversation dead, let me use your name."

"Look, I gotta sing here."

"Well, you know how to make me hang up."

"Fine, use my name, live in health. I'm told he swings high, so maybe you'll duck. We'll talk later about what this costs."

"Thanks."

He said, "Aaaahh," and hung up, but he was singing again before the connection was severed.

I sat there in the car, feeling distinctly uneasy about the rest of the evening, just daring the wind to kick up again. If it had, I'd probably have called it all off, but it stayed as still as it apparently does when it becalms sailboats in the Doldrums, so I went inside to try a Matcha Green Tea Kit Kat and ask Ronnie if she'd mind my leaving her there for an hour or so.

It was a very expensive, very noisy, very famous-face, and not very good Italian place on San Vicente in that weird little boutique area before it curves to the right to meet up with Wilshire. I'd eaten there once and sworn not to come back, but here I was, breaking my promise to myself.

"Had any wind?" I asked the parking guy as he handed me the ticket.

He said, "Huh?"

I said, "Park it close. Get it to me within a minute, it's an extra twenty."

The noise clapped invisible hands over my eardrums as I went in. I paused, ignoring the maître d' as he shouted over the din for my name. The place was packed with second-string talent, and there he was, sitting with another man at a table for four, up against the wall. I said, "There's my party," and zigzagged between tables that were so close together the diners could have eaten off the dishes of the customers on either side. They didn't hear me coming, so they were unprepared when I pulled out an empty chair and sat down. That put the two of them—the other one was the *Spinal Tap* reject who checked under the beds—across from me with their backs to the wall. Looking startled.

The Slugger, who'd been staring at a very watchable waitress two tables away, said, "What the fuck?"

Up close it was difficult to imagine him as the man I knew him to be. He was slender, with a strong jaw, cold blue eyes, and a patrician nose. The swipe of gray hair over his forehead was tinted slightly blue and meticulously cared for. He looked, in fact, a little like a fussier, vainer Charlie Watts, whose elegant older-guy appearance I'd long hoped I'd grow into.

I said, "Hi." Then I took out the stamp, in its transparent envelope, and held it up.

His eyes froze on it.

I said, "I'm here to apologize, I'm here to talk business, and I'm here to get your property back to you. But first I need you to get rid of Sad Sack, to my right."

"You don't pull up a chair uninvited and tell me who sits at my table."

I put my hand behind my ear and said, "Pardon? You know, if the hired help went out and played in the street for a few minutes, I could slide in next to you and we could talk." I waved the stamp back and forth.

His eyes went back and forth with it, and then he gave a single nod. "Stumpy," he said. "Beat it."

I said, "Stumpy?"

"Don't push it," the Slugger said. "Even if you and me turn out to be friends, he'd still do you for an afternoon highlight."

Stumpy got up, making a little more noise with his chair than was strictly necessary, and stalked away, bumping other people's chairs as he went.

"Stumpy's in a huff," I said.

"Get to it," he said. "I'm hungry." He was watching the waitress again as she threaded between the tables, and he wasn't looking at the food. In what seemed to be an unconscious gesture, he reached up and fingered the fringe hanging across his forehead.

"Okay. First, mea culpa, which is Latin for 'I'm guilty.' I stole this stamp from you, not knowing who you were. So now I find myself in kind of an awkward position."

"I'd say so," he said, his attention back on me.

"So what I thought I'd do, I'd make a kind of double restitution. I'd get your stamp back to you and pay you forty K to do a hit."

"Whoa," he said. "You think you can walk in here and *hire* me? Even if I were the kind of person you could hire to do a hit, which I'm not, how could I know you're not wired up the ying-yang? How could I know this whole thing isn't a setup?"

"Do you know Irwin Dressler?"

"What're you *talking* about? Of course I don't know Irwin Dressler. How would I know—"

"Well, I do," I said. "And he'll vouch for me."

He looked around the room, his eyes snagging on the waitress for a moment. "Yeah? I don't see him."

"Then you know what he looks like."

"Sonny," he said, "everybody with more than four parking tickets knows what he looks like."

"Okay, here's how we can work it." I reached behind me, watching him stiffen, and pulled out my wallet so I could show him the only driver's license I have that's got my real name on it. He leaned forward to look at it. He looked at it so long that I started to get nervous, but when he sat back, the look on his face wasn't suspicious, so maybe it just took him a while to process information.

"So?" he said. "Junior. And you're razzing Stumpy about *his* name?"

"This is who I am," I said, tapping the license. "Junior Bender. Now, here's what we'll do. You take a picture of me with your phone, okay?"

He squinted at me, wondering where this was going. "I can handle that."

"And I'll give you the cell-phone number of one of Dressler's bodyguards, who's pretty much always with him. You send the picture to him with two questions: 'What's this guy's name, and do you trust him?' Got it?"

"Oh, sure. And I'm really sending it to some mook who sends it back and says, 'Hundred percent,' and I'm supposed to think—"

I said, "You said you know what he looks like, right?"

He examined the question for trick clauses and then said, "Yeah."

"Fine. I'll have Dressler's guy ask Dressler to hold up the phone with my picture on it, sort of cheek to cheek, and he'll take a picture of Dressler holding *my* picture and send that back with the answer. How does that sound?"

"It sounds, um . . ."

"Okay, here's a last fillip."

"Who's Philip?"

"*Fillip,*" I said, spelling it. "It's like an extra, a little boost. Just before you take my picture, you tell me to do something, whatever, so you know the picture Irwin will be holding will be the one you just took, not something I arranged a year ago, wearing the same clothes and all. It's not very plausible, but what the hell. Okay?"

He thought about it for so long that Stuffy or whatever his name was pushed his way through the door and into the room, and the Slugger, who saw him before I did, waved him back out. While he was doing that, the food arrived.

"Can I eat his?" I said.

"I don't give a fuck." He smiled at the waitress and got one back. When she was out of earshot, he said, "Okay, we'll do it." He raised the phone. "Hold the fork up." I held the fork up. Then he asked me for Tuffy's phone number, took so long to key in the text that I'd eaten half of Stuffy's food by the time he finished, and pressed to send it.

"Now what?" he said.

"This is good," I said. "Best thing I ever ate in here. Probably tastes better when someone else is paying. Now we wait until your phone buzzes or does the cha-cha or whatever it does."

I passed him the bread basket, but he waved it away, so I took the last piece of bread. His pasta didn't look as good as Stuffy's chicken. I said, "His name is Stuffy?"

"Stumpy," he said. He twirled some noodles on a fork, but he had his eyes on the phone, and then he dropped the whole thing, fork *and* food, onto his plate and grabbed the phone with both hands. He looked at it, and when his eyes came up to mine, they might have belonged to a different person. He looked frightened.

I said, "Can I see?"

He turned the phone to me. Dressler, one cheek pressed to the phone he was holding, on which was a tiny me, hoisting a fork. A very small hand was reaching up to take the phone away from him. The words beneath the picture were: HE'S JUNIOR BENDER. I TRUST HIM. IN FACT, I LIKE HIM. A LITTLE.

The Slugger said, "Who do you want me to do?"

"Twenty thousand now," I said, sliding the envelope with half of Stinky's money in it across the table. "The other twenty and the stamp when it's done."

He hesitated, licked his upper lip, and then nodded. "Suicide," he said.

"If your guy can make it convincing. Like I told you, he leaves the studio at seven and goes home. The house is empty until then, most of the time, and I gave you the combinations for the alarms. Just make sure your guy leaves the gun and it isn't traceable, so it's plausible the dead man might have owned it."

"Got boxes full of them," he said.

"Well, good," I said. "Attention to detail is essential to success."

"Okay, we're on. Any refinements?" He waited, his Montblanc fountain pen poised over the small leather notebook in which he'd been making notes.

I said, "Excuse me?"

"Options? Extras?"

"No. Dead will be fine." I pushed back my chair, meaning to stand, but instead I said, "No, wait, I'm wrong. Just before your guy pulls the trigger, I want him to say, so it's the last thing Granger ever hears, 'This is for Suley.'"

"S-O-O—"

"No." I got up from the table. "*Suley*, S-U-L-E-Y."

The slugger wrote it down and shrugged. "Sounds the same."

I said, "But it's not," and my tone brought his eyes up to mine. "Even if he's just saying it out loud, I want her name spelled right."

32
A Lower Standard

Ronnie had finally gotten her Korean food, and she wolfed it down as though she hadn't eaten anything since the first time I promised it to her, all those nights ago. Still full of Stumpy's roast chicken, I'd just picked at mine. We were in Soot Bull Jeep on West Eighth, in K-Town, and when we came out, burping garlic, she said, "So what's the surprise?"

I still hadn't committed entirely to the plan, but the question gave me the shove I needed. "It's about a mile from here."

She said, "And I'm going to need my toothbrush?"

"If I get lucky."

She slipped her arm through mine, and my heart did a little change step. She said, "Did you see the expression on Tyrone's face?"

"I did."

"I see something like that," she said, "and know that you set it up, and how much you probably had to do to arrange it, and it almost makes me willing to hold you to a lower standard."

I said, "I would love to be held to a lower standard."

"Well, if we're going to be an item, as they used to say,

I should probably be willing to forgive a lapse here and there."

"Lapses 'R' Us," I said. I opened the car door for her and said, "Does this count, too?"

"A really infinitesimal amount. This is the kind of thing that might make me overlook you chewing with your mouth open. Occasionally."

"Do I chew with my—"

"No, silly. Just giving you an idea of scale."

I got in and started the car. Took Eighth a couple of blocks and made a left. Blew out a bunch of air.

"Lungs are sounding good."

"Great, great."

"Although sudden, window-rattling sighs don't really inspire confidence."

"I'm just nervous."

"Nervous. Where *are* we going?"

"I think it's better if you just see it."

"Want me to close my eyes until we get there?"

"Great idea."

So she did, and I said, "Keep them closed," when I pulled down the driveway into the underground garage. When I got out of the car, I said, "Don't open them yet."

"I'm not walking in a strange place with my eyes closed. I'm wearing heels."

"Up to you."

A moment later she said, "Oh," a syllable packed with disappointment. The garage took up an acre and was lit just enough to allow a person to make out large objects, at least if they were light colored and moving. I led her to the scratched and battered elevator doors and pushed the cracked call button, and when we got in and she saw the gouged walls and the graffiti and the single, dangling sour-milk fluorescent tube, her mouth tightened.

I waved at the recessed camera.

She said, "What?"

"The guards," I said.

"To keep people in, I assume."

I pushed UP, and the elevator did its programmed little stutter and groan and creaked its way into motion. Ronnie stood closer to me and put her hand on my arm. "If this thing drops," she said, "I'm jumping straight into the air and doing everything I can to land on you."

"It won't drop," I said. "That's all stage effects."

"Really. For what purpose?"

"You'll see."

We fell into a silence that thickened significantly when the doors opened on the third-floor corridor. There were water stains on the ceilings and cracks in the walls, and here and there the tacky maroon carpeting, stickier even than the rug at the Dew Drop Inn, was flaked with plaster that seemed to have fallen from the ceiling.

"Special effects?" she said.

I said, "Uh-huh."

"Shame they left out the dead junkie hunched over his needle in the corner."

"They spoil," I said. "We're in between dead junkies right now."

We reached the door of Apartment 302, and I keyed the first lock and then the second. Before I opened the door, I said, "I've never told anyone about this before."

"And I can see why."

"Not even Rina. Not Kathy, not Louie. No one."

She was looking up at me.

"Just you," I said, and I opened the door.

Two well-spent hours later, we were in the living room, me in my bathrobe and her in one of my shirts, both of us drinking wine and looking at the aspirational lights of the Los Angeles skyline. She said, "A *library*."

"I knew you'd like it."

"So this is your . . . your bolt-hole. You're living in those motels and you have this place waiting for you."

"It's where I'll go when it all comes down."

"If," she said.

"When," I said.

"And you told me about it."

"I love you," I said.

"It sounds so *bald* when we're together. It's easier on the phone." She snuggled closer to me. "But . . . uhh, me, too."

"And I've still got a million questions about you, but this isn't a quid pro quo arrangement. I brought you here because I trust you and I love you, and I promise never to ask you those questions again until you're ready to talk about them."

She went to kiss me on the chin, but I got my mouth down there in time and said, "I win."

"You know," she said, "not to wave off all those nice things you just said, but you promised *last* time that you wouldn't ask me about—"

"Yeah, but this time I mean it."

She tilted her head to the right, regarding me. "So you didn't mean it the first time?"

"Sure I did," I said. "But this time I'll mean it longer."

33
USDA Prime

Three days later Jeremy Granger owned the news. MOVIE MOGUL FOUND DEAD was the biggie, plus the cluster stories: DEAD TYCOON'S WIFE MISSING and DOUBLE MYSTERY IN HOLLYWOOD, although none of it had actually happened in Hollywood; and after the cops announced they'd found the towels I used to clean up Suley's blood, right where I'd left them in the linen closet off the second-floor drawing room, the headline I'd waited for appeared: GRANGER: MURDER-SUICIDE?

That last one became the topic of endless, mindless on air and online discussion that grew into a firestorm after the cops revealed that the use of luminol in the drawing room had revealed traces of blood on the floor and on the candlestick, obviously unconnected with Granger's death, since he'd been shot, or shot himself, downstairs in his home office. Suley's parents, who were described as being "distraught," had let the cops swab them for DNA to match the blood on the towels, but even before the results came in, a great many conclusions had been jumped to. TMZ used the murder-suicide possibility as an excuse to run a lurid history of Granger's mansion—titled, naturally, HOUSE OF HORRORS—that swallowed the whole thing without chewing and linked it to the spirit of the suicidal Thud for good measure. Hollywood Ghouls and Ghosts, which led the credulous on tours of the city's plentiful suicide, murder, and overdose sites, complete with color postcards, added the house to their itinerary.

"You heard about it?" the Slugger said on the other end of the phone the day the first stories broke.

"Hard to avoid it. Good work."

"You can bring me my stuff tonight, and you can buy the dinner, too."

"You got it. What time?"

"An hour." It was 7 P.M.

"Where? I want to go somewhere with a bar. You know, hoist one and then get a table to eat."

"Ricochet in Beverly Hills. You know it?"

I did. It was one of the most expensive restaurants in the city, a one-percenter pickup joint par excellence. "Sounds great," I said. "See you there. Make it eight fifteen, though. I've got something I have to do."

"Fine. Hey, don't forget the stamp."

"I promise," I said. "I'll put it directly into your hand. Will Stumpy be there, or can we do without him?"

"Just you and me," he said. "He didn't know about our arrangement, and I can't think of any reason to tell him about it."

"Man after my own heart," I said.

"Not yet," the Slugger said, and we shared a hearty laugh.

"You keep the twenty K he'll be carrying," I said into the phone as I stood outside the restaurant. "He'll have the stamp in his pocket, and that's mine. I'll give you the last ten K when you hand me the stamp."

"Yeah, yeah, yeah. Just come in here and let's get it over with."

I pocketed the phone and went in.

The bar was packed, and the Slugger was already at his table. He looked antsy, like he was half afraid I wouldn't show, and his eyes went to me the moment I started across the floor.

"The twenty," I said, putting an envelope on the table, "and the Gandhi."

He pried it open and glanced inside. "All tied up neat," he said. "You satisfied?"

"Couldn't be better."

"Amazing, about the wife disappearing and the blood and all," he said, looking at me with an edge of interest I hadn't provoked before. "Almost like you knew about it in advance."

"Nah," I said.

He licked his lips. "I just mention it, you know, 'cause you wanted my guy to say her name and so on."

"Purest coincidence," I said. "How'd he take it?"

"In the right ear."

"I meant the mention of her name."

"Oh, yeah. He wet himself. Although he could have done that before, I guess. My guy wasn't real clear on the timeline."

"No," I said, "I suppose he wouldn't be."

"Even a pro," he said, "they tend to be a little wound up when the target's that close."

"I'm actually glad to hear that."

"Listen," he said. He flicked a corner of the envelope, hesitating. "I don't suppose you'd be willing to give me, like, an endorsement? To . . . you know." He pointed a finger in the air, and his eyes darted past me, toward the bar, and rested there for a moment. He fingered his fringe reflexively and came back to me.

"Already did," I lied. "Told him you exceeded all expectations."

"Was he . . . um, was he in on the deal?"

I gave him a reproachful look and zipped my lips closed.

"Right," he said, "right, right, right. *Right*. Forget I asked." He looked past me again, and I could see the spark of interest in his eye.

"Well, listen," I said, "as much as I'd love to chew the fat with you, I'm going to have to bail on dinner. There's an extra three hundred in the envelope because I said the meal would be on me, but when *some people* call you, you've really gotta go."

"Got it," he said. "Say hi for me. Love to meet him someday."

"Maybe I'll set that up," I said, but he wasn't paying attention to me.

"Is that fine, or what?" he asked.

I turned to see the very pretty girl sitting at the bar, caught in mid-smile. "Not bad."

"Not *bad*? That's prime," he said. "USDA Prime and pretrimmed. You think?"

"I guess," I said, "if you like hippies. Have a good evening."

Before I was out of the restaurant, Eaglet was in the seat I'd just vacated.

I sat in the car for a moment, figuratively taking my moral temperature. I didn't feel good about what I'd done, but then I remembered Jejomar, and I couldn't honestly say I felt very bad either.

I dialed the phone and once again got the voice-mail lady. She never takes a day off, never gets hoarse. "Stinky," I said, "you can go home now. It's all over."

Then I started the car and pointed it toward K-Town, and Ronnie.

Afterword

The basic ideas for my books usually assemble themselves spontaneously in my mind, but this one was even more random than usual.

The first thing I had was the title, which came to me out of nowhere when I was jogging about two years ago. Just the two words, *King Maybe*, no meaning; what I liked about it was the combination of absolute power and absolute equivalency. It seemed to me that kings might say "yes" and "no" all day long, but there was something unkingly about "maybe."

I parked the title while I finished the book I was writing then (*The Hot Countries*, I think), and at some point I realized that King Maybe was a studio executive who derived an almost sadistic pleasure from keeping people on the hook by deferring his decision whether to make their film. So I had a show-business book with a powerful villain, and the Suley story started to shape itself.

And then, in a single week, I got five emails from readers politely upbraiding me for not having written as many burglaries in the last two or three books as they felt they had a right to expect. I realized that I agreed with them, and decided that *King Maybe* would be a show-business book that was essentially all burglaries. Plus Suley. (This is as close to an outline as I ever have.)

When I finally sat down to write it, it was immediately apparent that the characters demanded a say in the story. One of my favorite writers, the wonderful Colin Cotterill (if you haven't read his Dr. Siri books, your life is not complete), gave an interview in which he said that the problem with writing a series, after a while, is that he shows up to write and realizes that the characters have been holding meetings without him and have developed firm ideas about what they will and won't do. That was the case here. What I had envisioned as a string of sensational burglaries, immaculately planned and executed by a master thief, turned into one disaster after another. And Ronnie kept elbowing her way in.

So you've just finished the book that my readers and my characters bullied me into writing. I hope you like it. I do, but I'm usually the last to know.

As always, lots of music accompanied the placing of the words on the page. For the burglaries, I put together a playlist of the darker cuts from all of Arcade Fire's albums (which means I left out three or four songs), Neil Young's "On the Beach" and "Rust Never Sleeps," some Calexico and Fratellis and Franz Ferdinand, plus a bunch of Ravel and my current go-to for suspenseful scenes, Beethoven's late quartets.

For the material centered on Rina and Patsy and Anime and Lilli, it was all women, all the time. There's so much good rock, country, and just plain music by female singer-songwriters right now that I might write a book that's *all* women just to take advantage of it. I owe special thanks to Aimee Mann, Broods, Frou Frou (and Imogen Heap, solo), Lucius, Courtney Burnett, Rachael Yamagata, Ingrid Michaelson, Haim, the ever-present Tegan and Sara, Sky Ferreira, Karin Berquist of Over the Rhine (what a voice!), Mindy Smith, and two amazing young country songwriters, Kacey Musgraves and Ashley Monroe. One great talent after another.

And one more time, thanks to the people at Soho Crime for putting up with both me and Junior and making the books better in every regard: Bronwen Hruska; the formidable and usually correct Juliet Grames; marketing maestro Paul Oliver; Rachel Kowal; Abby Koski; Amara Hoshijo; and anyone I may inadvertently have left out. To my own eagle-eyed proofreader, Everett Kaser, and to the best copy editor a boy can have, Maureen "God Is in the Details" Sugden. Everything is easier when you're playing on a great team.

Last, it would be graceless not to thank Junior's new building consultant, who helped him survive this story and whose inside knowledge of houses will keep both him and me from making egregious errors in other books: the scrupulously honest (luckily for you) Peter "Tiptoes" Sanderson.